PRAISE FOR ME

"With her wonderful characters and resonating emotions, Melissa Foster is a must-read author!"

—*New York Times* bestseller Julie Kenner

"Melissa Foster is synonymous with sexy, swoony, heartfelt romance!"

—*New York Times* bestseller Lauren Blakely

"You can always rely on Melissa Foster to deliver a story that's fresh, emotional, and entertaining."

—*New York Times* bestseller Brenda Novak

"Melissa Foster writes worlds that draw you in, with strong heroes and brave heroines surrounded by a community that makes you want to crawl right on through the page and live there."

—*New York Times* bestseller Julia Kent

"When it comes to contemporary romances with realistic characters, an emotional love story, and smokin'-hot sex, author Melissa Foster always delivers!"

—*The Romance Reviews*

"Foster writes characters that are complex and loyal, and each new story brings further depth and development to a redefined concept of family."

—*RT Book Reviews*

"Melissa Foster definitely knows how to spin a tale and keep you flipping the pages."

—*Book Loving Fairy*

"You can never go wrong with the heroes that Melissa Foster creates. She hasn't made one yet that I haven't fallen in love with."

—*Natalie the Biblioholic*

"Melissa is a very talented author that tells fabulous stories that captivate you and keep your attention from the first page to the last page. Definitely an author that you will want to keep on your go-to list."

—*Between the Coverz*

"Melissa Foster writes the best contemporary romance I have ever read. She does it in bundles, tops it with great plots, hot guys, strong heroines, and sprinkles it with family dynamics—you got yourself an amazing read."

—*Reviews of a Book Maniac*

"[Melissa Foster] has a way with words that endears a family in our hearts, and watching each sibling and friend go on to meet their true love is such a joy!"

—*Thoughts of a Blonde*

Maybe We Will

MORE BOOKS BY MELISSA FOSTER

LOVE IN BLOOM ROMANCE SERIES

SNOW SISTERS

Sisters in Love
Sisters in Bloom
Sisters in White

THE BRADENS

Lovers at Heart, Reimagined
Destined for Love
Friendship on Fire
Sea of Love
Bursting with Love
Hearts at Play
Taken by Love
Fated for Love
Romancing My Love
Flirting with Love
Dreaming of Love
Crashing into Love
Healed by Love
Surrender My Love
River of Love
Crushing on Love
Whisper of Love
Thrill of Love

THE BRADENS & MONTGOMERYS

Embracing Her Heart
Anything for Love

Trails of Love
Wild, Crazy Hearts
Making You Mine
Searching for Love
Hot for Love
Sweet, Sexy Heart

BRADEN NOVELLAS

Promise My Love
Our New Love
Daring Her Love
Story of Love
Love at Last
A Very Braden Christmas

THE REMINGTONS

Game of Love
Stroke of Love
Flames of Love
Slope of Love
Read, Write, Love
Touched by Love

SEASIDE SUMMERS

Seaside Dreams
Seaside Hearts
Seaside Sunsets
Seaside Secrets
Seaside Nights

HARBORSIDE NIGHTS SERIES

Catching Cassidy
Discovering Delilah
Tempting Tristan

STAND-ALONE NOVELS

Chasing Amanda (mystery/suspense)
Come Back to Me (mystery/suspense)
Have No Shame (historical fiction/romance)
Love, Lies & Mystery (three-book bundle)
Megan's Way (literary fiction)
Traces of Kara (psychological thriller)
Where Petals Fall (suspense)

Maybe We Will

Silver Harbor, Book One

MELISSA FOSTER

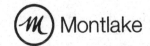

Published by Montlake, Seattle

www.apub.com

Amazon, the Amazon logo, and Montlake are trademarks of Amazon.com, Inc., or its affiliates.

ISBN-13: 9781542027182
ISBN-10: 1542027187

Cover design by Letitia Hasser

Cover photography © Jen Brown/Of Stardust and Earth Photography

Printed in the United States of America

For all the brothers, sisters, sons, and daughters who have gone above and beyond for their families

CHAPTER ONE

THIS FREAKING HILL is going to kill me!

Abby winced against the sliver of guilt slicing through her for joking about death and pushed herself to run up the steep residential sidewalk toward the main drag on Silver Island. She was not a runner by any stretch of the imagination, but from time to time she needed to escape the monotony and stress of working as a cook in a busy New York restaurant. When that happened, she became one. Or maybe *jogger* was a better word for her sluggish pace. It was easier to run on her treadmill at home in New York, in the comfort of her apartment, where she could watch television or read. She'd forgotten how hilly her hometown was. But she'd spent half the night arguing with her older sister, Deirdra, and she needed to work out her frustrations.

Deirdra had kept Abby up, badgering her to accept an offer they'd received from an investor to purchase the Bistro, their family's beachfront restaurant. But their mother's unexpected death three months ago had caused Abby to take a long, hard look at her life, which was nothing to write home about. She'd felt stuck in her job and in the quasi relationship she'd let go on for far too long. So she'd stepped out of her comfort zone and had thrown caution to the wind, quitting her job and ending the relationship, and she'd come out the other side feeling better than she had in years, despite having no plan for her future in place. Abby was still trying to figure out how to tell Deirdra she'd quit her job, because she knew her sister would give her a hard time about being irresponsible. But Abby saw her decision as an act of self-care—and probably the most responsible decision she'd made in ages. It wasn't like she was broke and had given up her apartment. She had a nest egg that would cover her rent for a while.

She wasn't quite sure *what* her plans were, but she definitely wasn't ready to sell the Bistro. In a few hours they were meeting with their mother's closest friend, Shelley Steele, who was the executor of her will. Shelley had been like a second mother to Abby and Deirdra when they were young, and she'd graciously allowed them time to wrap their heads around their mother's death before dealing with her final wishes.

When Abby reached Main Street, the flat terrain felt like heaven. She slowed to a walk, peering through the windows of the shops as she passed. It was the end of April, not yet tourist season, and the streets were quiet, the sidewalks empty. She had always loved the island's quaint small towns, with their inviting wooden benches and flower boxes, which were starting to bloom. Her family's Sunday-evening strolls down Main Street were some of her fondest memories. Her parents would hold hands as their father captivated them all with his thick French accent, telling stories about when he'd first come to the island and bought the Bistro and how much both had changed. Abby had been the epitome of a daddy's girl. She'd adored his sense of humor and kindheartedness and had wanted to be just like him. Back then, her mother had been full of life, and her parents had been so in love, it had emanated from them and had felt indestructible. Unfortunately, after their father died from a heart attack, their mother had found solace in alcohol, forcing nine-year-old Abby and eleven-year-old Deirdra to grow up far too fast.

Sadness pressed in on Abby, and she picked up her pace, jogging the rest of the way through town and along the winding roads toward Silver Harbor. The expansive patios and the pool at the Silver House, which stood sentinel on a bluff overlooking the harbor, came into view. She looked past the mansion-turned-sought-after-resort to the sunlight glittering off the inky water, the waves kissing the shores of Sunset Beach, and her worries fell away. Boats were tethered to the marina, and more were anchored in the harbor like rebellious teenagers refusing to come home. While she'd eventually left the island to start her life, growing up here, she'd always felt like a marina boat, following the rules and making the best of it, sticking around the island long after Deirdra had gotten scholarships and left to make her mark on the world.

Feeling the pull of the Bistro, she pushed herself to run the few extra blocks to take a quick peek before heading back to her mother's house. Unlike the Silver House, the Bistro, a renovated boathouse, was built *on* the flat terrain of the sandy beach. The back faced the parking lot, and the front overlooked the water.

Abby's breath caught at the sight of THE BISTRO sign perched tall and proud on steel legs attached to the double-peaked roof. The sign had been there since her father had first opened the restaurant several years before she was born.

Surrounded by the scents of the sea and memories of her parents' laughter, which had once seemed ever present, she made her way to the side patio, taking in the shuttered windows and the CLOSED FOR THE SEASON sign hanging on the weather-beaten siding. She could still recall images of her father with perfect clarity, his long white hair tied back in a ponytail, his matching beard unkempt, and his gray-blue eyes dancing with happiness as he wandered through the restaurant, joining guests at their tables for brief chats. Memories of her mother always took her back to her youth, when Ava de Messiéres's sandy hair was shiny and beautiful and a gap-toothed smile was always at the ready.

Her eyes shifted to the beach in front of the restaurant, where she and Deirdra used to play. The rickety, weathered gray fence that had once held colorful lanterns had been consumed by bearberry bushes as untamed as her hair. Memories of better days floated around her as she stepped off the side of the patio and onto the sand. Even in her sneakers, she loved the feel of sinking into the sand. She rounded the front of the building and was surprised to see a man sitting at a table reading a newspaper in the shade of the covered patio. It reminded her of her father, who used to read every page while he drank his coffee in the morning. *But who reads actual newspapers anymore? And where did you get that table and chair?* A travel mug from the Sweet Barista, her friend Keira Silver's coffeehouse around the corner, sat on the table beside a book and a delicious-looking croissant. He'd made himself right at home, in his crisp short-sleeve button-down shirt, which revealed enticingly defined but not overly muscled arms, khaki pants, and loafers. *Loafers? On the beach?* A gold watch clung to his wrist, another anomaly. His toffee-brown hair was brushed back, giving her an extraordinary view of his clean-shaven, handsome face as she stepped closer. His chiseled jawline and aquiline nose were a little too familiar, though she couldn't place where she'd seen him. He looked a lot like a distinguished David Beckham—*Yum*—but he wasn't tattooed. Was that why he looked familiar?

He lowered the newspaper, his serious dark eyes finding hers as he said, "Good morning."

His rich voice gave her goose bumps. His lips quirked up in amusement, and she realized she was standing on the beach *right* in front of him, hands planted on her hips, blatantly *staring*. "Hi. I, um . . ." She chided herself for sounding flustered and a little embarrassed and threw her shoulders back as she said, "You know this is private property, right?"

"Yes, I'm aware," he said, setting the newspaper on the table as if he had all the time in the world.

"Do you always make yourself at home on other people's property?"

He arched a brow. "How do you know I don't own this place?"

She was amused by his attempt to seem important. "I'm pretty sure you don't."

"Are you? Well, then, you're probably right." He leaned forward and crooked his finger, motioning for her to come closer.

It had been so long since a man had caught her attention, much less since she'd been *beckoned* by a hot guy, and her pulse quickened like a schoolgirl's. Only she was a grown woman wearing a sweaty tank top with FLIPPIN' AWESOME written across the chest and a picture of a spatula beneath it, which quite possibly made her *look* like a silly schoolgirl.

"I'm staying at the Silver House, but I'm not fond of crowds," he said conspiratorially. "I bought this table and chair at a store around the corner, and I've been camping out here in the mornings. If you promise not to tell, I'll share my raspberry-and-Bavarian-cream croissant with you."

"Ah, draw me into your web of deceit with the allure of one of Keira's pastries," she said in a low voice, mentally shuffling through magazines and commercials, trying to figure out where she'd seen him before. "Normally I'm a rule follower, but I like your style, Chair Guy. I'll keep your secret."

He cut the croissant in half and pushed to his feet, bringing to light his six-foot-plus stature. His identity hit her with the impact of jackpot-winning bells, and before she could reel in her excitement, "You're the guy from the Nautica underwear ads!" came roaring out.

His brows slanted.

"Oh *God*. You're *not* him, are you?" She covered her face. "This is *so* embarrassing," she said as she lowered her hands.

"Not for me. I'm taking that as a compliment. In fact, if you feel the need to narc someone out for trespassing, please say it was that underwear model and not me."

She was glad he had a sense of humor. "They'd probably drag you in anyway. You look just like him."

"I'll take your word for it." He waved to the chair and said, "Join me?"

"I can't. Thanks, though. I have to go meet my sister."

He gathered half of the pastry in a napkin and descended the steps to the beach. His eyes remained trained on her, making her pulse quicken again. He handed her the napkin-encased croissant and said, "If you run this way tomorrow, I'll have a whole pastry waiting for you."

"*Oh.*" There was no hiding the surprise in her voice.

"Not all criminals are bad guys. I'm Aiden, by the way." He offered his hand.

"I'm Abigail de Messiéres. *Abby.*" She shifted nervously on her feet, wondering what had possessed her to say her full name, as if she were someone special. "It's nice to meet you."

When she put her hand in his, he lifted it to his lips and kissed the back of it. "It's been a pleasure, Abigail. I hope to see you tomorrow, and remember, if I get dragged into jail, you're now an accomplice. I go down, you go down."

Butterflies swarmed in her belly at the way he said her name and the low, seductive way he said that last part. She couldn't remember the last time she'd gone *down* with anyone. "You play dirty, Chair Guy."

"Only for *very* special people," he said with a wink. "Thanks for brightening my morning, Runner Girl. I hope to see you tomorrow."

She walked away, nibbling on the sweet croissant, but she couldn't resist taking one last peek over her shoulder. Aiden was standing on the side of the patio watching her. Butterflies took flight in her stomach as he flashed that sexy grin and waved.

Real smooth, Abby.

She hurried toward the street. He was probably just as bad for her as the croissant—and even more delicious.

By the time Abby made it back to her mother's house, she'd devoured the croissant despite the butterflies nesting in her belly and mulled over her conversation with Aiden at least a dozen times. It had been so long since she'd flirted with a guy, she was kind of proud that she hadn't made a complete fool of herself. *Well, except for the underwear model debacle.*

She walked down the narrow dirt road to her mother's driveway on the outskirts of Silver Haven, feeling lighter than she had when she'd left. But the sight of Deirdra's car parked in front of their funky four-bedroom, three-bath bungalow brought a knot of tension. While Abby didn't even own a car, her control-freak sister had brought hers with her on the ferry.

Their mother's house also had a one-car garage with an apartment above it and a gorgeous view of the water, which Deirdra called their *saving grace.* The house looked as haggard as her mother had when Abby had visited over the holidays. The picket fence was missing boards, the lawn was long and uncared for, the vegetable and flower gardens overgrown with knee-high tangles of weeds. The white siding on the house was so dirty it looked gray, but the wide front porch still held memories of Abby singing with her mother as her father stood at his easel painting with the wind in his hair and the familiar spark of happiness in his eyes.

Deirdra had it all wrong.

The view she deemed as their saving grace was something everyone on that side of the island had. It was gorgeous and it added to their property value, but to Abby, her cherished memories were the *real* saving graces.

She held on to those treasured thoughts as she breezed through the front door, humming as she walked into the crowded living room, refusing to stress over Deirdra's mood or the boxes and piles of magazines, records, books, and other things littering the floor. It was as if time had stopped when their father passed away. Their mother had never gotten rid of any of his belongings. Abby had already begun going through the living room, but she didn't want to think about how difficult it would be to go through the other rooms. She was glad Deirdra would be there with her. She'd been embarrassed when her mother's friends had stopped by over the last couple of days, bringing casseroles and pies and all sorts of other food, and had seen the mess. The freezer and refrigerator were packed full, and the counters held so many dishes, it looked like they were having a potluck gathering. You'd think her mother had *just* passed away. But that was life on Silver Island, where everyone pulled together during difficult times. Her mother's friends had all known of her alcoholism, and Abby remembered the carefully choreographed dance of talking around the elephant in the room when she'd see them at the Bistro or around town. Thankfully, they had never looked down on her or Deirdra because of it.

Abby found her sister pacing in the cozy, though outdated, kitchen with her cell phone pressed to her ear. They shared the same brownish-blond hair color, but while Abby's was coarse and rebellious, always appearing a little messy, Deirdra had been blessed with silky hair that looked perfect at any length. Her natural waves fell just past her shoulders. As always, Deirdra was ready to take on the day, although she looked like she was going out for drinks in the Hamptons in her skinny jeans, white-and-blue-striped shirt, a pink blazer with the sleeves rolled up, and sharp strappy sandals.

"Damn it, Malcolm, this is the *one* week—" Deirdra pursed her lips, anger simmering in her mossy-green eyes. Malcolm was her stern sixty-year-old boss. "No. I need to be *here*." She paused, listening. "*Fine.* I'll see you Friday afternoon." She ended the call and grumbled, "*Bastard.*"

"What's wrong?"

Deirdra put her phone in her pocket, closing her eyes. She straightened her spine and lifted her chin, her eyes opening as a calm came over her like a curtain. The momentary *slip* in her behavior was pushed aside as if that part of her didn't matter. But it did matter. Abby missed the unpredictable side of her sister, which she'd lost when their mother had started drinking.

"The shit hit the fan, of course." Deirdra's gaze softened, and she said, "I'm sorry, Abby. I know I promised to help you go through Mom's things this week, but this is my—"

"It's okay," Abby said, cheerily masking her disappointment. Deirdra was a corporate attorney for a major Boston tech company. Abby knew how much pressure her sister was under and how overwhelming her schedule was. It had only gotten worse since her promotion last year. Even though they were very different by nature, they usually enjoyed each other's company, and they used to make time to see each other one weekend each month, but ever since Deirdra's promotion, those get-togethers had been few and far between. They hadn't seen each other since their brief visit with their mother over Christmas.

"I can handle going through Mom's things. Like I said last night, I'm here for however long it takes, so I have plenty of time."

"Even the junk room?" Deirdra arched a brow.

The famed *junk room*, aka the Bermuda Triangle, was down the hall from the kitchen. Abby was pretty sure it was meant to be the master bedroom because it protruded from the back of the house, had two walk-in closets, a full bath, and three walls of nearly floor-to-ceiling windows, offering exceptional views of the water. They had used it as a playroom when they were young, and even back then the closets had been packed with boxes. Sometime after their father died, it had become the junk room—a catchall for everything from outgrown toys and clothes to broken furniture.

"That might take a bulldozer," Abby joked. "I don't mind doing it alone. I was just looking forward to spending time with you, beyond the Mom stuff and the restaurant." She lifted one shoulder and said, "I miss you, Dee. You know what? After you're done with whatever you're dealing with at work, if you can't come to see me, I'll come to Boston and hang out for a weekend."

"Thank you for understanding, but I'll be back my next free weekend. I don't want to leave you with this nightmare."

"It's only a nightmare to *you* because you resent Mom so much. What's happening at work, anyway? What's so dire that they need you back so fast?"

Deirdra gave her a deadpan look. "You know my work is confidential."

"Really? I'm your *sister*. Who am I going to tell?" Abby opened the fridge and dug out a water bottle. "Fine, keep your lips sealed and I won't tell you about the hot guy I met when I was out running." She opened the bottle and took a drink as she sauntered out of the kitchen.

"If you're talking about Wells Silver, I'll slaughter you for even looking at the hot two-timer," Deirdra called after her.

Abby had gone out with Wells briefly in high school, until she'd found out that he was also seeing her best friend, Leni Steele. They'd both ditched his cheating ass. She went upstairs to her bedroom, remembering the chicks-before-dicks pact she and Leni had come up with after that. But while Silver Island had three primary schools, it had only one high school, and before long they'd forgiven Wells for his indiscretion. Mostly, anyway. Leni still carried a chip on her shoulder about it.

She turned on the shower, and as the water heated, Aiden's sexy smile and serious eyes pushed to the forefront of her mind. She touched the back of her hand, thinking about his warm, soft lips and the spark of heat in his eyes when he'd said, *I go down, you go down.* Her body shuddered with the tease of something more.

She stripped off her clothes and stepped into the shower, wondering if she'd misconstrued *heat* for *mischief.* Even if she had, a girl could fantasize, couldn't she? She closed her eyes, letting the water rain down her face and body, and imagined Aiden's dark eyes and tantalizing lips and his rich voice whispering in her ear, *Only for very special people . . .*

CHAPTER TWO

"I CAN'T BELIEVE you're wearing a dress. I haven't seen you in a dress in years," Deirdra said as they climbed out of Deirdra's car at the Bistro, where they were meeting Shelley. "You look great, but I swear to you, if that's for Wells . . ."

"It's not for Wells. We haven't seen Shelley in months, and I want to look nice for her." Abby wasn't about to tell her that she'd dressed up in case she ran into Aiden again. It felt good to wear something pretty. She'd paired a floral sundress with a dressy button-down, which she'd left open, and wore cute ankle boots. She felt young and fresh, which was a big change from the woman who stood behind ovens for sixty-plus hours each week. She was never going to give up being a chef, but maybe she could fit in a few days each month of doing something just for her. "Besides, look at what you have on. Who wears a blazer at the beach? That can't be comfortable." She thought of Aiden's khakis and loafers and *almost* allowed her mind to put the two sharp dressers together. But she wasn't that generous.

"It's soft and extremely comfortable, thank you very much," Deirdra said as they walked around to the front of the restaurant.

Abby's hopes deflated at the sight of the empty patio. She imagined him hauling the table and chair he'd brought back to his room at the resort with his newspaper and book tucked under one arm. She'd been silly to get her hopes up. What did she think? That a handsome, charming guy like him had nothing better to do than sit on a patio all day to see if she returned? He probably had women at his beck and call.

"Don't you think it's weird that Mom needed Shelley to go over her estate with us?" Deirdra asked, pulling Abby from her thoughts. "It's not like she had anything more than the house and the business."

"I'm thankful Shelley was there to help her. But everything Mom did was weird, don't you think? She never even told us she was sick. I keep thinking about the last time she called, two weeks before she died. She was saying goodbye, but she never gave us a chance to say it back."

When Shelley had called to let Abby know their mother had passed away, Abby had asked her why their mother hadn't told them she was sick or given them a chance to come home and be with her to say goodbye. Shelley had said that she didn't want to be more of a burden to them, and she hadn't wanted them to remember her as bedridden and sickly. She'd said it was bad enough that she'd been drunk for half their lives. On some level Abby appreciated that, but to Deirdra it was another strike against their mother.

"That was Mom," Deirdra said. "Selfish as the day was long."

Abby was hurt by Deirdra's cold tone. "She missed Dad."

"So did *we*, Abby. It was her job to take care of us, not the other way around."

Same talk, different day.

Abby opened the door to the restaurant, and they stood in the entryway, taking in stacks of dusty tables and chairs, candle votives, and other restaurant paraphernalia. The wallpaper looked ancient, not elegant as she'd remembered. The rafters that had once held fancy lights were covered with cobwebs, as if the romantic decor of their youth had been only a dream. With the windows boarded up, the room felt cold and desolate, as ignored and cluttered as their mother's house.

"It smells like a mausoleum," Deirdra said.

"It's musty. We'll air it out." She propped the door open and headed inside. "Are you coming?"

Deirdra stood in the doorway, arms crossed, a look of disgust on her face. "You can't be serious. We're not sitting in there. It's awful. I say we lock it up, take that offer, and run."

Abby sighed. "This was Daddy's *dream*. Don't you remember how he taught us to cook here? Friday nights dancing with him on that very patio? Watching him and Mom mingle and dance? How can you want to leave all that behind?"

"It's called living in the present, Abby. Dad's been gone for nineteen years." She softened her tone and said, "I know how much you miss him. I do, too. But you've worked hard to get where you are at your job, and this is a money pit. The whole thing needs to be redone. Not to mention that neither of us knows a darn thing about running this place."

"Excuse me?" Abby said sharply. "I've been a cook for years, and we worked here every night from the time we were nine and eleven and *all* summer, *every* summer. I basically ran the place after graduating from high school. We know enough to make it work."

"You're *such* a dreamer." Deirdra shook her head and walked away. She stood at the edge of the patio with her back to Abby, arms crossed, gazing out at the water.

Abby was used to their differences, but that didn't mean she enjoyed arguing with Deirdra. She went to her, but rather than argue, she watched the sandpipers along the shore and let the sounds of the waves calm her.

"It's a mistake, Abby," Deirdra said softly. "I love you, but I can't give up a six-figure career for memories I'd like to forget."

Abby felt like she'd been poked with a hot needle. "You want to forget Dad?"

Deirdra turned with glassy eyes and said, "No, of course not. But everything after he died?" She nodded solemnly. "Everything but you."

Tears rose in Abby's eyes.

"Excuse me . . . ?"

They both turned at the unfamiliar voice, meeting the cautious eyes of a tall woman with jet-black hair cut just below her ears and porcelain skin. She looked like the lead actress from *Blindspot*. Her gray sweater hung loosely over her lithe frame. Her legs went on forever, and her cropped jeans revealed a swath of pale skin decorated with a colorful tattoo a few inches above her flat, black leather ankle boots.

"Hi," Abby said.

The woman looked down at an envelope she was fidgeting with, and Abby noticed tattoos on the back of her hand and snaking out from the edge of her collar.

"I'm looking for Shelley Steele." Her voice was as cautious as her green eyes.

"Shelley?" Abby said, exchanging a curious glance with Deirdra. "She should be here soon. I'm Abby and this is my sister, Deirdra. We're actually meeting with Shelley this morning. How did you know she'd be here?"

She looked down at the envelope in her hand again, her finely manicured brows knitting as she held it out to them, her unsure eyes moving between Abby and Deirdra. "She sent me this letter and asked me to come here."

Deirdra took the envelope and read the letter with a pinched expression. "This says our mother left you something in her will. Your name is Cait Weatherby?"

Cait nodded.

Deirdra looked at Abby, her silent question—*Do you know her?*—hanging between them. Abby shook her head. Deirdra handed Cait the envelope and said, "How did you know our mother?"

"I didn't," Cait said softly.

"You didn't know her at all and she left you something? Are you *sure*? Ava de Messiéres?" Deirdra sounded out their last name slowly—*de mess-ee-ay*. "She was tall, about my height, and skinny, with shoulder-length sandy hair and a gap between her two front teeth like Lauren Hutton."

Cait shook her head again.

"Have you ever been here before? Maybe you met her in the restaurant," Abby suggested. "She could have taken a liking to you. Are you an artist?"

"This is my first time on the island. I'm a tattooist and body piercer at Wicked Ink on Cape Cod." There was a quiet strength behind Cait's voice that was at odds with her fidgeting hands. She slid one arm across her stomach and leaned her other elbow on her wrist, her knuckle grazing her chin, as if she needed a barrier, a shield of protection.

"Okay," Abby said. "I don't know if our mother had hidden tattoos or piercings, but it wouldn't surprise me. She could have been one of your clients."

"Sorry I'm late!" Shelley exclaimed as she flew around the side of the building, a whirlwind in jeans and a blue clingy top, carrying a thick messenger bag. "The meeting at the winery went on forever." She was a big, beautiful woman with long auburn hair and bangs that made her look like she was in her forties rather than fifties. She had a zest for life, a heart of gold, and a contagious smile.

"*Shelley.*" Abby hugged her, and Shelley enveloped her in the maternal warmth Abby knew she'd never get enough of. "I've missed you."

"I've missed you, too, sweetheart." Shelley embraced Deirdra and said, "I've missed you, too, honey."

"Me too, Shelley. Thanks for taking care of Mom's will."

"I loved her, and I love you girls." Shelley turned to Cait with a warm smile and said, "You must be Cait Weatherby."

Cait nodded.

"I'm Shelley, and, darlin', it is a pleasure to meet you."

Shelley embraced her, but Cait stood rigid, her face a mask of apprehension. When Shelley let go, Cait's breath rushed from her lungs, as if she'd been holding it.

"I assume you girls know each other now?" Shelley asked, her eyes moving between the three of them.

"Yes," Abby said. "But we're confused. Cait said she didn't know Mom, but the letter said Mom left her something?"

"That's right, honey. Why don't we go inside and sit down," Shelley suggested.

"That's a big *no*," Deirdra said. "It's pretty bad in there."

"We can bring chairs and a table out here. Come on, Dee. I'll wipe them off." Abby hurried into the restaurant, and Deirdra and Cait followed her in.

The three of them set up a table and chairs on the patio. Abby and Cait wiped them down while Deirdra took a call from Malcolm. When they finally gathered around the table, Shelley seemed a little uneasy with the three of them looking at her expectantly. The buzz of the unknown reminded Abby of the day many years ago when Shelley had sat her down and told her that her mother was *not* her responsibility and that she needed to study hard and get a scholarship so she could one day leave the island and build her own life. Deirdra had been in her first year of college and doing just that, but at the time Abby couldn't imagine leaving her mother, who, though she was a functioning alcoholic during the day, at night was nearly drowning in her sorrows and threatening to take everything else down with her.

"I've been thinking about this day for months, since Ava told me she was sick," Shelley said. "The first thing you need to know is that I *did* ask Ava to do this herself, just as I'd wanted her to tell Abby and Deirdra that she was sick and her diagnosis was terminal. But she wasn't strong enough. She felt she'd already been enough of a burden on you girls when you were growing up, and she couldn't . . . well, she couldn't do any of it."

"Do *what*, Shelley?" Deirdra asked matter-of-factly. "Please cut to the chase. We're all adults here."

"You're right." Shelley inhaled a deep breath and said, "Here goes. Deirdra, Abby, when your mom was seventeen, she got pregnant, and her parents made her give up her daughter." Her eyes moved compassionately to Cait. "Cait, honey, you are Ava's eldest daughter."

The earth shifted beneath Abby, and her gaze locked on Cait, who looked like a deer caught in headlights, her lower lip trembling. Abby mentally cataloged her features. *Tall, lean, green eyes.* She had the same high cheekbones as their mother, the same curve to her lips. Was that jet-black hair her natural color?

"What?" Deirdra snapped. "Mom never said anything about having another child."

Shelley covered Cait's hand with her own, giving it a reassuring squeeze. "I know she didn't, and I know this is a shock to all of you, but it's true. Your mother didn't want to give up her baby. *Cait.* But her parents were overbearing, and she was only seventeen. She had no other option. Her parents arranged for a private adoption, and even at seventeen your mother knew Cait would have a better chance at a life with her adoptive family than she would with a teenage runaway, which is what she would have had to do at the time to keep her."

A tear slipped down Cait's cheek, and she quickly wiped it away. Deirdra looked stuck somewhere between stunned disbelief and frustrated confusion, so Abby picked up her chair and moved between Deirdra and Cait. She put her arm around their half sister and said, "Are you okay?"

Cait nodded. "I've just . . . I've always wondered why I was given up for adoption."

"Of course you have, honey." Shelley squeezed her hand again and said, "Ava loved you very much. I wish I could have convinced her to do this, to meet you, but Ava was an alcoholic, and she wasn't strong enough to handle it. I think she knew she was sick long before she was diagnosed, because she told me all of this before she saw the doctor the week after Christmas."

"How did she . . . ?" Cait asked softly.

Shelley's eyes dampened. "Metastatic liver cancer. By the time she saw the doctor, it had spread throughout her body. She passed a few weeks later."

More tears spilled down Cait's cheeks. Abby stroked Cait's back and said, "I'm sorry you never got a chance to meet her."

"Maybe she's better off that way," Deirdra said.

"What Deirdra means," Abby said, glowering at Deirdra, "is that the last several years were hard because our mom was drinking, but when we were young and our father was alive, our mother was amazing."

Cait looked at Shelley and said, "Did Ava run away from her overbearing parents?"

"Yes," Shelley said. "She left home shortly after the adoption was finalized. She landed here on the island a little less than a year later and got a job working for Dee and Abby's father, Olivier." His name was pronounced *O-liv-e-ay*. "Once they were married, Olivier helped Ava track you down. But Ava made the very brave and very difficult decision not to disrupt your life by trying to get you back. And I'm so sorry, Cait, but Ava wasn't sure who your father was. She said it could have been one of two of the teenage boys she was hanging out with back then, but she'd lost touch with them when she moved."

Cait lowered her eyes.

Abby's heart was breaking for her. What was she feeling, hearing about her birth mother for the first time and knowing she couldn't meet her? Learning she had two sisters? Abby was excited to get to know the sister she never knew existed, despite the skepticism on Deirdra's face. She knew how that skepticism could burn, and she also knew Deirdra would come around, so she put her energy into making sure their new half sister was okay.

"It looks like today is our lucky day," Abby said cheerily. "We have another sister to get to know."

Cait's eyes shot up to hers, and her lips twitched into an uncomfortable, disbelieving smile.

"No offense, Cait, but I have to ask a hard question," Deirdra said. "How do we know for sure that Cait is actually Mom's daughter?"

Shelley pulled a thick packet of documents out of her bag and said, "It's all right here. Copies of the adoption papers, her birth certificate, all of your mother's legal documents—birth and death certificates, social security card, medical records. The paper trail is there, Dee."

Deirdra began scanning the documents.

"Ava left the house and the business to the three of you in equal shares, along with her life insurance money." Shelley put another stack of documents on the table and said, "She didn't have much insurance. It comes out to about twelve thousand dollars each."

Cait shook her head, fidgeting with the envelope she'd brought with her, her gaze trained on it. "You two can have my shares. I didn't know her." She looked up and said, "But I would like to hear about her."

"Of course," Abby insisted. "But she left those things to you, Cait. They're *yours*."

Cait's eyes shifted warily to Deirdra.

"She's right. They're yours," Deirdra said in a softer tone. "You might have noticed that I have some resentment toward our mother, but it's not aimed at you. I'm sorry if I came across *lawyerish* or cold." She smiled and said, "I am a lawyer. I may not be as warm as Abby is, and I don't get mushy over memories the way she does, but I'm not a cold bitch. So I'm sorry."

Shelley looked at Deirdra and said, "I see you've still got your father's penchant for honesty."

"Except she doesn't cushion things as well as Dad did," Abby said, earning a smirk from Deirdra and a silent smile from Cait. "Cait, you also need to know that there's a hefty offer on the table from an investor who wants to buy the Bistro."

"Oh? In that case, it looks like you girls have even more to talk about today," Shelley said as she gathered her things.

"I can't stay," Cait said softly. "I have to get back to work."

"Oh, okay. Do you think you can come back tomorrow or another day? We have a lot to talk about, and I really want to get to know you," Abby said, hoping Deirdra hadn't scared her off for good.

Cait was quiet for a long moment, shifting nervously in her chair. Abby couldn't begin to imagine what was going on in her head. Hoping to sway her decision with the lure of sisterhood, she said, "You can stay with us. We haven't cleaned out Mom's room yet, but you can stay in the apartment above our garage, help us go through Mom's things, and learn about who she was."

Cait smiled cautiously. "Thanks. I'd like that. I'll talk to my boss tonight about getting a few days off and will try to come back tomorrow."

"*Great*," Abby said, thrilled that she wanted to try to come back.

Deirdra said, "I'm here until Friday morning. I'd like to get to know you, too, if you can get time off."

Relief swept through Abby, and she saw that relief mirrored in Cait's expression.

"Okay." Cait pushed to her feet and said, "It's all overwhelming. I think I'll go back to the ferry and try to wrap my head around everything. Can we exchange phone numbers in case I can't get time off?"

As they exchanged numbers, Shelley said, "Do you need a ride to the ferry?"

"Yes, if you don't mind. Thank you," Cait said, sounding more at ease. "I took an Uber here."

"No problem." Shelley turned to Abby and Deirdra and said, "Jules is anxious to stop by and see you."

Shelley had three daughters, Sutton, Leni—Abby's bestie—and Jules, and three sons, Jock, Archer, and Levi. Jock, Archer, and Jules lived on the island.

"We know," Abby and Deirdra said in unison.

"She sent a group text trying to set up a girls' night." Jules was the queen of group texts. "But everyone is so busy, we haven't been able to coordinate schedules."

"My little social butterfly keeps the island girls hopping," Shelley mused. "Just you wait, Cait. Jules will sweep you into her net, too."

"That ought to be interesting." Cait picked up her chair and said, "Is it okay if I help put these things away before we go?"

"Of course," Shelley said.

As Abby and Cait carried their chairs inside, Abby said, "Cait?"

"Yeah?" She turned, her eyes moving over Abby's shoulder to Shelley and Deirdra talking on the patio.

"I was wondering if you have other siblings . . . or if you *want* siblings . . . ?"

"I don't have any siblings, but . . ." She stood up taller, her gaze filling with confidence. "I know your mother threw us all for a loop—"

"*Our* mother, Cait. I don't see you as an outsider."

"Right. Okay. Thank you, but I don't want you to feel like you have to include me in the business, the inheritance, or your lives. You don't have to get to know me just because your mother made a mistake."

"First of all, don't refer to yourself as a mistake. Second, as far as the business goes, it's one-third yours. Whatever happens to it will be one-third *your* decision." She was surprised by her vehemence, but Abby didn't like anyone feeling uncomfortable . . . *ever*, and this was her sister. "If our mom thought you were a mistake, I don't think we'd be standing here right now. I don't feel pressure to get to know you. I *want* to get to know you. We're sisters, Cait, and that means something to me. It's a special connection, and yes, it's new for all of us, but it's not unwanted. *You're* not unwanted. Are we? Deirdra and I?"

Cait's lips pressed into a firm line as she shook her head. "I don't have any siblings, but I don't want pity."

Abby knew all about not wanting to be pitied. When she was younger and all her friends were playing and she and Deirdra were helping their mother at the restaurant because it was either that or starve, she hadn't wanted pity, either.

"The hell with pity." Abby rarely cursed, but this called for it. "How about friendship?"

"I could use a few friends."

"Good, because so can we. My sister—*our* sister—and I are workaholics, but Deirdra is even worse than me. And now you know she's not a warm and fuzzy person. But she's pretty fantastic anyway, and before Mom spiraled into alcoholism, Dee was a whole different person. We both were. Maybe you can help us find ourselves again."

"I barely know who *I* am half the time," Cait said flatly.

"That makes two of us. And you know what? Mom did throw us all for a loop. She was good at that, so maybe I'm used to it. But we share a mother, and who knows what else we have in common. We could have gone our whole lives without knowing about each other. Bringing us together was a *purposeful* move on her part." Abby looped her arm around Cait as they walked toward the door and said, "You were no mistake, Cait. You're our *gift*, and maybe we're yours."

Cait's eyes pooled with emotion.

"Shelley said she has something else for us," Deirdra said as she carried a chair into the restaurant.

"Okay. Let's get the last chair and the table inside first."

As they walked outside, Cait said, "You're not freaked out by all this?"

"Sure I am. But when you grow up with an alcoholic parent, you learn that you can handle a lot more than you ever thought possible. Besides, my boring life needed a little upending."

"Maybe we do have a few other things in common," Cait said.

Abby carried the last chair inside, and then the three of them moved the table, and she locked up the restaurant.

"Okay, ladies. I know your heads are probably spinning, but Ava left you each one more thing." Shelley pulled three envelopes out of her bag and handed one to each of them.

Abby's chest constricted at the sight of her name written in her mother's loopy handwriting on the front of the envelope. She thought back to the notes her mother used to put in her lunches, but like everything else, that had stopped after Abby's father died. She pressed the envelope to her chest, reveling in the good feelings, hoping the letter would shed more light on Cait and their mother's thoughts in her last few weeks.

"I'll get right on opening it," Deirdra said sarcastically as she shoved the letter into her purse with the other documents.

Cait stared at the envelope, running her fingers over her name.

Shelley touched her arm and said, "It must be weird to see your birth mother's handwriting for the first time."

A spark of amusement rose in Cait's eyes, and she said, "Almost as weird as meeting my sisters for the first time."

When they hugged Cait goodbye, she was more at ease than she'd been at first. Abby waved from the parking lot as Shelley drove away with Cait.

"Wow, Dee," Abby said. "We have another sister."

"Did she look like Mom? I think she looked like Mom. Her cheekbones, her eyes?"

"I noticed that, too. I can't believe Mom never said anything."

Deirdra rolled her eyes. "Why are you always surprised by her inability to do the right thing? She failed us for nineteen years." She leaned against the side of the car, looking at the restaurant, and said, "We're going to sell this dump, right?"

Abby knew they would never agree, but maybe they didn't need to. Deirdra had worked hard for her career, and she seemed to love it despite the endless hours. Abby had long ago become disenchanted with the reality of working under someone else's thumb. She gazed at the Bistro, seeing something so different from what her sister saw and remembering happier times—times that even all these years later, she'd never again come close to experiencing. She didn't want to forget them.

She wanted to bring them back.

A flutter of excitement rose inside her, and she realized that what Deirdra saw as a burden, she saw as their legacy.

"I can do this, Dee," she said confidently. "I can bring Dad's restaurant back to life, and you won't have to give up anything."

"I hope you're kidding. Abby, you've come so far. Let this go. You'll lose money hand over fist, and I don't want to see you get hurt, or lost, or go broke."

"I've been hurt before and still landed on my feet. I was lost when I first went to New York, but I found my way, and I might go broke, but I believe in myself. I think I can do this and turn a profit. I *want* to do this, Dee."

Deirdra motioned toward the car and said, "Get in."

"Where are we going?"

"Back to the house to talk this shit out. Then I have a week's worth of work to do in two days, so we need to figure out how I can get it all done while guzzling a bottle of wine."

CHAPTER THREE

"WHAT ARE YOU planning to check off your list today?" Aiden's sister, Remi, asked over the phone Thursday morning.

The dreaded list.

He adored his sister, who was twelve years his junior and whom he'd raised after they'd lost their parents in a tragic car accident. Remi had grown up and become an A-list actress, but ever since she'd fallen in love last year and taken a step back from acting to marry her onetime bodyguard Mason Swift and they began fostering two girls—or as Remi said, ever since she'd *gotten a life*—she'd been on a mission to force him into getting one, too. It wasn't like he didn't have a life. He had a good one, which he enjoyed, even if it was consumed with work. He owned and invested in businesses and real estate all over the world. But he'd do anything for Remi, which was why he was on Silver Island in the first place. She'd swindled him into taking his first nonworking vacation, and he'd let her pick the location.

The truth was, he'd been ready for a brief vacation. A day or two without work, which was about how long he'd lasted before researching the Bistro and putting in an offer to purchase it. It was too good of an investment to pass up, not that he'd clue Remi into his business dealings. He hadn't even told his business partner, because Remi had ears everywhere, and she'd somehow managed to get him to agree to a four-week work-free vacation. She'd also given him a list of things she wanted him to do while he was on his work-free vacation, and she wanted him to provide *proof* in the form of pictures.

He had no idea what the hell he'd been thinking when he'd agreed to her cockamamie plan.

"I don't know yet," he said as he opened the bag from the Sweet Barista and began setting out breakfast on the patio of the Bistro. Yesterday he'd met the owners of the Silver House, Alexander and Margot Silver and their son Fitz, and last night he'd joined them for dinner. The Silvers had been happy to lend him a few things for his breakfast with Abby—a white linen tablecloth, a vase for the rose he'd bought, a sugar bowl and creamer pitcher, and two elegant place settings. He'd made it clear that he wanted to avoid island gossip and would appreciate their keeping his request under their hats. They'd been more than happy to comply.

Remi huffed out a breath. "You'd better get on that, don't you think? If you think there are no ramifications for not completing the list, you're wrong, Mister."

"*Remi,*" he warned in his best older-brother voice, which hardly ever worked anymore.

"Don't *Remi* me. I want you to be happy. You gave up your whole life for me. You were just starting out when Mom and Dad died, and I appreciate everything you've done. But I'm married now, Aiden, and I've got my own family to take care of. You're finally *free*. You can have a *real* life now."

"I have a real life, and I don't regret a second of how I've lived it." That was true, but her words brought a moment of discomfort. After years of managing Remi's acting career, watching her every move, and protecting her, he had struggled with handing over the reins to her and her husband.

Remi sighed. "You're so frustrating. You don't regret it because you've never done anything *to* regret. Don't you see how that's a problem,

Aiden? You're pushing forty and you've never messed up. You've never thrown caution to the wind and done something stupid."

"Like ditching my bodyguards?" he challenged.

Remi had driven him crazy with her acts of rebellion, ditching several bodyguards before he'd hired Mason to watch over her. But Mason had done more than watch over her. He'd shown her how to experience life in all the ways she'd wanted, but in a safe and protected manner. It was no wonder they'd fallen in love.

"Yes, exactly like that!" Remi said excitedly. "Sometimes you have to break the rules. Look at me. I found the man of my dreams, and maybe you'll find the woman of your dreams if you step outside your comfort zone."

"I *am* out of my comfort zone," he reminded her.

"No, you're standing on the edge of your comfort zone doing everything you can to figure out how to cross the boundaries I've set up. Now you know how I felt for all those years. But I'm not trying to keep you safe. I want you to go out and be a regular guy. Not Aiden the father figure or Aiden the older brother. Not Aiden the manager of my acting career, and not Aiden the investor and billionaire. Just be *Aiden*, the amazing guy who gave up his life for me at twenty-four and never got a chance to have a social life or chill out."

Aiden wasn't a chill-out type of guy. He was a take-charge, make-shit-happen businessman who had built an empire while raising Remi and managed to pull it off without it ever being at her expense or compromising his business.

"Can you please do that for me?" Remi pleaded.

"Sure, Rem," he said distractedly, pacing the patio of the Bistro, hoping Abby would show up. He hadn't been able to stop thinking about the intriguing brunette with flyaway hair, a smile that brightened everything around her, and mesmerizing green eyes that were so big and beautiful, it was hard to look away.

"Good, but if you pull what you did yesterday, I swear I'll come there and force you to relax. I know those weren't your hairy feet in the sand. I bet you're still wearing your loafers and a button-down shirt instead of the casual clothes and flip-flops I bought you."

He looked down at his short-sleeve navy button-down, khaki pants, and loafers and said, "Hey, now, you stop right there. I'm wearing the shirt you gave me."

"I guess miracles do happen. But I bet your feet haven't touched sand yet, have they? How much did you have to pay that guy to get him to let you take a picture of his ugly feet?"

He chuckled and looked out over the water, the cool breeze kissing his cheeks. He had to hand it to her. She had picked an extraordinary spot for his vacation.

"I can't believe you're *laughing*. This is serious, Aiden. You need to learn to relax. Isn't that the whole reason you and Ben groomed Garth and Miller to take over?"

Garth Anziano and Miller Crenshaw were two of the best directors Aiden and his business partner, Ben Dalton, employed. About two years ago, when Aiden and Ben had been on the cusp of taking over an international hotel chain, Remi had a stalker situation that needed to be dealt with. At the same time, Ben had found out he had a daughter and finally confessed his feelings for his best friend, Aurelia. Aiden and Ben had promoted Garth and Miller, and they'd taken several of their larger portfolios, alleviating much of their travel and time-consuming oversight. Though Ben had done a fine job of stepping back to spend more time with his new family, once the stalker situation was handled and Remi had taken a break from acting to get married, Aiden had jumped back in with two feet, filling his every second with work.

"I bet Garth would like to slap you upside your head for stepping on his toes," Remi said sharply. "And don't think Carrie didn't call me two seconds after you called her asking for your messages yesterday."

Carrie Worthington had been Aiden's assistant for ten years, and she'd weathered Remi's rebellion with him. She was in her late thirties, fiercely loyal, sharp as a tack, and one of the few people who could keep up with his busy schedule. Unfortunately, that loyalty hadn't stopped her from shutting him down when he'd called and reporting the call to Remi. Luckily, his attorney was still taking his calls, which was how he'd been able to get the offer on the Bistro drafted and submitted.

"How much did you pay *her* to lock me out of my own company?"

"I didn't have to pay her," Remi insisted. "She worries about you, too. You know neither of us would ever jeopardize your business. By the way, she told me that you've already booked every minute after your vacation. You're going overseas? We all *know* what that means."

It meant he would work from sunup until well past sundown, just the way he liked it. "Remi, you know how important the quarterly meetings are. I'm *not* putting them off for this game of yours."

"It's not a *game*, Aiden. Carrie and Ben agreed to help me with this and make sure nothing slips through the cracks at your work, because everyone we know wants you to chill before you drive yourself to an early grave." Her tone softened, and she said, "I know you're not all I have anymore, but that doesn't mean I don't need you around. And you have two foster nieces who need you, too."

"Then why did you exile me to this island?" *And why did I let you?*

"Because that's how much I love you. Oh, that reminds me! I have to tell you what Patrice did last night . . ."

As Remi went on about her adorable foster daughter, Aiden walked to the side of the patio and caught sight of Abby riding a bike into the parking lot. Riding a bike was on his to-do list from Remi. He'd thought it was a frivolous idea, but as Abby climbed off hers, flashing that gorgeous smile he'd thought about all night, it was starting to look pretty damn good—and so was *she* in those sexy cutoffs and a white sweatshirt with CHILL emblazoned across her chest in black, as if Remi had conjured her out of thin air and sent her to him.

He waved as she locked up her bike, and Remi's voice brought him back to their conversation. He'd lost track of what she was saying.

"Hey, Remi. I've got to go. I'm having breakfast with a friend. Kiss the kids for me, okay? Tell them I miss them, and I'm going to give them great gifts when I get back."

"A friend? You made a friend! You *are* doing my list! I want a picture!" Her expression turned serious. "Wait a second. Is this a business friend or a *friend* friend?"

"Since you forbade me from doing business, what do you think?" he said, feeling mildly guilty for putting in the offer on the Bistro when he'd promised not to conduct business. But as he watched Abby's hips sway as she approached the patio, that guilt went out the window.

"Yay!" Remi cheered. "Male or female?"

"*Goodbye*, Remi. I love you." He ended the call and slid the phone into his pocket. "Good morning, Abby. No run today?"

"Hi." A mischievous smile curved her lips, and she said, "I'm not really a runner. I only do it when I'm stressed out. I was wondering if you'd actually show up."

"I was wondering the same thing about you. I'm glad you came." He put a hand on her lower back as they walked along the side patio. The breeze picked up the summery scent of her perfume: coconut and sunshine.

When they stepped around the corner to the front, her jaw dropped, delight gleaming in her gorgeous green eyes. "Who *are* you?"

"Just a guy on vacation having breakfast with a beautiful woman." He pulled out a chair for her, making a mental note to try harder to be a *regular* guy. He'd spent so many years being guarded and professional, he wasn't even sure he knew how to be a regular guy anymore. But there was something unexpectedly exhilarating about not being known for his wealth or Remi's celebrity and Abby riding up on her bike, delightfully surprised by nothing more than coffee and a croissant. Maybe his sister was onto something.

She studied him as they sat down, giving him a moment to do the same. She had the prettiest golden-brown hair hanging in thick waves to the middle of her back, a little wild and messy, parted in the center, with one slim braid peeking out from either side, and the type of smile that said *You're new and this could be fun!* That smile reeled him right in, making him want to know more about what she found fun. A spray of adorable freckles dotted the ridge of her left cheek, as if they were marking her as special, begging to be touched, or maybe kissed.

"This is incredible, Aiden. But where did you get all this?"

"Here and there. I have a better question. Where did you get that sweatshirt? I need to get one just like it to appease my younger sister."

"That was a smooth subject change," she said teasingly. "Does your sister like to chill?"

He put his napkin in his lap and said, "She thinks she does, but the truth is, she's too busy to chill. She and her husband run a program that provides duffel bags and quarterly birthday parties for foster kids, and they're working on adopting their two foster daughters." He smiled, thinking of the two girls who had instantly stolen his heart. "Patrice is five and cute as a button. She's an inquisitive little thing, and calls me Uncle Aiden, which is pretty great. Olive is fifteen going on twenty-five. She's an amazing kid, but she wears her heart on her sleeve, which worries me. I wish I could put their hearts in Bubble Wrap, you know? Or maybe a lead box, until they're old enough to get past all the heart-breaks girls go through. They are the lights of Remi's life." As Remi's name left his lips, a heavy dose of shock settled in, giving him pause. He'd spent years protecting Remi's identity and he'd never talked about her personal life with someone he'd only just met. He gazed across the table at the woman who had somehow slipped past his guard without even trying and wondered what other powers she possessed.

"It sounds to me like they light up your life, too," she said sweetly.

"Yes, without a doubt. I love those girls as much as I love my sister."

Her gaze moved over their table, and she said, "Why do I have a feeling you spoil them rotten?"

"Who, me? *Nah.*" He took a drink of coffee and noticed her eyeing his blueberry Danish. He'd brought her a raspberry-and-Bavarian-cream croissant, as promised. "Do you like blueberry?"

"Was I that obvious?" Her cheeks pinked up. "I was wondering if you were a *sharer.* As much as I love Keira's croissants, I'd do anything for one of her blueberry Danishes."

"*Really?*" He arched a brow, making a mental note to stock up on blueberry Danishes. "I like a woman who goes after what she wants."

A cute little laugh tumbled out, and she said, "I didn't mean *that.*"

As he cut the Danish in half, she cut the croissant in half, sneaking glances at him, and said, "My sister and I used to do this all the time."

She picked up half of the croissant to give to him at the same time he lifted his plate, allowing her to take her half of the Danish.

Her infectious smile grew even larger as she said "Sorry" and put the croissant back on her plate. She lifted her plate as he had.

"Don't apologize for being yourself. It's refreshing, and I'm taking mental notes. My sister tells me I need to relax, and I'm starting to think maybe she's right." He took the half she'd picked up and set it on his plate. "It's been a long time since I've had breakfast with a woman who wasn't a business associate. I've kind of forgotten how to turn off my work etiquette."

She took her half of the Danish and said, "It's been a long time since I've had breakfast with anyone other than my sister. We're total finger foodies."

Finger foodies? She was too damn cute. "This sister of yours sounds like a big part of your life. You must be close. Do you work together?"

"No, but we took care of each other when we were growing up." She bit into the Danish and moaned. "You are a *god* for sharing with me."

"You should probably set that bar a bit higher," he said, and bit into the Danish. "*Mm.* You were right. This is fantastic."

"I know my baked goods." She sipped her coffee, and her eyes lit up, her every emotion on display. "I need to ask Keira where she got this new coffee. It's delicious."

"Actually, I wish you wouldn't do that. I'm a bit of a coffee connoisseur. I went to three coffee shops before I found Keira's, and all of them served something that could pass for coffee, but . . ." He shook his head. "Keira's was better than the rest, but this coffee is made from my personal stash of beans from northern Indonesia. Keira made me promise not to tell anyone she was doing me a special favor by making it for me each morning."

She tilted her head and said, "So you're a coffee snob."

"I prefer *connoisseur.* Let me guess. Keira is your sister."

"Okay, we'll go with your fancy word, and no, Keira isn't my sister. She's a friend I grew up with here on the island."

"Ah, the plot thickens. So you live here and know all of the island's secrets."

"I know *most* of the island's secrets, but only because my best friend, Leni, has siblings who still live on the island. She keeps me up to date on all the gossip. But I live in New York, and my sister, Deirdra, lives in Boston. How about you? Where do you call home?"

"I'm trying to figure that out. I guess LA is considered home, but I'm not there much. I'm in finance, and I travel a lot, living out of hotels."

She took a bite of the Danish, making another appreciative sound, and *man*, he liked those sounds.

"Tell me, Runner Girl, why were you so stressed yesterday?"

"Oh my gosh. *So* much has happened since I saw you, it seems like it was ages ago. For starters, this was my mother's restaurant. She passed away three months ago." A hint of sadness tainted her voice. "Two days ago we received an offer on the Bistro, and the night before I saw you,

Deirdra had kept me up half the night trying to convince me to sell it, which is why I was stressed."

Well, *hell*, his life just got a little more complicated, and there was no denying the tug he felt at the tinge of sadness he'd heard in her voice, which outweighed the minor complication. "I'm sorry for your loss. I know how hard it is to lose a parent."

"Thank you. We weren't that close these last few years, although I was closer to her than Deirdra was. Our father died when I was nine and Deirdra was eleven." The sadness returned, thicker this time. "It's a strange realization to accept that they're both gone."

"Oh, Abby." He reached across the table and caressed the back of her hand, bringing her eyes to his. Her skin was soft as a rose petal, her gaze even softer. He had the urge to move his chair closer, to let her know she had a shoulder to lean on if she needed it. But he stayed where he was and said, "My parents are gone, too. We lost them when Remi was twelve. I was twenty-four at the time, running the Los Angeles division of my father's company. I raised her from then on. I understand what you're feeling, but I think *strange realization* is putting it mildly. I loved my parents deeply. If I hadn't had Remi to raise, I probably would have lost my mind for a while. But she was so young and vulnerable and so very heartbroken. I didn't have the opportunity to fall apart, and that was definitely a good thing."

"Aiden . . . ? I'm so sorry. Looks like we have more in common than I would have guessed. I adored my father, and my mother was great when he was alive, but that was so long ago. She was never the same after he died, and neither were we. Deirdra and I pretty much had to raise ourselves after that and pick up the slack here at the restaurant."

His heart took another hit, a bigger one, the kind that was usually reserved for Remi and the girls.

"Deirdra has a lot of resentment toward my mother. Plus, she's a corporate attorney and busy all the time. In fact, she's working today from our mom's house while I get started cleaning up the restaurant, and she has to go back to Boston tomorrow morning for a meeting. Needless to say, she thinks the Bistro is a money pit and wants to sell and leave the bad memories behind."

It could be a money pit in the wrong hands. It might not look like much, but it was sitting on prime waterfront real estate and worth every penny of his three-million-dollar offer. For the first time in his life, Aiden hoped his offer would be turned down.

"And you?" he asked. "What do you want to do with it?"

"I want to *keep* it," she said excitedly. "I know our mother was a mess after our father died, and that sucked. There's no other way to put it. But I have years of happy memories of my parents, and those are the ones I hold on to. My mom was once so happy and in love, it radiated from her. I used to think I wanted to be happy like she was when I grew up, and work in a restaurant, cooking like my dad. But then I realized I don't want to be her type of happy, because she wasn't enough for herself after he died, and I get that. My father was an amazing man. He was French, and when he wasn't behind the stove, he'd pull up a chair to chat with customers while they ate dinner. I watched their faces light up when he stopped by their tables, like he was some kind of celebrity or a member of their family they hadn't seen in a while. He knew everyone, and if he didn't know them when they walked in, he did by the time they left. My mom was the sun to his moon. She was as friendly and outgoing, but she also watched out for him. When he'd talk for too long, she'd put a hand on his shoulder and say, 'Is my Olivier bothering you?' and of course the customers would say no. But my dad would take the hint, and he'd say something like, '*Mon amour* misses me.'"

If Aiden knew one thing, it was that there was no room for emotions in business decisions, and Abby was clearly leading with her heart. Had she even reviewed the restaurant's financials or worked up any future projections? Did she know what the operational costs were to run the business? Did she have the capital to fix the place up? To hire staff? Her sister called the place a *money pit*. Had Deirdra studied the data and made that call, thinking it smarter to sell? Every iota of his being wanted to warn Abby, to walk her through the necessary steps of due diligence before she made that big a decision, but that wasn't his place. He was supposed to be Aiden the regular guy, not Aiden the investor, so he took a drink of coffee, swallowing those urges down deep.

Abby licked blueberry off the edge of the Danish and took a bite. Pleasure rose in her eyes, stirring a wave of awareness within him, awakening *Aiden* the *man*. His mind took a turn down a different road, wanting to see a different type of pleasure in her eyes.

To distract himself from the lust simmering inside him, he said, "It sounds like your parents were wonderful together."

"They were, and I know my father sounds intrusive. But he wasn't." Oblivious to the sinful thoughts she'd sparked, she ate another bite of her Danish and said, "*Mm. So, so good.*"

God, this woman . . .

"It's hard to put into words what it was like to be around my father," she said. "It was like he sprinkled magic everywhere he went. I thought all restauranteurs were like him. But I learned the truth years later, when I left the island, went to culinary school, and became a chef. After working in restaurants in New York City for a few years, I realized life in the kitchen was pretty bleak and stressful."

"Then why keep the Bistro?"

Her gaze moved around them, as if she were making sure no one else would hear her answer, and said, "Because I'm convinced the restaurant still has a bit of my father's magic in it, and I want to bring it back to life. I think this might be my destiny. After my mom died, I took a long, hard look at my life, and I realized I wasn't happy. So I quit my job, even though I had absolutely no idea what my next move would be. I mean, I knew the restaurant would be ours, but I wasn't completely sure I'd want to run it until yesterday, when I jogged over that hill and saw it. Then I *knew* it was meant to be." She sighed and relaxed into the chair.

Abby was starry-eyed with her talk of magic and romanticizing her situation. While her dreaminess was appealing, Aiden had seen this a hundred times in business, and it almost always led to bad decisions that cost people everything they had. He heard the warnings in his head, but even though the businessman in him thought quitting her job without a plan was completely irresponsible, there was something so appealing about this woman who believed in herself enough to take that big a chance, he wanted to cheer her on.

"But yesterday we also found out that we have a half sister named Cait who lives on Cape Cod," Abby said lightly. "And it turns out that our mother left the restaurant and the house to the three of us in equal shares."

Aiden looked for hints of anger or resentment, but Abby's eyes were clear, and there were no tension lines anywhere on her beautiful face. Surprised, he said, "It sounds like your situation is no longer as cut-and-dried as you'd thought. Shouldn't you be running today? That sounds pretty stressful."

"I know, right?" She took a big bite of her croissant, her smiling eyes watching him as she ate. "I should be super stressed, but when I met Cait, I didn't feel freaked out. I don't really know what I felt. Excited to have another sister and sad for having never known her, of course, and a bit worried because Deirdra and I are a lot to take in. What if she doesn't like us? What if we don't like her? Honestly, I know we'll like her, or at least I will, because I already do. I mean, she's our *sister* and that's huge."

"I can't imagine anyone not liking you, but I have to ask a big question that's none of my business. Have you verified this through DNA?"

"You sound like Deirdra. She was skeptical, too, but our mother provided documents that verify everything."

"You should make sure it's all valid."

"Deirdra read through them last night, and it all appears to be in order. So now there's Cait to think about. And believe me, she was just as shell-shocked yesterday as we were. But at least Deirdra and I have had time to adjust to our mother being gone. Cait has not only *just* learned who her birth mother was, that she has *two* sisters, *and* that she's now the proud owner of one-third of this property and the house, but also that her mother is gone. She can never ask the questions I'm sure she has. I don't know what Cait wants to do about any of this, but she's meeting me here so we can get to know each other, and she's got the next few days off so we can start to figure things out. And here I am, knowing you for less than an hour and airing all my dirty laundry. Way to go, Abby!" she cheered. "I'm sorry, Aiden. I guess I really needed to talk about all of this, and you're the lucky recipient of my ramblings. Maybe you *should* have your running shoes on so you can take off and never look back."

And there it was, the difference between Abby and most of the other women he came in contact with. The others worked hard to impress him, but Abby was just being herself, and he liked that a whole hell of a lot. She was also a talker. He'd never been into talkative women, but the sound of Abby's voice was so much sweeter than the silence he usually craved.

"And miss the next episode of the *Abigail-Deirdra-Cait Chronicles*? No way. This is far more fun than anything I've done in a long time." He held her gaze, heat and curiosity swirling in the space between them. He had the urge to cradle her face in his hands and press his lips to hers, to taste all that she was and all that she hoped to be.

But just as those thoughts stirred darker ones, a blush stained her cheeks, as if she were thinking them, too. She looked out at the water, breaking their connection, and said, "Boy, I've missed being here." Her eyes flicked to his. "But it's never quite been like this."

They made small talk as they finished eating, and then she stood up in those sexy little shorts and said, "I should get to work. I'm sure you have a big day planned."

"Huge," he said with a grin. "I'm a regular sloth on vacation."

"Do you want me to help you clean up or take any of this back to the person you stole it from?"

He chuckled. "I think I can handle it. It was nice sharing breakfast with you, Not So Much of a Runner Girl."

She flashed that effervescent smile and said, "Right back at ya, Chair Guy."

Abby's heart was going ten types of crazy as she unlocked the restaurant door. Did she really just have breakfast with that great guy? That great *gorgeous* guy? What alternative world had she woken up in? Her life was never this exciting. She stole one last glance at the man who had completely disarmed her from the moment she'd sat down. He was stacking their breakfast dishes. He looked up and winked, sending the butterflies in her belly into a wild flurry.

"Thanks again," she said, and walked inside wondering if she'd ever see him again. She breathed deeply, trying to calm her nerves as she flicked on the lights. The musty scent and the sight of chairs stacked on tables brought her mind back to the enormous task before her. She'd stocked up on cleaning supplies and had dropped them off last night. She picked up one of the buckets, and as she wove around tables, heading for the kitchen, her thoughts trickled back to Aiden and the intense way he'd listened to her rambling on about her family. He probably thought she was nuts, wanting to keep the Bistro and spilling her guts to a stranger. Although, for some reason, he didn't feel like a stranger.

Just outside the kitchen, she passed the cracked and weathered counter where her father used to keep the cash register and could practically hear the faint *ding* of the drawer opening. She pushed through the double doors, taking in the familiar stainless-steel appliances as she set the bucket in the sink. If she tried hard enough, she could still hear the clanking of dishes, the sizzle of meats searing, and the kitchen staff calling out to each other over sounds of the Eagles, the Allman Brothers, and other classic bands playing from the only station her father's old boom box could tune in to without static. Luckily, classic rock was his favorite, and it had become Abby's, too. The songs were hallmarks of her youth, welcome reminders of how fun work could be.

Her phone vibrated with a text. She pulled it from her pocket and read the group message from Jules. *Hottie alert! The grapevine is buzzing for all the single ladies! Mrs. S can't stop raving about some guy named Aiden who is staying at the Silver House.*

Knowing Mrs. Silver, she'd already given him the third degree and vetted him for her single daughters. Abby wasn't going to respond and become part of the island gossip, but she liked knowing that Mrs. Silver thought enough of him to give him her stamp of approval, which wasn't easy to achieve. With Abby's luck, she'd never even see him again.

She pocketed her phone, returning her attention to the grungy kitchen and her father's boom box. Her father used to keep it on the shelf above the dishwasher, but she couldn't see the back of the shelf, so she hoisted herself up on the counter like she had as a young girl, letting out a *whoop* at the sight of the dusty black boom box with the cord wrapped around one side. She set it on the counter as she climbed down and blew the dust off the top, feeling like she'd won the lottery. Glancing at the dial, she realized her mother hadn't changed the station, which made her happy.

She filled a bucket with water and carried the boom box and the bucket into the restaurant, shocked to find Aiden standing inside the doorway looking around with a serious expression. In his button-down shirt and loafers, he could have walked off the pages of a yachting magazine. For some reason, seeing that beautiful man standing among the dingy effects of a life gone by—a life she wanted to resurrect—made her happy. She'd noticed that he hadn't shaved, and a dusting of scruff covered his jaw and upper lip. She'd also noticed how tempting his lips were. And now she was practically drooling.

Schooling her expression, she said, "Aiden?"

His face snapped in her direction as if she'd startled him. "Hey there. So this is it, huh?"

"This is it." She set the boom box and bucket down. "I know it doesn't look like much, but at one time, it was . . ."

"Your father's dream?"

She loved that he'd not only listened but had understood the things she hadn't specifically said. "Exactly. He came to the States when he was twenty-five on a mission to find his future with nothing more than a backpack and a small inheritance. He met a woman named Metty at an airport who had grown up on Silver Island, and she told him all about it."

"Ah, he followed a beautiful woman."

"No, actually. Metty was on her way to Chicago, but he was enamored by her description of the island, so he changed his route, came here, and got what we locals call *island fever*. This building was just a rundown boathouse at the time, and he bought it for a song. But you should have seen how beautiful he made it. That glass wall behind you is made of folding glass doors. The whole wall opens up, all the way across. It's hard to tell right now because they're covered by the barn-style doors on the outside to protect them from getting pitted over the winter. When they're open, the sea breeze comes into the restaurant, and there's *nothing* like it. You probably haven't ever seen anything like them before. They're pretty rare and expensive."

He cocked a grin and said, "I think I know what you're talking about."

"Yeah? It looks so different without the windows and doors open. But when I was growing up, we had three enormous imported French chandeliers that looked like they belonged in grand hotels and different types of colorful eclectic lights, like you'd see in a beach bar, all hanging from the rafters. My father called the whole lot of them *lights of love*. The tile floor was also imported from France. He was so proud of the lights and the tiles. He had Parisian rugs strewn around the room, and elegant café chairs. *Nothing* matched, but somehow it all worked together to give this place the most romantic feel. My mom sold the chandeliers and rugs when we needed money over the winters, and I guess I never realized the colorful lights eventually went, too." She thought about how sad she'd been when her mother had sold those things and realized she'd taken over the conversation *again*. "Oh my gosh, Aiden, I'm so sorry. I'm doing it again, rambling like a fool. What are you doing here, anyway?"

He lifted his hands, which held a bag from the Sweet Barista and a to-go cup. "You said Cait was coming from the Cape to meet you, so I went to grab her something in case she missed breakfast. I know how traveling can upend a schedule."

"That was *so* nice of you." There was no hiding her shock or her appreciation. "But you didn't have to do that. She won't be here for a few hours."

"In that case, why don't we put the Danish aside for her and you can have the coffee." He handed her the coffee and set the bag on a table. Then he rubbed his hands together and said, "What can I do to help?"

Holy cow, she'd never met anyone like him. "You said you have a *huge* day planned and that you were supposed to be relaxing."

"Yeah, well, I think we've established that I'm not great at relaxing. I grew up following my father around our old farmhouse, fixing things, tinkering, and doing odd jobs. I'm practically an expert at stripping wallpaper off the walls. I can show you how to do it and help you get the rest of this stuff cleaned up."

"You're on *vacation*. You must have better things to do."

His brows lifted, and he said, "I did my time relaxing and trying not to work. But Remi has relegated me to this island for an entire month on a work-free vacation, and she swindled my assistant into handling my calls and my business partner into keeping me out of business dealings while I'm here. And if that's not bad enough, she even gave me a list of things I have to do while I'm here. An entire *list*. She called it my Let Loose list."

Amused, she said, "Your sister sounds awesome. Maybe I should talk to her about doing that for Deirdra."

"I don't advise it. Bored workaholics can be dangerous creatures. They've been known to hang out at pretty women's bistros."

"Lucky me. Why didn't you say no?"

"Easier said than done with my sister, which is why I need you to *please* give me something to do before I lose my mind. I have three more weeks to get through."

"Somehow I doubt a man like you can't find something more interesting to keep him busy." She crossed her arms and narrowed her eyes, wondering whether he was serious. "Can I see your sister's list?"

He pulled out his phone, poked around on it, and handed it to her. "It's like I'm a kindergartener, right?"

"Aiden's Let Loose list." She chuckled. "What is *this*? It says to send *proof*."

"She wants pictures," he said with a shake of his head.

She scanned the list.

- Go on a bike ride
- Fly a kite

"I haven't flown a kite in years," she said excitedly. "That's so fun!"

- Spend the afternoon on the beach
- Collect shells and build a sandcastle
- Spend time in the water
- Make a friend—NOT business related

"Oh my gosh. I love your sister. You can check off *make a friend.* That's *me*." She wiggled her shoulders, earning an amused and extremely sexy grin.

- Visit Fortune's Landing lighthouse

"She's very specific. We have a few lighthouses on the island. I haven't been to any of them since I was a little girl. I remember the one at Fortune's Landing because the stairs seemed like they went on forever. I'd love to go in it again."

- Wish upon a star
- Visit the winery
- Read a novel

"Our friends own the winery," she said. "That'll be fun. And I can recommend a great novel for you to read. It's called *It Lies*, and the author lives on the island. It's super scary."

Aiden's lips quirked up. "Not much scares me."

"We'll see," she said, and continued reading the list.

- Window-shop
- Eat a huge ice cream sundae
- Nap in a hammock
- Go to a bonfire
- Eat with your hands

"Eat with your hands. *Done!*" She continued reading, wondering why *she* wasn't doing all these things, too. It was the perfect list for a beach vacation.

- Watch the sunset

- Watch the sunrise
- Take an evening walk
- Flirt with a woman

"I'm pretty sure you can knock this off, too." She pointed to *flirt with a woman*, and a low laugh rumbled from his lips.

- Feed a seagull
- Go skinny-dipping
- Eat dinner with new friends. NO talking business!
- Have a picnic with a friend (preferably a female)
- Go dancing
- Get your groove on. NOT your business groove!

She looked up, catching him watching her with an amused expression.

"Crazy, right?" he said.

"*No.* I want to live by your side for the next three weeks. I *love* picnics, and I haven't had one—or done most of these other things—in a really long time. I'd like to do all of them. Well, except maybe the last one, unless grooving to music is an option. Not that I don't want to get my groove on with you, because I'd totally be into that."

He flashed that devastating grin, and she realized what she'd said.

"Oh my gosh. I didn't mean that the way it sounded."

"That's a shame." He chuckled, making her laugh, too.

"*Ugh.* Just . . . never mind. Forget skinny-dipping, by the way. I haven't gone since I was a teenager, so that's all *you*, big guy."

"Skinny-dipping alone? What fun would that be?" He reached for the phone, his hand engulfing hers, and he stepped closer. The woodsy scent of sandalwood embraced her, and his piercing stare rooted her in place as he said, "I bet you're excellent at skinny-dipping *and* getting your groove on."

His seductive tone brought a rush of desire.

"I have to admit," he said, holding her gaze, "I like the idea of you living by my side for the next few weeks."

Me too.

"The only way to check these things off my list is to prove it with a picture. Would you mind if we took a selfie together?"

She couldn't resist teasing him. "How do I know you won't use it for some *other* purpose?"

"Because I don't need a picture for that. I've got the image of you in those skimpy shorts etched into my mind."

"Oh boy, you are good at the flirting thing." And she loved it!

"Good to know, because I rarely do it. Is that a *yes*?"

She nodded. "Why not?"

"Not the *hell yes* I was hoping for, but I'll take it," he joked. He pulled up the camera on his phone, slipped an arm around her waist, tugging her against his side, and said, "Smile, gorgeous."

He smelled delicious. His body was firm and broad, and they fit together as perfectly as a puzzle, like she belonged at his side. How could she do anything *but* smile?

"That should make your sister happy," she said.

"The heck with my sister. That one's *mine*."

She tried to ignore the quickening of her pulse and poked his ribs, feigning a scowl. "You said it was for your sister."

"It is, I promise. I just wanted to get a rise out of you because I love your facial expressions. You wear your heart on your sleeve, like Olive, and that's a rare and delightful quality."

Her heart stuttered. "But you said you were worried about her because of that."

"Because I don't want her to get hurt. I'm not worried that I'll hurt you, Abby."

Abby wanted to believe that, but her mother had lied to her so often, she was hedging her bets.

He pocketed his phone and said, "Why don't I open the shutters and those barn doors so we can air this place out."

"You don't have to help."

"Didn't we just agree that I'm helping you today and you're sticking by my side for the duration of my vacation, helping me with all those things on my list?"

"You're serious?" She wanted to do a happy dance, but she couldn't believe he was willing to give up his vacation time to help her clean the filthy restaurant.

"Do you think I know how to fly a kite or where I can go skinny-dipping without ending up in jail?" He pointed at her with a devious glint in his eyes and said, "A person's word is gold, *Smiley*. That's the first rule of good business, so think twice before backing out on me."

His endearment only made her smile harder. "Are you kidding? It's a win-win for me. I get the use of your muscles to help clean up this mess, *and* I get to have fun doing things I haven't done in years with a guy who knows how to pull coffee favors. I'm *in*. But do you want to go change or something? That's a really nice shirt, and it might get ruined."

He looked down at his shirt and shrugged. "You're probably right." He began unbuttoning it, revealing a dusting of chest hair and lickable pecs.

Lust pooled low in her belly. "Wait! Stop. You . . . *um* . . . Don't do that. Button up. I'll buy you a new shirt if it gets ruined." Her words came out too fast and flustered, causing him to laugh. "Don't *laugh* at me. You're like one giant distraction! How would you like it if I took *my* shirt off?"

A wolfish grin appeared, and he said, "I definitely would *not* tell you to stop."

She rolled her eyes, but she loved his sense of humor. As he rebuttoned his shirt, she said, "You are not some regular guy here on vacation. Regular guys don't look like you, carry around imported coffee beans, and set up breakfasts fit for a queen."

"Aw, come on, Abs. I'm a regular guy who has a touch of class and likes good coffee."

Abs? No one had called her that since she was a little girl, and she loved it. Guess he didn't think of her as a stranger, either.

He rolled his shoulders back and said, "And I will reiterate my earlier sentiments. You need to *raise* your bar on your *man standards*. A beautiful, smart woman like you should be used to being treated like a queen."

"Maybe we should take a picture of me blushing and send it to your sister to prove how well you flirt." She motioned toward the back of the restaurant and said, "Let's go, Coffee Guy. You need tools to take care of the shutters."

With the windows and folding doors open, the brisk sea air swept through the restaurant, clearing the musty smell and bringing back the scents of Abby's youth. Hours passed with chatter and laughter and the sounds of classic rock making their hard work feel more like play. Aiden was funny and charming, singing along with the songs just as she was. When he walked by, he'd take Abby's hand and twirl her around, do a dance step or two, then go back to scrubbing a table or chair. She'd learned that his parents had listened to oldies in the car when they'd taken family trips. They talked about tourist attractions on the island and how different it was from the city, and she made him laugh with stories of temperamental cooks, persnickety customers, and the trials and tribulations of working in upscale restaurants in the city.

She looked across the room, where he was hard at work wiping down the legs of a table, and she felt happier than she had in a very long time. It made her giddy. He was so easy to talk to. She couldn't remember the last time she'd had this much fun. He looked up, catching her watching him, and she couldn't help but smile, and then went back to cleaning. She kept her eyes trained on the chair as he headed in her direction, her pulse quickening with his every step. He walked past her, and just as she let out the breath she hadn't realized she was holding, he swatted her ass with a rag. She squealed and darted away. He chased after her, swatting her again.

She dodged the hit and hollered, "Don't you dare!"

She spun around to retaliate, laughing so hard she slipped and stumbled forward, landing against his chest. His arms circled her, strong and possessive, and that wolfish grin returned. Their eyes connected, silencing their laughter. Neither one blinked. She wasn't even sure she was breathing. The air around them electrified, her thoughts urging her to throw caution to the wind, go up on her toes, and kiss him.

"Um, Abby?"

Abby's head whipped to the side at the sound of Cait's voice. Cait stood in the doorway, her eyes wide as saucers. Abby tried to step back, but for a split second Aiden held tight. Just long enough to let her know he didn't want to let go. Then his hand slid down her back, lingering there, as she said, "*Cait.* Hi."

Cait looked warily at Aiden. Her eyes narrowed, finding Abby's again, and she said, "Everything okay?"

No. My heart is racing. I nearly kissed a man I barely know—and I wish I had kissed him because now it'll be all I'll think about for the rest of the day. Abby bit back those words nervously and said, "Yeah, of course. Come in." She glanced at Aiden. His expression was as intimate as the kiss she wanted. Swallowing hard, she tried to focus on Cait, and said, "This is Aiden. He was helping me clean up."

Aiden's hand slipped from her back, and he said, "Hi. You must be Cait. It's a pleasure to meet you." He crossed the room and offered his hand.

Looking tough in her leather jacket, jeans with tears on one thigh, and black Converse sneakers, Cait glanced at his hand, but she didn't shake it. She lifted a cautious gaze and said, "It's nice to meet you."

"I like your ink." Aiden nodded toward the tattoos on her neck.

Her arm snaked across her middle, as it had yesterday, and she leaned her other elbow on her wrist, touching her neck tattoos with her fingers, nodding a silent thank-you.

Aiden's gaze shifted to Abby, and that zing of electricity returned. "I should get out of your hair and let you ladies get acquainted. Thanks for letting me help out. I had a great time."

She didn't want him to leave, but at the same time, she wanted to get to know Cait and figure out why she was so cautious. "Thanks for breakfast and for helping me clean up."

"Do you think a particular owner of this place would have an issue with me leaving my table and chairs out front in exchange for breakfast tomorrow? I still need to get that *finger foodie* picture."

A shiver of delight skated through her. "I think she can handle that."

Appreciation shone in his eyes. "Excellent. Then I'm off to buy a book and a kite. If you two get bored around four or five o'clock, I'll be the guy wrestling with the kite down the beach."

Abby watched him leave, her eyes traveling from his broad shoulders to his slim waist, lingering on his perfect butt until he was out of sight, wishing *she* could wrestle with him on the beach. Her body tingled in anticipation of seeing him tomorrow morning.

"Need some ice water?" Cait teased.

"No." *Yes!* Abby hugged her, noticing Cait returned her embrace this time. "Thanks for coming. I'm so glad you're here."

"Me too. Was that your boyfriend?"

"No. I just met Aiden yesterday. We had breakfast together today, and then he showed up with breakfast for you and jumped in to help me clean."

Cait's brows knitted. "Breakfast for *me*?"

"Yeah. Nice, right? I mentioned you were meeting me, and he showed up with coffee and a blueberry Danish for you. The Danish is over there." She pointed to a clean table. "But I drank your coffee. Sorry."

"No worries," she said as Deirdra walked in.

"Did you guys just get a delivery or something?" Deirdra asked. "Because I saw one *fine*-looking man walking away from here toward the Silver House with his arms full."

"That was Abby's date," Cait said.

"He wasn't my *date*," Abby insisted, and Cait arched a brow. "Okay, *fine*. I guess he was my breakfast date, but then he showed up to help me clean. He's a new friend, a—"

"Guy you want to have your way with?" Deirdra asked, sending Abby's body into a needy frenzy at the thought. "Because if you don't, I wouldn't mind working off some stress with him."

Abby narrowed her eyes and said, "Hands off, Dee. What are you doing here, anyway? I thought you had to work."

"I do, but I felt guilty leaving you guys with this mess." Deirdra looked down at her jeans and T-shirt and said, "I'm ready to work. Had I known you had a hottie on your hands all morning, I'd have kept working."

"They looked like they were ready to christen these tables when I walked in," Cait said, snagging the Sweet Barista bag off the table.

Abby gasped. "We did *not!*"

"Then you're not as smart as I thought, because I definitely would have," Deirdra said. "Cait, did you go to Keira's?"

"I have no idea who Keira is, but Abby's guy brought this for me. Want to split it?" She held the bag out to Deirdra.

"No, thanks," Deirdra said. "I already ate about half a Bundt cake that someone dropped off at the house. So, what's the scoop with the guy?"

"No scoop. His name is Aiden, and he's here on vacation." Abby wanted to gush about their fancy breakfast, how easygoing he was, and how much fun she'd had, but she wasn't ready yet. Her body was still humming from their *almost* kiss, and she wanted to enjoy that before facing any more of an interrogation. She went to get the broom and said, "We can talk about him later. Let's tackle some of these dust bunnies."

Deirdra looked at Cait and said, "That means there's *something* juicy going on between them, but she doesn't want to share."

"How can you tell?" Cait asked.

"Because when little Miss Warm and Fuzzy avoids people, she's holding secrets. How long can you stay, Cait?"

"I have to go back Sunday for work."

Abby looked up from where she was sweeping, glad Cait could stay a few days, and said, "You can stay with us at the house. As I mentioned, there's an apartment above the garage. It's fully furnished and even has a kitchen, although I'd rather you ate with us so we can get to know each other."

"And we can ply Abby with alcohol to make her spill her secrets," Deirdra said, earning a genuine smile from Cait.

Deirdra and Abby had talked last night about Cait. They had a million questions, but they agreed that if she showed up to help today, they wouldn't grill her. Instead, they'd try to get to know her a little at a time, to help put her at ease.

Abby was surprised to see Deirdra jumping in to help clean, especially since she'd made several rhetorical remarks about having an offer on the table to sell the Bistro as is, but she was thankful just the same. They talked as they worked, tiptoeing around each other's lives and breaking only to eat the pizza they'd ordered. They learned that Cait had worked at Wicked Ink for the last few years, had grown up in Connecticut, and hated pepperoni. It wasn't much, but it was a start.

Hours later, Deirdra collapsed into a chair and kicked her feet up on the chair beside her. "I'm fried. I haven't done this much manual labor in forever."

Cait leaned on the mop handle, looking as worn out as Deirdra.

As a cook, Abby was used to being on her feet for hours, but she'd forgotten how long it took to *clean* a restaurant. And this one needed deep cleaning. Some of the grime was so caked on, she wondered if her mother had ever wiped down the furniture after Abby had moved off the island. It was taking forever to clean between the grooves on each of the intricately carved café chairs. But it was worth it. The tile floor sparkled, and the warm wooden tabletops gleamed.

But that was only the tip of the iceberg. The grout in the floor needed repointing, the wallpaper needed to be scraped off, and the whole place needed to be painted. They hadn't even begun tackling the windows and rafters, much less the kitchen, office, and bathrooms— although they did scrub one stall of the ladies' room so they could use it. That morning she'd noticed that the patio needed repointing, and some of the stones needed to be replaced, too. The siding needed to be repaired and replaced in a few areas, and the whole building could use a good power washing. The overgrown bushes and broken fencing were projects in and of themselves. But none of that deterred her joy of watching the restaurant start blooming to life like a seedling finally seeing the sun.

"I feel like I have grime from head to toe. I want to take a shower and flop on the couch to get some of my work done. What do you say, Cait?" Deirdra asked.

"I'm good with that," she said. "I'd like to lie down and read for a while. I didn't sleep well last night."

"I don't think any of us did," Abby said. Her thoughts had bounced between her sisters, their mother, and Aiden all night. She should be exhausted like they were, but she felt invigorated and far too excited to flop on a couch. She pulled out her phone to check the time—*4:40*— and wondered if Aiden was still flying a kite. "I rode my bike here, and I'm not ready to flop just yet. Can I catch up with you guys in a little bit?"

"Going to find Aiden?" Deirdra waggled her brows.

There was no stifling her smile. "Maybe."

"Abby, how do you know you can trust him?" Cait asked.

The question took Abby by surprise. "Well, he raised his younger sister, so that says a lot about him. And I highly doubt a creeper would set up breakfast on that patio out there with a white linen tablecloth and real china."

Deirdra's eyes opened wider. "He did that? See, Cait? I told you she had secrets to tell."

"No secrets, but yes, he did. And then he jumped in to help me clean in his nice clothes. I don't really know what to make of him yet, but there's something about the way he listens and the things he says that make it easy to trust him. He's in finance, so he has *that* kind of personality, you know? A little tightly wound and *very* much a gentleman. But I could tell there was a lot more to him. He knew the lyrics to all the songs on Dad's favorite station, and he danced a little, twirling me around, and . . . I want to get to know him better and strip back some of those layers to see who he is. It's not a big deal," she said more casually than she felt.

Deirdra barked out a laugh. "I bet you'll find a very *big deal* after you strip the layers off that man."

Abby rolled her eyes.

"Whatever you do, be careful," Cait said softly. "Lots of men know how to act to gain a woman's trust while they spin a web around her. Once they've got her where they want her, that's when they show their true colors."

"I hear ya, girlfriend," Deirdra said.

The warning in Cait's eyes worried Abby. Had someone hurt her? Was that why she had scrutinized Aiden so closely? "Sounds like you've run into a few bad guys."

Cait put the head of the mop in the bucket and said, "Haven't we all?"

CHAPTER FOUR

AIDEN WAS ALL knotted up, like the damn kite lying in the sand beside his chair. He'd gotten so frustrated trying to get the kite to catch wind, he'd given up—and he was *not* a quitter. He was used to going after what he wanted, overcoming every obstacle, and surpassing every goal. The trouble was, he didn't give a damn about the kite. The only thing he wanted to go after wasn't a *thing* at all. She was a beautiful free spirit with the most stunning green eyes he'd ever seen. When Abby had stumbled into his arms, he'd gotten lost in those emotive eyes, swept up in the flecks of gold and amber in them, like sparks of hidden treasures, which was what she felt like in his arms. He wanted to bask in Abby's carefree nature, get caught up in it and go wherever she took him. Before meeting her, he'd been *this close* to telling Remi he was done with this charade of a vacation and was heading back to work. But the prospect of spending time with Abby changed that.

If only it were that easy. He knew Abby needed time with Cait and Deirdra to figure out their new normal. He didn't envy her position, and he had the strongest desire to help her weed through the mess her mother had left behind. But he wasn't there to take over and lead her down wiser paths, which left him sitting on a beach with a book in hand, anxiously passing the hours until tomorrow morning, when he could see her again.

He tried again to focus on the horror novel Abby had recommended, wondering if she'd read it. He'd pegged her as more of a chick lit reader. He read a few pages, then gazed out at the water thinking about Abby's smile and how much he'd enjoyed getting to know her and helping her in the Bistro. He looked down at the book again and couldn't remember the last time he'd sat on a beach and read.

"Waiting for a boat to come in?" Abby asked as she walked up behind him.

He set down his book, a surge of adrenaline pushing him to his feet. "Abs," he said with surprise. Her hair was a little frizzy and tousled, and her white sweatshirt was smudged with dirt, but her smile was as fresh as a new day, and she looked even more gorgeous than she had that morning. "What are you doing here?"

Her eyes drifted over the kite. "By the looks of it, I'm rescuing that kite from ending up in the trash."

"The last time I flew a kite was with Remi when she was a kid. Now I remember why. It's definitely a two-person job. How did things go with Cait?"

"Good, thanks. I like her. A *lot* actually. As you probably noticed, she's quiet and a little skeptical of people, but she warmed up quickly. She's sweet and funny, and she worked her butt off. We didn't talk about anything too important yet. But I'm sure we will tonight. She's going to stay at the house with us. Deirdra showed up to help right after you left, which totally shocked me. I guess today is full of surprises."

"Sweet and funny must be a family trait." He reached for her hand without thinking too hard about why he felt the need to be closer to her and brushed his thumb over her knuckles, enjoying the way her breathing quickened with his touch. "And you're here, which is the best surprise of all. But shouldn't you be with them?"

"They're tired and wanted to relax. I . . . ." Pink stained her cheeks. "I thought I'd see if you needed help with the kite."

"The kite, huh?" He arched a brow.

"Well, yeah. I said I'd help you with your list, and you said you were going to struggle—"

"Wrestle," he corrected her, enjoying her adorable rambling.

"*Wrestle*, right. I pictured you out here tangled up in string, and I didn't want a good kite to go to waste."

"Well, we can't have that, now, can we?" He stepped closer, and she lifted her eyes, full of wonder and *want*, confirming that he hadn't imagined the heat between them earlier. It took all of his control not to lower his lips to hers and taste what he was sure would be the sweetest kiss of all. But he'd been with enough women to recognize how different he felt around Abby, and he didn't want to fuck up whatever this was between them, so he said, "I'm jealous of that kite right now."

"Yeah?" she asked breathily.

"Oh *yeah*. Knowing you want to get your hands on my kite does all sorts of interesting things to me." He was walking a dangerous line. If he didn't step away, he was going to haul her into his arms and kiss her, and he might not be willing to stop. He reluctantly let go of her hand and tore his eyes away, looking at the kite. "Think it's salvageable?"

She picked up the kite and cocked her head at the knotted string. "How did you even do this?"

"The thing is possessed. All I did was try to hold up the kite and run, but it kept twisting and falling and . . ." He shrugged. "*That* happened."

"Stupid kite," she commiserated, and plunked herself down in the sand beside his chair. "I'll teach it a lesson." She began working out the knots.

"You can sit in the chair."

She looked up at him, the late-afternoon sun reflecting in her eyes, and said, "I'm an island girl. Sand is my go-to comfy place."

"In that case." He sat beside her in the sand, pulled one knee up, and leaned his arm on it, watching her unravel the knots like a pro. "You're good with your hands."

She pressed her lips together, as if she didn't want him to realize she'd taken his words another way. Little did she know, Aiden hadn't flirted like this since he was in college.

"Deirdra was good at getting things tangled up when we were kids. Someone had to be good at untangling them." She tugged at a knot, eyeing his shoes, and said, "Do you always wear loafers and nice clothes?"

"Not all the time. I sleep naked."

Laughter tumbled from her lips. "Don't tell me *that*."

"You asked." He chuckled and picked up the book she'd recommended. "Have you read this?"

"Yes, and I'm so glad you got it. Isn't it good?"

"I'm only about a third of the way through, but yes. It's very well written. I didn't peg you as a horror reader."

"I read everything, but I grew up with the author, Jack Steele. I had to read it. He goes by the nickname Jock now. He and his twin brother, Archer, used to scare everyone all the time just for fun. That's how you knew they liked you. Jock recently moved back to the island and got married at his family's winery. I can introduce you at some point if you'd like." She untangled another knot, and a spark of excitement shone in her eyes. "*Hey*, isn't the winery on your list?"

"If it's not, we'll add it. I want to see all the sights that make your eyes light up like that."

She looked up from the string and said, "Your lines are better than any I've ever heard."

"Because they're not lines, Abs. I'm being honest."

"What*ever*." She shook her head and said, "The winery is a *must* see. It's got the best views on the island. Archer runs it with their parents, Steve and Shelley, and Jock's wife, Daphne. Daphne handles their events, and Shelley runs the tours. Shelley's like a second mother to me and Deirdra. She's the one who told us about Cait." She stretched the string and wound it around the spool, looking like she wanted to say more about that, but then she said, "There we go. Good as new. You're lucky it's not tourist season yet. The beaches get packed. You wouldn't have room to run with your kite. Why did you choose this time of year to go on vacation, and why *here* instead of someplace warmer?"

"It was a good time to take off work, and as I said yesterday, I'm not fond of crowds. I let Remi pick the location, so here I am."

"Well, I think you brought this unseasonably warm weather with you. Ready to fly this baby?"

"Absolutely." He stood up and helped her to her feet.

"Thanks." She held up the shocking-pink kite and said, "Interesting color choice."

"I was on FaceTime with Patrice when I was shopping, so I let her pick it out. Pink is her favorite color."

"That was sweet of you."

"My brother-in-law says I'm *niece whipped*. They blink those innocent eyes at me, and I can't say no. I think they learned it from Remi."

"Well, let's make them proud and get this kite up in the air." She held the kite and handed him the spool. "You have to be the one to fly it since it's on *your* list, so I'll be the runner."

"That's fitting, Runner Girl."

They made a quick assessment of the wind direction, and Aiden let out some string as he walked down the beach. When he looked back, Abby stood with her head slightly tilted, one hand shading her eyes. The breeze swept her hair away from her face, and the bright pink kite was blowing against her bare legs. She looked utterly gorgeous. He pulled his phone from his pocket and took a picture.

"*Hey!*" She put a hand on her hip. "You need proof that *you* flew the kite, not me."

"That one was for me!" he shouted.

"Fair's fair!" She whipped out her phone and took a picture of him. Damn, he liked her style. "Ready?"

She nodded, and he jogged forward, watching over his shoulder as the kite left her fingers and sailed into the air. She squealed, jumping up and down, and ran toward him, yelling, "Keep going!" Just as she reached him, the kite nose-dived. *"Nooo!"*

They both laughed, and then they tried again and *again*, until finally the kite sailed high into the sky, swooping and flapping with the wind. Abby cheered. "Yay! We did it!" She whipped out her phone and took pictures of him flying the kite. "Wave to Remi!"

Her enthusiasm was contagious. He couldn't remember when he'd had so much fun. "We're a team! Get over here and get in the picture, Abs."

She ran over, her thick mane lifting off her shoulders. He pulled her in front of him, wrapping his free hand around her waist, holding the spool with his other hand as he peered over her shoulder at her phone. Their smiling faces filled the screen.

"Gorgeous," he said, drinking in her summery scent. "Take the picture."

"We need to get the kite in the picture."

"Take this one first. I like it." As she took the picture, the screen reflected her widening smile, showing him how much *she* liked it, too.

"Are you always such a picture hoarder?" she asked.

He squeezed her tighter, loving the feel of her curves against him, and said, "Only with my nieces."

"Then I consider myself lucky."

"Did you say you want to get lucky? I'll add that to our list."

"Aiden," she said breathily. She angled the phone so their faces fit on the screen with the kite high in the sky behind them and took the picture. "I got it!"

She turned, and her hand landed on his chest, her eyes twinkling up at him. Heat flared beneath her touch. Could she feel it, too? Her eyes held his, and he knew he should step back, take things slow, but for the first time in forever he felt joyful and lustful at once, and he wanted to hold on to that feeling, to etch it into his memory bank. Her lips parted, her breathing shallowed, and everything else faded away. Without thinking, he put his other arm around her, the kite string sliced between them as the kite spiraled into the waves.

Abby gasped, her fingers pressing into his chest as she spun out of his grip and ran toward the water. "*No!* Your kite! It's soaking wet."

The hell with the kite. He wanted to get *her* wet.

"It's okay. We already flew it." He wound the string around the spool as a crashing wave carried the kite up the shore.

"But we were doing so well," she said as he pulled the drenched kite from the water. "I still have some time before I have to meet my sisters. We could do something else that's on your list."

He pulled out his phone and couldn't resist saying, "Give me a sec to add *get lucky* to it first."

A pretty flush raced up her cheeks, and she swatted his side, reaching for the phone. But he threw his arm up over his head and said, "First you want to get your hot little hands on my kite. Now you want to get them on my list? What's next? My book? My chair?"

"Your *ass* if you're not careful," she said.

"That's even better."

She tried to give him a disbelieving look, but while her pursed lips valiantly attempted to stifle her unstoppable smile, the heat in her eyes gave the truth away. She planted her hand on her hip, a mannerism he was beginning to anticipate, and definitely enjoyed, and said, "I was thinking we could tackle the *sundae*."

"Good idea. You need to cool off before you get all gropy with me." He hooked an arm around her neck, chuckling as he tugged her against his side, and they made their way up the beach.

They left the kite by his chair and walked the few blocks to the ice cream store, passing beautiful pristine cottages with manicured gardens and picket fences.

"What was it like growing up here? Beach parties all summer long?"

"For some people. My memories are split into before and after my father died. I was too young for beach parties when he passed away and our lives were upended. But before that, my parents were usually at the restaurant, and Deirdra and I were free to ride our bikes all over Silver Haven, which is this part of the island. But even as a kid I loved cooking, and from the time I could reach the stove, my father taught me to cook in the restaurant. So most of the time I'd play with friends after school for a while, then go to the restaurant and do my homework at breakneck speed so I could spend the rest of the time cooking with my dad."

"That sounds like a great childhood."

"It was. But after my father died, my mom got *lost*." When they reached the corner, she pointed to the left and they walked that way. "I think my father was like the blood that fed her heart. We found out yesterday that she'd had Cait as a teenager and left home after her parents forced her to give her up for adoption. My mom was only eighteen when she came to the island and started working as a waitress in my dad's restaurant. He was twenty-nine, and the way they told it, it was love at first sight, with fireworks and full-body tingles. But they waited a year before they finally acted on their feelings, and they were married a year later. He adored her, and he became her entire world. He was her true love, her friend, and to some extent her father figure, because he was always watching out for her."

"That's quite an age difference."

"I know," she said with a sigh. "But who's to say what's right or wrong when it comes to love?"

"Certainly not me. But at eighteen or nineteen there's no way I could have known what I wanted for the rest of my life. How old are you, Abs?"

"Twenty-eight. You?" she asked as they crossed the street.

"I'm thirty-eight. Our age difference isn't much different from your parents'. But somehow it feels different when you're older."

"I understand what you're saying. We learn and change so much between our teens and midtwenties. I can't believe I'm nearing thirty."

"And I'm closing in on forty. I have no idea how it happened so fast. I look in the mirror and see my father's face. Aging doesn't bother me, and it feels good seeing some of my father in me. But I've sidetracked your story. I'm sorry. You said your mother got lost after your father died. What did you mean by that?"

They came to a main drag, which was lined with cute shops with colorful awnings.

"The ice cream shop is at the end of this street with the red-and-white-striped awning." As they headed in that direction, she said, "What I meant about my mother getting lost was that she started drinking and never stopped. She could function well enough most of the time, but nights were hard. I think she must have missed my father so much she needed to escape the pain of it. Needless to say, mine and Deirdra's lives changed dramatically. By the time we were teenagers, while our friends were at those beach parties you asked about, or surfing, or out buying fancy prom dresses, doing all the normal teenager things, Deirdra and I were helping at the restaurant, making sure the bills were paid, and putting our mother to bed at night."

"Oh, Abs." He slid his arm around her waist, pulling her close. "That's awful. I'm sorry you went through that. I can't imagine how hard it must have been. It's no wonder Deirdra is resentful, and shocking that you're not. That's a lot for two little girls to take on. You were younger than Olive. I can't imagine her having to take on that kind of responsibility."

"It's funny, when we were in the thick of it, we just fell into step, you know? Our mom needed us, and we didn't think too much about it at first. We figured out what needed to be done and we did it. Deirdra is two years older than me, and I remember her complaining all the time about how unfair it was and how disappointed and angry she was at our mom. She couldn't wait to leave the island. She got scholarships, and when she left to attend Boyer University in Upstate New York, she tried to get me to go with her and finish high school near there. But I couldn't leave my mom."

"That's a real testament to who you are, Abs."

"I guess. Shelley tried to help as much as she could, sending her kids over to bus and wait tables and ordering food from the restaurant to keep money coming in. But by the time Deirdra left for college, business had dwindled and my mom wasn't doing anything to help herself. She'd promise to stop drinking, then sneak alcohol. After going through that a few times, I learned to stop having expectations—about her or anyone else in my life. Without expectations, I can't be let down."

"What about Deirdra?"

"Are you kidding? Her schedule is insane. She cancels plans all the time. It's not her fault, and I know she feels guilty when she cancels." She sighed and said, "Anyway, about my mom. I don't know if she loved my father so much that she was truly lost without him, or if he was her guiding light in more ways than I knew. But I know that I never want to be in a position where I rely so much on a man that I can't stand on my own two feet without him."

He understood why she tried not to have expectations, though it made him sad to think she didn't have anyone in her life she could rely on in that way. "Well, you've certainly set yourself up for independence."

"Yes, I have, and it works for me." She stopped at the ice cream shop and said, "Scoops used to be my favorite ice cream shop. It was sold a few years ago, but I've heard the ice cream is still homemade. Let's get that sundae before I bore you to tears."

"I'm not bored in the least. I like learning about you and what's made you into the woman you are, and I'd like to hear the rest of the story after we order the biggest sundae they've got."

"You must be hungry."

"The bigger the sundae, the more time I get to spend with you." He pulled open the door and followed her in.

They ordered a five-scoop sundae—three of Abby's favorite flavors: strawberry, chocolate chip cookie dough, and pistachio, and two of Aiden's: chocolate-cherry swirl and vanilla crunch—with hot fudge and caramel toppings, whipped cream, nuts, chocolate jimmies, and two cherries. They took the sundae outside and sat beside each other at a table in front of the ice cream store.

"This is a *lot* of ice cream," Abby said. She ate a spoonful, and pleasure rose in her eyes, as it had with the Danish. "*Mm.* This is just what I needed."

He had a feeling *Abby* was just what he needed. "I haven't had an ice cream sundae since . . . I have no idea when." He ate some ice cream and said, "So, what made you finally leave the island?"

She licked the sweet treat from her spoon. "You don't forget a thing, do you?"

"Not usually."

"I forgot, you're a finance guy. You're probably as meticulous as Deirdra is about details." She ate another bite, then said, "I was running myself ragged and getting nowhere. I *wanted* to get away and move on with my life, but every time I thought about leaving, I was swamped with guilt. One day Shelley pulled me aside and said that the life I was living wasn't the life either of my parents wanted for me and that I needed to get off the island and move on. She said the island would take care of my mom. I didn't understand why she said it wasn't what my *parents* wanted for me instead of just what my father had wanted for me, but it wasn't a suggestion. It was a definite push, and for some reason, hearing it from her made a difference. She wasn't my sister, who was stuck in the trenches with me, or my mom, who I couldn't look at without wanting to help. Shelley and I talked two or three times, maybe more before I finally decided to put in applications at a few restaurants in New York City near where Leni was living while she was attending college. When I finally got hired, Shelley and her husband, Steve, lent me money for culinary school, and a month later I made the move. I was lucky to have them watching out for me. And you know what? They never overstepped or made my mother feel like she was a bad parent, and I know that must have been hard for them. I also know they tried many times to get my mom to go to rehab, but . . ." She shook her head. "You can't force sobriety on anyone."

"It's a shame that she wouldn't go, but I'm glad Shelley and Steve were there for you. It must have taken a great deal of courage to move that far away and start over, leaving your mom behind, when it's clear how much you loved her and how hard you tried to hold your family together. Was it terribly difficult?"

She finished the spoonful of ice cream she was eating, a sea of emotions swimming in her eyes, and said, "It was a lot of things. I was happy to be free from the worries of home one minute, and then the next I was frantic again about my mom trying to make ends meet by herself. And there were times when I was too busy to think about anything other than school and work, which made me feel even guiltier when I finally slowed down enough to think about home and what I'd done."

"What you'd done? You mean leaving?"

"Yes. It was hard to escape the guilt. But at the same time, I had this overwhelming feeling of achievement that I had *never* felt before, and it was the most extraordinary feeling I'd ever had. I was out on my *own*, sharing an apartment with Leni, going to school, working as a waitress, and *creating* the life I wanted instead of being a cog in my mother's wheel. Even though I had helped my mother keep the restaurant afloat, and I made sure she was okay, at least as best I could, I never felt that sense of accomplishment when I was home." She ate another spoonful of ice cream, staring absently across the street as she said, "I came home a lot to check on my mom, and I remember the third or fourth time I came back, I really *saw* the full picture of the life I'd left behind and how dysfunctional it was."

He put his hand on hers, and when her beautiful eyes found his, he said, "You were in survival mode for all those years—not just for yourself, but for your mother, and in some ways, I'd bet it was also for your father. He was gone, and you took over as your mother's caretaker. But as her daughter, you couldn't be *him*. Abs, you have the biggest, kindest, warmest heart, and you obviously put it all into your mom and keeping the business going." That huge heart of hers called out to him on so many levels, it had him questioning the most important things he believed in, the very foundation on which he'd built his empire. "That must have been devastating, seeing your mother's downfall for what it was and accepting the loss of your childhood. To finally see and understand the magnitude of what it sounds like others must have seen all along. I wish I had known you then, so I could have been there to help you through it all. I'm glad you were living with Leni and had someone you trusted when those walls came tumbling down."

"That's exactly what it was like. Every bit of what you said. I had built walls between myself and reality in order to push through each day, and it was as if someone hit them with a sledgehammer. When I got back to my apartment, I broke down and cried. I cried for so long that night, Leni came into my room and lay on my bed, holding me as I wept. It was then, as my heart was breaking and I finally let the sadness out, that I realized I'd been so busy holding our lives together with bubble gum and Scotch tape, I had never grieved for my father. I think I cried for a week, holding it all in when I was at work and school, then falling apart at night. It was cathartic to finally grieve, and it allowed me to gain enough perspective to fit the various parts of my life into place, like a puzzle." She tapped different parts of the table as she said, "Over here was my childhood with both of my parents. And over here was life with only my mom and Deirdra, and over here was my life after Deirdra left. Then *all* the way over here"—she touched the other side of the table—"was the new life I was building, and it was separate from the others, yet somehow it carried pieces of those other lives with it. Once I put all those pieces into their places, I felt so much better, like I was *finally* gaining control of my life. I vowed to never build those walls again, and that was when I finally understood what Shelley had meant when she'd said my parents wouldn't have wanted that life for me. She meant the woman my mother had been *before* we lost my father, and that made sense because my mother *loved* me and Deirdra so deeply. Before my father died, she was always hugging us, singing, and dancing. And I know she loved us to the very end of her life, but it was different. Not enough to save her."

"You must have missed that part of her desperately."

"I did. I still do. Some of my favorite memories were sitting on the front porch singing with my mom while my dad painted, doing arts and crafts, and gardening. God, do I miss gardening. My mom was so proud of her vegetable gardens, and it made me proud to be part of them. I used to get so excited when we'd go out with our floppy rubber boots and weed the gardens and collect baskets full of vegetables. I'd stand on a chair at the sink and help my mom wash them while she talked about what dishes my father would make with them. He always made a big deal about using the vegetables we grew, and he'd make a show out of inspecting them and choosing the best ones. Then we'd go to the restaurant and he'd whip up a special, elegant meal with all the trimmings using the vegetables he'd chosen, and the four of us would eat it. My dad would put our drinks in wineglasses or champagne flutes. Gosh, it was so elegant."

She looked dreamily at Aiden and said, "You know what? It was very much like our breakfast this morning." She seemed to think about that for a minute with a faraway look in her eyes. "I can't believe I didn't think about that earlier. Anyway . . . gardening was a *huge* part of our lives before we lost my dad, and then, like everything else, it died with him. You asked me about resentment earlier, and I didn't resent my mom the way Deirdra does, but everything my mom did made me sad. She had terminal cancer and passed away within a few weeks. She never even told us she was sick, so we never got to say goodbye. I guess that made me mad, but not nearly as much as it crushed my heart. I was devastated, but then she brought Cait into our lives, and that is helping to heal the hurt."

"Jesus, Abs . . ." He wanted to hold her, to soak up all the years of hurt she'd felt so she'd never feel it again.

She pointed her spoon at him and said, "I swear, every time I'm around you, I blab like a conversation hog. I never spill all the details of my life like this. You must have put truth serum in my coffee and sprinkled it on the ice cream or something, and you're actually listening to every word I say."

"I learned a thing or two about females while raising Remi, like how to keep my ears open and my mouth shut. It was either learn to hear what she wasn't saying or continue to annoy the hell out of her by responding in all the wrong ways."

"You are a very wise man."

"I don't know about that, but I think you open up to me for the same reason I do to you. We sense the similarities in our lives. I was so busy raising Remi, I didn't fully grieve for our parents until Remi got engaged about a year and a half ago."

"Oh, Aiden." Sadness rose in her eyes. "You held it in for that long?"

"I was busy making sure Remi was okay." He took Abby's hand, holding it between both of his, and said, "I thought Remi and I had been dealt a tough hand, but you lost the father who meant so much to you, you lost your mother first to drinking, then for good, and in between, you lost your childhood. And now you want to resurrect their restaurant." Fighting his instincts with everything he had, for the first time ever, Aiden made a business decision with his heart instead of his head and said, "I know I should probably keep my thoughts to myself, but I think you should turn down that offer for the Bistro."

"You *do?*"

The hope in her eyes made his heart beat faster. "I do. The restaurant is too big a part of you to let it go. You're a remarkable woman,

Abby, and if anyone can make a go of bringing their dreams to reality, I believe it's you."

"I'm not that remarkable. I just keep plowing forward and hope things turn out okay."

They were both quiet for a beat, their eyes never wavering from each other. Aiden swore time stood still as "Abigail de Messiéres" slipped from his lips like a secret. *The woman who is rocking my world by doing nothing more than being herself.*

She swallowed hard, desire and something much deeper gazing back at him. Her tongue swept over her lower lip. Her eyes flicked to the sundae, then back to him. "Do you want . . . ?" Her nearly whispered words trailed off as he leaned forward.

"Yes, I *want.*" He touched his lips to hers, light as a feather, testing the waters.

Her lips were warm and sweet, and she didn't pull away. He slid his hand to the base of her neck, and when her lips parted, he deepened the kiss. His tongue slid over hers, tasting, *taking*, heat surging through his body. She grabbed his shirt, tugging him forward, giving him the green light he craved. He wrapped his arm around her waist, hauling her closer, bringing her knees between his legs. His other hand pushed into her hair, and he claimed more of her with every swipe of his tongue, plunging deeper, exploring, *possessing*. She made the sexiest noises, setting his entire body ablaze. She was still clutching his shirt with one hand when her other hand landed on his thigh, and he fought the urge to move it higher so she could feel what she was doing to him. Her mouth was heavenly and sinful at once. He'd promised himself he'd go slow, but as the cool evening air hit his heated flesh, there was no slowing down their feast of passion. She was as lustful and greedy for him, pushing forward, taking as eagerly as she gave. This wasn't just a kiss; it was a release of tethers, a kiss that put all others to shame, and he never wanted to stop. He slowed his efforts, savoring every sensual second, the feel of her hand on him, the taste of her desire on her tongue.

The sounds of voices trickled through his haze of desire, and he realized he was making love to her mouth in front of an ice cream store. He forced himself to break their connection, leaving both of them breathless, but he kept her close, kissing the spray of freckles on her cheek; then he touched his forehead to hers and said, "Sorry, Abs. I got carried away."

Abby could barely breathe, much less speak. She'd *never* been kissed like that before. Her lips tingled from the force of their passion, her skin burned from his whiskers, and his taste lingered in her mouth like her new favorite addiction. He ran his fingers through her hair and pressed a kiss to the corner of her mouth, to her cheek, and to her lips again, alighting sparks beneath her skin, and he put just enough space between them so they could see each other's faces.

He looked as blown away as she was as he said, "You okay, sweetheart?"

"Mm-hm. Better than okay. Can we put *that* on your list? *Daily*, please. This is going to be the best three weeks ever."

He kissed her smiling lips again, and when her phone dinged with a text, a groan escaped before she could stop it.

"It's okay," he said with a chuckle. "We'll have plenty more of those. I promise. You should check your text in case it's important."

"Sorry." She pulled the phone from her pocket, saw Deirdra's name on the message, and checked the time before reading it. She'd been gone for more than *two* hours? She quickly read her sister's text. *Where are you? We're starved. Is he holding you captive with his BIG DEAL?* She'd added an eggplant emoji. *Do I need to kick some hot-guy ass or are you enjoying it?*

Aiden lifted his chin. "Everything okay?"

She angled the phone so he wouldn't see the message and said, "Yes. It's Deirdra. I didn't realize I'd been gone for so long. I'm really sorry, but I have to get back." She thumbed out a response. *Sorry! Lost track of time. Be home soon. Start dinner without me, and no kicking ass. He's amazing!*

"Do you want to take the sundae with you? Eat it on the way?"

She put her hand on her stomach and said, "No, thanks. I'm stuffed."

"We'd better get a picture for Remi, or you might have to do this all over again."

That didn't sound bad to her!

He pulled out his phone and put his arm around her. "You know the drill, beautiful."

She loved it when he called her *beautiful* and *Abs*. Heck, she loved everything he said and did.

He took the picture, careful to include the remnants of their sundae, and Abby realized her cheeks were still flushed and there was no hiding the desire in either of their eyes. She liked that, too.

"What's your number, Abs? I'll send you the pictures I took," he offered.

She gave him her number and checked out the pictures as he forwarded them. Her eyes shone, and her smile overtook the pictures. She looked truly happy in every one of them. She'd almost forgotten what that looked like on her and, she realized, what it felt like, too. She sent him the pictures she'd taken as he threw out their sundae.

"You sure do make us look good." He pocketed his phone, taking her hand as they headed down the sidewalk, and pressed a kiss to her temple.

How could something as little as holding hands and a temple kiss feel as big as that toe-curling kiss?

When they got back to her bike at the Bistro, he drew her into his arms without hesitation, and she loved that, too.

"This has been the best day I've had in so long, I'll never forget a second of it," he said, his eyes searching hers. Could he see that she felt the same? "Are we still on for breakfast tomorrow?"

"Definitely."

His lips curved up, and he lowered them to hers, but while she readied for another earth-shattering devouring, he brushed his lips over hers, light as a feather. She closed her eyes as he held her tighter, and his tongue slid slowly, erotically, along her lower lip. "So sweet," he whispered, making her knees go weak. He touched his lips to hers again, taking her in a slow, intoxicating kiss that went on so deliciously long, a needy noise escaped her lungs. She felt him smiling, but he didn't break their kiss, and *boy*, she really loved that, too.

When their lips finally parted, she was clinging to him, and he embraced her, like he didn't want to let her go, either. His head dipped beside hers, and he whispered, "Abigail de Messiéres, you might be my undoing."

CHAPTER FIVE

ABBY COULD STILL hear Aiden's voice whispering in her ear as she walked into her mother's house. The living room and kitchen were empty. She called upstairs, "Dee?"

"We're in Mom's room," Deirdra called out to her.

Abby went upstairs to their mother's bedroom and found Cait and Deirdra sitting on the floor by the hope chest. "Hey. Sorry I'm so late."

Deirdra smirked. "That smile is even goofier than when you came home after kissing Wells for the first time."

"Wells was a *boy*, and I never did much of anything with him. Aiden is a big, delicious, tantalizing *man*. Of course I look ridiculously goofy."

Cait was looking at her like she'd lost her mind as Deirdra said, "Don't tell me little Miss No Time for Orgasms got down and dirty already."

"No, I did *not*. But I'm not saying I wouldn't have. He's . . ." She sighed, trying to come up with the right words, but she'd never met anyone like him before. She hadn't even told her last boyfriend of almost a year half of what she'd shared with Aiden in a day. He listened so intently. There was no way to fake *that* or the way he looked at her like she was special. "I don't know," she finally said. "He's pretty darn wonderful. We flew the kite and went for ice cream."

"I bet." Deirdra smirked. "You look like you enjoyed licking his *cone.*"

"Deirdra!" Abby should be used to her sister's openness about sex, but every now and then she was still shocked by her.

"Sit with us. You can share all your mushy details later, when I have a glass of wine in my hand," Deirdra said. "Did you know Mom sketched?"

"Mom didn't sketch; only Dad did."

Cait handed Abby a sketchbook with a beautiful color sketch of a child's face. There was no mistaking the similarity to Cait's big green eyes, but the fluff of light-brown hair didn't match. She flipped through several pages of sketches of the same little girl. The sketches looked nothing like Deirdra's or Abby's baby pictures. "You think Mom drew these?"

"And these." Deirdra pointed to several other sketchbooks between her and Cait.

Cait went up on her knees and pointed to the child's hair. "See the *AM? There.*"

"Each of the sketches has them," Deirdra said. "Ava Michaels, Mom's maiden name."

As Abby lowered herself to the floor and looked at the other sketches, she found their mother's initials hidden in every one of them. "I don't understand. I thought Mom gave you up for adoption when you were born."

"She did, but we found these letters from Cait's adoptive mother." Deirdra pointed to a pile of envelopes. "It looks like once Mom and Dad tracked down Cait's adoptive mother, she kept in touch with Mom and sent a letter giving her an update on how Cait was doing along with a picture every month like clockwork. The first letter had a bunch of pictures from the months she'd missed."

Cait handed Abby a stack of photographs and said, "The letters stopped when I was four, which is when my mother passed away."

"Oh, Cait. I didn't know you lost your adoptive mom. I'm so sorry." Abby hugged her. "You were so young. Do you remember her?"

"Sometimes I think I do," Cait said. "But I was so little, I have no idea if they're real memories or something I dreamed up from the pictures I have."

Abby's heart ached for her. "I understand what you mean. Do you think your father didn't want to keep sending the pictures because it made him sad about losing your mom?"

She shrugged. "He's kind of a dick. He refused to talk about her and moved us from Rhode Island, where we were living, to Connecticut."

Abby sighed. "*God*, that sucks." She looked at Deirdra and said, "You should apologize to Cait for what you said about her being better off not knowing Mom. She grew up without a mother, and that had to hurt to hear."

"I already did," Deirdra said.

"Good." Abby was grateful that her sister's disdain for their mother hadn't marred her heart irreparably. She looked through some of the pictures of baby Cait, with her chubby little legs and big green eyes that weren't quite as wary as they were now. "You were an adorable baby, which isn't surprising, given how beautiful you are."

Cait looked down bashfully, with an appreciative smile.

"Abby, why do you think Mom didn't tell us that she sketched? She was *good*," Deirdra said. "She probably could have made a living off her artistic talents."

"Maybe because it appears she only sketched Cait. And if that was the case, then I'm sure it wasn't something she wanted to bring up with us. What would she say? *Hey, girls, you have a sister out there?* Remember, Shelley said Mom was *forced* to give up Cait. I'm sure Mom missed her every day and felt guilty about the whole situation." She handed Cait the sketchbook and said, "That's your proof of how much our mother loved you, right there. That and the fact that she brought us all together. Did you guys read your letters from Mom? Maybe she explains some of this." Abby hadn't read hers yet. As much as she wanted to, it was the one special thing that her mother had given solely to her, and once she read it, there would be no more secret messages. She wasn't ready to be done yet.

"No, and I won't for a while," Deirdra said. "Have you read yours?"

"Not yet, but I will."

"Me too." Cait ran her fingers over the sketchbook and said, "I must have gotten my ability to draw from her."

"That's true! And you got her green eyes, her cheekbones, her height, *and* her figure. Did you design your tattoos?" Abby asked.

"Most of them, and I tattooed the ones I could reach." She ran her hand down her arm, then crossed it over her middle.

"What do they represent?" Abby asked. Her tattoos were unlike anything Abby had ever seen. They were a mash-up of buildings and trees, animals, shapes, webs, and shades of color, all beautiful in their uniqueness.

"Lots of different things. Things I've gone through, friends I've had. Do either of you have any tattoos?"

"I do," Deirdra said.

"You do not," Abby said, peering into the hope chest at the hidden pieces of her mother's life.

"Want to bet?" Deirdra challenged. "I got one when I was in Atlantic City with Sutton a couple of years ago."

"And you never told me? Let me see it." Abby scooted closer to Deirdra. "Where is it?"

"That's for me to know and you to find out."

"God, you're such a brat. Why bring it up? Just to torture me?" Abby asked.

Deirdra glanced at Cait and said, "It's fun torturing her, isn't it?"

Cait leaned closer to Abby and whispered, "She doesn't really have one."

"Oh my gosh! Seriously? You two are *already* ganging up on me? Dee, you're such a bad influence. You didn't even give her a few days to settle in."

Cait bit her lower lip, and Abby gasped. "It was *your* idea?"

"I've never had sisters to joke around with," Cait said. "Deirdra said you wouldn't be mad."

"I'm not mad. I'm pleasantly surprised, actually. I want you to feel like part of the family."

"She doesn't ever get mad at *anything*," Deirdra said. "Mom never told us she was sick, and that pisses me off to no end, but Abby rationalizes it all."

"I was more hurt than mad. I think she had her reasons," Abby insisted. "Plus, mad is so ugly. I hate being mad as much as I dislike the word *hate*."

Deirdra proceeded to spout off a laundry list of things she thought should anger Abby and didn't. "What gets your panties in a knot, Cait?"

"I don't know," Cait said as she gathered all of the sketchbooks into a pile. "Jerks. People who judge others when they shouldn't. I work with this girl at the tattoo shop, Aria. She's got social anxiety, and sometimes people treat her like she's invisible, or worse, they treat her like she's got a disease. That really pisses me off."

"Mean people suck," Deirdra said. "Do you like where you work and the people you work with?"

"I love them." She said it so easily, it seemed at odds with how wary she appeared. "They're like family to me."

"How long have you worked there?" Abby asked.

"Several years," Cait said as she picked up the pile of sketchbooks to put into the hope chest.

"You can have those sketchbooks and the letters and pictures," Abby offered. "Right, Dee?"

Deirdra pushed to her feet and said, "Cait can have all of Mom's stuff as far as I'm concerned."

"Are you sure you don't want to keep some of her sketches?" Cait asked Abby.

"I'm sure. I never even knew she could draw, and those are pieces of your life. I'm starting to think Mom loved so hard, that every time she lost someone, she lost a piece of herself."

"That's a thing," Cait said. "My boss, Tank, lost a piece of himself when his younger sister died."

"That's horrible." Abby didn't even want to imagine how hard it would be to lose Deirdra or Cait, even after knowing Cait for only a couple of days. "I wonder what else is hidden among Mom's things."

"We didn't find anything else interesting in the hope chest," Deirdra said.

Abby went to the closet, her mother's bohemian-style clothes bringing back a mix of good and bad memories. The wide-legged pants she wore to Abby's second-grade play, the long batik dress she wore on so many strolls through town, Abby could practically still see it swishing around her legs. The floral sundress Abby and Deirdra had nearly ripped trying to get it off their mother one night when she was drunk. She leafed through batik skirts and funky pants, dresses of varying lengths, all splashed with multiple colors, and withdrew her mother's favorite dress, with a yellow bodice and a long, flowing patchwork skirt and held it out for her sisters to see. "Dee, remember Mom dancing in this that night down on the beach when we cooked lobster over the fire?"

"Yes, I remember," Deirdra said sharply. "Can we *not* do this right now? I know you want—and probably *need*—to go through all of your mushy memories, but I'm overloaded, and I don't have the brainpower to deal with it at the moment."

"Okay." Abby put the dress back, glad Deirdra had at least spent some time going through their mother's hope chest with Cait. "I've got time. I'll get through it and will relive my good memories with Cait if she wants. Why don't we go downstairs and hang out?"

"Good idea. So, Cait, do you have any hobbies?" Deirdra asked as they headed downstairs.

"I draw and I like to hike. I like the water, but I don't get out much. I love animals, and I volunteer at Tank's brother's animal rescue sometimes. What about you?" Cait asked as they followed Deirdra into the kitchen.

Deirdra set three wineglasses on the counter and began pouring. "Work and wine, that's my life."

"It doesn't worry you? The drinking?" Cait asked.

"I'm all talk about the wine part. I almost never drink unless I'm here." She handed Cait and Abby glasses and said, "Here's to long-lost sisters."

They tapped glasses and sipped their wine.

"I'm glad Mom brought us together," Abby said as Deirdra took the foil off a blueberry pie. "Do you think we should have a goodbye ceremony for her now that we're all together?"

Deirdra shook her head. "She didn't want one. You can do something, but count me out."

Abby should have expected that. "Cait?"

"I didn't know her, so I don't feel like I need that closure. But if you want support, I can be there for you."

"I appreciate that, but I was just thinking out loud. I don't even know if I'll do anything." Abby sipped her wine and said, "But I'm looking forward to learning more about you. Your pet peeves, the quirky things that make you special."

Cait's brows slanted. "Did you call me quirky?"

"I meant it in a good way. I'm quirky. I laugh when things aren't funny, and I ramble when I'm nervous. I blurt things out when I shouldn't," she said, thinking of the underwear model debacle. "And Deirdra is *definitely* quirky. She's got a thing about the number four."

"Oh my God. Really?" Deirdra shook her head.

"What? You do. You can't take two bites of anything. It has to be four, eight, sixteen."

"Why?" Cait asked. "Do you have OCD?"

"No. It's a good luck thing."

"She won't even tell me why she does it," Abby said. "And she's got other quirks, too. She's got a wicked chip on her shoulder, and she's *never* afraid to go up against anyone."

"It's true, but that's a strength, not a quirk," Deirdra said, handing them each a fork and carrying the pie to the table.

"I haven't even eaten dinner. I can't eat pie." Abby grabbed a lasagna from the fridge and put a piece in the microwave.

"While you were licking Aiden's *cone*, we polished off a chicken casserole," Deirdra said. "It was delicious."

Abby leaned against the counter as her food heated up, thinking about Aiden and his *cone*, and suddenly she was itching to talk about him. "Not as delicious as Aiden's kisses."

"I knew it! You slept with him, didn't you?" Deirdra grinned like she'd caught Abby with her hand in the cookie jar.

"*No.* We just kissed."

"Well, that's still a big deal." Deirdra ate a bit of pie and said, "This is the first guy Abby has kissed since she broke up with her quasi boyfriend right after Mom died."

"So? It's not like you've been out there kissing guys for the last three months," Abby said.

"How do you know I'm not just keeping the details of my sex life to myself?" Deirdra said snarkily.

"Unless you're making out with Malcolm, which is gross, then I think you're all talk because you work more than I do." Abby carried her lasagna to the table and said, "It's not that I wouldn't have liked to have met someone great, but I was working sixty-plus hours a week. I had no time for anything else." She wiggled her shoulders and gloated a little. "Besides, Aiden was worth the wait, and after all this time, I deserve to have some fun."

"That you do," Deirdra said. "You deserve to have a lot of fun, Abby. You always did for Mom what I didn't have the patience for. You're a freaking saint in my book."

Deirdra handed out compliments as if she had a limited supply of them, which was why Abby felt like a kid gathering them up and pocketing them like treasures. "Thanks, Dee. Do you have a boyfriend, Cait?"

"Nope." Cait shook her head and dug into the pie.

"Do you work a lot of hours?" Deirdra asked.

"Sometimes," Cait said.

"Do you date a lot?" Abby asked.

"Not really," Cait said. "I'm not looking for a guy, but I've found a lot of guys are too talky for me or too into themselves."

"You want the strong, silent type. I like that," Deirdra said.

Cait scooped up another forkful of pie and said, "I don't care if a guy is strong or not. If I'm going to get close to someone, I want them to be trustworthy and smart enough to know excuses aren't usually worth the breath needed to make them and to choose to do the *right* thing ninety-five percent of the time."

"Why only ninety-five percent of the time?" Abby asked.

A slow smile crept across Cait's lips. "I'm pretty sure men are not as smart as women, and five percent is all the leeway they're going to get."

Deirdra pointed her fork at Cait and said, "I like the way you think, Cait Badass Weatherby."

A glimmer of happiness rose in Cait's eyes.

They fell into easy conversation, talking about what their lives were like growing up. Cait's father was a CEO of a manufacturing company, a well-respected pillar of the community who worked long hours and appeared to be adored by everyone . . . except Cait. Cait said she'd taken off right after graduating high school and had rarely seen him since. Abby told her stories about their mother, and she was glad that Deirdra interjected positive comments as often as she made jokes at their mother's expense. She hoped one day Deirdra would find peace with that whole situation, but for now all Abby could do was try her best to keep reminding her that their mother wasn't always the woman she'd been after their father died. They ate half of the pie and Abby ate her lasagna. They laughed about silly things they'd done over the years and cried about times they'd been disappointed or hurt. Hours passed like minutes, and before they knew it, it was after midnight.

"I have a breakfast date tomorrow with my hot renovation helper. I'd better get some sleep." Abby pushed to her feet and said, "Cait, Deirdra's leaving in the morning. Do you want to come with me and have breakfast with Aiden?"

"No, thank you. I'll grab something here. It seems like Ava must have had a lot of friends. Your freezer and fridge are packed full."

"We can thank the Bra Brigade for that," Deirdra said.

"The Bra Brigade?" Cait asked.

"Shelley's mom, Lenore, started the group when she was a teenager. She and all her friends would pick an out-of-the-way spot and sunbathe in their bras. But as the island got built up and more populated, those secret places became few and far between. There are all sorts of stories about people stumbling upon them." Abby laughed softly and said, "I love Lenore and Shelley, and all the ladies who take part in the Bra Brigade, but as a teenager, the idea of your mom hanging out in her bra was mortifying."

"Ava did it?" Cait asked.

"A few times, believe it or not," Deirdra said.

Cait grinned. "Have *you* ever done it?"

"No way," Deirdra said.

"I have," Abby confessed. "Me and Leni and her sisters joined them a few times. It was really fun. They're some of my fun memories with

Mom." She yawned and said, "Did Deirdra show you the apartment and get you set up with clean sheets and towels?"

Cait pushed to her feet and said, "Yes. It's perfect, thanks. You said you live in New York? When do you have to go back?"

Abby's nerves pinged to life. She hadn't told Deirdra that she'd quit her job, and she sucked at lying, so she pulled up her big-girl panties and said, "Well . . . I *did* work for a restaurant in New York City, but I recently quit."

"You *quit*?" Deirdra flew to her feet. "When?"

"Right before I came here. It's not a big deal. I have savings, and I knew I'd need the summer to go through Mom's stuff. Now I have time to figure out my next move."

Deirdra scoffed, starting to pace. "How could you be so impetuous? You have rent and living expenses. You don't even know if the Bistro can stay afloat."

"I didn't quit for the restaurant!" Abby didn't mean to raise her voice, but she couldn't stop herself. She knew Deirdra was upset because she cared about her, but she'd had it with other people trying to take control of her life. Forcing a calmer tone, she said, "I'm twenty-eight years old, Dee. I don't need permission to make a life change. I quit because I wasn't *happy*. I hated going to work every day, and I was stuck in a spiral of nothingness. For God's sake, I was seeing a guy I barely liked as a friend. That should tell you something. I've been miserable for a *long* time."

Deirdra crossed her arms, her jaw tight, and for a second Abby thought she saw hurt in her sister's eyes, but it disappeared as quickly as it had risen.

"Why didn't you tell me you quit?"

"Because I knew this would be your reaction, and I didn't want you to worry. I'm a big girl. I can make my own decisions. And it wasn't impetuous. Impetuous would have been quitting a year or two ago, when I *wanted* to quit. But I didn't. I made sure I had money in the bank to hold me over, and I still threw money into my retirement account right up until my last paycheck, like you told me to."

"That's why you want to run the Bistro? Because you don't have another job?" Deirdra asked. "Do you realize we can sell that shithole to that idiot investor and we'd each make a million bucks? Even after taxes, you wouldn't have to go back to work for at least a few years."

"I don't care about the *money*, Deirdra, and I *like* working. And so do *you*."

Deirdra threw her hands up. "You think I care *only* about the money? I don't give a shit about the money. You spent years cleaning up after and taking care of Mom, and you have worked your ass off to make something of yourself. I'm so fucking proud of you, Abby. I don't want you to get started and realize it was a mistake. I don't want you to get hurt or go broke because you have this fantasy about bringing back what can't ever be brought back. The magic in that restaurant was *Dad*. Don't you get that? And he's *gone*, Abby. He's been gone for nineteen years, and he's never coming back."

"I *know* that. I miss him every day." Abby swiped at the tears running down her cheeks, vaguely aware of Cait standing beside them, like she would jump between them if things went too far. "I want to run the Bistro because I love it with all of my heart and soul. You might hate this place, but I *don't*. I remember Mom and Dad happily running the Bistro, and I *know* I can bring it back to what it was. This isn't me being impetuous, Deirdra. This is me feeling like I've finally found my destiny."

"We are *so* different," Deirdra said. "You think you can make lemonade from lemons, but I'm an attorney. I see what happens with lemonade every damn day. It goes bad and grows mold just like the lemons. I can't fight like this tonight. I still have hours of work to do. I'm going upstairs."

Deirdra stalked out of the kitchen, and Abby flopped into a chair, wiping her tears. "Sorry, Cait. Welcome to the ugly side of sisterhood."

Cait sat beside her. "Don't be sorry. You two just showed me exactly what makes each of you special. I like yours *and* Deirdra's quirks."

Abby dried her eyes. "Then maybe you're as crazy as we are."

"Oh, I definitely am. We all are in some ways."

"And by the way, what kind of awful sister am I? I should be asking *you* if you want us to take the offer."

"I grew up with money and I know it can't buy happiness," Cait said. "I'd like to get to know our mom through the restaurant and through you and Deirdra. I know Deirdra won't be a fan of mine for saying this, but I'm glad you want to keep it."

"Thank you."

"Deirdra made good points, though, and boy, you're lucky. She obviously loves you so much she's terrified of you getting hurt, because it'll hurt her, too."

More tears slid down Abby's cheeks. "I know," she said, her voice cracking. "But I need to follow my heart."

"That's all Deirdra was doing, too," Cait said carefully. "You said you thought Ava loved so hard she lost a piece of herself every time she lost someone she loved. I think Deirdra does, too, but she protects herself by being stronger than everyone else. I think she feels guilty about leaving when you stayed to help Ava, and every time she's here, it's a reminder of that as much as it's a reminder of how Ava let her down. I think that's why Deirdra runs away. And maybe that's why she's still trying to protect you, because she couldn't back then. I could be wrong, but that's my take on her."

That brought more tears. "I don't want her to worry about me."

"Well, that's never going to happen," Deirdra said as she walked back into the kitchen with a sorrowful expression. "There were a few kernels of truth to what you said, Cait. But, Abby, I also want to protect you because you're a dreamer, and you have a gigantic—sometimes foolish—heart that refuses to believe life will shit on you time and time again. I know you believe you don't allow yourself to have expectations, but believe me, you can't help but have them. It's who you *are*. You believe and trust even when you think you're not. And that's good, Abby. Lord knows I'm fucked up in that department."

"You're not fucked up," Abby said, wiping her tears.

"I am, but I'm not going to let that mess you up anymore. You've had enough of your dreams stolen out from under you. We both have. I'm sorry for going off like I did. I don't want to steal your dreams. I love you, Abby." Tears spilled from Deirdra's eyes, drawing more tears from Abby. "I'm sorry I feel differently than you do about this place, but that's my shit, not yours. You can have my inheritance to use toward the restaurant, and I support you one hundred percent. If your lemonade gets moldy, we'll clean up Mom's old garden and grow more freaking lemons."

Abby pushed to her feet, tears streaming down her cheeks, and threw her arms around Deirdra. "Thank you! Thank you so much! I'll call the attorney in the morning and let him know we're turning down the offer. I love you, Dee."

"I love you, too, you starry-eyed pain in my butt." Deirdra wiped her eyes.

"Cait? Are you one hundred percent sure about turning down the offer?"

"Two hundred percent," Cait said.

"Thank you. I won't let you down." Abby pulled her to her feet and hugged her. "I'm so glad you didn't run away from our craziness."

"Speak for yourself," Deirdra said. "I'm not crazy."

Cait arched a brow and said, "What was that, *little* sister?"

"So this is what it feels like to be outnumbered," Deirdra said.

Abby put an arm around each of them and said, "No, this is what it feels like to be a family in the making."

CHAPTER SIX

"LOOK AT YOU, wearing a T-shirt and sneakers!"

Aiden's heart took off like a freaking jackrabbit at the sound of Abby's voice across the Bistro parking lot Friday morning, where he'd been pacing, anxiously waiting for her. He spun around just as she put down her bike's kickstand. She looked gorgeous, with her hair all windblown, wearing skimpy gray shorts and a black sweatshirt.

"You've even got the whole backward-baseball-cap thing going on," she said playfully as he closed the distance between them. "*Now* you're starting to look like a regular guy on vacation. Well, you would if regular guys looked like underwear models."

"I came dressed to work," he said, earning one of her magnificent grins. He reached for her hand and said, "Get over here, Abigail Best Lips on the Planet de Messiéres."

He drew her into his arms and took the kiss he'd been craving since last night. She wound her arms around his neck, pressing her soft curves against him, allowing him to savor and *linger*. When their lips parted, he kept her close and said, "How are you, beautiful?"

"Better now," she said breathlessly.

She'd snagged his hat and put it on her head, looking adorably sexy, which seemed to be her constant state. They walked around the Bistro hand in hand to their table, where breakfast from Keira's awaited. He'd arranged their chairs closer together, rather than across from each other, which allowed him to touch her hand or lean in for a kiss as they talked. He'd never needed to be near anyone. He liked his primarily solitary life, but he was drawn to Abby like a moth to a flame as she chatted excitedly about how things had gone with her sisters and how thrilled she was to have their support.

"I emailed the attorney this morning and turned down the offer on the Bistro. I swear it felt like a gorilla climbed off my back."

As worried as Businessman Aiden was about Abby having the financial means to take on the restaurant, Island Aiden was pleased that she would have the chance to follow her dreams. "Good. I think you did the right thing."

He leaned in for a kiss as a sharply dressed, attractive brunette came around the corner of the building, and Abby jumped to her feet. "*Deirdra.* What are you doing here?"

Ah, the older sister.

"I came to say goodbye and to check out the guy who's treating my sister to fancy breakfasts." Deirdra extended her hand and ran an assessing eye over Aiden as he rose to his feet. "Hi. I'm Deirdra, Abby's sister."

"*Aiden*," he said, shaking her hand and doing his own three-second assessment. Navy skirt, white silk blouse, expensive heels, pin-straight posture, chin up. The lawyer in her was rearing its powerful head, letting him know she was there on a mission. "It's nice to meet you, and I'm sorry to hear about your mother's passing."

"Thank you," she said.

Abby hiked a thumb toward the door and said, "If you guys will excuse me for a sec, I'm going to run inside and use the bathroom."

As Abby headed inside, Aiden waved to her chair and said, "Would you like to sit down?"

Deirdra sat down and crossed her legs, her eyes locked on Aiden as she said, "Since Abby's going to be gone only a minute, I'll make this quick. I don't know what your deal is, but if you have your eye on Abby because you think she's a sugar mama due to her inheritance, you're barking up the wrong tree." She broke off a piece of Abby's muffin and popped it into her mouth, as if to say *Take that*.

He liked knowing she had Abby's back, and he respected the hell out of her for taking a stance, even if she was way off base. "I admire your candor and your gumption, but I assure you, Deirdra, my interest in Abby is nothing but honorable."

Deirdra half laughed, half scoffed. "We both know that's not true. She's a gorgeous woman, and I saw the sparks flying between you two."

"I said honorable, not saintly."

She seemed amused by that and broke off another piece of muffin, accentuating her words with it as she said, "Listen, Abby's got a heart of gold, which is worth more than all the money in the world. So keep that in mind, because people have been known to kill for less."

"You don't mince words, do you?"

She smiled and said, "Not usually."

"I don't, either. You should know that I'm not the kind of guy that goes out looking for flings, and I'm not into drama. I like Abby a lot. I'm as drawn to her positivity, warmth, and intelligence as I am to her outward appearance, but I have a younger sister, so I completely understand where you're coming from. I'm not out to hurt Abby, or anyone for that matter. I'm here for three more weeks, and hopefully Abby and I will enjoy that time together."

Abby came out the front door, her bright eyes landing on him. How could anyone hurt such a sweet, beautiful woman? He pushed to his feet and said, "You can have my seat, Abs."

"That's okay, Aiden. I have to go, or I'll miss the ferry." Deirdra hugged Abby, whispering something Aiden couldn't hear. When she turned to say goodbye to him, her expression was warmer, her tone kinder. "Nice chatting with you. Enjoy the rest of your vacation."

"Thank you. I hope we'll see each other again."

Deirdra raised a brow, her eyes shifting to Abby as she said, "We'll see."

She turned to leave, and after she was out of earshot, Abby said, "Sorry I had to leave you two alone. My coffee went right through me. Did Deirdra grill you? If she did, I'm sorry. She can be blunt."

"She was great," he reassured her, and he meant it. "I'm glad she's looking out for you."

"Does that mean she didn't scare you off?"

Scare him off? That was laughable. He was *so* taken with her, when Remi had texted last night to see if he'd made any progress on his list, he'd *wanted* to share his happiness with the sister who had sent him to the island. He'd sent Remi a few of the pictures they'd taken with the caption *Made a new friend. Flew a kite and ate a sundae. See? I'm doing your list. Love you.* He'd been forced to endure a mini inquisition, and while he hadn't responded to most of her questions, he'd given her a little something to chew on—*Her name is Abby, and we met when she was out for a run. I'm having breakfast with her tomorrow morning.* He'd never talked to Remi about any of the women he went out with, and the fact that he wanted to tell her about Abby was not lost on him.

"Let's put it this way: I was so anxious to see you today, I was up at dawn, read the newspaper twice, and was still so pumped with adrenaline, I went for a quick jog on the beach." He pressed his lips to hers and said, "It's going to take a lot more than a protective sister to keep me away from you."

Later that afternoon, Aiden stood on the makeshift scaffolding he and Abby had made using ladders and wide planks of wood, wiping cobwebs from the rafters of the Bistro and watching Abby wiggle her hips to the music playing on her father's boom box. She and Cait were removing wallpaper across the room. They'd been cleaning all day, and neither of them had complained even once. He liked getting to know Cait as Abby was. She was interesting and careful, what he called *a watcher*, someone who observed for a while before letting her guard down.

Abby glanced over her shoulder with an expression that was tentative and somehow also full of hope and desire. He had no idea how she could pull all of that off with a single glance, but that hope reminded him of something he'd read and wanted to share with her.

"Hey, Abs, I forgot to tell you that I read about the Best of the Island Restaurant Competition in the *Island Times* this morning. Have you thought about entering?"

"No, but have I told you that I like that you read the newspaper, even though it's as outdated as Myspace?"

"Are you saying I'm old?"

She and Cait laughed.

"No," Abby said. "My father used to scour the newspaper every morning and get his fingers all inky."

"Don't knock the ink," he said. "It's a relaxing way to start the day."

"By the time you leave the island, you'll have a whole new concept of relaxation."

"I bet you both will." Cait tossed a piece of wallpaper onto the pile at their feet.

Aiden chuckled.

"Deirdra has *definitely* rubbed off on you," Abby said to Cait as she peeled off another strip of wallpaper.

"What do you think about the competition, Abs?" Aiden asked.

"It costs a small fortune to enter, and it's only four weeks away. I'll never be ready in time." The competition was held the week before Memorial Day, and the winner would be announced Thursday morning, before the crowds arrived for the holiday weekend.

The entry fee was only seven hundred dollars, which told him something about Abby's finances, spurring questions about how she was going to afford the start-up costs to launch the restaurant. If her finances were that tight, she could definitely use the advertising that came with the grand prize.

"The restaurant only has to be aesthetically pleasing when the judges come through. You don't have to be open to the public or even fully staffed to enter," he said, parroting what he'd read. "It's basically a tasting competition judged by four food critics out of Boston and New York."

"I don't know. There are so many things to consider, like how all of this hard work is going to turn out and whether the community will embrace a reopening, or if our mom ruined that for us." Confidence rose in Abby's eyes, and she said, "Don't get me wrong. I *hope* people love the restaurant and my cooking, and I'm determined not to fail. But what if I'm wrong and I can't rekindle my father's magic? What if the magic of the restaurant died with him?"

"Trust me, Abby," he said. "You have your own brand of magic. I didn't know your father, but I can't imagine anyone lighting up a room the way you do."

Cait looked curiously at him, and Abby looked a little dreamy-eyed, but he was only being honest. He'd seen businesses made or broken by attitudes. If Abby's cooking was half as good as her personality, she had a winner on her hands.

"I mean it, Abs. You don't have to be your father. Be yourself."

"I appreciate that, and I feel like I"—she looked at Cait—"*we* can really do this. But I think I need to give it a year before I try to win a competition, especially the biggest one on the island. I'm still kind of in the *Holy cow, I'm really doing this* stage."

Abby was too passionate about the restaurant to half-ass it. There was no way she'd make it anything less than the *best* it could be. He needed her to see that this could be the opportunity *she* needed to put the Bistro on the map, but Remi's voice trampled through his mind—*Just be Aiden . . . not Aiden the investor and billionaire*—reminding him to take off his business hat and be a regular guy. He sucked at being a regular guy. How was he supposed to turn off instincts that were as innate as breathing? Instincts that could help Abby and keep her from making mistakes? She needed what winning the competition could offer.

Doing his best to put on his regular-guy hat, he said, "I thought you might be interested since, according to the article, the winner will be featured on the front page of the *Island Times* and in the *Best of* segment of the *Cape Cod Times*. The winner also gets six ad spots in the *Island Times* over the twelve months following the competition, and their logo and the *Best of* banner will be featured on the Silver Island website and the *Times* website. That's a *lot* of free advertising."

"I know, but as much as I believe in myself, paying a big entry fee and possibly not winning won't do anything good for me. I'd be known as the restaurant that *didn't* win the competition. My parents never bought into competitions or any of that type of thing. My father built this business on word of mouth. The Bistro doesn't even have a logo," Abby said as she pulled off another strip of wallpaper.

Aiden was trying not to push, but he believed in her and couldn't bite his tongue without making one last effort to open her eyes to the realities of running a business in today's marketplace. "Yes, but your father was running the restaurant when the island was much smaller and just starting to grow," he said as he climbed down the ladder. "He got in on the ground floor of the biggest developmental years the island has ever seen, and the restaurant lost all of that traction when your mother was running it. You're starting from a different jumping-off point. It's a different world. You can't rely on word of mouth the way he did."

"He's right," Cait said, tossing another strip onto the pile. "Even in the tattoo industry, we need to have a presence everywhere—online, in bars, local businesses . . ."

Abby's shoulders dropped with a heavy sigh. "I'll add marketing to my to-do list. I don't know much about it, but I can do some research and ask my friend Leni for help. She does marketing for her cousin's PR firm."

"I can help, too, if you'd like," Cait offered. "I help Tank with the website, marketing, and social media for Wicked Ink. I can also design the logo if you'd like."

"That would be fantastic," Abby said.

Aiden couldn't shake the feeling that she should enter the competition, but he realized he didn't even know when she was planning to open the restaurant. "Have you thought about a launch date?"

"I was hoping *you* would be my launch *date*," she said playfully.

"I'd be honored." He leaned in for a kiss and said, "Since I'm leaving the weekend before Memorial Day, does that mean you changed your mind and want to try to get this place open before the competition? In time for the summer rush?"

"No way. Not for the competition. It's too soon." Her brow furrowed, but her eyes filled with endless hope again. "But am I crazy to think we can be up and running by the middle of June? That's only"— she looked at the ceiling, bobbing her head as she silently calculated time, lips moving—"seven weeks away."

God she was cute. "Not at all. If you had to, you could clean it up and have a soft opening, then hold a grand reopening when you're ready."

Abby shook her head. "I have a hard time doing things halfway. For my own sanity, I'd need to have it ready for the big *shebang*."

"I like the way you think. I've got nothing but time right now and very capable hands." Hands that hadn't done manual labor in so long and suddenly craved it. He'd forgotten how it felt to use his body to make things happen instead of his mind, just as he'd forgotten what it felt like to truly crave a woman's touch, the kiss of her lips, and that look Abby was giving him right now. "We've got this, Abs. Right, Cait?"

Cait looked at Abby and said, "I've only known you a few days, and I already know there's *nothing* you can't do if you set your mind to it."

Abby looked thrilled. "Okay, then! We've got seven weeks to get this place open. Oh my gosh, you guys! Seven weeks! We need to work *fast*." Her smile suddenly faded. "Wait. *Aiden*, you won't be here to celebrate our grand opening."

"I just said I'd be your date, and I always keep my word. But you could toss in some added incentive and promise me a moonlight walk on the beach after the grand opening."

She beamed at him. "You've got it."

Her gaze shifted to the entrance of the restaurant, and Aiden's followed as a clean-cut guy strutted in like he owned the place. His wily eyes surveyed the room, landing on Abby. An amused smirk crawled into place. Aiden stepped forward just as the guy threw his arms out to his sides and said, "There's the hottest cook around. How's it going, sweet lips?" With an arrogant wink, he added, "Still kiss as good as you cook?"

Abby's smile conveyed a twist of annoyance, making Aiden's protective instincts surge. He wanted to step between them, but this guy obviously knew Abby well, and he fought the urge, giving her space to handle him.

"Wells Silver, to what do I owe this pleasure?" She set down the scraper and wiped her hands on her shorts as she walked toward him.

Aiden remembered Fitz mentioning his brothers and sisters. He wondered if Fitz, who had come across as laid-back and professional, was as cocky as Wells when he wasn't at the resort.

"I heard you were back in town, and I thought I'd come by and say hello," Wells said, eyeing Cait. "Well, *hello* to you, too."

Cait narrowed her eyes and straightened her spine, staring him down.

Good girl. Don't let this douchebag intimidate you.

Abby rolled her eyes. "Get your eyes off Cait and give me a hug."

Aiden gritted his teeth. He didn't want that guy's hands anywhere near Abby. Wells made an *mm-mm* sound as he embraced her, but Abby pushed him away, still smiling as she said, "Same old Wells. You never change."

"Take another look, babe." Wells motioned to his athletic body, his biceps straining the fabric of his tight T-shirt. "I've been working out harder since the last time I saw you."

"You're a goof. Let me introduce you to my *sister*, Cait."

"Hi," Cait said a little coldly, her eyes never leaving his.

"Sister?" Wells looked puzzled.

"Yes. We just found out that we're sisters. Isn't that great?" Abby's unyielding positivity tugged at Aiden.

"In that case, *sis*"—Wells raised his brows at Cait and said—"if you want someone to show you around the island, I'm your guy."

"*Ugh.* Give her a break, Wells," Abby chided him. "She knows you two-timed me and Leni in high school."

You dated this guy?

"There was enough of me to go around, and you were both hot," Wells said.

"Dream on." Abby turned to introduce Aiden, but before she could get a word out, he slid his arm around her waist, showing the guy how far Abby had come, and offered his other hand to Wells. "I'm Aiden. Nice to meet you."

"Good to meet you, too." Wells shook his hand, curious eyes moving between Aiden and Abby. "You're not from around here."

Aiden held his gaze. "That's right, but I'm sticking around for a while."

"Cool." Wells pushed a hand through his thick hair and said, "Stop by the Rock Bottom Bar and Grill sometime and I'll buy you a drink. It's down by Rock Harbor Marina."

"You a bartender there?" Aiden asked.

Wells chuckled. "I own the place. I was actually coming by to offer my condolences again. Did you get the flowers I sent you after your mom passed, Abby?"

"I did, thank you. That was sweet of you."

Maybe he isn't a total douchebag.

"Yeah, I remember things weren't always easy, but still. I can't imagine losing my mom." Wells sounded genuinely compassionate. "I also wanted to see if you were interested in selling the restaurant. I know your mom was having a hard time of it the last few years, and I thought I'd take the place off your hands. At a fair price, of course. Save you the time of having to clean it up before putting it on the market."

There was no way in hell Aiden was going to let this guy take Abby's dream away. "Abby's keeping it," he said firmly, then immediately chastised himself for stepping in and taking over. He softened his tone and said, "Right, Abs? That's your plan?"

"Yes, that's my plan. I appreciate the offer, Wells, but I'm excited about digging my heels in and bringing the restaurant back to life."

Wells looked around with a skeptical expression. "It's going to take quite a bit of cash to bring this restaurant around."

"Sweat equity goes a long way," Abby said.

"And she has money," Cait said. "Deirdra and I are helping her."

Aiden wanted to give Cait an *attagirl*, but he bit his tongue. He'd had no idea that Cait was helping her financially, and by the look in Abby's eyes, she might not have known, either.

"Cool," Wells said with a nod. "Good luck. I wish you the best, Abby, and if it gets to be too much, you know where to find me."

"It won't," Abby said lightly, her effervescent smile returning. "But thank you."

"Guess I won't see you at the Best of the Island competition this year. Maybe next year, after you've gotten this place spiffed up," Wells said.

"You're entering?" Aiden asked.

Wells inhaled deeply, his chest expanding like he had something to prove, and he said, "You're looking at the reigning king for the past three years."

"How about that? Sounds like your competition has been too light." Aiden couldn't help pushing the guy's buttons.

"The competition is good. But we're better," Wells said arrogantly. "Like I said, come by anytime and see for yourself. Dinner's on me. I'm going to take off, but it was nice meeting you, Aiden." He flashed what he probably thought was a coy grin at Cait and said, "Hope to see more of you, Cait," and headed out the door.

"We need to get you into that contest, Abs."

"Why?" Abby asked.

"To beat that guy."

"Aiden's right—that guy needs to be brought down a notch," Cait said. "I've been thinking about it, and I want you to keep my share of the money we inherited to help with the restaurant. After everything you said last night, I agree with Deirdra. You've had enough of your dreams stolen from you. We all have. I'd like to help this one come true. Even though you don't want to do the competition, I still want to see this place—and *you*—succeed, and that takes money, so . . ."

"Oh, Cait, you don't have to do that," Abby said. "I have some savings, and mine and Deirdra's inheritance. You must have dreams of your own you want to follow."

"I don't. My dream was to find out who my birth parents were, and now I know who my mother was. That's all I needed. This is new for both of us, and I'll understand if you don't want me to be involved, but these last two days are the only time in my life that I've felt connected to something or someone outside of Tank and his family. I was going to ask if you'd mind if I continued coming here a few days each week to help you fix up the restaurant."

"Really?" Abby exclaimed. "I would *love* that. I'm so glad that you feel good about being here. You belong here. This is *so* exciting! We're all partners now. You, me, and Deirdra. Deirdra's a silent partner, obviously, and you can be as involved or as silent as you'd like. I know you have another job and a life on the Cape, so don't worry, I won't put *any* pressure on you. I'm thankful for whatever time you want to spend here, and with me. It makes the Bistro feel even more like a family restaurant. And you know what? Wells and his deep pockets can kiss our butts."

"Damn right." Aiden couldn't help saying, "I can't believe you dated him."

"It was *brief* and we were teenagers. He's a little full of himself, but he's a good guy," Abby said. "We may not have a lot of money, but we're determined, and trust me, I know how to squeeze pennies out of a shoestring budget. We're going to make this restaurant *the* place to be!" She hugged Cait and said, "This calls for a celebration! What are you doing tonight, Aiden?"

"Looks like I'm taking two beautiful women to dinner."

"I have a better idea," Abby said. "You've been helping for two days already. Let me repay both of you by cooking a special dinner, one of my dad's recipes. You'll love it. I promise."

"Sounds like a plan, as long as you let me help." Aiden slipped his arm around her waist again and said, "I make a pretty good sous-chef."

"Deal. *Cait?*" Abby asked.

"I suck at cooking, but I like eating, and I can set a mean table."

"Yay!" Abby rubbed her hands together and said, "I have to make a grocery list!"

Abby had a bounce in her step all afternoon. By the time Cait headed back to the house and Aiden walked Abby to her bike, he was beyond smitten with his fiercely determined and insanely sexy girl.

She took off his hat, which she'd worn all day, and squinted against the late-afternoon sun. "Thanks for letting me wear this."

"I want you to have it. You look better in it than I ever could, and I like seeing you in something of mine." He put his hat in the basket on her bike and gathered her in his arms. "Why don't you give me that grocery list and I'll bring everything over after I shower."

"You don't have to do that. I need to go to the grocery store and the organic shop in town."

He eyed her bicycle with the white basket on the front and said, "I'm not sure you can fit everything in that pretty little basket, Bike Girl. And you might not realize it yet, but tomorrow your shoulders are probably going to be sore from all that wallpaper removing. Go home and pamper yourself. Let me do this for you."

"You've done so much already," she said sweetly.

"Not nearly as much as you've done for me these past couple of days, Abs." He pressed his lips to hers in a tender kiss and said, "I'd like to do this for you."

"What have I done for you besides make you work your butt off?"

"You reminded me what it's like to enjoy life and do something other than think about finance." He kissed her cheek and said, "And you've shown me what it's like to get all worked up thinking about a beautiful"—he kissed her neck—"sexy"—he brushed his lips over hers—"incredibly adorable and contagiously happy woman."

He framed her face with his hands and lowered his lips to hers, kissing her as thoroughly as he'd been dying to do all day. She went up on her toes, and he took the kiss deeper, getting lost in her taste, her already familiar scent, the slide of her tongue over his. One arm circled her, holding their bodies flush, and his other hand threaded into her hair. God, he loved her hair, so long and lustrous. He tugged gently, angling her mouth beneath his and intensifying his efforts. She moaned, her fingers pressing into the back of his neck as she melted against him, surrendering to their passion. That trust brought a heightened sense of arousal *and* affection. He wanted to sweep her into his arms and carry her up to his hotel suite, strip her bare, and love every inch of her beautiful body, showing her just how incredible he thought she was. But he would never ask her to miss time with Cait when her sister was there for only two more nights.

It took all of his resolve to deny them both the pleasure he knew they'd find. He drew away slowly, but he wasn't ready to give her up and leaned in for more, quickly getting carried away, his hands moving down her back, clutching her gorgeous ass. Another tantalizing, needy sound escaped her lips. *Fuuck.*

"*God*, Abs," came out craggy and lustful, but he couldn't do it, couldn't walk away. Like metal to magnet, their mouths crashed together in another sensual kiss, which seared through him like an inferno. Desire throbbed through his veins as she pressed against his arousal. He tore his mouth away, both of them panting. "You feel so good. I could kiss you all night."

She clung to him like she never wanted to let go, her eyes pleading for more. *"Me too."*

The desire in her voice nearly did him in. He was a man who dealt in hard facts and tangible reasonings. He had no idea of the *why*s or *how*s they were so swept up in each other so fast, and he didn't care, because nothing in his life other than taking care of Remi, which was in a whole different realm, had ever felt so *right.*

He kissed her again, slow and sweet, full of unspoken promises to go along with the one she heard when he said, "Soon."

Abby wasn't good at pampering herself, and she didn't want Aiden to see the mess her mother had left behind, so when she got home, she skipped the pampering, threw open the windows, and went to work cleaning up the living room. Cait pitched in, despite Abby telling her she'd already done enough and should relax. They picked through their mother's records, choosing some of their favorites from the seventies, and played them while they cleaned. Abby enjoyed working with Cait and talking about their mother without Deirdra rolling her eyes or disparaging her. Cait soaked in every word, the good and the hard to hear. She was loosening up, and they worked well together.

When they were done cleaning, Cait showered while Abby made the pastry dough for dessert and put it in the fridge to chill. She showered quickly, but choosing an outfit proved time-consuming. She went through several options, wanting to look good for Aiden but not like she'd tried too hard. She'd turned into some sort of teenage girl, popping into Cait's room to show off each one. *Does this look okay? Is this too much? Does this color make my butt look too big?* At first Cait wasn't sure how to respond and told her everything looked good. But once Abby clarified that this was what sisters did and she needed to be blatantly honest because sisters trusted each other, Cait let loose. She nixed the outfits that were too bright, said one made her look too thick in the waist, and others definitely looked like she was trying too hard.

After the fifth or sixth outfit, Cait threw up her hands and stalked into Abby's closet, searching through her clothes, and put together an outfit Abby never would have come up with herself—dark blue textured leggings, a comfy short-sleeve gray shirt with a wide V-neck that showed a hint of the swell of her breasts, and a gray and white flannel shirt. *Flannel.* She'd forgotten that shirt was even in there. Abby rolled up the sleeves while Cait ran into their mother's bedroom, returning with several of their mother's bracelets and a long gold and blue dreamcatcher necklace, all of which Cait and Deirdra had found yesterday while Abby had been out with Aiden. They'd paired the outfit with Abby's tan ankle boots, and based on the lascivious looks Aiden had been giving her since he'd arrived and they'd begun cooking, she looked as fantastic as she felt.

Thank you, big sis.

Music filled the air, giving their evening a festive feel. As promised, Aiden had gotten everything on Abby's shopping list. They were making beet salad with pine nuts and one of her father's favorite classic French dishes, Poulet Vallée d'Auge—chicken cooked in apple cider, flambéed with Calvados brandy, and topped with sautéed buttered apples and a rich cream sauce. For dessert, she'd decided on something simple: a banana tarte tatin, a puff pastry with caramelized bananas and a dollop of cream spiced with her father's favorite rum.

Aiden was a great help, chopping and stirring, while Cait opted to set the table and take notes as they talked about the things they still needed to do at the restaurant. Abby couldn't believe Aiden wanted to help them get the Bistro ready for the grand opening any more than she could believe how attentive he was while they cooked, brushing kisses on her temple or touching her back. He somehow managed to lavish her with those intimate, special touches without crossing any inappropriate lines that might make Cait uncomfortable. She loved how he included Cait in their conversations, too, making sure she didn't feel like a third wheel. It was as if he'd been schooled in how to be a perfect gentleman, another thing she definitely wasn't used to but really enjoyed.

"Okay, this is what I have so far for the Bistro." Cait rattled off the list of exterior and interior repairs and the cosmetic modifications, like painting and repointing the floors and patio, while Abby browned the chicken. "My boss's cousins own Cape Stone. I'm sure they'd give us a great deal on fixing up the floors and patios. They do amazing work, as long as you have no issues being around bikers."

"Like the Hells Angels biker *gang*?" Abby asked cautiously.

"No. They're members of the Dark Knights motorcycle club. It's different from a gang. They do good things for the community to keep it safe," Cait explained. "They're really great guys, and as I said last night, they're like family to me. I thought I should ask because at first glance they're probably not what you're used to. They're tough, tatted-up guys."

"You have tattoos, and I adore you," Abby pointed out. "I have nothing against bikers. Leni's twin brother, Levi, is a member of the Dark Knights in Harborside. As long as it's a reputable company and we get a good price, that's all that matters. Let's see what kind of deal you can get."

"Great, and once we get started in the kitchen, I guess we'll know about appliances," Cait said.

"What about the menu?" Aiden asked, looking deliciously handsome in dark slacks and a polo shirt.

Abby noticed he'd worn leather sandals instead of loafers, too. He really did listen to everything she said.

"I definitely have to update it," Abby said. "It hasn't changed since my dad was alive. Mom had the waitstaff tell customers what was no longer available."

"Does the Bistro have an up-to-date inventory system?" Cait asked.

Abby turned the chicken over in the pan and said, "If you call a legal pad and a pencil a system, then sure."

Aiden winced.

"I know, right? Mom never liked computers. My dad had a manual ledger system for inventory and payroll, but my mom—*our* mom— never got the hang of it," Abby explained. "I showed her how to do it before I moved away, but she hated dealing with finances. Lord knows what state the books are in now. Shelley saw how it was stressing me out when I'd visit, and eventually she convinced me to step back and let her help. Honestly, it was a relief at that point. I'll have to start reviewing the financial and inventory records and think about automated systems."

"I can help," Cait offered. "Tank's parents own the Salty Hog, a restaurant and bar on the Cape, and I've been helping out there on and off for several years. Ginger and Conroy, Tank's parents, aren't all that fond of using computers, and I'm kind of a math and computer nerd, so I updated their general accounting, payroll, inventory, and staff scheduling programs. I can get you all the specs on the systems we used, but I didn't see a computer at the restaurant, and you'll need one to run them."

"Add a computer to our list," Abby said. "I had no idea you could do all that. That's wonderful. Thank you."

"A fellow *mathie*. I love it." Aiden held up his wineglass and clinked it with Cait's. "Were you in the math club in high school?"

Cait shook her head. "I wasn't in any clubs."

"I was a super nerd," Aiden said. "Math club, debate club, student council, homecoming king . . ."

Abby nudged him and said, "Homecoming king is *not* super nerdy."

"I didn't say I was *only* nerdy."

"That means you were a popular kid who also happened to be smart." Cait sipped her wine and said, "*Whoa*, apparently you're a super-nerdy popular guy who knows wine. This is delicious. What kind is it?"

"Chateau de Meursault, Meursault Charmes Premier Cru," he said casually, as if he weren't talking about a couple-hundred-dollar bottle of wine.

"Chateau *what*?" Cait asked.

He chuckled. "It's chardonnay from France. I figured it would go well with the meal."

"So you're a coffee snob *and* a wine snob?" Abby teased as she moved the browned chicken to a plate and added leeks and shallots to the pot. She hadn't cooked for people she cared about, instead of customers, in so long, she'd almost forgotten how good it felt.

"Can't fault a man for having good taste," he said.

"Okay, Chair Guy, but that's a really expensive bottle of wine. Where did you find it?"

He set down his wineglass and said, "I asked around."

"I bet you asked Margot or Fitz Silver, right? They're always helping their guests."

He flashed a dirty smirk, holding her gaze as he said, "A gentleman never tells."

Abby could get lost deciphering all the naughty, unspoken promises in that smirk. The man was not only good at flirting—he was a master at it. She forced herself not to think about what else he was a master at and said, "Would you mind stirring this while I get the lighter?"

"Sure." He kissed her temple so innocently, it had the opposite effect.

She dug around in the drawers, so caught up in the heat between them, she momentarily forgot what she was looking for until she saw the long-handled lighter. She snagged it and said, "Thanks, Aid," as if he hadn't set her insides on fire. She moved the pot off the burner, added the liquor, and picked up the lighter to flambé the brandy.

"That's it, baby, light my fire." He flashed a wicked grin, and in the next breath, as the flame flickered, he put his hand on her back and said, "Careful, babe."

"I can handle a little flambé," she said, as the brandy burned blue.

Aiden glanced at Cait, who was intent on whatever she was writing. He brushed his hips along Abby's back. The feel of his hard body and his tempting rugged scent sparked a flood of desire as he whispered, "I have a feeling nothing's too hot for you."

She swallowed hard, trying to concentrate on cooking instead of the dirty images popping up in her head of the two of them tangled up in the sheets.

He dragged his hand along her lower back, his fingers grazing her ass as he stepped beside her and casually sipped his wine, leaving her lonely lady parts begging for more, and said, "I like watching you cook."

She cleared her throat to try to pull her mind out of the gutter and jumped on the safer subject. "I was just thinking about how much I'm enjoying cooking for you and Cait. I can tell that you're no stranger to the kitchen."

"Remi and I lived on mac and cheese for months after my parents were killed, until I got my arms around schooling and parenting and could breathe enough to think straight. I learned to cook from my friend YouTube."

"Smart thinking. It sounds like you're one heck of a good brother," Abby said.

"We got by," he said humbly, and glanced at Cait, still focused on whatever she was writing. "How about you, Cait? You said you suck at cooking. Is it not your thing?"

Cait looked up and said, "My father wasn't around much, and when he was, teaching domestic skills wasn't a priority. I can make a half-decent burger and a few other things. But I'd love to learn how to cook one day."

"I'll teach you how to cook. I can show you some of Mom's favorite recipes," Abby said. "In fact, why don't you put down the list and help? I can show you a few things now."

They watched the flambé until the flames died down. Abby returned it to the stove and had Cait measure and pour the cider into the pot. "We're going to bring this to a boil, then simmer it until it's slightly reduced, so just a few minutes."

Aiden jotted down the things they needed to add to their list for the Bistro as she walked Cait through each step of the rest of the recipe, explaining why they turned the flame up or down and other things that would help her get a grasp on cooking. While dinner was in the oven, Abby changed the record to ABBA, and the three of them finished making the dessert she'd started earlier. When "Dancing Queen" came on, Aiden twirled Abby and pressed a kiss to her lips. He reached for Cait, but when he twirled her, she remained stiff and awkward. The second he let go of her hand, she turned away, blushing furiously.

"I'm sorry, Cait," Aiden said gently. "I didn't mean to embarrass you."

"We're all friends. No need to be embarrassed," Abby reassured her.

Cait turned, looking embarrassed and amused at once, and said, "I don't know how to dance."

"Well, we can help with that," Aiden said. "My mother taught me to dance from the minute I could tell my left foot from my right. I'll show you a few steps."

He reached for Cait's hand, charming Abby even more with the kind gesture.

Cait backed away, shaking her head. "No thank you."

"Want me to show you?" Abby asked.

She smiled briefly and said, "Thanks, but not right now."

"Okay, but don't be embarrassed. There are a million things I can't do, like sing or draw or roller-skate."

Aiden pulled out his phone. "I'm adding roller-skating to our list."

"You know how to roller-skate?" Abby asked.

"Babes, I raised a young girl. I had to keep up."

"Would you teach me how?" Abby asked.

"Absolutely." He glanced at Cait and said, "Want to get in on this game? Learn how to skate with Abs?"

Cait looked at Abby.

"Please, Cait? I'll do it if you do it," Abby added encouragingly. "We can skate in the parking lot of the Bistro. Deirdra is a great skater. I bet we have some of her old skates around here somewhere."

"Okay," Cait relented.

"Excellent. I need to get skates, which might take a few days. Cait, I know you're leaving Sunday. When will you be back?" Aiden asked.

"I talked to Tank earlier about my schedule. I think I can come back Friday for a few days."

"We can skate and spend Mother's Day together. This is going to be awesome!" Abby said, then quickly realized she was *assuming* Aiden wanted to spend that day together. "Aiden, I'm sorry. I should have asked you about Mother's Day before getting too excited. Do you usually spend it with your sister?"

"She has her own family to spend Mother's Day with. I'd like to be here for you, if that's okay? Unless you and Cait would rather spend it alone? I'm okay with that, too, of course."

Her heart swelled. "Cait?"

"All three of us have lost our mothers. I'm totally fine with spending it together if you are."

"I am, thank you." Abby was elated. "I wish Dee were here. She'd have so much fun with us."

"You could invite her," Aiden suggested.

"She's in the middle of a huge case at work. She won't come, but I'll text her anyway."

The kitchen smelled heavenly, and when they finally sat down to eat, Abby's nerves tingled as Aiden's dark eyes moved over the beet salad, perfectly browned chicken surrounded by creamy sauce, mushrooms, and chunks of potatoes and garnished with sprigs of thyme and bay leaves.

"Talk about presentation," Aiden said. "I feel like I'm in a five-star restaurant."

"It looks like the cover of a cookbook," Cait added.

"Thank you." Abby waited anxiously as they took their first bites, and the blown-away look on their faces made her giddy.

"*Mm.* Abs," Aiden said as he finished his bite. "This is incredible. *Delectable.* The sauce is rich and sweet, and the chicken is savory with a hint of spice. It's absolutely perfect, and I'm not just blowing smoke because my talented date cooked the meal."

"I've never eaten anything like this. It's . . . I don't even have the words to describe how good it is, but I can show you," Cait said, eating another big bite.

Abby was elated and relieved. "I'm *so* glad you like it. Thank you!"

Aiden took another bite and said, "Babes, this is really spectacular. If you can whip up something this gorgeous and delicious on a whim,

I can only imagine what you can do with a planned menu and all of the accoutrements at your fingertips."

"Does that mean you think my sisters and I can really make a go of this?" she asked nervously.

"Not just make a go of it, Abs. You'll outshine every other restaurant around."

She let out a squeal. "I'm so excited!"

Aiden raised his glass and said, "To new partnerships, new relationships"—he put his hand on Abby's leg, giving it a squeeze—"and new beginnings."

They all clinked glasses.

Their easy conversations and good-natured ribbing were everything Abby had always dreamed her life would include. They lingered over dinner, and as they savored dessert, Aiden and Cait spoiled her with more praise. She wished Deirdra were there, eating the food they'd made together, talking about their parents' restaurant, and filling the kitchen with positivity and laughter, just as it had been when both of their parents were alive. Abby felt her father's magic all around them as the happy moments of the last few days took root beside some of her favorite childhood memories, and she knew without a doubt she was finally on the right path.

When they finished eating, Aiden said, "Abigail de Messiéres, if we keep this up, I'm going to have to hit the gym *and* start running daily."

"You and me both," Cait said, standing up to clear her plate.

"I'll get the dishes." Aiden pushed to his feet and began stacking plates.

"You don't have—"

"Abs, you're worse at relaxing than I am. I've got the dishes. I'm good at this."

"Then how about if Cait and I clear and you wash?" Abby suggested.

"Sounds like a plan. But first we need to take a picture of the three of us to prove to my sister that I had dinner with new friends."

Abby waggled her finger at him. "Oh, no you don't. We talked about business, and she specifically said no talking business. I haven't met your sister yet, but if I ever do, I don't want her thinking that I let you skirt the rules."

Aiden glanced at Cait, nodding in Abby's direction, and said, "Who's the super nerd now? Did you know she was so straitlaced?"

"I'm not straitlaced," Abby insisted.

"Your mouth is twitchy. I think you're fibbing, which means you suck at lying, and that makes you a rule follower," Cait said.

Abby rolled her eyes. "Whatever. I don't want his sister to hate me."

"I'm pretty sure it would be impossible for anyone to hate you, Abs. But we won't send her a picture. I don't want to be a bad influence. At least not about something so innocent." He winked and said, "Besides, you won't hear me complain about spending *more* time with you two." He set the plates on the counter and drew Abby into his arms for a quick kiss. "I'm the luckiest guy on this island."

Aiden washed the dishes as Abby and Cait cleared the table. As Abby dried the last pot, Cait's phone rang. She pulled it from her pocket and excused herself to take the call. Heat sparked in Aiden's eyes. He swept Abby into his arms, and his mouth descended on hers in a kiss as urgent and greedy as she felt, unleashing the heat that had been simmering all evening. "I've been waiting all night to kiss you," he practically growled, and reclaimed her lips, backing her up against the counter as he took the kiss deeper, sending her body into a frenzy of desire. Their hands moved feverishly over each other's bodies as they feasted on kisses like they'd never get enough. His hips pressed forward, sending need pulsing through her core. She grasped at his shoulders as he tangled his hands in her hair, taking the kiss intoxicatingly deeper, *rougher*. Her thoughts fragmented, and as if he felt the change, a gruff, hungry sound escaped his lungs, searing into hers. He grabbed her shoulders and tore his mouth away, leaving her breathless and confused. But then Cait walked into the kitchen, her head down as she thumbed out something on her phone, and she realized Aiden must have heard her coming.

Thank God.

Abby had been lost in a sea of scintillating sensations, which were still vibrating through her body and wreaking havoc with her brain. She tried to school her expression, to find her voice, but her lips burned, desperate for another kiss as Aiden stepped beside her.

He slid an arm around her waist, whispering huskily into her ear, "I think I'd better take off before I get us both into trouble."

She didn't want him to leave. For the first time in her life, she wanted to run toward trouble, but her lust-fogged brain refused to string words together.

"Well, ladies, thank you for a wonderful night," he said, drawing Cait's attention and finally kicking Abby's brain into gear.

"It was fun," Cait said, and looked down at her phone again.

Aiden brushed his lips over Abby's cheek and lowered his voice. "See you in the morning for breakfast before we get to work?"

"You're sure you want to spend another day in the trenches?"

"Abs, stop asking. I don't do things I don't want to do." He brushed his thumb over her cheek and said, "I very much want to help you and spend more time with you."

"Okay, but if you're going to keep helping me, then we're playing hooky Sunday after Cait leaves and tackling your Let Loose list."

He embraced her and whispered, "That list is not the only thing I want to tackle."

CHAPTER SEVEN

SATURDAY PASSED IN a flurry of cleaning and stolen kisses. Aiden had finished removing the remnants of the wallpaper at the Bistro, while Abby and Cait had scoured the kitchen. They'd found a few loose cabinet doors, which Aiden had tightened, and a broken shelf, which he'd replaced. More problematic was the discovery that the largest of the range-oven units was on its last legs. Aiden's first instinct had been to make a few phone calls and buy Abby the best unit on the market, but he'd once again held back. At least as best he could. While he couldn't step in and take over, he had suggested making an inventory of appliances and equipment and researching repair and replacement costs in order to put together a maintenance budget. It was a move in the right direction and a way he could help Abby avoid mistakes without stepping on her toes. She and Cait had jumped on the suggestion, working on it for the rest of the afternoon. Since Cait was leaving in the morning, he hadn't wanted to monopolize Abby's evening, so after Cait had gone back to the house, he and Abby said goodbye in the parking lot. What had started as a kiss had turned into a full-on make-out session, complete with groping, grinding, and lascivious noise making.

Long cold showers were becoming Aiden's nightly activity.

He and Abby had spoken on the phone after Cait had turned in for the night. But once again, what had started as whispers of looking forward to seeing each other again had turned into reliving moments when they'd snuck kisses in the office of the Bistro. He had no idea why he couldn't control himself around Abby, but he'd ended up telling her the truth—that he'd like to take her to his suite, strip her naked, and touch, taste, cherish, and *enjoy* every inch of her body until he knew it by heart. They'd both ended up hot and bothered, and if Cait had not been at the house, Aiden would have been at Abby's door seven minutes later.

Instead, he'd dragged his horny ass into another cold shower to relieve the storm of sexual tension Abby always left behind.

They'd planned on meeting at ten this morning, after Cait caught the nine forty-five ferry, for their day of playing hooky. Waiting had been hell. He parked in front of Abby's quaint bungalow at ten on the dot.

As an investor, he owned commercial and residential properties all over the world, and usually his first thoughts at any new location revolved around quantifying the value of it. But as he climbed out of his rental car, that was the last thing on his mind, just as it had been Friday night when he'd arrived for dinner. He imagined Abby as a young girl running around the yard with her sister and singing on the porch with her mother while she gazed adoringly at her father as he painted. He spotted a fenced-off area that must have once contained the gardens she'd raved about toiling in with her mother. Grasses and weeds grew knee-high, tangled around the broken fence. He pictured Abby with a thick braid hanging down her back, rebellious strands of her beautiful hair sticking out all over, as she clomped around in shorts and rubber boots, carrying a basket bigger than she was.

A gust of wind swept up the hill, stinging his eyes and snapping him from his reverie. He tried to shake off the feeling of something burrowing deep in his chest as he climbed the front steps. The door flew open, and Abby's bright smile pierced the space between them, driving that burrowing sensation even deeper. Her peach sweater hung sexily off one shoulder, revealing a thin strap of lace and the swell of her breast and awakening his carnal desires. Her skinny jeans clung to her curves, with a fashionable tear in the upper thigh and another above one knee. He wanted to lick those smooth patches of skin. Her feet were bare, her toenails painted to match her sweater.

"*Damn*, babes," he said, dragging his eyes up the length of her as he stepped forward.

Her tongue swept across her bottom lip, leaving it slick and alluring, but it was the hunger in her eyes that had him reaching for her as she reached for him. Their mouths collided with the force of a hurricane. Their tongues tangled as they stumbled into the house, bodies grinding as he backed her up against the wall, untethering days of pent-up passion. She was right there with him, feasting on him as he devoured her. He imagined her hot, willing mouth traveling down his body. His hips rocked at the thought, and he groaned into their kisses. He pushed his hands into her hair, fisting them tight. She gasped, and he drew back, worried he'd hurt her, but *desire* raged in her eyes, not pain. She grabbed his head with both hands, pulling his mouth back to hers. *Fuck yes.* He kissed her fiercely, drawing back enough to nip at her lips and graze his teeth along her jaw.

When he sank his teeth into her neck, she said, "*Yesss*," breathy and needful.

She grabbed his ass, holding him even tighter. He angled his hips lower, pressing his hard length against her center, and recaptured her mouth in a punishingly intense kiss. Lust coiled tight and hot inside him.

"I thought about you all night," he said between urgent kisses. "In my arms. In my *bed*."

"Me too," she confessed.

Her cheeks were flushed, her eyes at half-mast. She was *stunning*. "I need more of you, baby."

Her eyes flamed. "Yes, yes, *yesss*."

He covered her mouth with his, kissing her slow and deep. But slow didn't last, and soon they were eating at each other's mouths, pawing at their bodies. He palmed her breast, brushing his thumb over the taut peak. Her head fell back with a sensual sound, and he kissed his way down her neck, lingering over the throbbing pulse at the base. Her hips rocked against him with every slick of his tongue. He trailed kisses lower, tracing the swell of her breast, and pulled the cup of her bra down, sealing his mouth over the peak.

"*Ah . . . Aiden,*" she pleaded.

"Tell me to stop and I will." *Please don't tell me to stop.* He righted her bra, anticipating a red light.

"*Don't* stop," she said softly.

His gaze shot up to hers, and the desire in her eyes nearly sent him to his knees as she panted out, "Don't you *dare* stop."

He crushed his mouth to hers, tugging up her sweater as she fumbled with the button on his pants. He tore his mouth away long enough to strip off her sweater and grabbed his wallet from his back pocket, throwing it in the direction of the couch. The next few seconds were a blur of clothes flying, desperate kisses, and urgent pleas as they stumbled toward the couch. She grabbed his shoulders, standing on one foot as they kissed, using her other foot to try to get free of her jeans and panties, which were stuck on one ankle. He bent to help and couldn't resist nipping at her ass cheek.

She let out a surprised *squeak*, giggling as she said, "*Aiden!*"

"When I'm not half out of my mind needing to be inside you"—he tugged off the offending denim and sexy silk—"I'm going to enjoy tasting every inch of your gorgeous body."

"Ditto," she said sassily.

He hauled her gloriously naked body into his arms and said, "I'm counting on it."

They tumbled to the couch, flesh grinding, hands groping, mouths *consuming.* The head of his cock throbbed against her wet center. She clawed at his arms, arching beneath him, her knees widening as he drew his hips back—and stopped cold. "*Fuck. Condom,*" he gritted out. He *never* lost control, had never been blinded by need like this before. It was as thrilling as it was terrifying. He reached for his wallet, trying not to think about what that lapse in control meant.

"Hurry!" she pleaded.

Her hands explored his hips and thighs as he tore open the package with his teeth and sheathed his length. He came down over her, their mouths connecting as he buried himself to the hilt with one hard thrust. Sparks of pleasure exploded inside him, spreading like wildfire through his chest and down his limbs. "*Jesus . . .*" he said against her lips. She was so tight, the pleasure was almost *too* intense. He needed to *move*, and reclaimed her mouth as they found their rhythm, but it wasn't enough. He thrust faster, kissed harder, and still he was ravenous for her. Being inside her hadn't taken the edge off; it had amped up every sensation, every emotion. She felt unbelievably good, as if their bodies had been made solely for each other's pleasure. He had no idea where that thought came from, but it lodged in his head, as *inescapable* as his desire to help her, to just be in her world with her. He pushed his hands beneath her, cradling her ass, penetrating deeper, deftly searching for the perfect angle to make her wild.

"*Aiden,*" she panted against his mouth.

He guided her legs around his waist, earning a long, surrendering moan. "I've got you, babe."

He moved quicker, *rougher,* homing in on the spot that had her inhaling tiny gasps. Her fingernails carved into his skin, heightening the pleasure engulfing him as she cried out his name, giving in to her climax. Her sex pulsed, her hips bucked, and greedy pleas streamed from her lips. His new favorite sound. When she came down from the peak, he kissed her softer, slower, whispering, "So beautiful, baby. You feel so good."

"*Again,*" she whispered.

Their bodies moved in perfect sync as he gave her what she needed, winding her up, up, *up*, until she soared free and loud and so damn sexy, he was going to lose his mind. She came down from her high, panting and greedy.

"*More*," she pleaded.

Desire roared through him like a runaway train. He couldn't get enough of her, and he drove harder and faster, trying to outrun the unfamiliar emotions consuming him. But there was no escape. Their bodies became slick with their efforts, her softness giving way to his hard frame. He felt fully *alive* for the first time in his life, and he never wanted it to end. He sealed his mouth over hers, swallowing her sounds, wanting to treasure them, for them to become part of him. Her thighs tightened around him, her body trembling, rising to meet his every thrust, her tight heat unraveling him second by second. He broke their kiss without slowing his efforts, needing to *see* if she felt it too. He gazed into the gorgeous green eyes of the only woman to have *ever* shattered his control, and the emotions in them swamped him.

"Abs," came out at the same time she said, "Aiden," full of lust and something much bigger.

"Come *with* me," he said rougher than he meant to, but he was on the verge of losing his mind.

He lowered his mouth to hers, and heat seared down his spine. He slowed his efforts, desperately trying to stave off his climax, but she clawed at his back, moaning and writhing as her orgasm slammed into her. "*Aiden!*" She buried her face in his neck. Her sex clenched and pulsed, dragging him under, stealing the air from his lungs, and shredding the last of his control as he surrendered to his own powerful release, her name flying from his lips like a prayer. "Abby, Abby, *Abby*."

They lay tangled together, their hearts hammering out the private beat that bound them as one. He lifted his face, and she blinked up at him, a small, disbelieving smile curving her lips. Sex had always been separate from the rest of his life, free from emotions. It was a release, a good time. But like everything else with Abby, this was different. *Special.* He wasn't ready to let her go, and he couldn't hold her on the narrow couch the way he wanted to. He kissed her lips, her cheeks, her forehead, and surprised himself by admitting, "I need to hold you."

He cradled her against him, lifting her within his embrace without breaking their connection as he sat up, her legs still straddling his waist. She wrapped her arms around him and rested her head on his shoulder, as if she belonged there. He reveled in the rightness seeping into his pores, wondering how he'd ever be the same again.

Abby was totally and utterly blissed out. She didn't know how long they embraced, but it felt endless and wonderful. When Aiden kissed her cheek and patted her butt, whispering, "I need to take care of the condom," she slid off his lap, instantly missing their connection. She watched him strut naked and beautiful across the room and disappear down the hall, surprised at how comfortable and safe she felt with him. She wasn't even embarrassed sitting on the couch naked as a jaybird. She rested her head back and closed her eyes, reliving the feel of him inside her, the weight of his body pressing down on hers, the masculine, passionate noises he'd made. He was so *intense.* His desire made her feel *wanted* and feminine like never before. And those kisses. *Lordy.* The man kissed like he'd been waiting his whole life *just* to kiss *her.* Goose bumps chased over her skin with the delicious memories.

She sensed his presence before she felt his fingers caress her cheek. She opened her eyes, finding him standing before her, his thick and very talented cock still half-erect, sending her body into an anticipatory celebration. *Down, girl.*

"Eyes up here, gorgeous." He flashed a grin and reached for her hand.

She smiled as he brought her to her feet and said, "You're the one dangling your goodies in front of me." She remembered the bite on her ass, and heat skated through her. She'd never had *fun* while being intimate with a guy, and now that she knew what she'd been missing, she wondered why that was.

He nipped at her neck and said, "You like my goodies, huh?"

"I'm not answering that for fear it'll bolster your ego too much." She giggled, and he swatted her ass. "Hey!"

He pressed his body to hers and said, "Well, I like *your* goodies a whole hell of a lot. How about we rinse off in the shower before we head out, and if you're lucky, I'll let you show me how much you like mine."

God, this man was going to do her in.

And *do her in* he did.

After their sexy shower, there was no shortage of kisses and gropes as they dressed and finally headed out for the day, all of which felt surprisingly natural.

"Grab a sweater, Abs. We might be out late."

She'd been independent for so long, she was surprised at how much she liked his thoughtful, caring nature. As she descended the porch steps, she said, "A sleek black BMW? Fancy wheels, Finance Guy."

"It's a rental, and it looks sleeker than it rides. Rental companies never have comfortable cars, so I thought asking for a luxury car would do the trick, but . . ." He shrugged.

"Well, it does the trick for me," she said, and noticed his trunk was open. "Hey, there's a bike in your trunk."

"Yeah. I wasn't sure if you'd want to ride bikes or take the car, so I picked one up on the way over."

How thoughtful. "Are you always this prepared?"

"I try." He lifted the bike out of the trunk, without a care about dirtying his tan pants or white linen shirt. "I thought we could start at the lighthouse and check out those stairs that went on forever."

She was touched that he'd chosen to start at the lighthouse, and not at all surprised that he'd remembered what she'd said. She'd already learned that he had the memory of an elephant. "After that phenomenal couch workout, I'm not sure I can ride the bike that far. Would you mind if we took the car?"

He set the bike next to hers at the side of the house and kissed her softly. "I think that sounds perfect."

As they settled into the car, she said, "So, we're starting at the lighthouse. What else do you want to tackle?"

He flashed that wolfish grin.

"You're a dirty-minded man, Aiden . . . ? Hey, Aid, I don't know your last name."

"Aldridge." He gave her leg a gentle squeeze as they drove away from the house and said, "You haven't known me long enough to realize this, but I want you to know that I'm only overtly sexual with you, Abs. You bring out parts of me I wasn't even sure I possessed anymore *and* sides of me I never knew existed."

"I feel the same way." The words came without thought, and that made her nervous, but it was true. "I've never felt this comfortable with anyone, not even the last guy I went out with, who was a friend first."

He took her hand, lacing their fingers together, and said, "How long did you two go out?"

"Almost a year, and his kisses never made me feel like I do when we kiss." She lifted their joined hands and said, "Even *this* feels vastly different."

"For me, too," he said, honesty shining in his eyes. "Why did you break up after all that time?"

"When my mom passed away, I took a long, hard look at my life and realized I had left the island searching for something that I never found. I wasn't happy with my job, my relationship, or quite honestly, *myself.* I allowed all of my dreams to fall away in order to earn a living, and I accepted less than I deserved in my relationship just because I wanted some sort of human connection. That probably sounds awful, but I was working more than sixty hours a week, and I guess I was lonely, so I turned to a friend. Paul and I had worked together a few years ago. He managed another restaurant, and we both had crazy schedules. We'd meet for drinks sometimes, and there had always been chemistry, so one night we took it further, and eventually we became a couple. Sort of. It was coupledom by convenience, and since we cared about each other more as friends than anything else, I never expected more from him, which meant I wasn't risking getting hurt. He's a nice guy, and he's *someone's* other half. But I knew he wasn't mine from the moment we got together. He's perfectly happy working for someone else, and whenever I brought up wanting to own my own restaurant, he said I should be thankful for the job I had and to stop asking for headaches. I couldn't have invested my heart in a man who didn't give value to my dreams. And I *was* thankful for the job I had, but thankful and happy are two different things. Does that make sense?"

"Yes, perfect sense," he said as they drove toward Fortune's Landing, which he must have already looked up, because he didn't ask for directions. His expression turned serious, and he said, "I usually don't share the details of mine or Remi's life with people outside of a small group of friends we think of as family, but I really like you, Abby, and I feel like we might be something special."

"Me too," she said, surprising herself with the confession.

"I have to ask that you keep what I tell you about Remi between us."

"Of course. You sound like she's in the witness protection program or something."

He smiled, but it was a troubled smile. "Before she took a hiatus from acting, it felt that way. In addition to my regular job, I managed her acting career."

"Remi was an actress?" As the pieces fell into place, she couldn't hide her surprise. "Wait! Your sister isn't Remi Divine, *is* she?"

"The one and only."

"Oh my gosh, I *love* her! You can't spring that on a girl." She sank back in the seat, grinning from ear to ear. "She's one of my favorite actresses. You don't mind if I sit here and fangirl for a second, do you?"

"Not at all. She's worth fangirling over."

"She's flat-out gorgeous, and everything she does on-screen is believable. I loved every one of her movies. And her name? Remi Divine. It's so glamorous. How did she come up with it?"

"Her real name is Remington Aldridge, but for safety reasons I didn't want her using her real last name. Our parents loved old movies with actresses like Marilyn Monroe and Rita Hayworth, and our mother used to talk about how *divine* they were. Remi chose her name to honor our parents."

"I love that," she said as troubling memories trickled in. "Wait, didn't she have a stalker before she got married? *Yes.* I remember now. Some crazy guy tried to attack her at a cabin or something, right? That must have been terrifying."

The muscles in his jaw bunched, and he squeezed her hand. "Yes, she had two stalkers, actually, and one attempted to hurt her. Needless to say, I'm glad she's out of the business now. I know the world sees her as Remi Divine, A-list actress and America's sweetheart. But to me, acting was what she did for a living, not who she was. She will always be my little sister, and the only blood relative I have left."

"Oh, Aiden, I'm sorry for acting like a ridiculous fan," she said, feeling horrible. "I had forgotten about the stalkers and everything you guys went through. I'm usually not that insensitive."

"That's okay. I know you're not. It was a natural reaction." He turned onto the coastal road and said, "There are some things I want you to know, so you'll understand why I kept it from you and what my life has been like since my parents died." His serious eyes shadowed with grief. "The day the stalker found Remi was the second-worst day of my life. The first being the day we lost our parents." He stared at the road, tightening his grip on the steering wheel. "Remember I told you that

I was running the West Coast division of my father's company when they were killed?"

"Yes."

"Well, Remi was taking ballet at the time, and she had a big recital that night. She'd always wanted to be an actress, and I'd pulled some strings to get backstage passes to a Broadway play so she could meet the actors. I'd come home to surprise her with the trip. Even though we were twelve years apart in age, we've always been close. Before my parents were killed, I tried to go home for all of her big events, and she'd call me every week with updates about her life. For a little girl with a typical existence, she never ran out of things to say. Every update included her latest achievement toward acting, which was usually something like she and her friends had held a mock audition and she'd nailed it." He laughed softly. "I've never met a more determined, hardworking child." He glanced at Abby and said, "Although from what you told me, you were just as remarkable."

She warmed with his praise. "Thank you."

"Anyway, that night when I arrived at our home in West Virginia, she was out with my parents. I called my father, and they were ten minutes from home. I got worried when they didn't show up after half an hour, but my dad was known for stopping on a whim to show us things, so I gave them the benefit of the doubt. But after forty-five minutes, something felt *wrong*. I called him again, and there was no answer, so I went looking for them. The house where I grew up was down a winding mountain road. It was a rainy February day, freezing out. I couldn't shake this heaviness all around me. I went up and down the road telling myself they were fine, but I swear I heard my father urging me to *keep looking*, to *find Remi*. And then I spotted the mangled shrubs and tire tracks where they'd gone over the embankment."

"Oh, Aiden."

He stared at the road as he drove, glassy-eyed, and said, "I threw the car into park and ran down the side of the mountain. I slipped and fell on my ass in the ruts from where the car must have rolled, and then I saw it." His voice cracked. "My father's car was on its side, mangled and crushed, partially twisted around a tree. I thought I lost them all."

He swallowed hard, squeezing her hand. Tears welled in her eyes as she imagined him coming upon the wreck.

"My memory gets foggy there. All I could think of was finding Remi. You know how they say in those situations you find strength you never knew you had?" His eyes dampened. "I tore at the broken glass and saw Remi hanging there with the seat belt across her chest, shaking all over and crying out for our parents. I managed to get her out. She was in shock, but I checked her from head to toe, and it was like an angel had been looking out for her. She had no broken bones, no big lacerations. She kept begging me to save our parents. I couldn't. They were . . ."

Tears slipped down Abby's cheeks.

"My father used to drill into my head never to let any *one* event define my life, and that night I knew what I had to do. I took Remi home and *then* I called 911 and reported the accident. I told them only our parents had been in the car. We lived in a small town, and I didn't want Remi to be known as the little girl who survived the accident that had killed her parents. I called in a favor with a guy I had grown up with who had become an EMT. His father was a doctor, and they checked out Remi and kept it quiet."

"Your instinct to protect her . . ." She wiped her tears. "Aiden, *that's* remarkable."

He shrugged. "I was only following my father's advice. There was nothing remarkable about it. I had nightmares for months, reliving all of it. But from that moment on, my life became about making sure Remi was okay. She'd lost the two most important people in her life at an age when her biggest worries should have been about cute boys and diaries. I wanted to keep our parents' spirit alive for her and make sure she grew up knowing she was loved and that, while we had lost our parents, she still had me and I'd always be there for her. I got her into therapy, and once she'd had time to mourn, I tried to carry on all the traditions my parents had, reading to her like my dad used to, making big deals of her birthdays, making sure she had friends and continued with dance lessons. Eventually the memories in the West Virginia house became too much, and we moved to my place in California. I didn't want her dreams of being an actress to die with our parents, so I got her an acting coach and made sure she had all the right opportunities."

"That must have been tumultuous for both of you, moving away from the comfort of the community and friends where you were raised."

"It was harder for Remi because she was so young. I did everything I could to help her make new friends and to nurture those relationships so she could regain a sense of community. And she did."

"What about *you*? That couldn't have been an easy transition, losing your parents? Suddenly becoming mother and father to your younger sister?"

"I got through it. I'm not going to pretend it was easy. I had no idea what I was doing."

"Did you have friends to turn to for help?"

"Not really. Before our parents died, I was so focused on running the LA division of my father's business, friends weren't a priority. And after I moved Remi to LA, I was too young to be peers with the parents of her new friends, and with a twelve-year-old girl to care for, I didn't fit in with other twentysomethings, either. My father's business associates and our parents' friends tried to help, that sort of thing, but I felt a need to shelter Remi from too much of that. As I said before, I didn't want her to be defined by their deaths, so I figured things out as best I could."

"She's really lucky she had you watching out for her."

"In some ways, yes. But I was overprotective, always afraid something would happen to her. If she went bowling or skating with friends, I went with them, even when she was a teenager. As you can imagine, she hated that."

"It's hard to be a teenage girl. But who could blame you for wanting to protect her?"

"That was my feeling. I may not have always made the popular decision, but I always made the decisions that I thought were best for her." As he turned onto the road that led to the lighthouse, he said, "And I now realize that as she got older, I protected her *too* much. When she finally got her big break into acting, I was right there every step of the way, managing her career, living wherever she was filming. Not only was I overprotective, but I also did too much for her. That's probably my biggest flaw, wanting to give her everything she deserved, everything she ever wanted. We were brought up with one general rule of thumb—if you have, you give to others, whether it's money or just helping things happen for them. That carried into every aspect of my life. It still does. It's a hard habit to break. But it was too much for Remi. When the stalker situation occurred, I had to travel for work, and I hired bodyguards for her. Unfortunately, Remi picked that exact time to rebel. She snuck out and outsmarted every bodyguard I hired, until I found Mason. She really met her match with him."

"Did that bother you? That you hired him to protect your sister and he fell in love with her?"

"Hell yes, it bothered me. Not to mention that she kept their relationship a secret from me at first. But he loves her to the ends of the earth, and they're good for each other. He's very protective of her, but he allows her the space she needs in a way that keeps her safe, while I had wanted to shield her from everything. Anyway, after the stalker incident was resolved, Remi, Mason, and I had a goodbye ceremony for our parents, which dredged up feelings I had been keeping locked down for a long time. Remi and I cleared the air, and when I told her that I blamed myself for our parents' accident, it broke her heart. The little sister I had raised put on my big-sibling hat and made me promise to see someone and deal with that guilt. For her, I got help."

Abby's heart broke for him. "And for *you*? That's a lot of guilt to carry around for so long."

"Like you when you were younger, I wasn't used to putting myself first." He turned into the parking lot and said, "But about a year and a half ago, when I started therapy, I realized I needed to let that guilt go. I'll never know if my parents could have lived had I not come home. But the bottom line is that I did go home, and they died. But I didn't cause the accident, and I've dealt with the guilt and grieving. I also realized how hard it was for me to step back and let Mason take over my role of protecting Remi. She didn't need me the way she once had. Remi and our close friends thought I'd race out and sow my wild oats or celebrate my freedom. But I'd done my fair share of playing around and being irresponsible in college. I had no more oats to sow, and I'd never seen raising Remi as a burden, so I wasn't looking to celebrate my freedom."

He'd given up his whole life for his sister, even more years than she'd given to her mother. And he was not only genuinely happy he'd done it, but he'd also helped Remi flourish and didn't carry an ounce of resentment toward her for all he'd given up so he could be there for her. Could he and Abby be any more alike? She felt like she'd met her soul mate. She should know better than to let herself think like that, but it was hard not to.

He parked the car and turned in his seat with a lighter expression. "My life had been completely defined by Remi's happiness, and I don't regret a second of it. But I needed to figure out who I was if I wasn't taking care of her. I had my own career, but I had no clue what the rest of my life should look like without her as the center of it."

"It takes a lot of guts to admit that," she said.

"Babes, you're involved with me, which means Remi will blab it all to you the first chance she gets."

"She sounds like a great sister. But I can only imagine how hard that transition must have been for both of you."

"For me, yes, but not for Remi. She's a pistol. She had no trouble spreading her wings, and I've since accepted my new role in her life as more or less just her big brother. But with extra time on my hands now that she's no longer acting and doesn't need me to travel with her or manage her career other than a few endorsements, I pretty much buried myself in work twenty-four-seven, which was great for business."

"But not great for *Aiden.* I bet Remi felt guilty that you'd given up so much for her, even if from where you were sitting it looked easy for her to make the change. I know how hard it is to be the person who needs something from others. I felt guilty as a kid when Shelley would send her kids over to help with the Bistro. Remember, Shelley is the one who finally pushed me to leave the island. *Remi* is your *Shelley.* It's no wonder she wanted you to get away, to get a life, and to learn how to relax. She knows you're too great a guy to let life pass you by."

"Either that or I'm a pain in her ass," he joked. "She was right. I hadn't just forgotten who I was apart from work and her, but I also no longer have a home base. She'd been that for me because wherever she needed to be, I went. That's why when you asked where I called home, I said I was trying to figure that out. The other thing you deserve to know is that while you had a friend with benefits, I was never that consistent. Relationships weren't a priority, and with Remi's career, I had to be extra careful about the women I let into my life. I trusted a few women who I'd hook up with from time to time. But I never told people about my relation to Remi. I had made that mistake at the beginning of her career, and women assumed Remi's celebrity status rolled over to me, which it did *not*, and I wouldn't have wanted it to. It's a full-time job scouring newsfeeds and shutting down paparazzi."

"I'm glad you trust me. I won't breach that confidence." She couldn't resist lightening the mood and said, "But now how will I *ever* see you as anything but actress Remi Divine's brother?"

He chuckled. "Since she's no longer acting, she's old news. You might want to end this date now and go track down another A-list actress's brother."

Loving that they could joke with each other, she said, "I think I'll stick around. You never know when she'll make a comeback."

"Lucky me." He leaned in and kissed her, his scruff tickling her skin. He took her hand and kissed the back of it, gazing so deeply into her eyes, it sparked a flutter in her chest. "I wasn't looking to meet anyone here, Abs."

"Neither was I."

"Then maybe we're meant to be, like you and the Bistro."

CHAPTER EIGHT

JUST AS ABBY had remembered, the lighthouse stairs felt like they went on forever, but she didn't mind. It wasn't unusual that they were the only visitors this time of year, and Abby was glad no one else was there. She and Aiden held hands, talking and kissing as they made their way up the narrow, winding steps, their voices echoing in the dimly lit chamber. Aiden appeared lighter after sharing his secrets with her. After hearing how secretive he'd had to be about Remi's identity, she couldn't imagine being the sibling to someone famous, wondering if people liked him for who he was or because of his sister. Knowing he was Remi Divine's brother didn't change how she saw him, but the fact that he'd trusted her enough to tell her definitely made her trust him even more.

"Does this bring back memories?" he asked.

"Yes. My sister and I used to race everywhere we went, including the lighthouses and windmills. We'd run up the stairs, leaving our parents behind."

He swatted her ass and said, "Then let's go. One. Two. *Three!*"

She ran up the stairs, squealing as he chased after her. When they neared the top, he took the steps two at a time, getting ahead of her, and turned, sweeping her into his arms. *"Gotcha!"* He backed her up against the cold concrete, showering her with kisses, her laughter echoing off the walls.

"Cheater!" She giggled.

"Aldridges don't cheat." He kissed her sweetly, but when he deepened the kiss, it quickly turned hungry and penetrating, and she melted against him, greedily enjoying every second of it.

When their lips parted, she put her arms around his neck and said, "Then what do you call trapping me with your big, *hard* body and kissing me breathless?"

He pressed his hips forward and said, "Careful, Abs. You keep looking at me like that and talking about my hard body and there'll be a lot more than giggles echoing off these walls." He lowered his lips to hers and scooped her off her feet.

"*Aiden!*" she said as he *carried* her up the steps. *Carried* her!

He pushed through the door at the landing, and a gust of salty sea air whipped around them. "What kind of a *win* would it be if I left you behind?"

Her heart filled up. "In a world where everyone is out for themselves, you want to win *with* me?"

"I've never craved intimacy with anyone, and with you, I can't get enough." He lowered his lips to hers, taking her in another sensual kiss.

"You're too romantic for your own good. I don't even know how to handle that," she said as he set her down.

"I've been called a lot of things—bossy, stubborn, a workaholic— but never romantic."

"Then that's another thing reserved especially for *me* on your work-free vacation. Just like your dirty comments," she said sassily, pressing her lips to his. "I like sharing secrets with you."

"I like everything we do." He took her hand, and they went to the railing.

The island bled into the inky water, sunlight glittering off the surface like diamonds.

"I had forgotten how pretty the view is from the lighthouses." The wind whipped her hair across her face. She gathered it over one shoulder and said, "I should have brought a ponytail holder."

"You did." Aiden put his arm around her, holding her hair for her.

She studied his peaceful expression and realized how naturally the little things he did came to him. How had he stayed single all this time? She knew the answer, of course, but she didn't know what he saw in her that made him want to share himself and the intimate details of his life with her. She thought she was pretty great, and she wasn't one of those women who felt unworthy or hated her body. But surely he had far more beautiful, financially well off, interesting women at his disposal. She knew those types of questions could never really be answered, at least not any more clearly than she could figure out what it was about him that had made her want to throw caution to the wind and meet him for breakfast the first time he'd invited her. Because *chemistry* was the most elusive, and possibly the most powerful, connector of all.

"I've never met anyone like you," she said honestly. "You're attentive and thoughtful, and you're a thinker, like my dad was. Sometimes you look so focused, I wonder what you're thinking about, and other times you're so funny. But it's like you see and hear everything, which I'm sure comes from raising your sister, because Lord knows girls are tough to figure out."

"Should I thank you, or are you trying to say I see and hear *too* much?" He pulled her closer and kissed her temple.

"I *like* who you are, Aiden. I like whoever or whatever version of you this person standing beside me is. The guy who gave up everything to allow his sister's dreams to come true and who jumped right in to help me with mine. But I hope you know that you don't have to work during your whole vacation. I can handle the restaurant and we can connect in the evenings."

"Helping you doesn't feel like work, babes. It's been a long time since I've worked with my hands, and I'm loving it. It takes me back to my roots, to memories of my parents and childhood. Only this is even more enjoyable because I'm with you."

"You know a lot about my childhood. What were you like as a kid?"

"I don't know. Weird, probably," he said as they looked out at the water. "I liked school, and I loved books of any kind. My father had a huge collection of novels, from classics to thrillers, and of nonfiction books on business and finance, which I devoured. I've had a knack for numbers since I was a little kid. I used to wake with the creak of his bedroom door and lie in bed until I heard him making coffee, and then I'd race into the bathroom and go as quickly as I could so I wouldn't miss any time with him. I'd head into the kitchen in my pajamas, and the smell of his favorite coffee was the best thing in the world."

"Was it the same coffee you drink now?"

"Yeah," he said. "It was the one thing he splurged on, and every morning he'd make me a really weak cup of it. So weak, it barely tasted like anything more than bitter water. He'd share the newspaper with me, and I'd scour it the way he did. I can still remember the thrill of feeling like a little man—*his* little man—preparing to take on the day, just as he did. We'd sit with the finance section of the newspaper, and he'd teach me a little more each week and ask my opinion like it mattered, even at seven or eight years old."

"Is that why you still read the newspaper? To hold on to the memory of your father?"

"Maybe. I never thought about why. I've just always done it."

"What did you dream of being when you were young?"

He cocked his head, meeting her gaze, and said, "My father."

"We're quite an original pair, aren't we?" She leaned her head on his shoulder, wishing she could always be this happy. She had a fleeting thought about protecting her heart and not jumping in too quickly, but she was already in too deep to pretend she wouldn't miss him when he left.

"My father was the best, most honest man I've ever known, and my mother was loving and supportive of everything we did. When my mom found out she was pregnant with Remi, it was a surprise for them. I'll never forget walking into her bedroom after I got home from school and finding her crying. For a split second I thought something had happened to my dad, but then she pulled me into her arms and told me I was going to have a sister or brother. She was laughing and crying, and when my dad got home, we celebrated. We talked a lot about how things would change with a baby in the house, and I remember thinking that I didn't care what changed. I was going to have a sibling. My friends all had brothers and sisters, and I was *finally* going to see what all the hubbub was about." He held her tighter and said, "I miss them every damn day. We lived such a simple life, and I miss that simplicity more often than not. My mother used to say *It takes little more than loving and hopeful hearts to make a happy life.*"

"I like that saying. It's true. But your life with Remi sounded complicated; no wonder you miss the simplicity."

"It was complicated. But my father made my career possible, and I wanted to make sure Remi had hers. My parents had nothing when they first married. It wasn't until much later that my father started dabbling in investing with a pittance from their savings. When my grandfather, who had raised my father, passed away, my father invested the life insurance money. It turned out he had a knack for it, and eventually he started the business."

"Your love of numbers comes naturally."

"I'm definitely a chip off the old block, and proud of it."

"What about sports? Did your dad play with you?"

"He wasn't a sports guy, but he tried. He put up a basketball hoop in the driveway and we'd play, but by the time I was fifteen I could run circles around him." He smiled, as if he were remembering playing basketball with his dad. "We had great parents, and I hope I make them proud."

She leaned against him and said, "How could you not?" They gazed out at the water for a long while, each lost in their own thoughts. But hers kept tiptoeing back to the fact that he was on vacation, and no matter how good they felt together, they were only temporary. "Where will you go when your vacation is over?"

"I've got business overseas for a couple of weeks."

"And then?"

"I might have to come back here. I'm getting a bit of island fever." He kissed the top of her head and said, "Or maybe it's Abby fever."

Her heart did a happy dance. "You should find a remedy for that ailment."

"I have." He turned her in his arms with a playful expression and said, "It's more *Abby*."

"Workaholic Aiden might have something to say about that."

"Three more weeks of this and Workaholic Aiden will have to claw his way back up to the surface."

They hung out at the top of the lighthouse for a little while longer, admiring the view and taking loads of selfies together, half of which were of them kissing. When they headed back down to the beach, they took a long walk. The air was chilly, but with the sun on Abby's cheeks and Aiden's arm around her, she was plenty warm. As they collected shells, which Aiden insisted they keep as a reminder of their day, Abby told him that she and Deirdra used to put the shells they'd collected on the porch and fill them with birdseed. They made a sandcastle, which was on his list, and they slipped off their shoes to put their toes in the cold water. Aiden took pictures of their feet in the water for Remi and gathered Abby in his arms for more kissing selfies.

After a while they flopped down on the sand. Aiden lay back, pulling Abby down with him, nestling her head on the crook of his arm and chest, and said, "I think this is what Remi was talking about, what I was missing out on. And what you were, too."

"What's that?"

"Carefree happiness. Just being in the moment, not worrying about the sister I was raising, or in your case, the mother you were taking care of."

"I haven't played hooky all day since before my dad died, and that wasn't playing hooky. That was being a kid."

"Exactly." He kissed her head and said, "I could get used to this, Abs."

She draped an arm over his stomach and said, "Well, look at that. Aiden does know how to relax."

"That's all your doing, babe. You make me want to seize every moment, to experience it *with* you, not from behind a desk. No one who knows me will believe that, so . . ." He whipped out his phone and took a picture of them lying on the sand, with her draped over him. "You sure do make us look good."

He showed her the picture, and she had the goofiest grin on her face. She had a feeling it would be there for the next few weeks.

They lay staring up at the crisp blue sky, serenaded by the waves crashing along the shore and the seagulls soaring overhead, talking about silly things like if they had superpowers what would they be.

"Teleportation," he said. "Then I could be anywhere you or Remi need me in the blink of an eye."

"Oh, I *like* that. You could teleport into my bedroom."

"I might never leave." He hugged her against her side. "What would your superpower be?"

"The power to heal."

"Damn, babes, you're more generous than I am. Your superpower kicked mine's butt."

"You're just as generous," she countered. "Your first thought was for your sister and me." She tipped her face up. He looked so blissful, she had the strange thought that *this* was what dreams were made of.

"Nice save." He kissed her and said, "Would you rather spend a day exploring a charming small town or lying on the beach?"

"Mm, that's a hard one. Probably the beach, since I never get to do it. You?"

"*Both*, because every beach town has cute shops."

"Wait. I want to change my answer to *both*. I didn't know that was an option."

"That makes you a copycat." He moved over her with a wicked glint in his eyes and said, "There's a penalty for that crime."

Yesss. "There's a penalty for that crime," she parroted in a high-pitched, mocking tone.

He tickled her ribs. "You're in big trouble, Runner Girl. You're paying *double* for that!"

After she *suffered* through a panty-melting make-out session that left them both high, they headed into town to grab some lunch and knock window-shopping off Aiden's list. They had lunch at Trista's café, sharing their sandwiches and a macadamia nut cookie for dessert, taking *finger foodie* pictures for Remi, and meandered through the shops on Main Street, holding hands and basking in the effortlessness of their coupledom. Aiden surprised her by buying birdseed to put in the shells they'd collected. He showed her things in various shops that he thought she might like for the Bistro, and his suggestions were perfectly aligned with everything she'd said as they'd cleaned the restaurant and she'd rambled on about her hopes of bringing her father's old-world charm and beachy chic together. The Bistro wasn't ready to be decorated, but she took mental notes about the items so she could buy them in the future.

Abby glanced at Aiden across the touristy shop they were exploring. He was looking through racks of T-shirts and tank tops. His linen shirt was wrinkled and dirty from lying in the sand. His hair was windblown, curling at the ends. He looked so relaxed, like a different guy than the clean-shaven, loafer-wearing man she'd met last week. She knew his finance-oriented mind never really shut off. He'd been making suggestions here and there about budgets and expenditures. She liked his serious, business-oriented side, which was always hovering, because she had that side, too.

Aiden looked up, catching her staring, and blew her a kiss. He said he could get used to this. She had a feeling she'd never get used to it. Aiden's affection was like a drug. Would she crave it? *Yes.* Appreciate it? *Absolutely.* But how could she get used to unconditional affection when it'd been so long since she'd experienced it?

He turned back to the shirts, and she went back to searching for something for him. She found the perfect navy-blue hat, with a picture of a lighthouse and I CHILLED ON SILVER ISLAND embroidered across the front in white. She snuck up to the register and paid.

Aiden sauntered up with one hand behind his back and said, "Are you done, ma'am? Because I have a purchase for a special lady in my life, and I'm afraid I need privacy to pay for it."

"You have a special lady in your life? Lucky lady."

"I'm the lucky one," he said as she walked away.

He came up behind her a few minutes later, speaking huskily into her ear. "Hey, sexy lady. You free tonight?"

"Sorry, but I'm taken," she said as they left the store.

"*Damn.* Then I guess I should return this." He pulled a pink tank top out of the bag and held it up. I RUN FOR GOODIES was written across the chest in white, with candy wrappers scattered below it.

"I *love* that! Thank you."

"I need to find a Sharpie so I can put a little caret before *goodies* and write *Aiden's.*"

"I like that even more! I got something for you, too." She took out the hat and handed it to him, earning one of his hearty laughs and a delicious thank-you kiss, which led to several more kisses.

"Abby!"

They startled apart, and Aiden put on his hat as Jules, Leni's younger sister, hurried toward them. Her sun-kissed-brown hair hung to the middle of her back, the top layer pinned up in her signature *water fountain* on top of her head.

"Hi, Jules." Abby hugged her and said, "I've missed you."

"I've missed you, too. I've wanted to stop by, but I'm so busy getting the shop ready for summer, and Grant has been monopolizing my *every* free moment." She lowered her voice and said, "Not that I'm complaining." Jules was engaged to Grant Silver.

"I bet. Jules, this is Aiden. Aiden, this is my friend Jules."

Jules checked him out with a rascally look in her eyes and said, "I heard there was a hot guy buying pretty girls breakfast on the island, but from the looks of the kisses I witnessed, maybe that gossip should be revised to buying *a certain pretty girl* breakfast."

Aiden put his arm around Abby and said, "It's nice to meet you, and it's most definitely a *certain* pretty girl."

"Well, in case Abby's ever busy, I own the Happy End gift shop, down there." She pointed to the end of the block and said, "The shop with the red door and the giraffes out front. I'm usually there by seven thirty, and I like my eggs over easy and my pastries as sugary as possible."

"I'll remember that," he said.

"I'm pretty sure Grant would take issue with a handsome guy bringing you breakfast." Abby looked at Aiden and said, "Jules is engaged to Wells's brother Grant."

"Since Wells is a self-proclaimed Best of king, does that make Grant a prince?" Aiden joked.

"God *no*," Jules said. "Grant is totally *my* prince, but if I were you, I would *not* call him that to his face. He's nothing like Wells. Wells is a shameless flirt and loves to talk about himself, but his heart is always in the right place. Grant is an ex–covert ops specialist, and *much* broodier than Wells."

"Why did Grant get out of that line of work?" Aiden asked.

"He lost his leg during a mission," Jules explained.

"Oh, I'm sorry. That must have been rough," Aiden said.

"It was," Jules said. "He had a hard time transitioning back to civilian life."

"Until Jules came along," Abby said, bumping shoulders with Jules.

Jules grinned. "That is true. I love my man so much, and now he's gone back to his artistic roots and rediscovered his love of painting and woodworking. Thanks to a little creative outreach, he's *already* made a name for himself. *Hey*, I have a great idea! We're going out to dinner Friday night with Jock and Daphne. You should join us so Aiden can meet them."

"Jock is an unusual name. Are you talking about Jack Steele, the author of *It Lies*?"

"Yes," Jules said. "He's my oldest brother, and Daphne is his wife. You'll love them."

He looked at Abby and said, "If you're okay with it, it sounds like a good time."

"Great, then we're in," Abby said, and then she remembered that Cait was coming back on Friday. "Jules, I don't know if you've heard or not, but Deirdra and I just found out that we have a half sister, Cait Weatherby."

"I *did* hear that. What a surprise, huh? What's she like?"

Abby told her all about Cait and about how much she liked her. "Would you mind if she came along? I'd love for her to meet everyone, too."

"Any sister of yours is a sister of ours," Jules said.

Abby's mind was three steps ahead, and she said, "Leni said she was coming in for Mother's Day weekend. She offered to help me with marketing for the restaurant. Do you know if she'll be here Friday night? It would be fun if she joined us, too."

"I think she said she's coming Saturday, but let me find out if she can come Friday instead." Jules whipped out her phone and said, "One group text coming up!"

They made plans to meet at Rock Bottom Bar and Grill Friday evening, and then Jules hugged them both and went on her way.

"She seems chipper," Aiden said.

"I love Jules. She beat cancer when she was little, and I swear she can find the silver lining in any situation. She's so happy that sometimes she just breaks out in song. She never gets the lyrics right. It's hilarious."

"I'm glad I had the chance to meet her."

"Me too." Abby's phone vibrated with a text. "This is probably her. She loves group texts." She pulled her phone from her pocket, saw Leni's name on the screen, and opened the message. *Why am I hearing about a new guy from Jules!? Of course I can come Friday night!*

"I'm sorry. This will only take a sec," Abby said as she thumbed out a response. *I swear Jules IS the island grapevine. He's awesome! Can't chat. We're on a date! Will text when free.* She sent the message and shoved her phone into her pocket. If she had it her way, she and Aiden would be too busy getting their *groove on* to text her later, but she'd fit a text in when she could. She smiled at Aiden and said, "What's next on our agenda?"

"Buying a hammock. It's on Remi's list."

"I'm pretty sure the Silvers won't let you hang that in your room at the resort."

He chuckled. "I was hoping you wouldn't mind if I hung it in your yard."

"That'll cost you," she said flirtatiously.

"*Mm.* That's one debt I'll enjoy paying back right after our six o'clock winery tour and tasting."

"You planned our *whole* day. I don't think you needed any help learning to relax."

He slid his arm around her waist and said, "But I needed a reason to want to."

They drove to the outdoor furniture store and headed into the showroom, which was bursting with colorful umbrellas, chairs, and tables in every style known to man, in fabric, wood, iron, and plastic. A middle-aged salesman directed them to the hammocks in the rear of the store.

As they made their way through the showroom, Abby said, "I have to start thinking about outdoor furniture for the Bistro. The furniture my mom was using was so ratty, Shelley had it hauled away for us." She pointed to a semicircular wicker couch with green cushions around a decorative metal firepit. "I've always wanted one of those conversation pits."

"For your house or for the Bistro?"

"Either. It would be cool to have a conversation pit like that at home, but we've been so worried about the restaurant, I haven't even talked with my sisters about what we're doing with my mom's house yet."

"How about at the patio of the Bistro?"

"There's a restaurant on the Cape that has that type of setup with the couches and a firepit out front, and customers love having drinks there and listening to the musicians they bring in."

"Couldn't you do that at the Bistro?"

Her brow furrowed. "My parents never had live music, but I guess we could think about doing it next year. I've got my hands full getting the restaurant up and running. There's so much to do. Finding musicians—much less affording them—and coming up with schedules is more than I can handle at the moment."

"That sounds like a good plan." He was glad she knew her limits.

"Aiden, *look*." She hurried across the room toward a set of stunning rattan café chairs and tables with simple yet elegant designs, which looked like they belonged in a French café. "These are similar to what my dad used when I was growing up." She ran her hands along the frame and scanned the information tag. "They're commercial grade, handwoven, *and* they're artisan-crafted in Paris! I *need* these. They're perfect!" she said giddily.

"I've got to admit, they'd really spruce up the place for the visit from the competition judges, which would work in your favor."

Confusion rose in her eyes. "What do you mean? I didn't enter, remember?"

"I know." He slipped his hands into his pockets and said, "But I might have entered on your behalf. I didn't want you to miss the deadline."

"Aiden!" she snapped, quickly looking around to see if anyone heard her.

Aiden waved off the salesman and said, "We're okay over here."

"We are *not* okay over here!" Abby waggled her finger at him, speaking in a harsh whisper. "Why did you do that after I said I wanted to wait a year?"

"Because after tasting your cooking, I knew you could win."

Her eyes lit up. "Really?" She must have realized she was smiling, because she scowled again. "That's no reason to go behind my back."

"I'm sorry, babe, but I believe in you, and the free exposure could be the difference between making it your first season and going under."

"I cannot believe you did that." She crossed her arms, her lips forming a tight line.

"I'm sorry I overstepped." He put his hand on her hip and, in a more serious tone, said, "But, Abby, I work with growing businesses every day, and I know what it takes to build a brand and a reputation. You want to re-create what your parents had, and with you at the helm, the Bistro has a real chance of succeeding. But you can only get so far without the right tools to back you up, including the far reach of marketing that the competition has to offer."

Her expression softened, but her eyes narrowed. "Does this have anything to do with one-upping Wells?"

"No," he said sharply, realizing how badly his idea had backfired. Abby wasn't a business associate, and he shouldn't have treated her like one. "This has everything to do with wanting to see you succeed. It's not just you anymore, babe. Deirdra and Cait are investing, too, and you know they're investing in *you* more than they are in the Bistro. I know you don't want to let them down, so why not pull out all the stops? *Win* that competition and work up a finite budget that includes your staffing, overhead, maintenance, and all the other costs, and *then* spend your money in the *right* places." He cocked a grin and said, "Beating Wells is the icing on the cake."

She sighed heavily, but the light in her eyes was slowly returning. "You really think I have a chance at winning? You haven't even eaten at the other restaurants on the island, and you've only tasted my cooking once."

"I've eaten at enough restaurants to *know* you can win."

"*Fine*," she relented. "Since you've already entered me, I'll do it. But I'm paying you back every penny of that entry fee."

He gathered her in his arms, relief pushing away the tension between them as he said, "I can think of plenty of creative ways for you to pay me back." He kissed her lips. "Like that." His hand slid down her back, and he squeezed her ass. "And that," he said, earning a genuine smile.

"You're so *bad*," she said heatedly.

"You haven't seen bad yet." He lowered his lips to hers, taking her in a tender kiss, and said, "Am I forgiven?"

"Yes, but *don't* step on my toes again. I need to be in control of my own business decisions."

"I respect that, and again, I'm sorry I went behind your back."

She stepped out of his arms and ran her hand along the back of a chair. "These really are perfect, aren't they?" She turned the price tag over and cringed.

"Steep?"

"Yeah." Her face pinched in concentration.

"I have lots of contacts. I bet I can get you a few sets at wholesale prices."

Anguish rose in her eyes. "I appreciate that, but I was really hoping to buy local. Now that I'm going to be living here full-time, I want to support other small businesses. You know, I scratch their backs, they scratch mine."

"That's an admirable goal, Abs. I don't know your financial situation, but I know about business, and overpaying is never wise. Especially at this stage of the game. You're likely to incur a lot of other unanticipated costs, like the oven unit needing to be replaced."

"I know. I've been thinking about that, and I think I can get away without replacing the oven right away. I have two, and that should be doable."

"Not for maximum efficiency," he said, immediately regretting it. The closer they became, the more difficult it was to bite his tongue.

She planted her hand on her hip, lifting her chin defiantly. "Sometimes you have to cut corners in the places customers don't see in order to beef up the areas they do."

"Abs, didn't you *just* agree that it was a good idea to come up with a budget and *then* spend your money?"

"Yes, and I will. *After* I buy these chairs. This is my decision, remember?"

He held his hands up in surrender and said, "Yes. You're right."

"Thank you."

While his unsolicited advice might have been out of line, he wasn't going to let her bury her dreams before they even got started. "You can buy them right after I talk to the owner or salesman and negotiate a better price. Markups in these places are astronomical."

"You are so . . ." She shook her head.

"Helpful?"

She rolled her eyes, a small smile tugging at her lips. "If this is what you did every time Remi made a decision, I can see why she pushed you to get your own life."

"Ouch." Aiden put his hands over his heart, although she wasn't wrong.

"That's not what I meant." She reached for his hand, holding it as she said, "You talk about my big heart, but you can't even bear the idea of letting me do something that you think *might* be a mistake."

"That's not my heart talking; it's good business. I don't mix business with pleasure." *At least I never used to.*

Heat sparked in her eyes, and she said, "Your creative debt-repayment options say otherwise."

Forty-five minutes later, Aiden had ordered a hammock, and Abby was the proud owner of six sets of bistro chairs with matching tables, which she'd scheduled to have delivered the week before the judging for the competition.

"I still can't believe you got twenty-five percent off!" she said excitedly, putting the receipt in her purse. "You're amazing, Aiden. I never would have thought to try to negotiate the price at a place like that."

"Don't forget, I threw in free dinner for him and his family once a month over the summer."

"I got a great deal on the perfect chairs. I'll feed him every *day* if I need to."

"*No*, you won't." Her stern look made him realize his mistake, and he said, "I mean, you *might* want to rethink that after you work up your budget."

"Maybe I will." She smiled and said, "I know you don't mix business with pleasure, and I can be stubborn, but would you mind helping me with the budget?" Before he could respond, she wrapped her arms around his waist, went up on her toes, and whispered, "I promise to pay *only* with *pleasure*."

As he lowered his lips to hers, he said, "Exception made."

CHAPTER NINE

ON THE WAY to Top of the Island Vineyard, Abby silently picked apart her conversation with Aiden about the chairs. She felt bad for getting upset when he'd only been looking out for her, even if he had overstepped by signing her up for the competition. He hadn't done it maliciously or for his gain, even if she wished he'd talked to her about it first. It had been so long since anyone had supported her like that, she'd had a knee-jerk reaction. She couldn't get over how vehemently he *believed* in her, and she worried she'd sounded ungrateful. A knot formed in her stomach as he parked in front of the cedar and brick winery.

He lifted her hand and kissed the back of it. "You okay? You're pretty quiet."

"Mm-hm."

He grabbed their sweaters from the back seat and came around to help her out of the car. "It's gorgeous here," he said, putting an arm around her.

The vineyard was located at one of the highest points on the island and gave way to miles of beautiful landscape, with roads snaking through cottage developments and cliffs that fell away to the deep blue sea. The late-afternoon sun illuminated the vineyards. The vines were bare but still beautiful. Abby wished he were going to be there later in the summer, when the vineyards would burgeon with bright green leaves and bundles of juicy grapes.

He turned a warm gaze to her, and his smile faded. "*Aw*, babe. What are those shadows in your eyes? You're not okay, are you?"

"You really do see everything," she said softly. "I feel horrible for the way I reacted at the store. I'm sorry I got so defensive. I'm used to doing everything on my own, making all of my own decisions—good or bad—and I guess I have a bit of a chip on my shoulder because of having to defend myself to Deirdra."

"You don't have to apologize. You were right, Abs. I overstepped. It's a bad habit of mine. I have a hard time stepping back when it comes to business and the people I care about. I'll try to keep my opinions to myself."

"No, I don't want that. It's been a long time since anyone looked after me in the way you did by entering me in the competition and trying to get me to make a smarter financial decision and wait to buy the chairs. Deirdra is protective, but like a big sister—it's a *duty* born of love, but a duty just the same. And Shelley watched after us, but more like an aunt making sure we didn't starve. She was always careful not to step on our mom's toes or interfere too much. I love that you believe in me, but I'm not used to having someone watch out for me because they *want* to, not because they feel like they have to."

He tossed the sweaters on the hood of the car and embraced her. "Sounds like we both have something to learn." He looked encouragingly into her eyes and said, "Maybe we can help each other. I know myself, and I'm sure to slip up again and overstep."

"And I'll probably go off on you."

He waggled his brows.

"Thank God you have a sense of humor. I'm sorry if I came off as a bitch back there."

He lifted her chin and pressed his lips to hers. "You weren't. You were a fierce businesswoman who doesn't need some old know-it-all stepping on her toes. What do you say, Abs? Do you want to try to navigate this unfamiliar bumpy terrain with me and see if two slightly stubborn people can find a comfortable middle ground?"

"Yes. I'd like that a whole lot."

He kissed her slow and sweet, and then he grabbed their sweaters and they headed inside for their tour. They were greeted with rich hardwood floors, warm wood and stone walls, and an exuberant, "Abby, Aiden!" from Shelley as she popped out from behind a display of wineglasses.

Shelley wore pretty black slacks and a floral blouse, and she was carrying Hadley, Jock and Daphne's adorable honey-haired daughter, who was clutching a stuffed owl in her hand. She hurried over to them.

"Hi, Shelley," Abby said.

Aiden said, "It's nice to see you again, Shelley."

"I didn't realize you two knew each other." Abby looked at them curiously.

"Aiden came in to schedule your visit," Shelley explained. "Abby, you remember my beautiful granddaughter, Hadley."

"Of course," Abby said. She had met Hadley over the holidays, when Leni had told her how Daphne's little girl had brought Daphne and Jock together and his love for them had helped him mend a ten-year rift with his twin brother, Archer.

"Hi, sweetheart," Abby said. "Do you remember me?"

Hadley buried her face in Shelley's neck.

"She's had a big day. Jock and Daphne are around here somewhere, probably *smooching*. You know how newlyweds are." Shelley caressed Hadley's cheek and said, "Hadley, can you say hi to Abby's friend Aiden?"

Hadley looked sleepily at Aiden and said, "Hi."

"Hi, peanut. That looks like a very special owl," Aiden said.

"*My* Owly." Hadley clutched the stuffed toy against her chest.

Daphne, a curvy blonde, walked out of one of the offices, wiping something from Jock's mouth, her back to Abby and the others. "Hold still for a sec. You have lipstick on your mouth."

Jock's dark eyes shifted to them, and he flashed an amused grin.

"What are you—" Daphne followed his gaze over her shoulder and blushed a red streak. "*Crumbs. Muffin crumbs,*" she said nervously. "He was eating muffins."

"I want a muffin!" Hadley thrust her arms toward Jock and said, "*Cawwy* me, Daddy."

They all chuckled as Jock took Hadley into his arms, his tall, broad frame making her look even smaller.

"Hi, Abby. It's good to see you," Jock said. "And you must be Aiden. I'm Jock, and this is my wife, Daphne, and our little girl, Hadley."

"It's nice to meet you both," Aiden said.

Jock shifted Hadley so she could rest her head on his shoulder and said, "I heard you two are joining us for dinner Friday night."

"Yes. I'm looking forward to it. I read your book and enjoyed it very much, but that was one heck of a scary ride. I wouldn't want to live in your head."

As Jock and Aiden talked about his book, Daphne and Shelley sidled up to Abby, and Daphne whispered, "Where did you find *him*?"

"He's scrumptious," Shelley said.

Now it was Abby's turn to blush. "I was jogging and saw him sitting on the deck of the Bistro."

"And he was so taken with Abby, he invited her to breakfast the next day," Shelley said excitedly. "He's been helping her at the Bistro ever since."

Abby stared at her curiously. "How do you know all that?"

"Aiden and I had a nice long chat about my daughter from another mother when he came by to schedule your tour. Oh, honey, he is *such* a gentleman. A real class act. They don't make them like that anymore. Except for my boys, of course," Shelley said.

"You guys seem happy together," Daphne said.

Abby didn't need Shelley's approval, but it sure felt good to have it. She glanced at Aiden, playing peekaboo with Hadley, and it turned her insides to mush. "Our relationship is still new, but he's all kinds of wonderful."

"And you deserve nothing less," Shelley said. "I know your parents are smiling down on you right now. All they ever wanted was for you girls to be happy, and your mom knew she wasn't strong enough to help you get there. But in some ways, what you went through with her made you the person you are, so maybe that's the silver lining."

"That's a nice way to look at it." Abby tucked away Shelley's thoughts to share with Deirdra and Cait another time.

Shelley glanced at the clock and said, "We'd better get a move on if you're going to get your tour in before sunset."

"Don't we have to wait for the rest of the customers?" Abby asked.

"This is a *private* tour." Shelley took her arm and said, "I told you your new man was a class act."

Abby loved that Aiden had requested a private tour.

"Yes, *go*." Daphne hugged her and said, "We'll see you Friday night."

Abby and Aiden followed Shelley through the winery as Shelley talked about grape cultivation and the winemaking process. Aiden kept his arm around Abby, whispering a mix of romantic and naughty things that made her warm and fuzzy one minute and hot and bothered the next. In between his secret whispers, he had complex conversations with Shelley about the history of winemaking, wine and grape varieties, oak species used for barrels, and a litany of other wine-related topics. Abby was fascinated by his knowledge, though she shouldn't be surprised. It was clear that Aiden was a man with a thirst for understanding and preparedness. She had a feeling he didn't jump into anything blindly. In fact, she'd bet her bottom dollar that he'd spent hours researching the history of the lighthouse, the best lunch café in the area, and even where to buy a hammock. That thought gave her pause. Had he chosen that specific outdoor furniture store because they sold Parisian café sets?

"What's going on in that beautiful head of yours?" Aiden asked as they followed Shelley down a corridor.

"A *lot*. I'm figuring out what makes you tick, putting together the Aiden Aldridge puzzle."

"When you figure it out, clue me in." He pressed a kiss to her temple and said, "I thought I knew who I was, but you're changing that."

Shelley smiled over her shoulder and said, "Keep up, kids. You'll want to see the vineyard before the sun goes down." When they reached the back door to the winery, she said, "Let me grab a few things from the kitchen. Back in a jiffy."

Shelley disappeared through a door, and Aiden said, "I love her energy." He put his arms around Abby and added, "Almost as much as I love yours."

He pressed his lips to hers just as Shelley returned carrying a big covered basket.

"Okay, *smoochers*," she said. "Follow me."

Abby put on her sweater, and they followed Shelley out the back door. The winery was U-shaped, with a gorgeous patio between the two wings of the building. The sun was making its descent, hovering in the distance, trailing ribbons of gold and fire-orange across the sky.

Shelley led them past the stone knee wall that separated the vineyards from the winery as Archer, Jock's twin, walked out from between two rows of vines. Archer was much brawnier than Jock, with a thick chest and bulbous biceps. He kept his brown hair military short, though he was never in the military.

Archer nodded at Abby and said, "Great to see you."

"It's good to see you, too." Abby embraced him. It was like hugging stone.

He lifted his chin in Aiden's direction, offering his hand. "Archer Steele. You must be Aiden. I like your style, dude."

Abby looked at Aiden's touristy baseball cap, wrinkled linen shirt and pants, and wondered if Archer was making fun of him. If he was, it didn't appear to bother Aiden.

"Thank you," Aiden said, shaking Archer's hand. "Your winemaking reputation precedes you."

Archer cracked a proud grin. "Thanks. We do all right."

"I'd say a gold Sommeliers Choice Award for your cabernet sauvignon is better than all right."

Leni had told Abby about the award he'd won last August, but Shelley hadn't mentioned it during the tour, and Abby didn't remember seeing the award or a plaque announcing it inside. Aiden must have noticed one, or done his research.

"We'll see how we do this year," Archer said. "Enjoy yourselves tonight." He glanced at Shelley and said, "You're all set."

"Thanks, honey. Tell your father I'll be right in." As Archer walked away, Shelley handed the basket to Aiden and said, "Everything you need is here. If you go right down that row and take a left at the end, you'll find the perfect spot for your wine tasting. And when you're done, leave everything where it is. We'll take care of it."

"Aren't tastings typically done here?" Abby pointed to the courtyard.

Shelley leaned closer to her and lowered her voice to say, "Honey, I think your new beau has already figured out that you are anything but a *typical* woman." She gave her a quick squeeze and said, "Go have fun. Stay all night if you want to."

As Shelley headed into the winery, Aiden said, "Let's go, babe. Our sunset awaits."

"Where are we going?" she asked as they walked between the tall vines.

"You'll see."

"*What* will I see? You're carrying a huge basket, and we're walking through the vineyard *without* Archer or his parents, which everyone knows is not allowed. He's more protective of these vines than you are of

Remi." Suddenly strings of lights strung from the tall posts of the vine fencing bloomed to life, illuminating their way. "*Whoa.* Aiden . . . ?"

He motioned to the end of the row and said, "Left, babe."

Abby stepped past the last of the vines and turned left. Her thoughts fell away at the sight of shimmering lanterns hanging on the tall wooden posts at the end of each row of vines, leading up to the most romantic picnic she'd ever seen. A rustic wooden table sat low to the ground atop a gorgeous decorative rug with large colorful pillows along one side for them to sit on. A bouquet of red, white, and pink roses graced the center of the table, with two elegant place settings and fancy wineglasses side by side. More lanterns twinkled in the grass.

"*Aid . . . ?*" she said, utterly *awestruck.* "I feel like I'm on an episode of *The Bachelor.* Where are the cameras?"

"No cameras. You're stuck with a regular guy chillin' on Silver Island with his beautiful girl." He put the basket and his sweater down, thrilled that the Steeles had made their picnic as special as he'd requested.

"I can't get over this. When did you have time to meet with Shelley and set this up?"

"When we were cleaning yesterday and I went on that coffee run."

She gasped. "You sneaky little fibber! You said the line was out the door."

"I didn't fib. The line *was* out the door. But since I supply my own coffee beans, all I had to do was call Keira and pick it up at the side counter, so I came here to meet with Shelley before picking it up. I just used my time creatively."

"Like your creative *repayment options?* Well, I hope you know that you didn't have to do this. I'd have been happy with grilled cheese on my front porch."

He took her hand, tugging her into his arms, and said, "Your easy nature is just one of the reasons you're becoming so special to me. I would have been happy with grilled cheese on your porch, too. But if the way you work on the restaurant is any indication of how you live your life—and I fully believe it is—then you're as much of a workaholic as I have always been. That's a great thing, Abs, and it's appealing to a guy like me, who enjoys putting my nose to the grindstone and rarely coming up for air. But you're helping me discover that perfect days like today are even better than burying myself in work. I wanted to do something special for you, and selfishly, I wanted to see that look on your face."

"What look?"

"The look of wonder, appreciation, curiosity. The look that asks why I did this, but at the same time, shows me how much you love it."

"Oh. *That* look," she said softly.

"Yeah, it's a great look, babe. Grilled cheese is awesome, and we'll have our grilled cheese dates, but this is what you *deserve*, Abigail de Messiéres, and I think it's time you stop telling me what I don't have to do and start enjoying what I *want* to do."

She looked at him for a long moment, as if she were mulling over his words, before saying, "You must have girls falling at your feet."

"*Jesus*," he said, frustrated. "I must really suck at this *wooing* thing. After everything I said to you, you still think I do this type of thing willy-nilly? For just any woman?"

"Well, *no*, but . . ."

"*But?*"

"I don't *know*," she said, her cheeks blushing. "I guess I'm not used to being *wooed*."

"Then *get* used to it. I might not be the best at chilling with my feet in the sand, but I was raised right. And at almost forty years old, I know the difference between spending time with a woman to scratch an itch and being with someone who makes me *feel* and *think* and *want* things I have never wanted before." He tossed his hat on the blanket, realizing he'd said more than he'd intended, and by the intense look on Abby's face, she'd *heard* every word. Well, *hell*. He didn't know how he felt about that.

That was a lie.

He knew *exactly* how he felt. He'd wanted her to hear it. But that was a slippery slope, and though he wasn't sure he wanted to plant his feet on stable ground, he wasn't looking for a landslide that could bury them both.

Forcing those unfamiliar and overpowering emotions down deep, he tried to play it off in a lighter way. "What do you say, Runner Girl? Think two workaholics can enjoy tonight without picking it apart, or are we going to stand here talking and miss our sunset?"

"We are *not* missing our sunset after how hard you've worked at my restaurant," she said emphatically.

"Attagirl. Now, get your sexy ass over here, and let's see what Shelley put together for us."

They sat on the pillows, and Abby peered into the basket. "Why do I have a feeling you told her exactly what to put in this?"

"I can't imagine *why* you'd think that." He took out a charcuterie tray with four types of cheese, prosciutto and four other types of meat, dried apricots, assorted berries, cherry tomatoes, baguette slices, artisan crackers, nuts, black olives, pickles, and three different dips.

"This visual feast is gorgeous enough to grace the cover of a magazine," Abby said as Aiden poured them each a glass of wine.

Loving her excitement, he handed her a wineglass and said, "So are you, Abby DM."

"You make me sound like a social media message. *Hey, did you get that Abby DM spam that's going around?*" They laughed and she said, "Oh my gosh, *Aiden*. If I'm Abby DM, you're *AA*."

"If Remi's comments about me hold any weight, you might need a support group after hanging out with me for a few weeks."

She popped a raspberry into her mouth and said, "I'm pretty sure I need a support group anyway. What harm can it do to add a little more crazy to an already wacky woman?"

"We'll soon find out." He lifted his glass and said, "Here's to you, Abs. You can spam my in-box anytime."

"Why, thank you, AA. I plan on doing just that, so maybe we should add *find a support group* to our list."

"I like that."

"What?"

"*Our* list instead of *my* list." He leaned in for a kiss.

They drank their wine and made tiny sandwiches, feeding each other tastes of their creations as they watched the sun setting in the distance. Everything they did together made him realize how much he'd been missing out on. He couldn't remember ever watching a sunset, much less enjoying a picnic.

After they ate, Aiden put his arm around Abby, and she settled in against him. He kissed her head, realizing how often he'd done it and how natural it felt.

"It's been so long since I've watched the sunset, I'd forgotten how beautiful they are," she said with a sigh.

"I know after your father died you were too focused on keeping a roof over your heads and worried about your mom to take time to watch a sunset. But did you watch many before your life was turned upside down?"

"Not as many as you'd think. Sometimes we'd watch them as a family if my parents could get off work. And after my dad died, I managed to sneak time in with friends, but I was too anxious and guilt ridden to enjoy it."

He kissed the side of her head, holding her tighter. "I'm sorry."

"It's different being back on the island without my mom to worry about. I loved her. I *truly* did, despite her alcoholism, and I don't mean this as harsh as it's going to sound, but the truth is, without the stress of worrying if she'll drink herself to death or everything else that goes hand in hand with alcoholism, I feel like I can finally breathe. I can finally see the island and all its beauty as I remembered it. Maybe I should feel guilty for admitting that, but I did my best to help my mom, and I believe she knew I loved her."

"Of course she did. You put your life on hold to care for her."

"She left us each a letter," she said softly, tracing his fingers with hers. "I haven't read mine yet."

"Why not?"

She sat up, and before she even said a word, he saw so many questions swimming in her eyes, he wished he had the answers.

"Because that letter is the *end* of everything," she said passionately. "Do I want her to apologize? To acknowledge the hurt she caused? Or am I past that? I think I am. I don't feel angry toward her, just hurt that she didn't tell us she was sick. But Shelley already explained that my mom didn't feel strong enough to face doing that, and I can understand that because I can't imagine knowing you're going to die and having to tell your children. But what if I'm wrong? What if she *doesn't* apologize and I'm *not* past it? What if the letter makes me mad? It's not like I can look her in the eyes and tell her what I'm feeling or what I need to hear. And what if she says something I don't want to know? Not that I think there are more family secrets, but who knows?"

He brushed a lock of hair from her cheek and tucked it behind her ear. "What if you read it and it's everything you never knew you needed to hear?"

"What if . . . ?" Her smile snuck out.

"I would give anything to have known my parents' final thoughts. But I understand your hesitation. I'm here for you either way, whether you decide to read it or not. And if you need to cry, yell, or stare out at the ocean and just be held, I've got a great set of ears and strong arms."

"You forgot *a comforting heart*." She held his gaze and said, "Thank you. I appreciate that. I don't know when I'll feel up to reading it, but

I know I don't want to read it around Deirdra. She has too many bad feelings toward my mom."

He took her hand in his and said, "That's probably wise. When I met Jock today, I asked him how he felt about moving back to the island, and he said he believed the island has a bit of healing magic if you're open to it. Now, if you ask me, as a man who believes in hardcore facts and statistics, I think it was that little lady in his arms and his beautiful wife who had worked their magic. But *if* he's right and *if* that letter holds words that hurt, then maybe being back on the island will help you heal."

"That's an old wives' tale," she said. "My mom used to say if you wish upon the right star, the island can help you heal and make your dreams come true."

"There's no harm in believing it, and wishing on a star *is* on my list." Aiden didn't believe in magic or wishes, but the hope brimming in Abby's beautiful eyes had him hoping he was wrong. "What do you say, Abs? Want to give it a shot?"

"Only if you'll wish with me. You can make your own wish, of course."

He took her hand and said, "On the count of three?"

"We have to close our eyes," she said excitedly.

She was so cute. She closed her eyes, her long lashes sweeping her cheeks. They counted to three, and he tossed his wish up to what he hoped were the most powerful stars that existed—*I hope all of Abby's dreams come true and her mother's letter leaves more love than loss behind.*

Aiden's phone dinged with a text message. "Excuse me." He pulled it from his pocket and saw Remi's name on the screen. "My sister," he said as he opened her message. *Are you still alive?* He shook his head and started to put his phone away.

She touched his hand, stopping him. "Don't you want to answer her?"

"And interrupt our first real date?"

"I don't mind. It's your sister."

"I mind—" Several more messages came in in rapid succession, and he quickly read them. *You haven't returned my texts since yesterday morning, and I realized that you didn't tell me anything about this Abby chick. What if she's psycho?* He turned his phone so Abby could read the message.

"Hey, I'm not psycho," she said as more messages rolled in.

Aiden, please answer me.

If I didn't answer you, you'd send an army after me.

Abby looked amused. "An army?"

"She exaggerates. Remi loves drama."

More messages came in rapid-fire. *Can you just tell me if you're still alive?*

OMG you're not answering. I'm calling the police.

Wait . . . is Abby even real? She added an angry emoji face. *Or is she like the hairy feet in the sand?*

"Hairy feet in the sand? Do I even want to know?"

"She wanted proof that I was relaxing, so I took a picture of some guy's feet in the sand and sent it."

"That's hilarious. Does she do this a lot?"

"She gets anxious when I travel. She's always been that way."

"You should answer her. She's obviously worried about you."

Another message rolled in. *Maybe you're getting your groove on. I hope you are!* She added a heart-eyed emoji. *But what if you're bleeding out in a ditch? What if she poisoned you?!*

I think I understand why you worry about me so much.

I'm getting you a bodyguard.

He chuckled at her persistence. "I could send her a message saying I'm alive and I'll call her tomorrow, which I guarantee will be met with a dozen more questions." He had never once introduced Remi to any of his lady friends, and he wasn't going to dissect the urge to introduce her to Abby. He went for it. "There's only one thing that will stop her, and that's full disclosure."

"Meaning?"

"Would you like to meet my sister over FaceTime?"

Excitement sparked in Abby's eyes. "Are you kidding? I would *love* to."

He navigated to his camera on his phone and pulled Abby closer for a selfie. "Babe," he said to get her attention. When she looked over, he kissed her lips and took the picture. "Okay, brace yourself for the whirlwind that is Remington Aldridge, aka Remi Divine."

"I'm sorry, Aiden. I know she's your sister and I shouldn't be overly excited, but I *am*!"

He kissed her smiling lips. "I love your enthusiasm. I watched Remi blossom from a broken twelve-year-old into one of the best actresses of her time. I'm proud of her. She deserves the fanfare." He sent the picture and said, "Three. Two. One—" A FaceTime call rang through with Remi's picture on the screen.

Abby's hand flew to her chest. "It's her!"

"Man, I'd give anything to get that response when I call you."

"Trust me, when your name pops up on my phone, you get a much better response. A *full-body* response." She tapped his arm and said, "Answer it before she hangs up."

He answered the call, and Remi's beautiful face appeared. People said she looked like Natalie Portman, but Aiden thought his sister was far more unique, with her slightly pointy chin, emotive eyes, and feisty personality. "Hey, Rem."

"Hi!" Remi's eyes lit up. "Is that Abby? Are you Abby? Holy cow, you look just like the singer Lauren Daigle." She hollered over her shoulder, "Mason! She's *real!*"

"Yes! I'm real. I mean, I'm *Abby*. It's nice to meet you. I'm a huge fan, and I promise I'm not psycho." Abby bounced beside him.

"Well, that's a relief," Remi joked. "Wait, my brother's not paying you to pretend to be his friend, is he? Because whatever he promised you, I'll give you double to tell me the truth."

"*Remi*," Aiden chided.

"What?" Remi snapped, but she did it with a smile. "How can I ever trust you again after those hairy feet? Where *are* you guys?"

"We're on a date," Aiden said.

"A date? I won't keep you long," Remi said excitedly, then called over her shoulder again. "Mason! Aiden's on a *date*!"

Mason's steel-blue eyes appeared over Remi's shoulder. "Hey, Aiden. Hi—"

"Abby. Her name is Abby," Remi said.

"Hi, Abby. I'm Mason." He waved a spatula and said, "Sorry, I was making a cake. Babe, let's let them get back to their date."

"In a sec," Remi said. "You didn't answer my question. Where are you on your date?"

"At a winery," Abby said. "We watched the sunset. You should see what Aiden did for us."

"Show me!" Remi exclaimed.

Aiden handed Abby the phone and watched as Abby showed Remi their picnic, the lanterns, and their gorgeous view.

"Look at the lanterns, Mason! The roses!" Remi exclaimed. "I had no idea my brother was so romantic."

"He's amazing . . ." Abby went on to rave about their day, describing it to Remi, from the lighthouse to the beach and lunch at the café, right down to their private tour of the winery, leaving out the part about him signing her up for the competition.

Remi asked dozens of questions, and Abby answered every one of them. They laughed like old friends, and Remi didn't hesitate to make fun of him.

"I bought him flip-flops, and he insists on wearing those nerdy loafers," Remi said.

"I like his loafers," Abby said as she walked over and sat next to Aiden. "And now I've monopolized your call with your brother. I'm sorry."

"Who is that?" Patrice asked as she climbed onto Remi's lap, looking adorable with pink bows tied to the ends of her braids. Her face lit up, and she said, "Hi, Uncle Aiden. Are you still on the island? Who's that girl?"

"Hey, Patty Cake," Aiden said, noticing Abby's dreamy-eyed expression. "I am on the island, and this is my special friend, Abby."

Abby waved to her. "Hi."

"Hi. I'm Patrice and I'm five. You can call me Patty, but only Uncle Aiden calls me Patty Cake. Do you like my bows?" She swung her head from side to side, sending her braids flying across her face.

"Yes. They're very pretty," Abby said.

"Olive, my foster sister, who I hope will be my real sister one day, is at her friend Catherine's house doing a science project," Patrice said. "She's gonna be mad that I met you and she didn't. Maybe you could call her, too."

"I'll catch up with Olive another time, sweets," Aiden said. "Love you, Patty Cake."

"Love you, too. Bye!" Patrice slid off Remi's lap and said, "Can I help bake?" as she disappeared from the screen.

"She is adorable," Abby said.

"Thank you. She's a pistol. You should meet Olive. She's a great big sister, but I swear she's an adult in a teenager's body." Remi glanced over her shoulder and said, "Speaking of adorable . . ." She moved the phone so they could see Patrice standing on a chair beside Mason as he poured cake batter into a pan. Patrice was feeding a cheese stick to their golden retriever, Nahla. Remi moved the phone so only Mason's butt was on the screen, and Aiden heard her sigh. She turned the screen so they could see her face, and she said, "I love my life so much. Who knew baking could be so sexy?"

Aiden looked at Abby, remembering the way they'd been caught making out in the kitchen the other night, and said, "Who knew?" earning a secret smile. "Can we get back to our date now, Remi?"

"Oh, sorry. Of course. I'd love to meet you sometime, Abby."

"I'd like that," Abby said.

"Let's exchange numbers and stay in touch," Remi suggested. "You can let me know if Aiden tries to work while he's on the island, so I can harass him."

"*Remi*," Aiden said sternly.

"I'm kidding!"

Aiden put his arm around Abby, pulling her closer, and said, "I have more pictures to send you, Rem, but can we do without the interrogations from now on? Abs and I would like to spend the little time I have here chilling, not answering texts."

"I never thought I'd hear you say you want to chill. Yes, of course. *Definitely*," Remi said. "I'm sorry if I'm overly excited, but I've never met anyone you've dated. I'm so happy! Abby, you have no idea how many of our friends have tried to set him up on dates. But he's usually all work and no play."

"On that note, I think we'll say goodbye. Love you, Rem. Kiss the girls, and tell Mason I said we'll catch up another time."

"Okay. I have one more thing to say to Abby." Remi schooled her expression and said, "I know Aiden doesn't open up easily, and he seems strong as iron, but he's the only brother I have, and he's not invincible, so please, *please* don't hurt him."

"I would never," Abby said.

Remi nodded. "Okay, because if you do, you'll have Mason to deal with."

"No you won't!" Mason called from off camera.

"Fine. Then you'll have *me* to deal with," Remi said. "Just be good to him. He can be dorky and a bit bossy, but he means well, and I know he works way too much, but he gave me the best life. One that I sometimes probably didn't deserve. He's a great man."

Abby gazed adoringly at Aiden and said, "I'm pretty sure you gave him a great life, too."

"I gave him headaches," Remi admitted. "But he loves me anyway."

Aiden took the phone from Abby, loving that she understood that while raising Remi hadn't been easy, it had made him happy. He looked at the sister who had become a wife and foster parent, and his heart felt full. But he needed to be bossy one more time. "I love you, Rem, but how about we take it down a notch."

"I'm good with that now that I know you're not locked in your hotel room working day and night." Remi whispered, "I like her, Aiden. Don't screw this up." She wiggled her fingers in a playful wave, blew him a kiss, and ended the call.

"Wow, she's really great," Abby said. "I totally forgot she was *the* Remi Divine. She's so normal and down to earth, and I love how she teases you. It's obvious how much she loves and appreciates you. And look at that dazzling smile she left you with."

He slipped his phone into his pocket and said, "I'm happy for her, and proud of her. She's a great mother. All I have ever wanted for Remi was for her to have a good, happy life and to be loved for who she is, not what she has."

"And for her to achieve her dreams, which you facilitated," Abby reminded him. "I know how good you are at helping others make their dreams come true. But what I don't know, and I'd really like to, is what your dreams are. What does AA dream about?"

He leaned in for a kiss and said, "Lately, a scantily clad brunette is front and center in all of my dreams."

She dragged her finger down his chest between the open buttons on his shirt and said, "As much as I love that—and trust me, I definitely do—I'm serious. I want to know what your dreams are."

"I've already got more than one man could ever need." And he'd trade it all for more days like they'd just shared. Working with his hands alongside Abby, getting to know her sister, and meeting a few of her childhood friends reminded him of how much he'd loved the simple way in which he'd grown up, without the pomp and circumstance of his wealth or Remi's celebrity. It had been a life surrounded by close-knit family and friends, not governed by deadlines, conquering the next deal, earning the next million, or worrying about every word out of his mouth so as not to reveal Remi's whereabouts or details of her life. He missed that simplicity more than he'd realized.

"That's the funny thing about dreams," Abby said. "They're not about need. They're about *what if*s and *wants*. What if you hadn't raised Remi? Was there something you wanted but never pursued?"

"I've always gone after what I wanted."

"Well, that's a start," she said skeptically. "But isn't there *something* you dream about or wish you had?"

He waggled his brows.

She poked his ribs. "I'm serious. You listen to me blab about my dreams all the time. Do I need to have you lie on a couch and pay me to get you to open up?"

"*You* lying on a couch might just do the trick," he said seductively.

"*Aiden.*" She tried valiantly to give him a serious look, but her smile was relentless, and he loved that about her. "Why are you holding back? We've been naked together, but *this* is too private for you to tell me?"

"No, Abs. It's not that it's private."

"Then what is it? Because I've never had sex on my mother's living room couch before, and I don't make a habit of showering with guys. Those things meant something to me, and you're making me feel like it meant less to you. And that's okay, but—"

He pulled her closer; the hurt in her eyes felt like a stab to his chest. "It meant something to me, too. It meant a *lot* to me, Abs. I'm not used to dissecting the part of my life I missed out on. I don't regret raising Remi. I channeled all of my dreams into her and into my business."

"I know. If anyone understands that, it's me. I don't regret being there for my mom, either. But that doesn't mean the dreams I had didn't survive. I had to clear the crap from my life in order to see them, but they were still there." She caressed his cheek, her eyes pleading with him as she said, "Let me in, Aiden."

He leaned into her touch. He'd never been a needy man, but everything was different with Abby. He *wanted* her affection, and he craved her soothing smiles and tender touches as badly as he hungered for her writhing beneath him in the throes of pleasure.

"Please?" she said. "Now is your time to think about yourself. Your sister has a great life, and she wants that for you. *I* want that for you, and I barely know you."

"God, you really have gotten under my skin."

"You're not the only one who can be pushy." She wrinkled her nose and said, "I like you a lot, Aiden, and I want to get to know you better. I want to know things about you I haven't wanted to know about anyone. I hope I'm not rubbing you the wrong way."

"You rub me in all the best ways." He kissed her, and the hope in her eyes brought his truth to the surface. "I did have dreams that I set aside."

"More like kicked to the curb, knowing you, but go on."

She truly did see who he was. "I wanted what my parents had. A family. A wife, a soul mate to come home to, to raise my own family with. Someone who understands how important Remi is, and that she and her family will always be a high priority in my life. Someone who won't resent my passion for work or my need to be who I am, quirks and all. My father used to say that the best part of his day was coming home, and every year that passed, I buried those hopes deeper. I feel guilty even bringing it up."

She put her hand on his and said, "I think you put that guilt on yourself, which I completely understand because it's a lot like the guilt I felt for wanting things of my own when I needed to be helping my mom. Aiden, that's totally normal."

"Yeah, I know, but I just . . ." He patted his chest over his heart with his fist, feeling the stab of guilt, and said, "I don't want Remi to ever hear that. I don't want her thinking that taking care of her cost me *anything*."

"But you know Remi is a bright woman. She sent you here. She's pushing you to get your own life, to have the things *she* knows you're missing out on. Whether you put it out there to her or not, she knows what you gave up, Aiden. She loves you, and when someone loves you, they see all of you, not just the parts you want them to see."

"Yeah," he said with a sigh. "But it feels wrong to say it out loud."

"That's because you're an admirable man with a huge heart who doesn't want to *ever* hurt his sister. I was thinking about how Deirdra and I were winging it for all those years, doing the best we could. We didn't have people to tell us if we were doing the right things or going about them in the right way. We had Shelley, but she was careful not to build up what we did for our mom too much, because although she knew Deirdra would take off as soon as she could, I think she worried that I'd never leave the island to start a life of my own if she made me feel like I was doing the right thing in too big a way. It doesn't sound like you had anyone to tell you what a great job you were doing with Remi, either, and I know how much I second-guessed myself. I bet you did the same. Those are the things that create more guilt. It's an awful cycle, and at some point we have to break it. Maybe talking about it, getting it out of your system, is the right way to do that." She cracked a smile and said, "Unburden yourself, AA. It does a body good."

And there it was, her uncanny ability to look past the clouds and find the light in everything and everyone around her. "You're a wise woman, Abigail DM." He leaned in for a kiss. "Want to know the other dream I put on hold?"

"Definitely."

"Boating."

"What kind of boats do you like?"

"Powerboats, sailboats. You name it, I love them. We grew up taking vacations on Cape Cod, and my father would always rent a boat. We'd go fishing and waterskiing. I loved being out on the water. When I moved to California to run my father's LA office, I thought I'd get a boat one day and spend every Sunday on it. I even had dreams of taking a month off and sailing somewhere. *Anywhere.* But I threw myself into work and never had the time. Then we lost my parents, and . . ." He shrugged.

"You buried your dreams so Remi could have hers."

"That, and I wanted to keep my father's reputation intact, to honor him at work as well. To this day I've *never* handed off any of his clients to my staff. *I* work with them, and they trust me to be there if they hit a crisis or need a shoulder to lean on, the same way they trusted my father. Boating got lost somewhere between Remi's dance and acting lessons and, later, auditions, traveling, filming, and my finance career."

"But now you have time for it," she exclaimed. "It's not too late to make either of your dreams come true. Do you still want a family?" She held his gaze, hope and wonder threading their way between them.

"Very much, but it's complicated. My work schedule is all consuming."

"Then that's something maybe you can work on over time. But you're in the perfect place to go boating. Let's put that on our list. Take out your phone."

He pulled out his phone and added *go boating* to the list.

"We had a dinghy when we were growing up," Abby said. "My dad taught me to sail on Lover's Cove, which is about a mile down from the Bistro. It was where he and my mom shared their first kiss and the one place we didn't have to worry about sharks. His dinghy is still in the garage. We'll have to get the sail fixed, and maybe a few other minor things, but we could use that."

A dinghy. She was so fucking cute and real, she made him wish he couldn't buy a fleet of luxury liners.

"Actually, I don't know what kind of shape the dinghy is in. We haven't used it since we were kids," she said. "But my friend Brant Remington is a boatbuilder, and he rents out all sorts of boats at Rock Harbor Marina, on the other side of the island. I bet we could rent a little sailboat from him. The boats there are much cheaper than the ones the Silver House rents out."

"Brant Remington. Got it," he said as he entered Brant's name in his phone. "Did you make out with him, too?"

"*No*, but he's super cute, so . . ."

"I'll give you *super cute*." He hooked his arm around her, pulling her into a hard, fast kiss.

"I wouldn't want you to think you've got me all sewn up as a sure thing," she said with a flicker of a tease in her eyes. "There are *plenty* of guys on this island who I have yet to lock lips with, and now that I'm going to be here full-time . . ."

"I'd better up my game." He pushed to his feet, navigated to the playlists on his phone, and queued up "Maybe We Will." He set the phone on the table and took Abby's hand, bringing her into his arms, swaying to the sounds of Noah Schnacky singing about getting to know each other and becoming more than friends and their late-night dance turning into their last first kiss, maybe even leading to forever. He whisper-sang about not thinking about the bad things that could happen and taking their time. Every word came straight from his heart, and the wanting look in Abby's eyes told him that each and every word landed on *hers*.

When the song ended and "Yours" by Russell Dickerson came on, he said, "I'm not always the best at expressing my feelings, but this song is for you, Abs."

"I love this song," she whispered.

They danced beneath the stars, surrounded by the sounds of nature and the scent of something rich and deep blooming between them. He kissed her slow and sweet, his breath becoming hers as he intensified the kiss, getting so lost in her, he no longer felt the cool breeze on his skin or heard the beat of the music. There were only the sounds of their kisses, the feel of her soft hands on the back of his neck, and her body moving sensually against his, and a resurgence of dreams Aiden wanted to explore.

He didn't know how many songs they danced to and couldn't repeat a single word of any but the first two, but by the time their lips finally parted, they were both breathless. Neither said a word as Aiden retrieved his hat and sweater and they followed the twinkling lanterns back the way they'd come, guided by emotions bigger than either of them.

CHAPTER TEN

THE RIDE HOME was a blur. Abby's thoughts of Aiden were as sexy and sinful as they were warm and wonderful, making her want to wrap herself up in him and never let go. Those feelings coalesced as she and Aiden stepped onto her front porch, and the boldness she'd possessed that morning when she'd practically dragged him inside to have her way with him gave way to nervousness. She shouldn't be nervous after their steamy couch romp and how much time they'd spent together, but the moonlit air sizzled with something much deeper and more meaningful than it had that morning. The secret Aiden had shared about wanting to be with someone, to have a family with someone who truly understood and accepted him could have come from her own lips. Abby wanted to be with someone who would love all parts of her, too, who wouldn't think her dreams were too silly or too lofty to even *try* to pursue. Knowing Aiden had shut away his dreams of having a family and had never let *anyone* see the parts of his heart he was hiding, as she had, made them even more right for each other.

No wonder I'm nervous.

His arms circled her from behind as she unlocked the door. He lavished the back of her neck with tantalizing kisses, heightening her anticipation. She didn't want to move for fear of him stopping. She closed her eyes, her hand stilling on the doorknob.

"The sooner we get inside," he said in a low, sexy voice, "the sooner I get to make you feel good all over."

She felt his body heat from shoulder to heel, his arousal temptingly hard against her bottom, as he reached around her to open the door, sending pinpricks of desire to all her best places. She dropped her things on the table, her hands trembling. Aiden closed the door and turned her in his arms. He gazed deeply into her eyes the way he had when they were dancing, like she was the only thing he saw. The only thing he wanted to see—and *devour*. Lord help her, because that look made her knees weaken, and the excruciatingly passionate kiss that followed made her entire body smolder.

Dizzy with desire, she took his hand and led him through the living room. They kissed on the way upstairs, which made her hotter and more nervous in equal measure. Before they reached the landing, he crushed her to him, taking her in a penetrating kiss that had her moaning and writhing against him, obliterating her trepidation. When their lips parted, his all-seeing eyes searched hers, and his slow grin told her that easing her nerves had been his intention. Aiden had *all* the right moves, and she couldn't wait to reciprocate.

He reclaimed her mouth as they stumbled up to the landing, down the hall, and into her bedroom. She reached for the buttons on his shirt, but he grabbed her wrist and shook his head. "We already experienced fast and furious, my beautiful girl." He lifted her hand and kissed her palm. "Now I get to enjoy pleasuring, *tasting*, and cherishing you."

He cradled her face between his hands, taking her in another deep, toe-curling kiss. Her entire body caught fire. He made a sinful, appreciative sound and said, "I adore kissing you." He brushed his thumb over her lower lip, his eyes dark as night. "One day soon I look forward to feeling your mouth on the rest of me. But *tonight* it's my turn."

The breath rushed from her lungs in a needy "*Yes.*"

No man had ever talked to her like that before, and she was surprised by how much she loved it, which was almost as much as she enjoyed the pleasure rising in his eyes. He kissed her again, taking his time stripping off her shirt, caressing and kissing her shoulders and neck so tenderly, her breathing shallowed. He dragged his gaze down her torso, leaving a hot trail of goose bumps in its wake.

"You're so damn gorgeous." He cupped her breast, brushing his thumb over the peak. His hungry eyes held hers as he said, "I'm going to enjoy every inch of you." He lowered his mouth a whisper away from hers, rolling her nipple between his finger and thumb, and said, "Making you come in ways you never thought possible."

He squeezed her nipple, and she gasped at the rivers of heat it caused. His mouth came coaxingly down over hers, kissing her painfully slow and impossibly intense. His hands pushed into her hair and fisted, causing a scintillating sting that twined together with the excruciating heat of their kisses, making her tremble and ache with anticipation. His mouth left hers in a series of tender kisses, each one making her beg for more, but he stripped off her bra and loved her breasts with his mouth, licking and sucking so perfectly, she felt it between her legs.

"Aiden . . ."

She grabbed his head, holding his mouth there, his every suck taking her closer to the edge. He moved one hand between her legs, stroking her through her pants, and *good Lord*, she was caught up in too many sensations. She couldn't stop the moans streaming from her lips. His hand tightened in her hair as he feasted on her breast and continued creating the most delicious friction down below. She squeezed her thighs together to keep her climax at bay, but that only spurred him on to intensify his efforts, and intensify he did—*all* over, sending her careening into an explosive orgasm. She grabbed at his hair, his shoulder, anywhere she could reach to counter her useless legs, gasping and crying out as pleasure consumed her.

She clung to him, coming down from her high like a leaf in the wind, sailing fast, then drifting slow, trying to catch her breath.

Embarrassment attempted to push its way in, but he wrapped her in his arms and whispered, "So beautiful," giving it no room to take hold.

He reclaimed her mouth, possessive and the slightest bit rough, kissing her so thoroughly, holding her so lovingly, she felt precious and safe. He kissed her until her breathing calmed, and then he stripped her bare, lavishing her with sweet whispers and tender touches. She helped him take off his clothes, getting all revved up again at the sight of his gorgeous naked body. He drew her into his strong arms, skin to skin, his thick cock nestled against her belly, and a longing, desperate sigh left his lungs, as if he'd been waiting forever to feel her naked body against his.

He held her with one arm around her waist, the other across her upper back, so close not even air could get through, and said, "*God*, Abs. We feel so *right*."

She wanted to tell him she felt the same, but the emotions in his voice, his now-familiar masculine scent, and the tenderness and strength in his touch were all too much. It was all she could do to make an affirmative sound. He kissed her again, slow and sweet. But their passion took over, turning the kiss urgent and greedy as he led her to the bed. He tore back the blankets and laid her down, taking a long, lascivious look at her. He made an appreciative sound, his eyes shining with pure, unadulterated lust, as he retrieved his wallet from his pants, withdrew two condoms, and set them on the nightstand.

"I don't know if I should praise you for thinking ahead or be offended that you brought *three* condoms with you when you picked me up this morning."

"You should definitely go with praise." He came down over her and said, "I knew being with you once would never be enough." He began kissing his way down her body. "I've got the rest of the box in the car."

She opened her mouth to respond, but his hands and mouth were everywhere at once, caressing and devouring her breasts, her ribs, her hips, working their way lower, and her thoughts scrambled. Her eyes closed, and she reveled in his strong grip on her hips, his mouth nipping and kissing along her thighs, his whispered words of appreciation making her want him even more. He trailed openmouthed kisses along her inner thighs, coming so close to where she needed him most, she held her breath. Her nerves sparked like live wires, sizzling beneath his tongue. She rocked her hips, and he spread his hands over her thighs, licking so close to her sex, a needy moan escaped.

"Aiden, *please.*" She looked down, and his eyes locked on hers, the pleasure in them as bold as his stare as he slid his tongue over her most sensitive nerves. "Oh *God.*" Her head fell back, and he did it again. She fisted her hands in the sheets as he continued licking and teasing, until she was moaning and trembling.

"So much sweetness," he said huskily, dragging his tongue along her sex.

He sealed his mouth over her sex, loving her there the way he'd kissed her, deep, slow, *intense.* She dug her heels into the mattress, and he lifted her bottom, using his mouth on the apex of her sex as he pushed his fingers inside her, stroking over the spot that made her lose all sense of time and place. She was caught in a web of arousal as he fucked her with his fingers and loved her with his mouth. She arched and writhed, inhaling through gritted teeth as he quickened his efforts, sucking the oversensitive bundle of nerves into his mouth. Zings of pleasure ricocheted through her, shredding her control. Her hips bucked, her sex pulsed, and she cried out, but he didn't relent. He homed in on the secret spot inside her, lingering there, teasing over it, every stroke sending her soaring anew, until a tsunami of pleasure tore through her and her entire body arched, and she collapsed, trembling and sated, to the mattress.

His hands slid up her waist and torso, holding her tight, *reassuringly,* making her feel adored and safe as he kissed her thighs and hips, whispering, "I've got you, babe."

He kissed his way unhurriedly up her body, and then his mouth found hers. He tasted of sex and sinful pleasures, and she wanted it *all.*

The head of his cock rested temptingly against her center. Her body ached to shift lower, to feel him inside her. "I need *you*," she begged against his lips, and the growl it earned sent fire through her veins.

He reared up on his knees, his eyes never leaving hers as he tore open the condom and sheathed his length. When he came down over her, aligning their bodies, he kissed her softer and gazed entrancingly into her eyes. The way he looked at her sent lightning through her chest, their connection as overpowering as it was reassuring. He pushed his arms beneath her, holding her like she was precious, and in his arms, she truly felt she was. She lifted her hips, taking in every glorious inch of him, sending shock waves rippling through her core. Passion glowed in his eyes as he lowered his mouth to hers, and they began to move, finding the rhythm that carried them away to a secret place full of warmth and passion where only they existed. Their bodies took over, moving to a frenetic beat. She felt the claws of an orgasm grasping for purchase. Her head fell back, and Aiden grabbed her hips, pressing her into the mattress as he thrust deeper, faster, his dark eyes as lost in them as she was. Her mouth fell open and her eyes slammed shut as her climax engulfed her. She writhed and whimpered, her body shuddering beneath him, as he came undone, gritting out a curse as his release claimed him. His body jerked and thrust, his arms squeezing her so tight, she felt every pulse of his cock. Nothing had ever felt so good.

When Aiden's head dipped beside hers, his body jolting with aftershocks, he kissed her cheek between heavy breaths and whispered, "*Jesus*, Abs."

They lay together until their breathing calmed, and then he took care of the condom. She used the bathroom, and when she returned, she found him sitting on the edge of her bed, naked, one elbow leaning on his leg, his hand shielding his eyes. She got a little nervous, not wanting him to leave. It was crazy how little time they'd known each other and how close she felt to him. She never would have believed it if it weren't happening to her.

"Come here, beautiful." He reached for her, guiding her between his legs, and embraced her, resting his cheek against her breasts. She ran her hands through his hair, and he pulled her down onto his lap. He kissed her tenderly and brushed her wild hair away from her face, too many emotions gazing back at her to decipher. "I'm a greedy bastard with you, Abs. I want to fall asleep with you in my arms and wake up that way."

"Yay for me," she said, wiggling her shoulders.

"God, Abs." His brow furrowed, but he was smiling, and it was such a complex, fitting look for who he was. "You are everything I never knew I needed."

She scooped up that little golden gift and tucked it away as she said, "Stay with me."

"You've had a lot of AA today. You sure you don't want me out of your hair?"

"I want you *in* my hair." She touched her lips to his and said, "And in other places, too. Get your naked butt in my bed, greedy boy."

He tossed her onto her back on the mattress and rolled over her, grinning like the greedy boy he was. "Careful what you wish for, sweetheart. This greedy *man* is ready for seconds."

CHAPTER ELEVEN

AIDEN HAD ALWAYS been a creature of habit, up with the sun and armed for work. Even as a boy he'd gotten up early seven days a week. He could still remember his father's serious eyes lighting up when he would pad into the kitchen in his pajamas and climb onto a chair beside him at daybreak, ready to learn anything his father had to offer. *Dad, why not read the paper when you get home at night instead of getting up early to read it?* His father had a habit of sitting back and looking him in the eye every time Aiden asked him a question, giving him his undivided attention. Aiden prided himself on learning that trait at an early age—giving everyone who crossed his path the same level of respect, no matter who they were. His father's voice walked confidently through his mind. *Because you never start a race from the back of the pack.* He'd set the newspaper on the table and leaned closer to Aiden, his smile softening his features as he'd lowered his voice and said, *And evenings are reserved for the thing that matters most: family.*

Aiden had gone years without thinking of those memories, but he didn't need to look far to know why his parents and the life he'd once imagined for himself had been on his mind a lot more lately. She was sleeping naked and safe in his arms, her cheek resting on his chest, and she was making the cutest snoring sounds he'd ever heard. She didn't wear her heart on her sleeve just when she was awake. It was right there in her peaceful expression as she slept. No part of him wanted to get up, much less read a newspaper or work a new deal. That should scare the life out of him. Hell, his inability to leave her last night should have sent him running for the mainland. She was not only stirring memories, but she was also causing him to take a good hard look at who he was and what he wanted in his life.

Abby snorted so loud, she startled herself awake. She looked around, probably trying to figure out what had caused the noise.

"Morning, gorgeous."

"Hey, you," she said sleepily. "What are you grinning at?"

"Your adorable snoring."

"I don't *snore.*"

"You absolutely snore, but it's cute. It's kind of a grunting-snorting sound followed by a contented hum."

"Ohmygosh." She buried her face in the side of his chest.

"I take it your ex never mentioned it to you?"

She opened the one eye he could see and said, "I'm not talking to you about some other guy while we're *naked.*"

"Good, because I'd like to pretend that no other man came before me. No pun intended."

"That's my game plan with you and other women."

"Babe, nobody could hold a candle to my snorting girl."

She made an appalled sound. "I seriously do *not* snort."

He rolled her onto her back and moved over her, kissing her freckled cheek. "It's okay, Abs. I like your snort-snoring and the contented little hum that comes afterward."

"I don't *do* that. And I *don't* snort." She laughed.

"You definitely snort." He kissed her lips. "You also grabbed my junk in your sleep. Not that I'm complaining."

"I did *not!*"

"Why do you think we ended up making love again at two in the morning? You were working me like a stick shift. Thank God I thought ahead and ran out to the car to get the box of condoms after the second time we fooled around."

Her cheeks flamed, but her smile never faltered. "Oh my . . . You're *terrible*."

"That's not what you were crying out last night as you—"

"*Stop!*" She wrapped her arms around him.

"Why? You don't like it when I talk about you *coming*?" He nuzzled against her neck, kissing her there.

"*Aiden*," she said, her voice thick with embarrassment.

He dragged his scruff along her cheek, earning a sexy moan. "I like when you come." He nipped at her earlobe and said, "I like hearing the noises you make."

"*Stop*," she said breathily.

He trailed kisses down her body, teasing her breasts.

"*God*, I love when you do that." She grabbed his head as she had last night, holding him there as he taunted her into a wiggling, needy mess. She pushed him lower, her hips rising to greet his talented mouth.

His eyes shot up to hers, and he said, "And I fucking *love* when you do *that*." He raked his eyes down her body, between her legs, and said, "*Mm. Breakfast.*"

Her knees fell open, and he gave her what she wanted, earning all the sexy sounds he adored. Then he loved her with his body, slowly and passionately, until they were both too satisfied and worn out to move.

After a lazy, sensual morning, they hung up the hammock, filled the shells they'd collected with birdseed, and set them out on the porch. Abby looked gorgeous in jeans and the tank top he'd bought her, with an open zip-up sweatshirt over it. They rode their bikes to the Silver House so he could change his clothes, and then they biked to the Sweet Barista, where Keira and Abby chatted up a storm. When Keira said she liked a man who knew coffee, Abby glanced at him and said she liked a man who savored his breakfast. The sexy little minx knew exactly how to turn him on.

After eating breakfast, they biked to the Bistro to work on the budgets, checking off *bike ride* from their list. Aiden hadn't ridden a bike since he was a kid. He'd forgotten how rejuvenating it was to feel fresh air whipping against his skin instead of stale air-conditioning within the confines of his car.

"It's really beautiful here," he said as they made their way around to the front of the restaurant and were greeted by a cool breeze coming off the water. He stepped off the patio into the sand and sat down. "Come sit with me. Let's enjoy the view for a few minutes before we get started."

"You're really good at taking time to enjoy your surroundings." As she sat beside him, she said, "Are you sure you're a workaholic?"

"Absolutely. You heard Remi. But I've got this new woman in my life who's changing me in more ways than I'd like to admit." He put his arm around her, pulling her against him. "She's even got me riding a bike, which I haven't done since I was a kid."

"That was fun riding together this morning. Did you rent the bike daily, or weekly?"

"I didn't rent it. I bought it." He looked at the overgrown bushes and fencing a few feet away, making a mental note to put landscaping into her budget.

"You said you hadn't ridden since you were a kid. Do you plan on riding it after you leave the island?"

"I hope so."

"Really?"

"Sure. You seemed to enjoy biking to work. I thought I should give it a try."

"I love riding my bike here. I tried biking when I first moved to the city, but it was terrifying trying to navigate the busy streets. Luckily, I love walking, and the subway was easy to use. You'll probably find this hard to believe, but I've never owned a car. I have my mom's car now, assuming Cait doesn't want it. I guess we can share it. I need to remember to talk to her and Deirdra about the car and the house, although I know Deirdra won't want either." She rested her head on his shoulder and said, "I'm rambling again. Sorry. How will you get your bike home? You said you're going overseas when you leave."

"I like your rambling, and I am going overseas. I was hoping my hot new girlfriend would let me keep my bike in her garage. It would give me a reason to come back to the island."

"A reason, huh? It's nice to know where I rank on your priority scale."

He took her chin between his finger and thumb, moving her face so he could see her eyes, and said, "You have *no* idea how far you've tipped my scale, Abigail de Messiéres." He kissed her, slow and sweet, and said, "But if you'd rather I take my bike with me . . ."

"I didn't say that. I'm just not sure you can afford my *high* storage fees," she said flirtatiously.

Man, he liked her style. "Maybe we can work something out."

"If this morning was any indication, I'd say the chances are pretty high that we can. Although, bikes often need maintenance, which might mean more visits, especially in the winter, when days are shorter and nights are longer. I might have to charge double for those months."

"You drive a hard bargain."

"Thanks to this new guy in my life, I'm learning to bargain to my advantage, and a *hard* bargain sounds like it might be worth looking into. But first we have a budget to tackle."

"I'd rather tackle you." He brushed his lips over hers and said, "Here in the sand. *Naked.*"

After a few steamy kisses and more sexy banter, they finally went inside and headed into the small, paneled office. Pictures of Abby and Deirdra as little girls were thumbtacked to a corkboard on the wall beside an old metal desk. Abby was adorable, with lanky limbs and thick, messy hair that hung nearly to her waist. Her eyes looked even bigger and greener in her tiny face, and her effervescent smile was just as beautiful as it was now. Deirdra looked happier then, too, before the situation with their mother had stolen her childhood. There were several pictures of their mother when she was young. She was tall, painfully thin, and unconventionally pretty, with sandy hair and a gap between her two front teeth. He saw hints of Abby in her cheeks and nose. On the desk was a framed picture of their family. Her mother wore a denim miniskirt and a white shirt. She had one arm around Deirdra, who held a fistful of flowers. Her mother's other arm was around their father, who looked nothing like Aiden had pictured. He had long white hair tied back in a ponytail and an unkempt beard to match. He wore sandals, his clothes were rumpled, and he had a bit of a belly. But his eyes danced with the same light Aiden saw in Abby's. Her father had one arm around his wife, and he was holding Abby in his other. Abby's hair was in long pigtails, and she wore red shorts and a white top. One arm was draped around her daddy's neck, and the other held the fingers of his hand wrapping around her knee, like she wanted to touch as much of him as she could. Aiden's heart felt full and sad at once. He longed for her to have her family back, and in that moment, he longed for his, too.

"Those were my dad's pictures," Abby said. "My mom never changed anything in here after he died. See how my mom was looking at my dad in that picture?" She pointed to the family picture on the desk. "That's what true love looks like."

Aiden was wrong. His heart hadn't been quite full before, because it just got fuller.

"Do you have more of these pictures of your family?" he asked.

"Yes, at my apartment in New York—which reminds me, I need to talk to my landlord. My lease is up in the fall, and I need to make arrangements to move my stuff here now that I've decided to stay. Just a few more things to put on my long to-do list."

"I'm happy to help if I can. You should get those pictures sooner rather than later and put them up at the house if that's where you're going to be. Keep those memories close."

"I like the way you think, AA. Do you have pictures of your family in your house?"

"Yes, several. I kept them up so Remi would always be surrounded by family."

She tugged at the hem of his T-shirt. "And so *you* would be surrounded by them, too, right?"

"Yeah, of course."

"At some point, we need to get you to think of yourself as being as important as your sister."

"You think so, huh?"

She stepped closer and kissed him. "I know so."

He gathered her in his arms for the millionth time, knowing he'd do it a million more. "You said you weren't used to having someone look out for you. Well, Abs, neither am I." He kissed her softly and said, "I think I like it."

While Abby spent the afternoon sorting through the Bistro's invoices to see which distributors her mother had maintained relationships with over the years, Aiden analyzed the financials. They were even bleaker than he'd expected when he'd put in the offer on the property. He didn't know Abby's financial situation, but unless her parents had had enormous life insurance policies, there was no way she'd be able to turn the property around without some help. His gut twisted thinking about breaking the news to her, but he couldn't let her continue to put her efforts into a business that would surely fail without proper funding.

"Aiden, look what I found."

"More recipes?" She'd found her father's handwritten recipe cards earlier and had been so happy, she'd gone on about them for twenty minutes.

"No." Abby handed him the Lifestyle section of an old *Boston Herald* newspaper from twenty-six years ago with a nearly full-page article on the Bistro. There was a picture of her father standing in front of the restaurant and several more of the interior. As he scanned the feature, she said, "I totally forgot about that article. My father told us that the food critic who wrote it had a son who was vacationing here. Remember how I said my dad used to walk around and talk to all the customers? Well, he hit it off with the guy's son, and that guy went back and raved to his father about my dad and the food here. When the food critic came out, he didn't tell my dad why he was there, but the way my father told the story, and from the article, which I probably read a dozen times as a kid, he fell in love with the atmosphere, my dad, and of course the food." She pointed to the pictures of the interior and said, "Look at the rugs, and see the chandeliers and lights? *Those* are the lights of love. You can't tell because the photos are in black-and-white, but all those eclectic-looking lights were different colors."

Aiden studied the enormous chandeliers as Abby went on about the lights.

"Weren't the chandeliers stunning? I loved how they had a narrow ring of gold at the top and a wider one at the bottom. It's hard to see them in those pictures, but those things dangling from the top and bottom rings are teardrop-shaped crystals, and those are strings of crystal balls draped between the top and bottom rings. Aren't they elegant? I loved how the actual lights looked like candles. I used to try to convince my dad to put colored bulbs in them. I loved them as they were, but since we had other colored lights, I always thought they'd be prettier with a dash of color."

"They're gorgeous, Abby," he said, hating that he had to give her bad news on the heels of her excitement.

"What a great surprise that was." She was positively beaming as she put the article with her father's recipes.

He tucked the images of the chandeliers away and forced himself to do what he had to. "That article is great press, Abs, but we need to talk about the financials."

♥ ♥ ♥

"I know we do, but now I have pictures of the lights and the rugs. Do you know how *great* this is?" She couldn't stand still and paced the small office. "I won't be able to afford them for a while because the chandeliers are so expensive. I think my mom got about four thousand dollars for each of them, and that was years ago. I'm sure they're much more now. I'll have to put a trip to France on my bucket list. But one day I'll buy some that look just like these."

She planted her hands on her hips and said, "I have a great idea. I'm going to talk to Leni about that article. Maybe if the restaurant does well enough, she can nudge someone important my way and the Bistro will get rediscovered." She'd texted with Leni about an hour ago, gushing about her and Aiden's date, how much he was helping her with the restaurant, and how compatible they were. But she'd been careful not to mention Remi. Leni was excited to meet him, and she'd been impressed that he'd signed Abby up for the Best of the Island competition. She'd actually given Abby a hard time for getting on his back about it. "Thank you again for entering me into the competition, which I still have to pay you back for. Don't let me forget to write you a check when we get home. Or I could send it with PayPal if you'd rather."

"Babe—"

"If I win the competition, it might bring people from the mainland. You've got a pretty good business head on your shoulders, AA."

"Thanks." Aiden reached for her hand, drawing her eyes to his, and it took her a second to realize he wasn't smiling. "I know you're excited, and I hate to do this now, but there's never a good time to discuss the financial side of a new business."

"An *existing* business," she corrected him. "We're just breathing new life into it."

"Right, and if you don't mind me asking, roughly how much capital do you have to put toward it?"

"With the money we inherited and my savings, about forty-five thousand."

He took both of her hands in his. His serious expression made her uneasy. "Abs, I'm afraid this place needs new lungs, not just new breath."

"What do you mean? You think it's not structurally sound?"

"No, that's not what I mean. But depending on what you decide, it might be a good idea to get an inspection."

"What do you mean, *what I decide*?"

"I've been trying to stay out of your way when it comes to making business decisions."

An incredulous laugh slipped out before she could stop it. She covered her mouth, then said, "Sorry. The furniture store and the competition . . ." She cleared her throat. "Never mind. Go on. I'm listening."

"These financials . . ." He shook his head. "Restaurants in general don't make large profits, so I wasn't expecting to find much. But, babe, I don't know how your mother earned enough money to live on, much less kept this place afloat."

"Is that what you're worried about? I've worked in restaurants my whole life, Aiden. I know they're not big moneymakers. It's not like I'm expecting to become a millionaire. I want to run my family business, and I know it's possible to make enough to live on. We never had a lot before my dad died, but we never *wanted* for anything. And after he was gone, we survived on a lot less. There's no mortgage on the house or the restaurant, and the summer crowd brings in enough to cover the winter months when the restaurant is closed."

"Under normal circumstances, reopening a profitable restaurant during high season should earn you a living. But I looked over the last few years, and it appears your mom was living off the good graces of the community. She had a handful of regular customers, most of whom tipped her outrageously, like fifty bucks on an eleven-dollar lunch, and her catering earnings are the same way." He moved the other chair from the corner of the room over beside his and said, "Come here—take a look."

She sat down, scanning the ledgers as he explained.

"If I didn't know better, I'd think the restaurant was a poorly managed front for a drug dealer." He grabbed a file full of old-fashioned, handwritten receipts.

She gave him a deadpan look.

"I'm kidding. But take a look. Once a month, like clockwork, she catered for BB, whoever that is."

"The Bra Brigade. It's a group of old ladies that sunbathe in their bras. Shelley's mom, Lenore, started it when she was young. Most of our friends' mothers are part of it. But that's not so strange that they'd have her cater a monthly get-together."

"No, but the strange part is that her fee for their luncheons was eighteen dollars a plate, which includes about ten percent profit. That's normal for catering. But see what they paid?"

When she saw the receipt, her eyes nearly bugged out of her head. "That's more than *double* the cost."

"Exactly. And they added gratuities on *top* of it. Look at this. Shelley hired your mom to cater what look like pretty big events under the winery's name. Birthdays, anniversaries, dinners for every holiday, *including* Saint Patrick's Day."

"But that doesn't make sense. Before this year, when they hired Daphne, the winery didn't host any events other than Lenore's birthday party and their regular tastings, which have never been catered."

"That's not the only thing that looks off. Your *lip locker*, Wells, hired your mom to cater the Christmas party for his restaurant for the last four years, to the tune of twenty thousand dollars a pop. And look at the bottom line for Shelley's events: an Easter celebration for fifty-seven hundred dollars and a birthday party at a cost of three thousand dollars. That must have been one hell of a party."

"What the . . . ?" Abby sat back, trying to figure out what was going on.

He waved to the other documents and said, "I can't even find pay-roll records of staff working here for the last several years."

"She hired college kids on and off when she needed them, but the restaurant wasn't very busy the last few years."

He shook his head. "I don't see *any* paid staff. There's a staff schedule—Rosa, Marie, Lenore, Gail . . ."

"Those are all Bra Brigaders."

"Okay, well, it looks like they worked for free."

"But none of this makes sense. Shelley took over the books a year or so after I moved away, and she never mentioned any of this."

"Like I said, I think your mom was living off the goodwill of the community. Look at the inventory receipts." He opened another folder and showed her order forms that were made out to the Bistro but paid for by the winery.

"Oh my God, Aiden." A lump lodged in Abby's throat. "When Shelley encouraged me to leave the island, she said the island would take care of my mom. *She* did this. She did this so I could move on." Tears welled in her eyes. "Why wouldn't she tell me?"

"Because she loves you, Abs. That's what love is, doing whatever you need to in order to take care of the people you love."

"I have to call her. *No.* I have to go see her. I need to understand why she'd take on such a burden for so long."

He reached for her hand again. "I think that's a good idea, but there's more, and I think it would be good for you to hear it before you talk to Shelley, just so you know for sure which way you're going."

She sat back and crossed her arms, bracing herself for Lord knew what. "Okay, give it to me. The good, the bad, and the ugly."

"The good news is that I still think this restaurant can not only pull a profit but blow every other place out of the water."

She grinned, despite knowing there had to be more bad news. "Me too."

"The not-so-great news is that while forty-five thousand dollars is an impressive figure, it's not nearly enough to cover inventory and staff for a restaurant of your size. Or for advertising, which I think you need now more than ever. You have the capacity to serve, what? Twenty tables?"

"Twenty-five with the outdoor seating. I'll borrow some money from Deirdra."

"That might be an option, but Deirdra didn't want to be involved at first, and I know she supports you now, but do you really want to take her hard-earned savings?"

Abby thought about that and shook her head. "You're right. This is my dream, not hers. She should keep her savings for herself. But I could take out a home equity loan or something."

"You could, but if the business fails, you'd lose the business *and* the house. Actually, the house is another thing I wanted to talk to you about. You said Deirdra probably wouldn't mind if you kept the house for yourself. As a finance guy who has seen a lot of bad blood get stirred up between family members when money was involved, I'd suggest that if you want to keep that house for yourself, you come up with a financial agreement with your sisters. Legally, they each own a third, and water-view properties are rare. If you sold the house, you'd probably make close to a million dollars. Split three ways, that's a good chunk of cash for each of you."

"I don't want to *sell* the house. Have you heard anything I've said about the good memories I have there?"

"I've heard every word, but you misunderstood what I was saying. I think it would be a mistake to sell the house. You love it as much as you love this restaurant, and I'd never suggest you sell either. But that home equity loan you mentioned? If you go that route, the money should rightfully go toward buying out your sisters if keeping the house for yourself is what you end up deciding to do."

"I don't know about Cait, but Deirdra definitely won't want my money," she said.

He arched a brow. "That's a big assumption. Are you sure? What if she gets married in a few years and wants to stop working but she can't afford to? What if she wants to buy her own house? Start her own business? You already have her inheritance. Is it fair to keep the equity that's rightfully hers?"

Abby moved to the edge of her seat. "Aren't you supposed to be on my side?"

"This isn't about sides, babe. This is business, and if you're going to be a business owner, you need to see it from all angles."

"Is that what you're doing? It's like you flicked a switch, and suddenly you're as curt and business-minded as Deirdra."

He cracked a smile. "I do have my business hat on. I want to make sure you know what you're getting into and that you're protected, but I apologize if I sound harsh. I don't mean to. But I would hate to see something come between you and your sisters, especially since you and Cait are beginning to form a friendship."

"I thought there was no room for emotions in business."

"There's not, but the part of me that cares about you doesn't turn off when I have my business hat on."

She flopped back in her chair and sighed. "I love that. But I *hate* this."

He scooted closer and put his hands around her waist, pulling her to the edge of her seat again. "I have a few suggestions."

"Are they as sucky as all the stuff you just told me?"

"I have a great *sucky* suggestion," he said seductively.

She smiled despite the cloud now hovering over the Bistro.

"We'll table that particular suggestion until you're in a better mood," he said.

"Good choice."

"I ran the numbers, and I estimate you'll need roughly two hundred thousand to make this place what you envision."

Her eyes nearly bugged out of her head. "Two hundred *thousand*?"

"It's not that big a number, and you've got forty-five, so you need about another hundred and fifty."

"*Thousand*," she said incredulously.

"Yes. I have a few bucks in the bank I can invest to help you out."

"A *few bucks*? This is more than a few bucks, Aiden, and you don't mix business and pleasure, remember? I'm not taking your money. Can you imagine what that would be like? I'd be forever in your debt."

A slow grin lifted his lips. "I do have creative repayment options."

She rolled her eyes. "*No.* I need to do this on my own, and we only just met. I could be a crazy woman who will drop everything and abscond with your money."

He chuckled and held up his hands. "Okay, have it your way. In that case, I think you should have your attorney approach the investor who wanted to purchase the property and pitch an angel investor deal instead."

"Maybe your calculations are wrong."

"They're not. It sounds like a big number, but do you want this place to take off? Or do you want to run it hand-to-mouth?"

"I want it to be a success, but that's way too much debt to take on."

"It takes money to make money, babe."

"Yeah, but that's *huge* money. I can't do that. It's too much. What if I started smaller? I could set up ten or fifteen tables and see how it goes the first year?"

"That would lower your overhead, but it would also lower your income, and you'd still need two months of operating expenses up front. We'd have to run the numbers, but I'm not sure it would reduce your overhead significantly enough to make the kind of difference you're looking for. And for Pete's sake, Abs, whatever you do, don't slight yourself. Make sure you hire another cook or two so you can take a break. I assume you'll want to enjoy living here again and have a real life, which it sounds like you missed out on back in the city."

"*Ohmygod*, Aiden. What was I thinking? A hundred and fifty thousand?" She felt sick. "Maybe Deirdra was right and this place is a money pit."

"In the grand scheme of things, it's not that much money to make your dreams come true."

"Maybe not to you since you deal with finances every day. But it is to me. I don't even know how angel investors work. Do they get to tell me how to run the business?"

"No. That's why I said an AI instead of a VC."

"VC?"

"Venture capitalist. Angel investors are typically silent partners, but VCs aren't. Financially they both work the same. They both take a percentage of interest in the company, and they usually take all of the profits until the initial investment is returned, and then they take an ongoing percentage."

Her shoulders slumped. "What's the use if I'm giving up my profit?"

"You wouldn't give up *all* of your profits forever. It comes down to if you want this business and how you want to run it."

"I definitely want it."

"Okay, well, if you go the angel investor route, you can define the terms and pitch a deal you can live with. I can help you with that—negotiate down the percentage and try to make sure you keep a percentage of the profits while they're earning back their investment. With the right investor, there are all sorts of ways to broker a deal like this."

"I don't know. It's all overwhelming. I need to think about it and talk to Deirdra and Cait. This is their business, too, and we're talking about a lot of money and a commitment that would last as long as we own the restaurant."

"Yes, but better to do it right than to get started and lose your pants."

Despite her mind going in a million directions she didn't want to think about, she couldn't suppress her smile as she said, "Losing my pants sounds like a heck of a lot more fun."

CHAPTER TWELVE

ABBY LAY IN bed staring at the ceiling Thursday morning, dissecting an idea for the Bistro that had been percolating all night. She and Aiden had spent the last few days cleaning the Bistro and endless hours going over budgets, forecasts, and all of the options for obtaining the money ad nauseam. She'd even gone online and researched restaurant expenditures, and everything Aiden said was right on the money. But any way she looked at it, the amount of additional capital she needed felt like an elephant sitting on her chest. Her mind was spinning with the complexity of the situation. They'd spent the last few nights cooking dinner together, listening to music, and getting to know each other better. Two nights ago they'd gone for a ride along the coast, and last night they'd bundled up and gone for a romantic walk to try to clear her head. She enjoyed every minute they were together, but the only time she'd been able to stop thinking about financing for the Bistro was late at night, when they'd tumble into bed and get lost in each other's arms, making love until neither one could think at all. *If only we could do that every time my mind went crazy,* she mused.

Aiden rolled onto his side and pulled her against his naked body, kissing her softly, stirring a flurry of anticipation inside her. She'd never found sex very exciting, but with Aiden *everything* was different and thrilling, from their talks and romantic walks to his kisses, dirty promises, and the fulfillment of each and every one of those delicious promises.

"Did you get any sleep?" he asked, running his hand down her back.

"I don't know, a little maybe. But I have an idea, and I think it's a good one."

He gave her butt a squeeze and said, "I have a good idea, too."

She felt him getting hard. She loved how much he wanted her and debated putting her idea on hold. He kissed her jaw, nipped at her neck, and her thoughts started to blur. She forced herself to say, "Wait, Aid. Your idea will make me forget mine, so maybe I should go first."

"Fair enough. As long as I don't have to let you go."

"Sounds like a win-win for me." But his kisses turned to sucking on her neck, and her whole body ignited. *"Wait, wait, wait."* She leaned back far enough to see his wolfish grin. "You can't do *that*. It's too hard for me to concentrate."

"I'll have to remember that the next time you're putting me in my place. What's your idea, beautiful? Whatever it is, I bet it's not nearly as fun as mine."

"I don't know about that. You seemed to get off on spreadsheets yesterday."

When she was studying the spreadsheets in the office of the Bistro yesterday afternoon, trying to figure out another way to approach the restaurant, Aiden had come up behind her and distracted her with kisses on the back of her neck. Kisses had led to caresses and titillating taunts that had her begging for more. He'd guided her hands to the edge of the desk, stripped her pants down, and made love to her from behind right there in the office, hitting that secret spot inside her as if he were using a heat-guided missile, and *oh*, how she'd loved it!

"No, babe. I got off on *you*."

Great. Now she was thinking about him taking her from behind. Her body thrummed with desire. He must have sensed it because his hand moved down her butt to between her legs.

He brushed his lips over hers and said, "Seems like you get off on me, too."

"*Aiden*," she said breathily. "Just give me three minutes to tell you my idea before I forget. Then you can have me." The grin that earned made her want to forgo the next three minutes, but this was too important. "I think I know how to cut down on overhead costs. What I loved about the Bistro was the feel of the place. I think I can put my own twist on that without losing anything. Let's say we're open from twelve to ten to serve lunch and dinner, but instead of sit-down lunches, we run window orders only. It would be easy to put an ordering window on the side of the building for walk-ups, and we can serve a lot more people per hour at a walk-up window than in a sit-down restaurant, where people linger and chat. During the summers, the beach is *packed*. I bet we could serve three times as many people an hour with enough staff. More if the lunch menu is standard beach fare—burgers, fries, fish tacos, shrimp quesadillas, and something that's easy but specifically made for our customers. Customers can still eat at the tables in the restaurant and enjoy the environment, or they can eat on the patio, or take it to go. But they'd clear their own tables and throw away the trash, alleviating the need for waiters and full-time bussers. Then we can close from four to five to clean the floor, wipe the tables, and reopen for sit-down dinners with more elaborate meals. For the first season, I'd start with only twelve to fifteen tables for dinner instead of twenty-five. That way we'll only need a few waitresses, bussers, and kitchen help. Dinners would sell for around twenty-five bucks a plate, plus we can serve liquor, which has a high profit margin. I was thinking about the menu, too. I could make special dishes on certain nights, Parisian fare, using my dad's recipes, and charge more for them. I have to run the numbers, but I think I could get away with much less capital doing it this way. What do you think?"

He looked awestruck, his brow furrowed, jaw slack, eyes sharp. "It sounds brilliant and makes a lot of sense for a beachfront restaurant. But based on the information I've gleaned about this area, I think you'll probably see far more people on an hourly basis for lunch than you anticipate, which could mean needing more kitchen staff. But that's a good thing, as long as you won't lose the aspects of the restaurant that you were so excited about. Those magical elements you were hoping to bring back to life."

"I love that you remembered that. I won't lose them. I can still decorate with the same romantic, bohemian vibe, visit with customers like my dad did during the dinner hours, and create a warm, friendly environment but without as much overhead. It's the best of both worlds. A new twist on an old type of magic. I was also mulling over what you said about making sure I still had time to enjoy life and not work myself to death, and I appreciate you bringing that up. I'll want to be at the restaurant most of the time, at least the first season or two, but I also want to enjoy living on the island again and spending time with friends, so I'll definitely need another chef."

"Good. That's important, Abby. You have a zest for life, and it would be a shame to miss out on that."

She lowered her eyes, hoping she wouldn't sound clingy, and said, "Last night you said you'd come back to visit after you leave the island. Did you mean that? Assuming we're still together?"

"Absolutely." He kissed her and said, "I've got to come back and see my bike."

"And pay your storage fee," she said, and he kissed her again. "I want to have time to spend with you when you visit."

"Abigail de Messiéres, are you putting *expectations* on me?"

"*No.* I don't mean it like—"

Her words were lost to the hard press of his lips.

"I'm kidding, Abs. Of course I want to spend time with you, but this is your business, and despite the man I am while I'm here on vacation, I really am a workaholic. You need to know that I will understand if you have to work *every* day. You should do whatever you want or need to do, and we'll figure the rest out."

"I appreciate that. But I've really enjoyed our time together, and if we keep seeing each other after you leave the island, I'll have plenty of time to work in between visits. I want to run the numbers and see what the bottom line is."

"Well, what are you waiting for? Get that sexy ass out of bed." He gave her a chaste kiss and swatted her butt. "But you'd better put panties and a shirt on, because right now the only number I'm thinking about is sixty-nine."

She threw off the covers and scrambled on top of him. "My numbers can wait."

Much later that morning, after pleasuring each other senseless and getting ready for the day, they ran the numbers for several scenarios and sat at the kitchen table hammering out a plan in which she would need only an additional seventy-five thousand dollars of capital.

"Do you feel better about this?" Aiden asked.

"Yes. This feels much more manageable. It's also terrifying, but as you said, it's an investment in my future and in making my dreams come true." She was still nervous, but mostly because she still had to run the idea of changing the restaurant into a window service during the day and a sit-down restaurant at night by her sisters. She didn't know what she would do if they weren't on board with the idea, but she'd deal with that when and if the time came. She also wanted to see Shelley and discuss the ins and outs of what she and the others had done for their family, but first things first.

Aiden pulled up a word processing program on his laptop and said, "Okay, let's get started on defining a pitch for the angel investor."

"Wait. I don't want to go the investor route. I don't think it's smart to give away profits to a company I don't have any connection to. It feels wrong. I want to get a home equity loan and use that."

"Abs, as a businessman I would never support an endeavor that I thought would fail. When I said I believed in you, I meant it, and I still do. So when I say this, know I'm saying it with my *personal* hat on." His tone was so serious, it made her uneasy. "This is the guy who takes up space in your bed speaking, not the finance guy."

In an effort to ease her nerves, she went for levity. "That's a very possessive designation."

"With you I'm a possessive guy." He took her hand, a smile tugging at the corners of his mouth.

"Yeah, you are. You take up space in my shower, too."

His grin broke free. "Careful, sweetheart, or we'll monopolize this table next."

"That sounds like a lot more fun than whatever you were going to say a second ago."

He scooted closer, holding her gaze and her hand as he said, "Babe, this house means the world to you. I see the way your shoulders relax when you walk in the door. Last night after our walk, when we were standing at the edge of the property, you were talking about gardening with your mom and how your dad used to tell stories about when he first came to the island. You said he knew this was the house for his family the first time he saw it, and I could hear how much it means to you. This house is the very fabric of the family you cherish. I will stand back and support whatever you decide, and Lord knows it's not my business, but if you take out a home equity loan and something goes awry, you risk losing both the Bistro *and* the house. Please think this through before you make that decision. I would hate to see you make a mistake that can't be undone."

She slid her hand free and put it over her stomach, nauseous at the thought of losing everything. "It's all I've been thinking about since yesterday. If I screw up, or something happens and this goes south, I'll have enough to deal with from disappointing myself and my sisters. I will put enough pressure on myself to try to keep that from happening.

I don't need the additional pressure of some investor breathing down my back, waiting for me to fail."

His jaw tightened. "That's not what investors do."

"Come on, Aiden. You're a finance guy. You must know they're sharks, investing with the hopes that companies will fail so they can take over."

"That's not how investors work, Abby." He squared his shoulders and said, "Not good ones, anyway. They help companies become even more profitable. If they do their job right, both parties come out on top."

"Yeah. I know that's what's supposed to happen. But it feels like they're sharks with giant teeth waiting for the little fish to slow down so they can gobble them up."

"Abby—"

"I'm sorry," she said sharply. "I know that sounds bad. But if this doesn't work, I'd rather lose it all to a local bank than to some investor I don't know, especially when it didn't feel right to go that route in the first place."

He drew in a deep breath, his eyes contemplative. "Then reconsider my offer. Let me invest. Let me help you."

"No way. If I'm not taking my own sister's savings, there's no way I'd ever take yours."

His expression softened, and he said, "Abby, I know what it feels like to leave childhood memories behind. Even though the memories were too much for me to stay in West Virginia, selling that house was the hardest thing I'd ever done at that point in my life. I'm trying to protect the things that mean the most to you."

He was fighting so hard to help her, a lump formed in her throat, but she had to follow her gut instincts. "I appreciate that, but I've made up my mind. Now I have to get my sisters on board."

♥ ♥ ♥

Aiden stepped outside to call Ben while Abby called her sisters.

Ben answered right away and said, "If Remi finds out I answered your call, she'll throttle me."

"I know, Ben, sorry. But I'm in over my head. I need some advice."

"You, in over your head?" Ben scoffed. "I highly doubt that. What's going on?"

Aiden paced the front yard. "I don't know, man. That's the problem. I met someone."

Ben didn't respond.

"You there?" Aiden looked at his phone to make sure the call hadn't dropped.

"Yeah. I was waiting for you to tell me what kind of business this person is in."

"I met a woman, you idiot."

"Seriously? Why didn't you lead with that? I wondered why you hadn't come back to work yet. I figured you'd be gone for a weekend at most, but when I asked Remi if she'd heard from you, she basically threatened my life if I reached out to you. So you met a chick. What's the problem?"

"She's not just some chick. *That's* the problem. Her name is Abby." He gazed out at the water and said, "She's so fucking adorable. When she gets excited about something, her entire face—*no*, the entire *room*—lights up. She knows what she wants, and she goes after it. She's a chef. She's hardworking, smart, energetic, funny, and sexier than any woman I've ever met. I'm really into her, Ben."

"So this *thing* is going to last another few days?"

"A *lot* more if I have it my way."

"Well, not too long. You're set to do the international Q2 meetings after your vacation. Is something worrying you? You want me to have Mason run a background check on her?"

"*No*," Aiden snapped, though he knew Ben was only watching out for him, the same way Aiden had watched out for Ben over the years. That's what partners did. But it still rubbed him the wrong way.

"Buddy, I know you're careful not to give away your hand, but you sure she's not a gold digger?"

Aiden rubbed a knot in the back of his neck, gritting his teeth, and said, "*Yes*, I'm sure. If you met her, you'd know in ten seconds that she's not like that."

"Women can hide a lot."

"Damn it, Ben. Trust my fucking judgment, will you? I just offered her two hundred grand and she turned it down."

"She must give one hell of a blow job." Ben chuckled.

"Forget it. Sorry I called."

"Wait, I was kidding. Dude, you're really off your game today."

"No shit. That's why I called." He took a deep breath and said, "I told her about Remi, about my parents."

Ben was quiet for a beat. "I'm sorry for messing around, man. I didn't realize how serious you were."

"Yeah, it kind of crept up on me, too."

"Talk to me, Aiden. What kind of advice do you need?"

"She's inherited a restaurant, and she has a shot at something magnificent. I believe in her with everything I have, and it's not based on anything other than a gut feeling, tasting her food, seeing her work ethic, and her passion for the business. I swear, Ben, she talks about her father having some sort of magic that made that restaurant shine. I see the same thing in her, and I know how crazy that sounds. But it's true. The problem is, she stands to lose everything if she doesn't handle it right. I want to step in and make sure it's all done perfectly, but . . ."

"But you know you *can't*, right? Please tell me you know you can't."

"I fucking know that, but I hate it."

"Aiden, I trust your judgment one hundred percent, but I have to ask you a hard question."

Aiden gritted his teeth against whatever was coming.

"You've known this girl, what? A week?" He didn't wait for confirmation. "Are you sure you feel something real for her and you're not just riding your white horse looking for a maiden to save now that Remi has flown the coop?"

Aiden closed his eyes, fighting against the knee-jerk response of telling Ben off and throwing his fucking phone into the ocean. "Yes, I'm *sure*," he finally said.

"Go ahead—you can call me an asshole for asking."

"No, it's a fair question, even though it makes me want to rip you to shreds. But it's not like that. She's capable and experienced. She doesn't need *saving*. She needs *guiding*, which I'm doing to some extent. But I'm going to fuck this up if I can't back off, and backing off is the last thing I want to do. I want to protect her, and at the same time, I have no fucking clue what I'm doing because I've never been in this situation before."

"Holy shit. I know exactly what you're doing."

"Then how about cluing me in?"

"You're breaking your number one rule. You're letting your emotions lead you."

Aiden sighed and looked up at the sky. "Right. *Fuck.* That's got to stop, but I don't want it to."

"Then don't. I've known you for years, Aiden, and you've never been like this about a woman."

"It's only been a week. I know better."

"You think you have control over this because you're a control freak with every aspect of your life, but I have news for you, partner. When your heart is involved, it's worse than when you were a teenager thinking with the head between your legs instead of the one on your shoulders. The heart is the fiercest competitor I've ever been up against. The best thing I ever did was take a chance and let Aurelia know how much I loved her. Now I have an amazing wife and two beautiful children, and even on the days when Bea and Christopher are cranky and driving us crazy, there's no place else I'd rather be. Those cranky days are still the best days of our lives. So let me ask you something. How do you feel when you're with Abby? Is your mind on work or on her?"

"I'm so damn happy with her. I never knew I wasn't happy before, but now I see the difference. I *feel* the difference, and, man, I like who I am around her. I don't feel like Remi's protector and surrogate parent. I don't think about work, and I don't feel like the man with the money that everyone kowtows to. I feel like a regular guy who is totally into this amazing woman. For the first time in my life, I feel *lucky*, Ben. Lucky to be included in her life. No deal could ever feel better than this."

"You're preaching to the choir, buddy. Aurelia and our kids are everything to me."

"Aiden!" Abby flew out the front door, beaming from ear to ear.

His heart boomed to life. "Ben, I've gotta—"

"I heard. Go, buddy. Be happy, and *don't* fight it."

Aiden pocketed his phone as Abby sprinted toward him, dropped the messenger bag she was carrying on the ground, and leapt into his arms. He spun her around as they kissed.

"I take it your talk with your sisters went well," he said, setting her on her feet.

"Yes, although not at first. If I didn't know better, I'd think you'd secretly called Deirdra because she gave me the same lecture you did about risking the house and the business."

"She stands to lose a lot of money if the restaurant fails."

"It wasn't that. She didn't want *me* to lose it, and not because of money. But because, like you, she knows how much all of this means to me. But she said this is my dream, and she's a totally silent partner in it. That I can do as I please and she'll support me. And I even talked to her about the house, because you were right about buying her and Cait out if I want to live here. That's only fair. But Deirdra doesn't want to do that, either. She said it's money she never had, and if one day we sell the business and the house, we'll split it all up in thirds. But for now, she said to do what I want and follow my heart."

It sounded to him like he and Abby weren't the only ones letting their emotions lead them. "That's great. What about Cait?" While he didn't believe a loan was the smartest financial decision, he was glad she and her sisters were happy with it.

"Cait," she said with a new light in her eyes. "She's on board with it all—the home equity loan, the window-ordering lunches and sit-down dinners, everything—the same way Deirdra is. They're so different, though. Cait is really laid-back, but she's smart, and she asked great questions, so I know she's not just telling me what I want to hear. She seems excited to come back, too."

"That's great news, Abby."

"Yeah, it is. I hadn't realized that Deirdra had reached out to Cait, but apparently they're talking or texting almost *every* day. I'm glad they're becoming friends, but if I know Deirdra, she's checking up on me through Cait."

"Does that bother you?"

She shrugged. "Not really. It's just weird. I'm sure she's curious about you, and worried about how I'm handling the Bistro, but there's never been a middleman in our relationship before. I guess I'm also a little jealous that Deirdra talks to Cait more than she talks to me right now, but I figure she and I have twenty-eight years of history, and they have a lot to catch up on." Her smile returned, and she said, "Deirdra can be really bossy, so maybe I'm more relieved not to be interrogated by her than I am jealous. In any case, I'm glad Cait is in our lives, and I think she's really glad to have us in hers, too."

"Navigating new sister dynamics can't be easy, but as time goes on, I'm sure you'll all find your places. I'm glad you have their support. So what's next?"

"The Sweet Barista for the only coffee that tastes good to me anymore—*thanks to you*—and something sugary and delicious. Then we have to go to the bank to apply for the loan. I called after talking to Cait and set up an appointment. I'm so nervous, and so glad you're helping, and . . . I'm rambling again. I'm also being pushy and assuming you are going with me to the bank. Do you want to take the day and go do something alone? Something fun? I can handle this myself."

He loved the way she bubbled over with excitement. "Are you trying to get rid of me, beautiful?"

"Hardly. I just don't want you to feel like you *have* to come with me. No expectations."

"Oh no?" He was unable to resist teasing her, because he liked her pushy, presumptuous side, and said, "I'll drop you off and head to the resort to check in with my office and get some work done."

"You will do no such thing. Don't make me tell Remi." She picked up her messenger bag, grabbed his hand, and dragged him toward the car.

He chuckled. "I forgot to mention that if you're going this route, you need to get a home equity line of credit, not a home equity loan. That way you're only liable for the amount you actually use and you're not paying interest on the rest."

"You're doing it again, Aiden. This is *my* thing, remember? I'll make that decision."

He gritted his teeth as he opened the passenger door and said, "Of course. Rule number one of business is to do your research."

She gave him a deadpan look. "I thought rule number one was that my word was as good as gold."

"There are a lot of rule number ones," he said as she slid into the seat. "Just google *home equity line of credit versus home equity loan* on your phone and make your decision from there."

As he walked around the car, he wondered where he could stop along the way to get earplugs and a muzzle, because there wasn't a chance in hell he'd keep his mouth shut in that meeting if every single thing in the transaction wasn't going to benefit Abby.

CHAPTER THIRTEEN

ON HER WAY to Shelley's house on Friday afternoon, Abby's thoughts drifted to Aiden, as they usually did. He was trying so hard not to step on her toes, he'd looked like it had physically pained him to keep his opinions to himself while she'd discussed financing options with the banker. When she'd finally asked for Aiden's opinion, the gust of relief that he'd expelled had been almost comical. But he'd asked a litany of questions Abby hadn't thought to ask, and the answers had proven that he was right about applying for a home equity line of credit instead of a home equity loan, confirming once again that he had her back, even though she knew he would have preferred she'd gone the angel investor route. They would find out next week if she was approved for the line of credit.

She climbed the front steps to Shelley's house feeling nervous and grateful and realized that Shelley's family had also always had her back. She'd spent as much time in Shelley's house as she had in her own before her father died, and she had great memories of sleepovers and play-dates with Leni. Her brothers would try to scare them or pull pranks on them, while her older sister, Sutton, would act like she didn't have time for them, even though they were only a couple of years younger than her, or she'd share her *vast* knowledge about life and they'd eat it up. Jules, who was three years younger than Leni and Abby, would insist on sleeping wherever they slept, and then she'd fall asleep twenty minutes into the slumber party. And without fail, sometime during the evening Shelley would wrangle as many of them as she could into baking with her. Her husband, Steve, would sneak into the kitchen for tastes of whatever they were making and steal kisses from Shelley. He always took the time to ask after Abby and her sister. Baking and chatting with Leni's parents had been one of Abby's favorite parts of their sleepovers, and after her father died, she'd missed those carefree times. She had no idea how to thank the woman who had done so much for her family, and at the same time, she wanted to tell Shelley she shouldn't have done it.

Gratitude and unease warred within her as she knocked on the door, still trying to come up with an appropriate thank-you.

Shelley opened the door, vibrant in a green wrap dress. "Hi, Abby. I'm so glad you called—"

Swamped with emotions, Abby threw her arms around Shelley, hugging her tight, and whispering, "Thank you. Thank you so much!"

"Wow. Now, that's a greeting. You're welcome, sweetheart." Shelley let go, but Abby held her tighter. "Honey, are you okay?"

"Yes," she whispered, but she held on for another minute, regaining control of her emotions.

When Abby finally stepped back, Shelley looked worried. "What on earth did I do to deserve that special thank-you?"

"You did things you shouldn't have so Deirdra and I could do the things you thought we should."

For a split second Shelley looked choked up, but she quickly schooled her expression and said, "I'm not sure I know what you're talking about, but I was happy to hear from you last night. You gave me a reason to make chicken and dumplings soup for lunch, your favorite. Come in."

Shelley believed food made from the heart fed a person's soul, and chicken and dumplings had been Abby's comfort food as a child. The meal was a dead giveaway that Shelley had already figured out why

Abby had come. But as Abby followed her toward the heavenly scent of homemade cooking, she had to hand it to her for keeping up the ruse.

Shelley handed her a bowl of soup and said, "I thought we'd sit out back and enjoy the sunshine while we chat." They carried their bowls outside, where a fresh pitcher of iced tea and two place settings waited for them on the patio table. They'd been blessed with an extended warm front, and daffodils were already starting to bloom. "I'm sorry you missed Leni. She ran over to Jules's shop."

"I knew she was going to be busy today. We've been texting," Abby said as they settled into their chairs. "We're meeting her tonight for dinner."

"Oh yes, she mentioned that. I love that all you kids still get together. Maybe she'll visit more often now that you're moving to the island."

"Maybe," Abby said, wrestling with what to say next. It was obvious Shelley didn't want to fess up to what she'd done, but Abby couldn't let it go. She'd have to ease into it. She ate some soup and said, "Thank you for making time for me, and for making this. It's delicious."

"You're very welcome. I wasn't sure what you wanted to talk about, but favorite foods go a long way. Your romantic new beau, perhaps? The Bistro? The sisterly surprise your mother left you?"

"Sure, all of those things. But, Shelley, Aiden and I went through the books for the Bistro the other day, and we found some rather unusual transactions. I thought you might want to tell me about them."

Shelley ate a spoonful of soup and said, "Not really, no."

"Shelley . . ." She didn't want to push, but at the same time, she *did* want to talk about it.

Shelley set down her spoon and put her hand over Abby's. "Honey, I promised you the island would take care of your mom, and I meant it. I only wish we had known how sick she was before it was too late, but with the restaurant closed for the winter, our visits were few and far between. She claimed she wasn't sleeping and begged out of our get-togethers. We all tried to reach out to her. Lenore, the other Bra Brigaders, Margot . . . But your mama was a proud woman."

"I wouldn't say *proud*, considering she let you do so much for her, and she let the Bra Brigaders work for free."

"Oh, honey. She never knew what we did, or about the ladies not being paid. Ava didn't look at the books. She trusted me."

For some reason Abby suddenly felt like she was going to cry. She took a sip of her iced tea, steeling herself against the guilt rising inside her, and said, "I'm sorry I wasn't here for her. I know you were with her in the end, and I understand why you didn't call us. I wish . . ."

"I know what you wish, sweetheart. You would have been there if you'd known, just as I would have called you if my loyalty didn't have to lie with her first. That might seem hard to understand. But as a mother, I know there are certain things some parents can't handle, and as I said when I met with you and your sisters, your mom had hit her limit."

Abby nodded. "Do you think if I had stayed on the island anything would have been different?" She'd asked Shelley all of these questions right after her mother died, but she needed to hear the answers again.

"Yes. You would have resented her as much as Deirdra does, and you would not have had the chance to become the amazing woman you are." She squeezed Abby's hand and said, "You couldn't have saved her, Abby. Nobody could have. We tried to get her help time and time again, but you know how that went, because you tried, too."

"But why did you *keep* helping her? Why didn't you . . . ?" She couldn't even force the words to come.

"Why didn't we give up on her?" Shelley asked carefully. "Because she was my friend long before she lost herself to alcohol. She was family, sweetheart, just like so many other people here on the island. I could no sooner turn my back on her than I could turn my back on you or Deirdra."

"But those parties and dinners? Wouldn't I have heard about you hosting some of those events?"

Shelley was quiet for a moment. "We didn't host them, honey. We had them catered for the assisted living facility to keep income flowing through the restaurant."

Tears welled in Abby's eyes, and she tried to will them away. "Thank you doesn't feel big enough, Shelley. You have a huge family, and you continually went out on a limb for ours. I need to pay you back."

"You *are*, Abby. Yours and Deirdra's happiness *is* our payback."

Abby swiped at the tears sliding down her cheeks, and Shelley stood up and pulled her to her feet, enveloping her in a maternal embrace. "Let it out, baby," she said, patting Abby's back. "You are loved by so many. It's okay. Just let it go."

"I'm sorry," Abby said through her tears.

"It's okay, darlin'. No need to be sorry." Shelley held her, doling out reassurances, along with the maternal love Abby had missed out on for far too long. She held her until she had no more tears to cry, and then she touched Abby's cheek and said, "You okay, baby girl?"

Abby nodded, but her sweet words made her eyes dampen again. "I'm sorry. I don't know why I'm so emotional."

"For years your life has been shaken up like a snow globe, and you've always been good at catching all those little pieces. But now those pieces are settling, and you're realizing the storm is over. That's why you're crying, and crying is good. It cleanses your soul, gets all that sadness out so your happiness has room to breathe." As they settled back into their seats, she said, "You know, before your mom started drinking, if the tables had been turned, I have no doubt she would have done the same for our family."

"She was so different before my dad died."

"I know, honey. I trusted your mother implicitly. She was a good friend. When you kids were little, she was always there for us. She got lost. I don't understand why or how, but I know she's in a better place now."

"I hope she's with my dad."

"I believe she is, and I'm sure he's taking good care of her." She sipped her iced tea, giving Abby a moment to breathe, and then she said, "Now that you know all of my secrets, perhaps you can share one of yours."

"What do you mean?" Abby asked as Shelley's mother, Lenore, came out of the carriage house where she lived. Lenore was everyone's surrogate grandmother, and Abby loved her dearly.

Lenore waved and headed their way. Shelley looked nothing like her mother. Lenore was tall, with a blond pixie cut, a flair for fashion, as evident in her wide-legged slacks and chic, colorful top, and a sense of humor as big and beautiful as her daughter's.

"The grapevine is buzzing about you and your new beau. Should we be booking a winter wedding?" Shelley asked.

"*Shelley!* We just started dating, and I *know* I'm crazy to be redoing and reopening the restaurant *and* starting a relationship with a guy who has a life somewhere else. But he's so damn easy to be with." That was the hardest part. Being with Aiden was easy, fun, and exciting. She felt like she'd known him forever, and she was already looking forward to spending time with him after he left. And every day she learned even more wonderful things about him, like how he thought of everyone else before himself. Despite asking Remi for space, he'd been keeping in touch with her via texts so *she* wouldn't worry about *him*, and he'd already bought skates for them *and* for Cait to use over the weekend. And then there were the other things, like that he enjoyed cuddling, and when he thought she was asleep, he whispered the sweetest, most intimate things, such as *You're so unexpected* and *How did I get so lucky to find you?* Her heart squeezed just thinking about them. She was learning things about herself, too, like the fact that *she* loved cuddling as much as he did and how deeply words alone, and Aiden's actions toward others, touched her.

"Sounds like I'm just in time for the good stuff," Lenore said, and Abby got up to greet her.

"Hi. How are you?" Abby said as they embraced.

"If the rumors are true, I'm not nearly as good as you." Lenore sat down and leaned her elbows on the table, setting her mischievous blue-gray eyes on Abby as she said, "So? Are the rumors true? Are you dating Mr. Coffee? Jules said he's scrumptious."

"Ohmygod." Abby felt her cheeks burning. "I am going to have to duct tape Jules's mouth shut."

"That won't stop her. She'll send a group text," Lenore said. "I love my Julesy."

Shelley tapped Lenore's arm and said, "I asked Abby if we should plan a winter wedding."

"Why wait for winter?" Lenore asked. "Fall weddings are beautiful."

"You two are *impossible*. We're only *dating*. He's on vacation, and believe it or not, he has a real life to go back to."

"Don't give me that nonsense," Shelley said. "That man set up a romantic evening with all the trimmings at our vineyard. That means something, and I see that blush on your cheeks, honey. There's no hiding your feelings for him."

"Mm-hm," Lenore agreed. "That's a hotsy-totsy glow if I've ever seen one."

"Oh my gosh." Abby covered her face. "I'm *not* talking about this with you two."

"Chalk one up for naughty Mr. Coffee," Lenore said cheekily, sparking a litany of jokes between her and Shelley, which sent them all into fits of laughter and reminded Abby of even more reasons why she loved living on the island.

There was nothing quite as embarrassing or as fun as being teased by people who had changed her diapers. The people who loved her despite her family's messes.

CHAPTER FOURTEEN

EVENING ROLLED IN with clear skies and a brisk breeze for their dinner with Abby's friends at Rock Bottom Bar and Grill, which overlooked Rock Harbor. Even though it wasn't yet tourist season, the parking lot was packed. Wells's restaurant was much larger than the Bistro, with ample indoor and outdoor seating and a boat dock with designated waitstaff so boaters didn't have to leave their vessels to eat. The rustic restaurant had a nice setup, but it was very different from the romantic environment Abby hoped to create.

As Cait climbed out of the back seat, Aiden took Abby's hand and pulled her into his arms, whispering, "How am I going to keep my hands off you in that dress?"

His affection and constant attention made her feel desired and feminine, and she'd wanted to look sexy for him. She'd gotten all dolled up in her favorite beige knit minidress and had paired it with knee-high leather boots. When he had arrived to pick her and Cait up, he'd taken one look at her and stumbled over his words, making Abby feel fantastic.

"The same way I'm going to have to keep my hands off you," she countered.

He was strikingly handsome in a dark gray button-down and jeans. Even in jeans he had a commanding presence, drawing the attention of everyone around him. Abby had noticed that in great detail last night when they'd gone to the market to buy fresh fish and vegetables for dinner. She'd never seen so many women ogle one man before, but he hadn't seemed to notice. He'd been too focused on sneaking kisses from her.

"Are you two done making googly eyes at each other?" Cait asked. She had arrived a couple of hours ago, and she looked pretty in black jeans and a peach sweater.

"*Done* sounds so final." Aiden draped an arm around Abby as they crossed the parking lot. "Ready to check out the competition, ladies?"

"If Wells opens his mouth when the judges are around, we're sure to win," Cait said. "The guy thinks he's the cat's meow."

"Abby, wait up!"

Abby turned at the sound of Leni's voice and ran to greet her auburn-haired bestie with a big hug. Leni always looked well put together, and today was no different. She wore a short navy blazer, a blue-and-white-striped shirt, and jeans. "I'm so glad you came!"

"You said you needed my help with marketing, and I had to check out the guy Jules and my mom are absolutely raving about *and* your new *sister*. I still can't believe you have another sister." Leni gave Abby a once-over and said, "Girl, you look smokin' hot. Your new man must be lighting *all* your fires."

"And then some . . ."

"Lucky you!" Leni glanced over Abby's shoulder and said, "Wow, your sister is beautiful, and *he* is drop-dead gorgeous."

"I know, right? You'll love them both." Abby took her hand, hurrying toward Aiden and Cait. "You guys, this is Leni. She's been my best friend since we were kids. Leni, this is Cait and Aiden."

"Hi," Cait said shyly.

Aiden extended his hand and said, "Aiden Aldridge. It's nice to meet you."

Leni's eyes widened for a split second, and then she shook his hand. "I'm looking forward to getting to know both of you."

As they headed inside, Leni held Abby's arm, falling a few steps behind the others, and whispered, "You didn't tell me you were seeing Aiden *Aldridge*. He's Remi Divine's brother and manager. Shea is Remi's PR rep." Shea Steele was Leni's cousin. "I've heard his name dozens of times in the office. Shea *raves* about how classy he is because he's not a jerk like other celebrity managers."

"*Shh.* I know," Abby said quietly. "But he doesn't want everyone knowing about Remi being a celebrity, so please don't bring it up. He wants to keep a low profile while he's here."

"Gotcha. My lips are sealed. Things are good, though?"

"*Amazing*," she said quietly. "In *every* way."

"I'm so happy for you."

Aiden held the door open, placing his hand on Abby's back as he followed them in. Abby was glad that Leni struck up a conversation with Cait right away. She was so good at making people feel comfortable.

Aiden whispered, "I bet you two could cause some trouble together," and kissed her cheek.

The hostess directed them to a table by the window, where Jules, Grant, Jock, and Daphne were talking. Jules let out a squeal and jumped to her feet. "I'm so glad everyone made it!" She threw her arms around Abby.

"That's my little pixie, sprinkling her happy dust on everyone," Grant said as he came around the table to greet them.

"I've missed her happy dust," Abby said as she hugged him. Abby loved how he called Jules *Pix* or *Pixie*, which suited her perfectly.

"And you must be Cait," Jules exclaimed.

"Let me introduce everyone before we get into a flurry of hugs and conversation." Abby took Cait's hand and said, "You guys, this is my *sister* Cait." She reached for Aiden's hand, unsure of how to introduce him. Was it too much to say he was her boyfriend? She chose a safer route and said, "And this is Aiden, aka man of many talents, including the best handyman around. I'm only going over names once, so take notes.

The happy-dust sprinkler is obviously Jules, and this shaggy brown-haired dude is Grant, her fiancé. The gorgeous blonde is Daphne, and the guy holding on to her like someone's going to abscond with her is her husband, Jock. And here come the family ties. Jules, Jock, and Leni are siblings. Got it?"

"Not even close," Cait said. "But it's nice to meet all of you."

"That's okay. We'll help with names," Jules said as she embraced Cait.

Everyone said hello as they took their seats around the table.

Aiden held Abby's hand under the table as he and Jock got reacquainted, and Abby chatted with the girls.

"Is it tough being a celebrity on this small an island?" Aiden asked.

Jock scoffed. "The only celebrity here is Grant. He's our local hero."

"Shit." Grant shook his head. "Hero, my ass."

"You have the medal to prove it," Jock said.

Grant said, "I've got a prosthetic leg that says otherwise."

"I'm sorry to hear about your injury," Aiden said.

"Thanks. What do you do, Aiden?" Grant asked. "Any military service in your background?"

"No. I'm a finance guy . . ."

Abby liked listening to Aiden getting to know the guys.

"Why do guys always talk about work? I want to know more about you, Cait," Jules said.

Cait was staring across the room.

Abby followed her gaze to Brant Remington, who was heading their way. Brant was *everyone's* friend, with wily eyes and a love of all things outdoors. Abby nudged Cait, startling her out of her lustful leer, and said, "I can introduce you."

"What? *No.* I wasn't . . ." Cait's cheeks burned red.

"Oh, *yes* you were," Jules said as Brant sauntered over. "We forgot to mention that we invited Brant to join us. I hope that's okay."

"Did I hear my name?" Brant flashed a grin, and the dimples that had gotten him dates with all the hottest girls on the island appeared. His wavy brown hair and year-round tan made his blue eyes *pop*.

"The Bee Gees are back," Abby said, pushing to her feet. "What have you been up to, Brant?"

Brant embraced her and said, "Stayin' alive, baby," amusing their friends, except Grant, who shook his head.

"We used to call Brant and Grant the Bee Gees," Abby explained to Cait and Aiden. "Aiden, Brant is the one I said you should talk to about renting a boat. Brant, this is my friend Aiden."

Aiden stood to shake his hand. "Nice to meet you."

"You, too."

"And this is Cait," Abby said. "Cait and I recently learned we're sisters."

Cait offered a tentative smile.

"Well, any sister of Abby's is a friend of mine," Brant said as he sat in the empty seat beside Cait. "Don't worry. I don't bite," he said, making Cait blush again.

"Unless you ask him to," Jock said.

"Damn right." Brant high-fived Jock across the table.

"You're going to embarrass her," Daphne said. "Don't worry, Cait. I'm a blusher, too."

"I swear you guys will never grow up," Leni said as the waiter came to the table. "I need a stiff drink if I'm going to survive dinner with these people."

They ordered drinks, and Cait looked relieved to have the spotlight off her.

"You okay? He's a nice guy," Abby whispered to her.

"I'm fine," Cait answered quietly.

"So what brings you to the island, Aiden?" Grant asked.

"My sister booked a monthlong work-free vacation for me. I was ready to pack it in and get back to work after three days." Aiden lifted

Abby's hand to his lips, kissing the back of it, and gazed adoringly at her as he said, "Then I met Abby, and she showed me how fun a no-work and all-play vacation can be."

"Go, Abby," Leni cheered, earning giggles from Daphne and Jules.

"Sounds like a dream vacation to me," Brant said.

"I feel island fever coming on," Jules said in a singsong voice.

"That's a real thing, Aiden. Watch out." Daphne snuggled closer to Jock and said, "I came for a weekend and knew I never wanted to leave."

Aiden and Abby exchanged a glance. She could tell by the spark in his eyes that he was thinking about what he'd said to her when they were lying in bed earlier that morning. *We've only been together for a week and a half, and already I can't imagine not seeing you every day.*

"I'm all for vacations, but I'd go nuts if I didn't keep busy," Leni said.

"Don't let Aiden fool you. He's a total workaholic," Abby said. "He might not be working in an office at his real job, but he and Cait have been helping me get the Bistro into shape, and Aiden has worked all day, almost every day since we met."

"How's that going?" Grant asked.

"There's a lot to do, but it's getting there, and looking better every day." She told them about how they were changing the restaurant into a window service for lunch and offering more elaborate sit-down dinners. Everyone thought it was a great idea, since that side of the island didn't have any walk-up restaurants along the beach.

The waiter came with their drinks, and they took a moment to place their dinner orders.

After the waiter left, she said, "I'm really excited to put our own spin on the Bistro. But it's stressful. *Someone* entered me in the Best of the Island Restaurant Competition." She grinned at Aiden. "I'm scouring my father's recipes to come up with the best ones to enter."

"Babe, you're going to win," Aiden said with such confidence, she almost believed him.

"That was really smart, Aiden," Leni said with a nod. "I'd have pushed her to do the same thing. Abby, if you win, you'll get months of free advertising, and that could have a big impact on your visibility. We can talk about that tomorrow when we go over marketing strategies."

"I can help with marketing ideas," Jules offered. "I know a lot about spreading the word on the island, and Daphne came up with great grassroots marketing ideas for the winery."

"That's true," Leni said. "Are you free for a few hours tomorrow morning, Daph?"

"Sure. I have a bridal shower at three, but I can do it before that," Daphne said.

"You guys really want to help?" Abby said.

"Yes," they said eagerly.

"Thank you. That's fantastic. Aiden and I have been working on budgets. Maybe you can take a look at those, too, in case we missed anything. Want to say ten tomorrow morning? Cait? Does that work for you?"

"Yes, perfect," Cait said. "I've got a few logo ideas, and I'd love to get everyone's input."

The others agreed, and Abby said, "I'm excited! This is going to be great. I really need to get my marketing in place in case I don't win."

Aiden kissed her temple and said, "You've got this, Abs. You're sure to win."

Grant leaned his forearms on the table, leveling a concerned stare on Aiden, and said, "No disrespect, Aiden, but you might want to temper your encouragement and help Abby keep her expectations realistic. Rock Bottom has won that competition for the past few years. Wells has an awesome chef."

Aiden's gaze never wavered from Grant's as he said, "That's what I hear, and it's very impressive. But have you tasted Abby's cooking?"

"No," Grant said.

Aiden turned to Abby. "Sounds like you need to have a tasting for your friends, sweetheart. If those closest to you don't know what you're capable of, how can they help spread the word?"

"Yes!" Jules exclaimed. "That's a *great* idea."

"Count us in," Daphne said. "I love taste testing, and if I want to ask you to cater the winery events, I should know how good the food is."

Abby was floored. "You guys would really want to come to a tasting? And, Daphne, you'd consider using me for catering?"

Her friends exchanged incredulous glances.

"Are you kidding? Of course!" Daphne exclaimed.

"Abby, you're moving back to the island and reopening your family's restaurant," Leni said earnestly. "Why *wouldn't* we want to support you in every way we can?"

Abby had lived in the city for so long, working too many hours to have any kind of personal life, she'd forgotten what it was like to have real friends who pitched in without being asked and cared about her like family.

"I don't know. Because you have *lives*," Abby said, overwhelmed with gratitude.

Jules began dancing in her chair and singing to the tune of the *Friends* theme song, "We'll be there for Abby!"

"*Nooo!*" everyone said at once.

Grant pulled her into his arms. "God, you're magnificent."

"Aw, I love you." Jules kissed him and quietly sang to the same theme song, "You're always there for me."

"You guys are too cute," Abby said.

"Don't say that. You'll give Grant a big head," Brant said, sparking a round of jokes.

Aiden put his arm around Abby and kissed her cheek, whispering, "Hey, sexy girl. Your friends adore you almost as much as I do."

His words coalesced with the hunger in his eyes, making her stomach flip.

"Okay, where were we? Abby?" Leni said, jerking Abby from the moment.

"The *tasting*. What do you think, Cait?"

"I think it's a great idea. Taste is subjective. It might be best to get a few opinions before deciding what to serve the judges."

"Kind of like dating," Brant said, earning a glare from Leni. "What?"

"Dating? Really?" Leni rolled her eyes.

As Leni and Brant bantered, Aiden leaned closer to Abby and said, "I hope it's okay that I suggested the tasting. I wouldn't have if I didn't think you could blow them away."

"I know. Thank you." His encouragement made her want to live up to his praise. She looked at her friends and said, "Okay, let's do the tasting."

The girls cheered.

"When are you thinking?" Leni asked.

"The competition judges are coming two weeks from Tuesday." Her pulse quickened. She hadn't realized how fast the deadline was approaching.

Aiden must have sensed her worry, because he squeezed her thigh and said, "We've got this, Abs."

"How can you be ready to open the restaurant that soon?" Leni asked.

"I can't. The restaurant won't be open to the public until a month after the competition, so I won't have to stress about hiring and training staff right away. But it needs to look its best when the judges come through, so I'm slammed getting all of the cosmetic stuff done. I'm having the building inspected, and the floors and the patio are being fixed, and I'm having an ordering window installed on the side of the building."

"Who's doing the work?" Grant asked.

"Cait got us a great deal with her friends who own Cape Stone and Cape Renovations. They're starting Monday and said they should be done by Wednesday evening."

"Cait, you know the Wickeds?" Daphne asked.

Cait nodded. "I work for Tank Wicked at Wicked Ink. I do tattoos and piercings."

"I'm from the Cape," Daphne explained. "My friend Chloe is married to Justin Wicked."

"I know Chloe. Justin is a really nice guy. She's very lucky," Cait said.

"Maybe you can give me a tattoo one day," Jules said, earning a curious look from Grant. "I'm thinking of getting a pixie throwing happy dust in the air, and I want our names written in the dust."

"Ah, Pix. I love that." Grant leaned over and kissed her.

"Jules, that's a *really* bad idea," Leni said. "Inking your significant other's name on your skin is a recipe for disaster. It's like you're testing the relationship gods, and it never ends well. Tell her, Cait."

"Sorry, Leni, but I know better than to judge anyone else's ink," Cait said.

Jules flashed a cheesy grin. "Besides, I don't believe in recipes for disaster. I believe in true love conquering all."

"You sound like my sister," Aiden said. "I hope you never lose that outlook."

"I won't," Jules said cheerily.

"That sounds like a big tattoo, Jules. I would be too afraid to get one," Daphne chimed in. "I can barely give blood without feeling queasy."

"I've got a few tats," Brant said.

Grant looked at him like he was crazy and said, "No you don't."

"When's the last time you saw Brant naked?" Abby asked.

Grant scowled.

Jock pointed at Brant and said, "You used to be afraid of needles. Let's see those tats."

"No can do, bro," Brant said cockily. "I'm pretty sure you don't want me dropping my pants right here at the table."

"On *that* note, let's keep your pants *up* where they belong and figure out the date for Abby's tasting," Leni suggested. "I want to see if I can make it."

"Oh, right. I got sidetracked," Abby said. "Let's see. Thursday, after the Wickeds are done, we're going to start painting the interior of the restaurant. That will take some time."

"We need to power wash the exterior, too," Cait reminded her.

"I can help you with that. I've got a pressure washer." Brant looked at Cait and said, "Are you painting, too?"

"Yeah."

Brant grinned. "Good. I'd like to see you in action."

Cait blushed again, only this time she smiled and shook her head.

"I can spare a few hours to help you paint if you'd like," Grant offered.

"I wish I could help, but I'm on a deadline for my publisher, and the words are not flowing as well as they could be," Jock said.

"And I'm swamped at the winery," Daphne added. "But I'm excited to help with the marketing tomorrow."

"Thanks, you guys." Abby looked at Grant and Brant and said, "Are you guys sure you don't mind painting?"

"I'm happy to help," Brant said.

"Your old man took me under his wing the summer I turned ten and taught me everything I could absorb about painting landscapes and portraits," Grant said. "It meant a lot to me and had a big impact on my love of painting. Spending an afternoon helping you bring that place back to life is the least I can do."

"I didn't know my dad did that," Abby said.

Grant took a drink and said, "He was awesome. We were at the Bistro one night when he was out there painting and I was in a crappy mood, pissed off about God knows what. I spent the whole time watching him from my seat, and when we were leaving, he called me over and struck up a conversation about how much he used to hate eating dinner as a kid because it took him away from what he really wanted to be doing, which was painting."

"He loved eating," Abby said with surprise.

"Yeah," Grant said. "I found out later it was his way of getting through to me, and it worked. That summer is one of my best childhood memories. He gave me an outlet, and I ran with it."

"I love knowing that," Abby said.

"Isn't my Grant wonderful?" Jules said. "So if you're painting next week, what does that mean for the taste-testing date?"

Abby looked at Cait and Aiden and said, "What else do we have to finish? We're working on the menu and logo design. I have to go through recipes and decide which ones hold the most promise. I'll probably try them out this week and next in case the recipes need to be tweaked. Why don't we do the tasting two weeks from tomorrow? Oh, wait. Aid, that's the weekend you leave, isn't it?" *Do we really have only two more weeks together?*

"I'll be around if you do it Saturday. I leave Sunday morning," he said.

She tried to ignore the sinking feeling in her stomach and said, "Oh, good. With all the effort you're putting into this, I didn't want you to miss it."

Aiden held her gaze, the reality of their situation hovering between them like an intruder. "You're going to kick ass in the competition." He looked at the others and said, "I hope someone will take a video when they announce her as the winner so I can see it."

"You bet," Cait said.

"So we're all set, then?" Abby said far more casually than she felt. "Maybe we can have a bonfire afterward."

"A bonfire, huh?" he whispered as her friends chatted about the bonfire and whipped out their phones to check their schedules.

"It's on your list."

"You're on my list, Abs, and taking off that sexy little dress is, too." He brushed his lips over her cheek and said, "I'm so proud of you for giving the Bistro your all."

"You make me feel like I can do anything."

"Because you can, sweetheart. But you know that. It's one of the things I find so appealing about you," he said as the waiter brought their meals.

And your encouragement is one of the reasons I'm falling for you.

The thought came with a side of shock. She braced herself for fear to chase that shock uphill until she couldn't breathe. But as her friends dug into their dinners, chatting animatedly and teasing her about having tough competition with Wells, she felt *happy*. The kind of happy she hadn't felt since she was young, when she'd looked forward to every day and hadn't had the need to construct virtual life rafts to keep from drowning in the realities of life.

She thought about how easily Aiden fit in with her friends. His laughter sounded carefree, not forced, his conversations effortless. Yet he was so engaged, it was clear that he cared about what her friends had to say when he asked about Grant's artwork, Jock's writing, and how they felt about moving back to the island after being away for so long. He and Brant talked about boats, and he asked Jules about how she got started with her business. He didn't leave anyone out, chatting with Cait and Daphne about the Cape and Leni about the city, where he apparently did a lot of work. Through it all, Aiden held Abby's hand, touched her shoulder or leg, kissed her cheek, and whispered sweet things, like how beautiful she looked and how much he was enjoying spending time with her friends.

It was as if he'd always been by her side, and she was completely and utterly swept up in him. How had that happened so fast? It was a little scary to realize those feelings came with expectations, but it felt right to trust Aiden, and it felt good to be happy and to accept the *wooing* he so expertly lavished on her. It felt good to have a stake in *them*.

"Excuse me, babe. I'll be right back." Aiden kissed her cheek, snapping her from her reverie.

She watched him disappear around a corner and wondered how it was possible that she already missed him. As if she'd summoned them, her friends all leaned in, looking at her expectantly.

"I *love* him," Jules said in a hushed voice, as if Aiden could hear her.

"He's a cool guy, Abby," Grant agreed. "You've got my approval."

"And he's a gentleman, like Jock," Daphne said.

"Agreed." Jock nuzzled against Daphne's neck and said, "Love you, baby."

"I like him, Abby," Brant chimed in. "He treats you like you're special, which is how a woman should be treated, and he seems genuinely interested in helping you succeed. I like that in a man."

"Maybe *you* should date him, Brant." Grant snickered.

Brant smirked and said, "Hey, if I batted for the other team, Abby would have some stiff competition."

"You're a dork." Leni threw her napkin at Brant. "I agree with everyone else, Abby. He's head and shoulders above the single guys I know."

Abby's heart was racing as she said, "He sure is. He's in a league all his own."

After taking care of the bill, Aiden went in search of Wells. He'd seen him come in earlier and stop by a few tables to chat with patrons before heading across the room. He spotted Wells chatting up a pretty brunette near the bar and took a moment to study the guy who, as a teenager, had possessed the arrogance and stupidity to two-time girls who had not only been best friends but also *his* friends. Wells had many reasons to be arrogant, from his good looks and wealthy roots to his restaurant's standing as the Best of the Island. But after seeing what he'd done for Abby's mother, Aiden knew there was more to Wells Silver than met the eye. Aiden knew establishments like the Rock Bottom Bar and Grill couldn't thrive without a smart businessperson behind the wheel. He knew plenty of smart businessmen who were jerks to women. Had Wells outgrown the womanizing habits that could take a man down? Or was he still an ass in that regard?

Wells kissed the brunette on the cheek, and Aiden watched him expertly work the room. He put a hand on the shoulder of a man eating by himself and talked with him for a few minutes. He chatted with couples and crouched by the chair of a woman who looked to be at least eighty, holding her hand and nodding with a compassionate expression. Wells spotted Aiden and headed for him with an affable smile.

"Good to see you, Aiden." Wells shook his hand and said, "I heard that Abby entered the restaurant competition. That's ballsy of her."

There was no doubt that the chef there knew his or her way around a kitchen, but Aiden had eaten enough of Abby's cooking to know she was head and shoulders above whatever Wells's chef cooked up.

"Abby is a confident woman, and she has every reason to be. Although I have to say, if the meal we just enjoyed is typical of your establishment, then the competition will be tough."

Wells inhaled deeply, puffing out his chest like a peacock. "Thank you. I pride myself on hiring the best."

Aiden wanted to say that the *best* was opening her own restaurant, but he wasn't there to verbally spar with Wells, so he said, "It'll be an interesting competition."

"Yes, but I'm betting you didn't seek me out to talk about the competition, did you?"

"No. I wanted to thank you for taking care of Abby's mother over the last few years."

"I don't know what you—"

Aiden held his hand up, liking him even more for his chivalrous efforts. "I'm a numbers guy, Wells. You can't have more than about seventy employees here, and even if I'm wrong and you have a hundred, I know what catering costs, and it's a hell of a lot less than what you spent each year for your holiday party."

Wells shifted his gaze away, looking contemplatively over the room before finally returning a thoughtful, humble expression to Aiden. "Please tell me Abby doesn't know."

"I'm sorry, but she does."

He shook his head. "I don't want her to feel funny about this. I don't know how much she's told you about her family—"

"We've shared a great deal. I'm aware of the issues with her mother."

"Then you know her mother didn't just fall on hard times. She dove into them headfirst, and Dee and Abby did what they could to make ends meet. They were smart to get off the island when they did. Abby would have stuck around forever if Shelley hadn't pushed her to leave. We take care of our own here, Aiden. I have good memories of going to the Bistro as a kid and being treated like family by Abby's parents. Her father was the reason I wanted to open a restaurant. I wanted to be like him, the guy who got to know people, who brought something good into their lives and didn't snub his nose at them."

When Aiden had met Wells's parents, Alexander and Margot Silver, they hadn't seemed particularly snobby. But whether Wells had issues with his parents or had simply taken a liking to Olivier wasn't Aiden's concern. Abby was.

"Is that why you wanted to buy the Bistro?" Aiden asked. "Because you admired her father?"

"No. I wanted to buy it because I knew Dee wouldn't lift a finger to help with her mother's things, and I didn't want Abby to get stuck trying to fix it up just to get rid of it. I had no idea Abby was serious about reopening the Bistro."

Aiden was glad to see there was even more to Wells Silver than he'd thought. "Thanks for watching out for her."

"No worries, man. Abby and Dee are good people. As I said, we watch out for our own." He crossed his arms and lowered his chin, setting a serious stare on Aiden. "What's the deal with you two? You're not going to leave her brokenhearted, are you? Because we don't take messing with our women lightly."

He and Deirdra would make a good pair. "Something tells me that you've caused your fair share of broken hearts."

Wells looked in the direction of their table with a regretful expression.

"Rest assured, Wells, whatever Abby and I decide will be for the best."

He met Aiden's gaze. "For her? Or for you?"

"The fact that you're asking me that means you don't know me well enough *to* ask that. I sincerely hope we have a chance to rectify that before I leave the island."

"Yeah, me too. I've got something for Abby. I'll bring it by the table in a minute."

Abby was telling a story about her father when Aiden returned to the table. He sat beside her, not at all surprised that everyone was as captivated by her storytelling as Aiden was by everything about her. He put his hand on her leg, craving the connection. His appetite for her was insatiable, but his need to simply *be* with her was even greater. He loved her radiant personality, her sense of humor, and the fact that she wasn't afraid to challenge him. He'd been staying with her every night, and yesterday she'd suggested he bring some clothes over, so he didn't have to run back to the hotel each morning. Before Abby, he'd have run for the hills at that suggestion, but he'd jumped at the chance for more time with her. Although he was preparing himself, because tonight he knew he might have to say good night at the door to give her and Cait privacy.

As if she sensed he was thinking about her, Abby glanced at him, smiling without missing a beat in her story. She placed her hand over his, squeezing his fingers around her thigh, as lustful and greedy as he was, which would make it even harder for him to sleep without her in his arms tonight. He thought about what Wells had said and what Wells would have no way of knowing. If Aiden were to break Abby's heart, he'd also be breaking his own.

Wells showed up at their table a few minutes later carrying a bottle of champagne and a bottle of tequila. He was his exuberant self, high-fiving the guys and flirting with the women. When he turned his flirtatious comments on Cait, she stared him down like he was public enemy number one. Aiden noticed Wells's eyes darting to Leni with every remark, as if he were gauging her reaction.

Brant lifted his chin in Wells's direction and said, "Mind layin' off Cait? She obviously isn't into what you're offering."

Cait's arm snaked around her middle, as Aiden had noticed her doing when she was uncomfortable. Her eyes flicked to Brant for only a second before leveling Wells with another serious stare.

"Why? To make room for you?" Wells scoffed.

"Okay, enough," Leni said. "Cait probably isn't used to guys playing dick wars."

"Actually, I'm used to much worse." Cait continued staring at Wells and said, "But I haven't gotten a read on this one yet."

"Are you saying you want to get your ink on my pages?" Wells countered.

"*Ugh*, dude." Brant shook his head.

"Your lines are getting worse by the day, bro," Grant added.

"Really?" Wells shrugged. "I thought that was pretty clever, but I'll get out of your hair. I just stopped by to wish Abby luck in the competition."

"Thanks, Wells. Dinner was incredible, by the way." A tease rose in Abby's eyes, and she said, "A little heavy on the basil, but to each his own."

Wells laughed. "We'll see what the judges have to say about that. I brought you something." He set the bottles in front of her and said, "Tequila to drown your sorrows while I'm celebrating my victory and champagne in case you want to celebrate with me."

Aiden knew from the cheesy grin on Wells's face that he was only joking, but Jules must not have picked up on it, because she said, "You have no shame, Wells Silver."

Wells winked at Jules. "I was kidding, darlin'. The champagne is in case you win, Abby. Good luck."

Abby got up and hugged him. "Thank you. Good luck to you, too."

Wells nodded to Aiden before walking away.

"I know he's all over the map," Daphne said, "but I love him. I think he's got a big heart beneath that flirtatious exterior."

"That's not all that's big," Leni said.

"Leni," Jock chided her.

"Damn, Len." Brant chuckled.

Leni sipped her drink and said, "Put your imaginations away. I was talking about his ego."

"What was that nod about?" Abby whispered to Aiden as the others talked.

"We had a chat and cleared up a few things. I also thanked him for taking care of your mom."

Her eyes went hazy with that look women got when they saw puppies and babies. "You did that?"

"Yeah, and, Abs, he wasn't trying to buy the place to get a leg up. He was trying to help you out. I think he's a good guy."

She leaned closer and whispered, "He's a good guy, but not quite as good as *my* guy."

Aiden had been praised by many, but he'd never felt better about himself than he did at that moment.

"I think we'd better settle the bill and get out of here before these two start tearing off each other's clothes," Leni said, and everyone reached for their wallets.

"It's all taken care of," Aiden said.

"How?" Leni asked.

"Did you pay already?" Jock asked.

"No way, man. We can help pay," Grant said.

"Don't worry about it." Aiden pushed to his feet and said, "You guys can get it the next time."

Everyone thanked Aiden as they headed out to the parking lot. The girls firmed up plans for tomorrow, and Aiden and Brant made arrangements to meet at the marina in the morning. After a round of goodbyes, Aiden, Abby, and Cait headed back to the house.

When they arrived, Aiden grabbed the tequila and Abby grabbed the champagne. She held the bottle over her head and said, "It's still early. Anyone want to get tipsy on the good stuff?"

The last thing Aiden wanted to do was leave, but he said, "I thought I'd give you and Cait some privacy and stay at the resort tonight."

"Don't leave on my behalf." Cait yawned and said, "I'm really sorry, Abby, but I worked fourteen hours each of the last few days to catch up with clients so I could get this time off. I was hoping to head up to the apartment and crash."

"Of course. We'll have plenty of time together. Get some rest."

"Okay." Cait headed up the walkway and turned back to say, "See you two at breakfast?"

Abby looked at Aiden, the invitation in her eyes clear and enticing. He reached for her hand and said, "Yes, Cait. See you in the morning."

As Cait disappeared through the door on the side of the garage that led to the apartment, Aiden drew Abby into his arms and said, "I don't want to make either of you uncomfortable. Are you sure it's okay that we're together while she's here?"

"Aiden, we're all adults, and it's not like she can hear us from her apartment."

"Good, because the thought of sleeping without you sucked."

"Want to get tipsy with me?"

"I've been thinking about stripping off your sexy dress all night. I'm already half-drunk on *you*." He lowered his lips to hers, taking her in the kiss he'd been holding back all night long. They stumbled up to the porch, stopping every few steps to kiss and juggle the bottles of alcohol.

She handed him the champagne, and as she unlocked the door, he kissed her neck, the desire that had been brewing all night burning hotter. When she ground her ass against his erection, he said, "Damn, baby. Keep doing that and I'll drop these bottles and take you right here."

She pushed the door open, tossed the keys on the table, and turned, her eyes dark as night as she said, "You've done enough *taking*. Tonight it's *my* turn to do as I please." She grabbed him by the collar and yanked him inside.

He nearly dropped the bottles as their mouths collided, but he managed to get them on the table. He toed off his shoes, their tongues battling for control as they stumbled through the living room. She fumbled with the buttons on his shirt, and he tugged off her sweater-dress and dropped it to the floor. Her bra came next, sailing through the air as they made their way upstairs. She whimpered in frustration, tugging at his buttons. Adrenaline and lust coursed through his veins. He grabbed his shirt with both hands and tore it open, sending the buttons flying down the steps. She gasped, eyes wide, and he *growled*, "Your panties are next."

She stripped them off before he could shred them, and he pushed off his jeans, kicking them down the stairs as they reached the landing. She bent to take off her boots, but he grabbed her wrists and backed her up against the wall, demanding, "Leave them on."

He crushed his mouth to hers, grinding against her, earning the sexy sounds that always made him lose his mind. He drew her wrists over her head without breaking their kiss and trapped them with one hand, holding them there as his other hand snaked down her body, groping her breasts, teasing her nipples to firm peaks. She writhed against him, gloriously naked, and he ached to be inside her. But he loved drawing out her pleasure, fondling her breasts, caressing the dip at her waist, and clutching the swell of her hips, reveling in her curves. He moved his hand between her legs, teasing over her slick heat, and she moaned into his mouth, bowing off the wall.

"You feel so fucking good," he said against her lips. "I can't get enough of you."

"I need to touch you," she pleaded breathlessly.

"You will, baby." He dragged his tongue along her lower lip as he dipped his fingers inside her.

"More," she pleaded.

He crushed his mouth to hers, devouring her as he stroked over the spot that sent her up on her toes. Her legs flexed, her breathing hitched, and she tore her mouth away.

"Oh, *yesss*," she cried out. "Don't stop."

He lowered his mouth to her breast, sucking and grazing his teeth over her sensitive skin, until his name flew from her lips. Her body pulsed around his fingers, and he captured her pleas, kissing her roughly as she rode the waves of her pleasure. He stayed with her, loving her mouth like he wanted to make love to her body as she came down from the peak. Her body melted against his. He released her wrists, and the feel of her hands on his shoulders and arms stoked the inferno burning him from the inside out.

"Christ, baby. I need to be inside you."

She tipped her face up, her eyes glowing with desire. She grabbed him by the arms as she stepped away from the wall and pushed his back against it. "You will be. When *I'm* good and ready." She grabbed his boxer briefs and stripped them down.

Holy hell, this woman . . .

She ran her hands up his legs, kissing his thighs. Her breath whispered over his eager erection, but she passed it by, rising to her feet, exploring his chest with her hands and mouth. He stifled a groan. Every slick of her tongue made his body throb, his cock weep. When she sealed her mouth over his nipple, using her tongue and teeth, he grabbed her head, fisting his fingers in her hair, hanging on to his sanity by a fast-fraying thread. She was so fucking sexy in those high-heeled boots as she sucked, kissed, and *bit*. Sweet Jesus, he'd never been so turned on. She was relentless, teasing him as she moved down his body and sank to her knees. By the time she wrapped her fingers around his thick length, stroking tight and perfect, his every muscle was corded. She dragged her tongue around the head of his cock and over the slit at the tip so exquisitely a curse fell from his lips. His body trembled with restraint as she teased and taunted. She grazed her teeth over his sensitive flesh, obliterating his ability to think of anything other than the need searing through his veins. He fought the urge to take control and drive into her mouth, but it was like holding back a freight train. Greedy desire stacked up inside him, pounding and aching until his skin felt too tight.

"*Abs*, I can't take it."

When she finally took him in her mouth, the pleasure was so intense, it spiked up his core, spreading through his chest like wildfire. His head lolled back and "*Holy fuck*" fell from his lips like a prayer. He clung to her hair as she worked him, sucking and licking and taking him right up to the edge of madness.

"*Abby*," he warned.

Her eyes flicked up to his as she swirled her tongue over the sensitive glans, wickedness staring back at him, challenging him. She lowered her mouth over his shaft, her eyes remaining trained on his as she worked him into a thrusting frenzy of need. He gripped the base of his cock with one hand, tugging her hair with the other, so she released his shaft.

"You need to stop or I'm going to lose it."

She licked her lips, lust swimming in her eyes, and said, "I *want* you to lose it."

He couldn't think, couldn't speak as she reclaimed his cock with a vengeance, working him faster, rougher, until his skin was on fire. She cupped his balls and tugged, catapulting him into ecstasy. Lights exploded behind his closed lids as his climax ravaged him. She stayed with him, taking everything he had to give, until he collapsed against the wall, panting, and lifted her to her feet. He held her against him, their hearts pounding erratically.

"Baby, baby, *baby*." He cradled her face in his hands and said, "Where did that come from?"

Her shoulders rose in the sweetest shrug he'd ever seen. "I wanted to make you feel as good as you make me feel."

"If I make you feel that good, then I deserve an award, because, baby, I've never . . ." It was too crude to say he'd never come so hard, but that wasn't all he'd stopped himself from saying. Abby had cracked open his heart and crawled inside before she'd ever put her mouth on him, and the urge to tell her was as strong as his desire to help her dreams come true. But while he was thirty-eight and ready for more, Abby was just getting started. It might be too soon for her, too fast, and their lives too far apart to put that kind of pressure on her.

Instead, he lifted her into his arms and carried her into the bedroom, determined to show her exactly how incredible and special she was.

CHAPTER FIFTEEN

"HEADS UP, GORGEOUS," Aiden said as they made the bed Saturday morning.

He tossed her a pillow, and as she placed it by the headboard, he walked around the bed and took her in his arms, gazing at her with the smile she knew by heart. He thought she wore her heart on her sleeve, but little did he know that he was just as transparent. She liked cataloging his expressions, like the certain look in his eyes when he needed to kiss her versus when he simply *wanted* to and another that showed a hint of worry when he had something heavy to talk about. Then there was the dreamy expression she didn't really know how to pinpoint except that when that look came over him, he was utterly relaxed and happy and kisses were not far behind. She'd seen that look a lot more often lately.

"I have to ask you an important question and I want you to think carefully before you answer."

His expression was so serious, it made her nerves prickle. "Okay."

"You and I are getting pretty close, wouldn't you agree?"

"Mm-hm."

"And we're fairly compatible."

"I'd say *very*, but okay."

"I didn't want to seem too presumptuous, since you don't love having expectations."

"I'm finding them much less scary lately."

"Good to know," he said, deadly serious. "So, we agree, we're *very* compatible."

"Ask the question already. You're making me nervous."

"It's a tough one. Do you like your pancakes with chocolate chips or blueberries? Or do you prefer them plain?"

She swatted his chest. "You're a brat! What does that have to do with how close we're getting and how compatible we are?"

"Nothing. I wanted to see where you stood now that I've met your friends."

"Seriously? I guess getting down on my knees in the hallway wasn't a clear enough indicator of how I feel about you."

His eyes darkened. "Baby, the minute we kissed, all thoughts went out the window." He pressed his lips to hers, taking her in a slow, sweet, excruciatingly delicious kiss. "See? Just like that. *Brain-dead.*" He hooked an arm around her shoulder, heading out of the bedroom, and said, "So, am I too old to be called your boyfriend? Because I like that a lot better than *handyman.*"

"I like it better, too. I didn't want to be too presumptuous when I introduced you."

"Be presumptuous. I told you I'm a possessive guy with you, and I meant it. So, pancakes?"

Overflowing with happiness, she said, "Are you really making breakfast, or was that all a ploy to see where I stood?"

"I'm really making breakfast." He stopped in the hallway and gazed deeply into her eyes, as if he were seeing her for the first time. He touched her face, shook his head, and said, "You are truly beautiful, Abs. Inside and out. Pretty soon you're going to be spending a lot of time cooking for other people. I want to do this for you."

The things he said, and the way he was looking at her, were *everything.* "Thank you."

They picked up the clothes they'd left strewn on the stairs on their way down, and a thrill darted through her with the memories of their lovemaking and how bold she'd been.

"You know, you could have just asked me where I stood."

"What fun would that have been?" He dangled her panties from his fingers and said, "Good thing Cait didn't see these."

Cait! How had she forgotten that Cait was joining them for breakfast? They'd taken their sweet time getting out of bed and then fooled around in the shower, taking even longer. She'd been beyond excited last night when they'd decided to surprise Cait with their skating adventure after meeting with the girls at the Bistro this morning. It felt very sisterly, and she was glad Aiden was going to be a part of it. But then he'd kissed her, which had led to all sorts of sensually scrumptious things, and she'd completely forgotten about seeing Cait this morning.

She finally understood why people said they were *screwed senseless.*

The smell of coffee hit her nose as she picked up her bra from the bottom step. She peeked into the kitchen, finding Cait sitting at the kitchen table with a cup of coffee in front of her and a cheesy grin on her face.

Cait waved. "Looks like someone had fun last night."

Aiden chuckled and plucked Abby's bra from her hands, bundling it with the rest of their clothes as Abby buried her face in his chest and groaned.

"Based on the clothing trail you left, I'd think you would be celebrating, not groaning," Cait said.

Aiden kissed the top of Abby's head and said, "I take full responsibility."

Abby pried herself from his chest and said, "Why do I feel like I got caught making out under the bleachers?"

"I've never done that," Aiden said with a devilish grin. "Shall we go find some? Add it to our list?"

They all laughed.

Aiden carried their clothes into the laundry room, and Cait said, "Relax, Abby. I'm your sister, not your judge. Besides, you two are good together. I'm glad it's not all work and no play." She lifted her mug as Aiden walked back into the kitchen and said, "I made coffee. It's not nearly as good as Aiden gets from Keira, but it won't kill you."

Aiden and Abby exchanged glances. Aiden had turned her into a coffee snob, too. No other coffee tasted good to her anymore. And now that she knew about his mornings with his father, she had a feeling nothing ever would.

"Aiden's making pancakes this morning. Why don't you and I go to Keira's and pick up some coffee and a newspaper?"

Aiden winked.

"Thank God." Cait dumped her coffee in the sink, looking cute in skinny jeans and a white T-shirt, and said, "I suck at making coffee."

Aiden kissed Abby and said, "You can take my rental." He dug his keys from the pocket of his jeans. "You never answered me about the pancakes, Abs. Chocolate chips, blueberries, or plain?"

"I'm a glutton. I want chocolate chips and blueberries," Abby said.

"A woman after my own heart. Cait?" Aiden asked.

"I'm good with both, thanks."

As they headed outside, Cait said, "Tank says I should never be allowed to make coffee."

"I'll show you how to make it, but between you and me, I can't get enough of that special coffee Keira makes for Aiden."

"Based on that twinkle in your eyes, I'd say you can't get enough of *him*, either."

"I think we've proven that women should rule the world," Leni said later that morning at the Bistro. Her auburn hair framed her face, and her green shirt set off her flawless, fair skin. "In a matter of hours, we've come up with a grassroots campaign *and* a big-picture marketing plan that fits your budget and should bring you excellent exposure."

"Your brain never fails to amaze me," Daphne said. She had come up with so many great marketing ideas, it was no wonder the winery already had a waiting list for events.

"It's almost like Leni does marketing for a living," Jules said as she pulled her hair into a ponytail, her cropped yellow sweater exposing the top of her high-waisted jeans.

"That's why they pay her the big bucks," Abby said.

Abby was overwhelmed by the generosity of her friends. They'd come armed with lists of ideas and contacts, worked through lunch—they'd ordered pizza—and had not only helped her devise marketing plans, but they'd also provided more ideas for the logo and nailing down the menu design. Cait's mock-ups for the logo were gorgeous, using soothing blues and browns with just a hint of gold, giving them a touch of class. Some were more elaborate than others, and all the girls agreed that they should go with a fluid, clean design, focusing on the name of the restaurant and giving it an upscale beachy feel. Cait was going to work up another idea for the logo this week using hers and Abby's favorite elements of the mock-ups she'd shared.

"Speaking of earning big bucks," Leni said. "Cait, you're incredibly talented. Would you ever consider doing graphic design for corporations?"

"No offense, but *no*," Cait answered. "I like doing my own thing."

Leni said, "I guess I'll scratch *recruit Cait* off my list."

"*Hey*, get your claws away from my sister. I just found her, and I'm not giving her up without a fight," Abby said, earning the biggest grin from Cait. "You guys are amazing. I can't believe it's all coming together." Excitement bubbled up inside her. "Holy cow, Cait. We're really doing this!"

They all laughed.

Abby took a deep breath and voiced the worry that had been nagging at her. "Hopefully I'll get approved for the line of credit I applied for, or else all of this will be for naught."

"What do you mean?" Leni asked.

"With the insurance money we inherited and my savings, we still didn't have enough capital to make it work. It's much more expensive than I realized. I need to have two months of capital up front so I can order food and pay staff. I don't know what I was thinking, but I should be okay if I get approved for the home equity line of credit. Thank goodness Aiden went with me to the bank. I almost went with a loan instead of a line of credit, which would have cost me a lot more in interest. I should hear if it's approved Monday or Tuesday. I keep telling myself they *have* to approve it, since our house is worth so much, but the truth is, I'm scared shitless. Without enough money for inventory, staff, and everything else it will take to get this off the ground, even if I win the competition, I can't open the restaurant unless I run it as a one- or two-person show, which would be impossible."

"Is there another way to get the money?" Daphne asked.

"Yes. There's an investment company that wanted to buy the restaurant, and Aiden thinks we could approach them for an angel investment deal instead of a purchase. He also offered to invest."

Cait's eyes widened. "He did?"

Abby nodded. "I said *no*, of course."

"That was smart. If there's one thing that can kill a relationship, it's mixing business with pleasure. Abby, how much money are we talking about?" Leni asked.

"A lot. *Way* too much for him to be offering. I really want to do this on my own, with my sisters. I don't want an investor hovering over me, much less to feel indebted to Aiden. I mean, it was sweet of him to offer, but like you said, it's not smart."

"He must really believe in you to offer you money," Jules said.

Abby sat back and felt a smile tugging at her lips. "He does, and it's the most incredible thing I've ever experienced. I can't wait to show him the menu design and logo ideas."

"Where is he today?" Daphne asked. "I thought he was helping you with all of this."

"He is helping, but he's supposed to be on vacation, remember? He and Brant were going sailing this morning." She wished she could have gone with them. She'd love to see Aiden piloting a boat, the wind bringing out his curls, and kissing him as they sailed swiftly through the water, the ocean breeze on their faces.

"You've got that dreamy look again, like you did last night," Jules said.

"It looks good on her," Daphne said. "Doesn't it?"

Abby rolled her eyes. "Stop." Her phone vibrated, and she pulled it from her pocket. Her pulse quickened at the sight of Aiden's name on the screen. *Hey, Abs, I'm running pretty late. Sorry. Can I meet you and Cait a few hours later? 6:00 at the Bistro?* A wave of disappointment washed through her.

"What's wrong?" Cait asked.

"Nothing. Aiden's running late." She thumbed out a reply—*Sure. Thanks for letting me know*—trying to quell the hurt of being pushed to the back burner, and at the same time, she knew it wasn't fair for her to be hurt. He had a right to enjoy his vacation, and skating with her and Cait probably wasn't nearly as fun as sailing with Brant.

Leni sat back and studied her. "And you're upset?"

"*No*, just disappointed. We had something planned that I was really looking forward to."

Leni held her gaze with a look only a best friend could serve up—the one that said something was going on, and she was going to get to the bottom of it. "You know, you dated Paul for a *long* time, and you were never this invested."

"Not everyone who dates is meant to be together forever," Abby said as she put her phone in her pocket.

"I get that," Leni said. "But you never put in much effort with Paul, and here you are, in the middle of *huge* life changes, moving back to the island and opening the restaurant, which would be enough to make *me* more closed off than ever, and you seem to be letting Aiden *in*."

"Ever heard of chemistry?" Jules asked.

Leni gave her a big-sister eye roll. "Yeah, I get that. Even though I only went out with Abby and Paul a few times, the difference in how she and Aiden look at each other and treat each other is obvious. But why are you willing to put in so much effort when your entire life is up in the air?"

"I don't know," Abby admitted. "I'm sure this will sound like I'm lying, but I honestly don't think I'm putting in more effort. I'm not shirking responsibilities to be with Aiden; we're doing it together. This thing between us isn't me rearranging my schedule to fit him into it. It's just *happening*. We met, we clicked, and we really like each other. I haven't ever had a relationship like this before."

"That's how it was with me and Jock," Daphne said. "Suddenly we did everything together, and life was fuller and better. I was a nervous wreck at first because he had trouble with little ones, and I have Hadley, but it was worth every second."

"But, Abby, what happens when he goes back to wherever he came from?" Leni asked.

Leni had always been straightforward, and Abby usually loved that about her, but she didn't want to think about Aiden leaving. "We haven't gotten that far, Leni. We've talked about still seeing each other, but you know me. I don't like to put expectations on people."

"The look on your face when you got that text told me otherwise," Leni challenged.

"In Abby's defense, how can you build a relationship without expectations?" Cait asked.

"That's exactly my point," Leni said with a softer tone. "Relationships take trust, and trust builds expectations."

Frustrated, Abby pushed to her feet and paced. "But not expectations of a future. It's not like I'm pining for a wedding ring. We just started seeing each other a little over a week ago."

"I can't believe you've only been together that long. You guys are so comfortable with each other," Jules said. "When you looked at each other last night and the other day when I saw you in town, it was like you two could read each other's minds."

"That's exactly how it feels," Abby confessed. "And I know it makes no sense, but we're *that* good together, and I'm happy for the first time in years. He *gets* me, you guys. He fosters my friendships, he values family as much as I do, and he supports my ideas. Although he pushes, too, like signing me up for the competition when I said I didn't want to do it."

Leni raised her index finger toward the ceiling and said, "He gets extra brownie points from me for doing that."

"Great. I'll tell him that," Abby said. "That's what I mean. His *bad* thing is a *good* thing. Is it a crime that I want to enjoy it and not worry about if we're going to last past these few weeks?"

"No, that's not a crime." Leni pushed to her feet, stepping into Abby's path, and said, "But the fact that you think we don't realize you're lying to us about not being worried is ridiculous."

"I am *not* lying," Abby said as a kernel of guilt lodged in her chest.

Leni crossed her arms and arched a brow, and Abby couldn't keep a straight face. Laughter bubbled out, and they all laughed with her. She stalked around Leni and plopped into a chair with a heavy sigh. "I'm screwed, aren't I?"

"If the panties and bra on the stairs this morning were any indication," Cait said sassily, "I'd say you got good and screwed last night."

"*What?*" Leni shrieked.

Daphne giggled, and Jules popped to her feet and began singing to the tune of "Hot in Herre" by Nelly. "He got a whole lotta, *ah, uh* . . ." She accentuated the last two sounds with hip thrusts. "She got a whole lotta, *ah, ah.*"

"*Nooo! Stop!*" Leni covered her ears.

The next few hours flew by with old-school girl talk, which was exactly what Abby needed. Jules and Daphne left midafternoon, but Leni stayed all day. She lectured Abby about trying to manage her expectations with Aiden, but she also raved about him again and reminded her that her cousin thought the world of him. She invited them to spend Mother's Day with their family, but Abby secretly had plans to make Cait and Aiden a delicious brunch, and she hoped to go through more of her mother's things. By the time Leni left, Abby realized once again that she'd made the right decision by coming home to rebuild her life. With Leni's and the rest of her friends' support, she would always have a shoulder to lean on.

As she and Cait locked up the restaurant, the late-afternoon sun shone down on them, and the sounds of the waves kissing the shore was music to Abby's ears. "Ready for your surprise?"

"*My* surprise?" Cait looked skeptical. "I should clue you in to the fact that I'm not big on surprises."

She draped an arm over Cait's shoulder and said, "You survived finding out you had two sisters. I think you can survive this."

They walked around the side of the Bistro, heading for the parking lot. Abby's heart skipped at the sight of Aiden with his Silver Island hat on and three sets of skates in his hands. That skipping warred with her earlier disappointment, which she'd all but forgotten about until now. It gnawed at her like a rat stuck in a maze.

Conflicting emotions swam in Abby's eyes, and Aiden knew it was because he'd been running late. He could only imagine how she'd feel when he told her he was leaving Monday morning. He had been having a great day until he'd received a call from George Pennington, the founder of Pennington Development Group, one of his father's old clients. His grandson Damon had taken over last year, and they were expanding the business in a new direction. Aiden had already invested heavily in the company, and now they needed more capital. Although Aiden believed in the company's potential, he preferred to keep his portfolio diverse and had already invested all he was willing to. George was taking his financial team on a *road show*—hitting four cities in five days, pitching to groups of potential investors to sell additional interests in the business—and they had a better chance of winning over other investors with Aiden on board for the presentations. Aiden had known about the road show two months ago, but while he'd suggested he go with them, they had initially turned down his offer. He wasn't surprised at their last-minute reality check. It was a much smarter business move to bring him along, even if the last thing he wanted to do was leave Abby.

"Hey there, stranger," Abby said.

"Hi, babe. Are you ladies ready for our roller derby?" Aiden asked lightly, though he felt anything but light.

"We're really doing this?" Cait asked as he handed her a pair of skates.

"Hell yes. You can't go your whole life not knowing how to skate." He pointed to the open trunk of his rental car and said, "Helmets and knee pads are in there."

"If I break an arm, Tank is going to be pretty upset," Cait said as they retrieved the rest of their gear.

Cait sat down on the grass to put on her skates, and Aiden kissed Abby's cheek, guiding her a few feet away. As they sat down to put them on, he said, "I'm sorry for running so late."

"It's okay."

"It's not okay, Abs, but it couldn't be avoided. I am sorry."

She focused on putting on her skates, but his chatty girl had gone reticent.

"Talk to me, Abs."

"I *hate* the way I feel right now," she said in a hushed and anguished tone. "I *was* disappointed because I was so excited to surprise Cait, and you knew that. But it's not like you canceled, and it's not like we have some great commitment. Not to mention that this is *your* vacation. You're supposed to be out having fun, not only doing things for me. I feel stupid for even being disappointed in the first place, but I was."

"You have every right to feel slighted, and I am so very sorry. Hell, I was disappointed in myself, but the delay couldn't be avoided. I had to get a few things done, and they took longer than I anticipated. I texted the second I realized I'd be late."

"I thought you were out sailing with Brant all day."

"That was the plan, but you know what they say about best-laid plans." He pulled on kneepads and put on his skates. As he laced them up, he said, "I also got some bad news today. One of my father's old buddies—a client of his—needs my help next week. He's in a pretty dire situation. I'm taking a five o'clock flight Monday morning to New York so I have time to swing by my place, change into a suit, and pack. I'm meeting my client in Manhattan at ten, and we've got meetings in New York, Chicago, LA, and Boston. I'll be gone until late Friday evening."

"Oh. Okay." Confusion joined the disappointment in her eyes, but she quickly put on a braver face and said, "I thought you lived in LA?"

"I've got a place in New York, too, because I work there often. I've got a few places of my own."

"A *few*?"

"Some people invest in 401(k)s. I happen to like real estate and businesses."

"Wow, okay. You weren't kidding about traveling a lot for work, were you?" She managed a smile and said, "Does Remi know?"

"No. This client doesn't work through my assistant. He called me directly. I'll call Remi at some point. She knows that I don't put off my father's friends or clients." He was pretty sure Remi would go off on him, but Abby didn't need to worry about that. He took her hand and said, "I hope you know that leaving is the last thing I want to do, and I'll bust my ass to get back as soon as I can. I hate that I'll miss helping you for these next few days. I was looking forward to painting with everyone."

"It's fine. I totally understand." A real, though tempered smile appeared, and she said, "You have a life, Aiden, and that's something we can't pretend doesn't exist."

"For the first time in my life, I wish I could. I'm sorry about being late today and about leaving Monday." He kissed her and said, "I'll make it up to you when I get back."

As he pushed to his feet, Cait crawled over to them, cutting through the remaining tension. She went up on her knees, planted her hands on her hips, and said, "You didn't think I was going to try to stand up in these things alone, did you?"

"Heck no." Aiden reached for her hand, bringing her to her feet. Cait clung to him as he helped Abby up. He put his arms around their waists and said, "A beautiful woman on each arm. I feel like the luckiest guy on Silver Island."

Cait smirked. "If I get hurt, you'll be the deadest guy on Silver Island."

Offering to teach two women to skate had been Aiden's first mistake.

He had only two hands, and while Abby had fairly good balance, when she got talking, she forgot to pay attention to skating, tripping herself up a multitude of times. Cait, on the other hand, was a walking calamity. When Aiden told her to *glide*, she did some kind of stomp-dance-trip step, stumbling so many times, he worried she might end up in the emergency room.

"I think I've got it!" Abby exclaimed. "Give me space."

Abby shooed them away, her knees buckling, and she wasn't even skating yet. She wobbled, her arms flailing. Aiden held on to Cait, dragging her back toward Abby. He reached for Abby just as she thrust her hand out, catching Cait's shirt, causing them all to lose their balance. Their legs shot up, arms flailing, *yelps* sounding, as they tumbled to a pile on the pavement.

"Everyone okay?" Aiden asked as Cait and Abby peeled themselves off each other and burst into hysterics.

"My ass hurts," Cait complained.

"At least it's hot!" Abby slapped Cait's ass, giving in to another fit of laughter.

Cait snort-laughed. "If you're into *bruises*!"

"Did you guys have a few drinks that I'm not aware of?" Aiden asked. They were a hot mess, but he was having a blast. He pulled out his phone and navigated to the camera as they cracked up and made more jokes.

They made silly faces and bunny ears, which made them laugh even harder. Abby put an arm around each of them and said, "Smile, guys. This one's going on the Christmas card."

Forgoing any more bruises, they decided to get some ice cream before heading back to the house. The delicious treat and the memories of their first trip to the ice cream shop, which had led to Abby and Aiden's first incredible kiss, went a long way to soothe the bruises that were probably forming on Aiden's ass. Or maybe it was the thought of fulfilling the promise he'd made to Abby of giving her a full-body massage later. He glanced at her in the passenger seat scrolling through the pictures he'd taken on his phone.

"Oh my gosh, look at this one." She leaned over the back of the seat to show Cait the picture. "You're laughing so hard."

"I guarantee I won't be laughing tomorrow. I'll be lucky if I can sit down." Cait shifted in the back seat.

Abby righted herself in her seat, chatting about the other pictures. "I'm sending this one to myself so I can send it to Deirdra." As she did so, she said, "And these are going to Remi right now. Don't worry, Aid. I'll tell her it's me texting from your phone."

He had never in his entire life let a woman do anything more than use his phone to make a call, and yet here he was, giving Abby full rein and loving every one of her comments, and her inclusion of his sister.

As he pulled into the driveway, his nerves knotted up. Abby was looking down at the phone when he parked in front of the house.

Cait opened her door and said, "Wow, Abby, I guess your lawn guys came."

"I don't have—" Abby looked up, and her jaw dropped. She opened the door and climbed out.

Aiden came around the front of the car in time to see her eyes light up. He'd spent the entire day power washing the house, cleaning up her front yard, rototilling the gardens so they would be ready for planting, and repairing the fencing.

"Look at the gardens. It's like they're brand-new, and the fence is fixed. Oh my gosh, the *house*. It's white again." Abby sounded like she might cry.

"Did our mom have a gardener or a handyman?" Cait asked.

"If she did, he sure let the yard go to he—" Abby looked at Aiden, understanding dawning in her eyes. "Did you hire someone to do this?"

"That would have been the smart thing to do, but *no*. I borrowed Brant's pressure washer and picked up a few other tools in town."

"Is this why you didn't go sailing?" she asked. "This is why you were late to meet us?"

Now she looked like she might cry, and his gut twisted. Had he done the wrong thing? Lord knew he was good at stepping on people's toes.

"The pressure washer stopped working, and I had to wait for Brant to come over to fix it," he explained. "I wanted to get it done today because tomorrow is Mother's Day, and I thought you and Cait might want to work in the garden together."

Abby covered her mouth, tears brimming. "Oh, *Aiden*," she said as her tears broke free. She threw her arms around his neck and kissed him. "Thank you. You can't imagine how much this means to me."

"And to *me*," Cait said softly. "Thank you, but you're not getting a kiss."

He pressed his lips to Abby's. "You're both welcome, and these are the only lips I need."

CHAPTER SIXTEEN

SUNDAY AFTERNOON, ABBY was wrist deep in dirt, with the sun shining on her face, and loving every second of it. She still couldn't believe Aiden had done so much to make her house and yard beautiful again. He was kneeling in the dirt a few feet away, chatting with Cait as they planted vegetables. After they devoured the surprise Mother's Day brunch she'd made, the three of them had gone to the nursery and picked out vegetable plants. They'd also chosen others to plant later in the season. Abby hadn't enjoyed Mother's Day this much since her father was alive. Deirdra had always had an excuse not to visit on Mother's Day, but Abby had made it a point to come home for the weekend. The holiday hadn't been easy for her mother. She'd missed Deirdra, and their father, which had led to more drinking. Aiden's thoughtfulness took what could have been a sad day and turned it into a day of coming together.

He looked over and winked, handsome and rugged in his Silver Island hat and shorts. She was wearing the baseball cap he'd given her the second day he'd helped at the restaurant. "I thought I felt your eyes on me. Do you need something, babe?"

Yes, your lips on mine, please.

She shook her head and said, "Just enjoying the view."

Last night, when he'd thought she was asleep, he'd whispered about how he didn't want to leave her and how that freaked him out a little.

She'd been tempted to let him know she was awake and tell him that she was thrown by the power of their relationship, too. But she'd lain still. She may have hoped she wouldn't form expectations, but they were blossoming anyway, and hearing his private thoughts had helped tamp down the anxiousness those feelings caused.

But he deserved to have his worries eased, too, so she said, "Actually, I was thinking about how much I'll miss you when you're gone. Other than my father, I don't think I've ever missed a man."

"I'll miss you, too," he said, emotions taking root between them like the vegetables they were planting. "We won't go long between calls."

Cait looked up from where she was working, her eyes hidden behind her sunglasses as she said, "If we're confessing, can I get in on it? I missed you guys when I was gone, and I never miss anyone. It was weird. Tank realized something was wrong and thought I had found a boyfriend and wanted to come check him out."

"We thought about you when you were gone, too," Abby said. "Aiden and I were talking the other day about how it felt weird when you were gone. I had joked about how maybe the stars were starting to align for the first time in our lives, and you were helping it happen."

"I like that thought," Cait said.

"I do, too. I guess this means I haven't totally failed in the new-sister department."

"You've got to be kidding. You and Deirdra are awesome," Cait reassured her. "I think Deirdra might have started texting me because she wanted to be sure you were okay and Aiden wasn't a jerk, but we've become friends. She's always so busy. I have no idea how she can live like that. I mean, we all work a lot, but we have downtime, too, and I have a bruised butt to prove it. But even at night she's working when she texts."

"Sounds like my normal life," Aiden said.

"We're all workaholics," Abby said. "But there's this new guy in my life who keeps giving me a reason to slow down and smell the roses."

She never would have taken an entire day just to enjoy being back on the island if not for him. And she was so glad she'd done it.

He blew her a kiss. "I can say the same for you."

Aiden's phone rang. He wiped his hands on his shorts and pulled it from his back pocket, glancing at the screen. "It's Remi. I guess Mason gave her the Mother's Day gift I sent." He pushed to his feet, walking out of the fenced area as he answered the FaceTime call.

Remi's voice exploded from the phone. "*Aiden!* Thank you! I love my gift so much!"

Aiden had shown Abby a picture of the gift he'd had made for Remi's first Mother's Day as a foster parent. It was a framed collage of family photographs from Remi's childhood, with a picture of Remi, Mason, and the girls in the center. The mat around the collage was made of paper ornaments Remi and her mother had made from the pages of their father's favorite books. Aiden had gone on to describe how much Remi loved making them, and he'd said that when they'd moved from West Virginia, she'd taken their father's books and their mother's crafting supplies. To this day, she continued making ornaments and had even taught the girls to do it.

It was such a thoughtful gift, Abby had fallen harder for the man who was nothing like the *regular* guy he claimed to be.

She didn't want to eavesdrop, but their voices were hard to miss. She heard Aiden talking to Patrice and Olive, the love in his voice inescapable.

"Abs, Cait," Aiden hollered. "Come say hello to my family."

Cait looked like she was going to beg out of it, so Abby dragged her to her feet.

Cait gave her an imploring look. "I don't want to impose. You're his girlfriend. You should go."

"You're my family, and he's my guy. Do it for me?"

"Fine," Cait said begrudgingly, though her smile told Abby she didn't really mind.

Aiden introduced Cait to Remi and the girls, and he introduced Olive, a pretty blonde with a sweet face and wavy hair that hung just past her shoulders, to both of them. Since Abby had already told Cait about Remi being *the* Remi Divine, she kept her fangirling to a minimum. But it was cute to see her gushing. While Patrice chatted about the breakfast they'd made for Remi, Olive kept looking at Abby and Aiden.

"Can you believe I ate *four* pancakes?" Patrice exclaimed.

"I believe you," Remi said, kissing Patrice's head. "You're my little pancake gobbler."

Patrice beamed at her. "And I'm Uncle Aiden's Patty Cake. Are Abby and Cait your girlfriends, Uncle Aiden?"

"He doesn't have *two* girlfriends at the same time," Olive said sharply.

Aiden chuckled and said, "Abby is my girlfriend, and Cait is her sister."

"Olive is my foster sister," Patrice chimed in. "I've had lots of foster sisters, but I love Olive, and I hope she'll be my forever sister."

"Me too, squirt," Olive said. She and Patrice did some sort of secret handshake, which made Patrice giggle. The girls turned to Remi, and she did the handshake with them, too, followed by a group hug.

"Hey, I want in on that secret handshake and hug," Aiden said, and the girls lectured him about not being a sister or a mom.

Cait nudged Abby and whispered, "He really loves them, doesn't he?"

"He does," she said as the girls giggled.

"They're lucky," Cait whispered. "All of them."

Abby stepped closer to her and said, "I think we're pretty lucky, too. *All* of us."

After chatting with the girls and Remi, and finally meeting Mason, they said goodbye and went back to gardening. They worked until they'd planted everything they'd bought, and when Cait went into town to run an errand, Abby and Aiden decided to check something off his

Let Loose list and sacked out in the hammock. The feel of Aiden's arms around her, the sure and steady beat of his heart against her cheek, and the warmth of the sun lulled Abby to sleep.

When Cait got home, they headed inside and went through their mother's bedroom. They boxed up her parents' belongings, most of which would go to Goodwill, and Aiden carried them out to the garage as quickly as they could fill them up. They each chose a few items from their mother's jewelry box as keepsakes. Abby kept the ring her father used to wear and her mother's necklace she'd worn the first night Aiden had come over for dinner. Even though Deirdra had been adamant about not wanting anything, Abby saved the necklace Deirdra had made for their mother when Deirdra was nine. It was strange picking through her parents' things, but it was also cathartic, getting rid of the clutter of bad memories and holding on to the good ones.

After they were done, Cait said, "Do you think you'll move into this room?"

"No. It would feel weird," Abby said.

"Even if you paint it and replace the furniture with your things from New York? Make it your own?" Cait asked.

"I don't know. It was still my parents' bedroom, you know? I'll do all those things—paint, get rid of their furniture, and move my things in. But I don't think I want to sleep there."

"Maybe you can make it into an office," Cait suggested. "Or a nursery one day?"

Abby had never imagined having a family of her own. Maybe that was because she'd never been with anyone like Aiden, who not only supported her professional dreams but also made a point of suggesting she set up a schedule that would allow time for her to enjoy being back on the island and living her life. Her thoughts drifted to a different type of future, one with Aiden and a family of their own. She knew she was getting way ahead of herself, but if Abby believed in one thing, it was the power of dreaming. Even if she didn't *expect* something to happen, she could still wish for it.

"Maybe one day," she said.

"Have you read Mom's letter yet?" Cait asked.

"No. I feel like I'll know when the time is right. I'm waiting for a sign, which is silly, but whatever."

"It's not silly. I haven't read mine yet. Deirdra hasn't either, but I have a feeling she might never read it."

"That would be a shame. Mom obviously had things to say to us."

Cait sighed. "I agree. I'm going to make a quick call. I'll meet you downstairs to take on the junk room?"

"Sounds good. I'll be right down."

Abby stood on the hardwood floor looking at her mother's bed, remembering too many painful nights when she and Deirdra had struggled to get their inebriated mother upstairs and had wrestled to get pajamas on the woman who should have been taking care of them. Nights of Deirdra sitting in the yard planning her escape while Abby cried herself to sleep. A lump lodged in Abby's throat as happier memories trickled in—bounding into the bedroom and launching herself onto the bed when her parents were sleeping, greeted with tickles, laughter, and *I love you*s. On the heels of that memory came the one of crawling into her mother's bed the night her father died. She hadn't thought about that night in so long, she'd almost forgotten the way her mother had clung to her, crying so hard it had scared Abby. Deirdra had heard them sobbing and had climbed into bed with them. For the life of her, Abby couldn't remember how soon after that her mother had started drinking. The days were too muddled with grief. Maybe she'd never even known when it had started.

"You okay, Abs?" Aiden asked as he came down the hall.

Abby blinked away tears and said, "Yeah. It's weird to miss so much of who my mom once was and to hurt so badly for the parts of her that I don't miss. I'm glad she's in a better place. I hope she's happier."

He put his arm around her and ran his hand down her back. "I can only imagine." Pressing a kiss to the top of her head, he asked, "Do you want to talk about it?"

She shook her head. "I'm okay. I've been so busy, I haven't slowed down enough to really think about it."

"Maybe you should take a few days off and let yourself think about all of those things. The good, the bad, the happy, the sad. Or even better, do it when I get back, so you have me to lean on."

"Thank you for not brushing my feelings under the carpet, but I think I'm okay." She leaned her chin on his chest and said, "Cait asked if I wanted to move into this room, and I guess that sparked a few memories."

"Do you want to?"

"Move into the room? *No*, but when I ship my things from New York, I'll clear all of the old furniture out and freshen the house up, really make it mine."

"That sounds like a great idea."

"Speaking of good ideas, it sounded like Remi loved her gift. Has anyone ever told you how incredibly kind and considerate you are?"

"Maybe this stunning brunette who's knocked me off my feet a time or two." He gave her a kiss and swatted her butt. "Better get a move on before I drag you into your bedroom and make you *mine* again."

"You say that like it's some sort of threat, when actually, it's a pretty enticing idea," she said as he picked up a box and they headed for the stairs.

His eyes darkened. "It wasn't a threat, just fair warning."

Cait walked past the stairway carrying a box and stopped, giving them both a chiding stare. "I know that look, you two."

Abby tried to stifle her smile, feeling like the cat that ate the canary.

"I'm only taking this box to the garage. I'll be back inside in one minute," Cait warned. "Try to keep your clothes on until we're done."

She headed for the front door, and Aiden cocked a brow. "I think she's getting the hang of this big-sister stuff."

"Isn't it great?"

"Yeah, almost as great as the way you light up around her. Is it ever like that with you and Deirdra?"

"Sometimes. But other times we just roll our eyes at each other. Did I tell you she's coming to the tasting?"

"I think you might have mentioned it six or seven times since she texted two hours ago." He leaned down and kissed her.

"You two almost make relationships look worth the effort," Cait said as she walked past the stairs.

"You're as stealthy as a ninja," Aiden called down to her.

"What do you mean *almost*?" Abby asked.

Cait shrugged. "I like my solitude more than I like anything else in the entire world."

Abby watched her disappear down the hall toward the junk room and said, "Is it just me, or is that kind of sad?"

"You're asking the wrong guy. Before you jogged into my life, I treasured my solitude more than anything other than Remi."

He carried the box out to the garage, and Abby joined Cait in the junk room. Once they cleared the room of old furniture, some of which was headed to the dump, the rest to Goodwill, they started going through boxes. Abby was shocked that her mother had kept things like their old school backpacks, homework assignments, and even Deirdra's old skateboards. She found Deirdra's roller skates, too—every pair, right down to the ones her father had given her in first grade.

"Deirdra was a skater. What were you?" Aiden asked.

She didn't even have to think about her answer. "A dreamer."

"Thank goodness some things never change." Aiden opened another box and said, "How about you, Cait? What were you like when you were younger?"

Cait tucked her hair behind her ear and said, "I kept to myself. I wasn't into any sports, but I loved to climb trees and take walks. I'd find a place in a field or a park and draw for hours."

"I wish Deirdra and I had known you then," Abby said.

"Me too," Cait said.

They found boxes of her father's clothes, his easels and other painting supplies, and several of his paintings. Abby told them more stories about her father, and she got a little choked up as they looked over his things.

"Cait, I know you draw, but do you paint?" Abby asked.

"Sometimes," she said as Aiden pulled another box from the closet and began going through it.

"Would you like my dad's easels and the other supplies? I'd love to keep them in the family."

"Really? Are you sure you don't mind?"

"It would make me happy, and I know Deirdra would feel the same way." Abby pushed the boxes over to Cait.

Cait put one of her hands on top of two of the boxes ever so lightly, as if they were fine pieces of art, and said, "Thank you." She sat like that for a long time, and as Abby started going through another box, she said, "I've been thinking about the Bistro. How would you feel if I painted a mural on one wall? Remember the story Grant told us about your dad painting on the patio? I have this vision in my head of your father standing at his easel and our mother sitting on a chair with you on her lap and Deirdra behind her chair, leaning her elbow on the back of the chair, with her chin in her palm. You're all watching him paint. I can't seem to shake the idea, but if you'd rather I didn't, that's totally fine."

"Oh, Cait, that sounds beautiful. But it wouldn't feel right if you weren't represented, too. You're a big part of the Bistro now, and of our family."

"But I wasn't there," Cait said.

"I have a feeling you were never far from your mother's thoughts," Aiden said as he handed Cait a journal he'd been looking through. "Based on the dates in that journal, I'd say the baby Ava is talking about is you."

"What?" Abby moved next to Cait and scanned the pages the journal was open to.

The lump that had clogged Abby's throat earlier was back in full force as she read her mother's innermost thoughts about loving the child she would never have a chance to know. Cait turned the page, revealing more of their mother's heartbreaking sentiments about longing to hold and to get to know her baby.

"She loved me," Cait whispered, tears spilling down her cheeks.

Abby, swamped by her own emotions, could do little more than take hold of Cait's hand and choke out, "She did."

Aiden knelt between them and gathered them both in his arms, holding them as they wept for the mother and daughter who never had a chance to be together and for the sisters who had finally become a family.

Much later that evening, after clearing out the junk room, which was a pretty impressive master suite, they got cleaned up for dinner, and then Aiden turned on one of Abby's father's records and set the table while Abby gave Cait another cooking lesson. They enjoyed a delicious chicken Parmesan dinner, and as they cleared the table, Aiden twirled Abby around the kitchen to the sound of the Allman Brothers. He washed the dishes and Abby dried, while Cait stood at the counter drawing in one of her sketchbooks and telling them about a new tattoo she was designing for a client. Aiden tried to focus on what Cait was saying, but he was sidetracked, trying hard not to think about leaving in the morning and how much he hated the idea of missing almost an entire week with Abby.

Deirdra called as they finished cleaning up, and Abby answered on speakerphone as she dried the last pot. "Hi, Dee."

"Hey. I just finished working and wanted to see how you were holding up today."

"Aw. Are you getting sentimental on me?"

"*Please*," Deirdra said. "Are you okay?"

"Yes, I'm good. Thanks, Dee. Cleaning out Mom's room was weird, but it's done, and remember how bad the junk room was? I have to show you what we did. You can actually see the floor. I'm going to FaceTime you, so accept the call."

Deirdra groaned, and then her face appeared on the screen. Her hair was pinned up in a messy bun, and she looked tired.

"There you are. Say hi to Aiden and Cait." Abby moved the phone so Deirdra could see them.

Cait waved, and Aiden said, "Good to see you."

"Hi, you guys," Deirdra said with a tired smile. "How are you two doing this Mother's Day?"

"It's been the best one I've had in years," Aiden said honestly.

"Me too," Cait agreed.

"Guess what Aiden did?" Abby raved about the work he'd done outside, how they'd planted all morning, and how excited she was to have a garden again.

"That was really nice of you, Aiden," Deirdra said, a tinge of suspicion in her tone. "How long are you there for?"

"Actually, I'm heading out tomorrow for the week," he said regretfully. "I'll be back Friday and will stay until the following Sunday, when my vacation is over."

"But we're not talking about that because it bums me out," Abby said. "Let me show you the junk room and Mom's room."

When Abby left the kitchen, Cait said, "You're *leaving*?"

"Unfortunately. A client has an issue I have to take care of."

Abby came through the kitchen chatting on her way upstairs. And just like that his heart did a double take. *Damn.* He'd gone his entire life not thinking twice about taking care of business, and in the span of less than two weeks, Abby had not only gotten under his skin, but she'd become such a big part of him, he didn't want to leave her.

"Will you be here with Abby while I'm gone?" Aiden asked.

"Yes, until Friday morning."

"Good." He knew Abby could take care of herself, but he liked the idea of her having Cait to keep her company.

Abby returned a few minutes later, still talking to Deirdra. "I was thinking about using the junk room for my bedroom, unless you or Cait want to use it?"

"Not me," Deirdra said.

"I'm cool with staying in the apartment when I'm here. I really like having my own space," Cait said. "Unless you want the apartment for something else?"

"No, I just didn't want to make plans until I checked with you," Abby said. "I'm going to make a few calls tomorrow to have the boxes, Mom's bedroom furniture, and the rest of the stuff picked up. I'll swap the living room furniture with mine when I have it shipped. I'm excited to give the house a makeover."

"I can see that. Look how happy you are, and how much you've accomplished," Deirdra said earnestly. "Mom and Dad would be proud of you."

"Do you really think so? You never talk like that about Mom," Abby said, her words laced with emotion.

"I know I don't. It's harder for me than it is for you, but yes, I think they'd be very proud of everything you're doing."

Abby teared up.

"Oh no. Don't get all weepy on me." Deirdra raised her wineglass and said, "How about we make a toast instead?"

"Hold on!" Cait hurried out of the living room and returned with the bottle of champagne and the bottle of tequila they'd left in the foyer the other night. "Looks like Wells Silver is good for something after all." She held up the bottles and said, "Tequila or bubbly?"

"The bubbly is to celebrate Abby's win." Aiden took the bottle of champagne and set it aside.

"Tequila it is, then," Cait said.

"I like a confident man," Deirdra said.

"He's *taken*. Claws off," Abby said as she took three shot glasses out of a cabinet and set them on the counter.

Aiden put his arm around Abby and said, "Happily taken, babes." He kissed her temple.

As Cait poured the shots, Abby set the phone on the counter where Deirdra could see them.

Cait handed them each a glass and said, "What are we toasting?"

"I think we should toast our mother for bringing us all together," Deirdra said.

"Hear, hear," Aiden said.

They cheered, tapped their glasses, and drank their shots, while Deirdra sipped her wine.

"Woo-hoo!" Abby shouted. "Fill 'er up. We need to toast Aiden's mom."

"Oh boy, here we go. Aiden, I hope you have strong arms," Deirdra said as Cait refilled their glasses. "You might need to carry Abby to bed tonight. She's a total lightweight."

Abby glowered at her.

Aiden hugged her and said, "I'll gladly carry you anyway, sweetheart." Abby snuggled closer, turning soft green eyes on him, and he felt something inside him click into place—as if he'd always been slightly off-kilter, and she'd finally set him right.

Abby raised her glass and said, "To Aiden's mom for bringing him into this world, and to his parents for raising such an amazing man."

The girls cheered, and they all drank.

The rest of the night passed with sisterly banter and stolen kisses. Abby was tipsy when they finally ended the FaceTime call and Cait headed up to the apartment.

Abby hung on to Aiden as they made their way upstairs and said, "You're really handsome. Have I told you that? Like, super-duper handsome."

"Thank you, beautiful."

"And *sweet*. I know guys don't like to be called sweet, but it's true. I mean, you're manly and *incredibly* strong. But you're also sweet to your sister, the girls, *my* sisters. You're sweet to *me*," she said as they headed down the hall to the bedroom.

"You're so damn cute, you make me crazy."

She stepped in front of him, walking backward into the bedroom as she worked the buttons on his shirt open. Her cheeks were flushed, her eyes glittering flirtatiously.

Aiden worried she'd had too much to drink and put his hand over hers, pressing it to his chest. "Babes . . ."

Her eyes narrowed seductively. "Aiden Aldridge, I know you are a gentleman, but I promise you, I am not drunk, and this is our last night together until Friday. You'd *better* let me get you naked."

"God, I adore you."

He lowered his lips to hers, savoring the taste of desire and happiness all wrapped up into one enchanting woman. They kissed as they stripped each other bare, touching and tasting each other's bodies. How would he go almost a week without holding her in his arms? He laid her on the bed and sheathed himself, gazing into her eyes as he came down over her. She wrapped her arms around his neck and hooked her heels around the backs of his thighs as their bodies slowly and perfectly became one. Another shift took place inside him, and she sighed, as if she'd felt it, too.

"Jesus, *Abby*." He cradled her face between his hands, overwhelmed by the feelings consuming him. She whispered his name, so full of emotions he wanted to drench himself in them and hear her say it every day for the rest of his life. He touched his forehead to hers, and his heart slipped out. "I'm falling so hard for you, Abby, and I don't want to stop."

She put her hand on his cheek, and he leaned into it, soaking in the feel of her as she said, "You were so unexpected. I think I tripped on day one and have been rolling ever since."

He lifted his head so he could see her face, and the emotions gazing back at him brought a thrust of his hips. *Fuuck.* He wanted to be so deep inside her, he didn't know where she ended and he began. He'd never felt so in *and* so out of control, but there was no stopping it now.

"You probably won't remember saying that in the morning, but I sure hope you do."

Her eyes sparked with something even more intense than before as she said, "I haven't forgotten a single moment we've shared or a single word we've said." Her lips curved up. "Not since the first time I saw you sitting on the patio of the Bistro in your fancy clothes and those *sexy* loafers, reading the newspaper."

Man, she made him smile. "Why does everyone hate my loafers?"

"It turns out, I have quite a thing for a particular guy in loafers." She lifted her head off the pillow and kissed him. "And an even bigger thing for that same guy naked."

"Abigail de Messiéres," he whispered against her cheek, "you have stolen my heart, and every other piece of me. I'm going to miss you." He lowered his lips to hers and spent half the night showing her just how much.

CHAPTER SEVENTEEN

ROAD SHOWS WERE grueling, though imperative, for companies such as Pennington Development Group, which had enormous potential but lacked capital. Aiden was normally laser focused during the presentation and investor Q and A, but today his thoughts were back on Silver Island with the sexy brunette he'd poured his heart out to last night and had reluctantly left in bed this morning. Abby had put on a brave face when he'd kissed her goodbye, but there was no masking the longing in her eyes or the ache in his heart as he'd walked out that door. He'd texted her on his way into the city, but he hadn't had a break since. The presentation lasted all day, as underwriters and members of the management team, including Aiden, as a representative of the company, introduced the opportunity to potential investors, analysts, and fund managers in an effort to interest them in investing. They covered the history, vision, and goals of the company, as well as its financial performance, projected growth, and earnings forecasts. When the presentations were over, he and the team went to dinner, and then they headed to the airport—next stop, Chicago, where they'd do it all over again.

After going through airport security, Aiden excused himself from the group to call Abby. It was already eleven o'clock. He hoped she was still up. She answered on the first ring, and he swore his entire body exhaled at the sound of her voice.

"Hi, Abs. Sorry to call so late."

"That's okay. How are you? How are your meetings going?"

"They're long, but they're going well. How are you, babe?"

"I'm good. It's been a crazy day here, too. I got approved for the line of credit, which is a huge relief."

"Awesome. I knew you would." He was proud of her for doing it on her own, but he gritted his teeth at the idea of Abby accumulating debt when he could write a check and give her everything she needed.

"Thanks. I'm thrilled. Justin and Blaine Wicked, from Cape Stone, worked all day and finished the patio and the flooring. They're incredible. Tomorrow their father, Rob Wicked, the owner of Cape Renovations, is coming with his guys to do the inspection and then start the ordering window and . . ."

She continued telling him about the renovations and the work she and Cait were doing, but the more she talked, the more he missed her, and if he didn't let that out, he was going to lose his mind.

"We're picking up the computer tomorrow. Cait touts herself as a tattooist, but she's a literal computer *genius*. I swear if we locked you two in a room, you could fix all of the world's economic probl—"

"Abs, I'm sorry to interrupt. I'm interested in everything you're saying, but *damn*, baby, I *miss* you. I need you to know that."

"Oh, *Aiden*," she said longingly. "I thought if I talked fast I wouldn't feel the ache of missing you so badly."

Wishing he could hold her in his arms, he said, "How'd that work out for you?"

"Sucky."

He heard her smile in her voice. "What have you done to me, Abs? Before I met you, I'd have memorized every word out of everyone's mouth in that meeting. But I couldn't concentrate on anything but wishing I could be there with you. How messed up is that?"

"Um . . . ? I *think* I'm supposed to say that it's pretty messed up, but I'm in the same boat. At least we're lost at sea together."

"Yeah." He leaned his forearm against the wall, dipping his head for privacy, and said, "I want you in my arms, Abby, in my *bed*. I want to get on a different plane and head back to Silver Island. I want to look into your eyes and hold you while you fall asleep. I want to hear you snore and soak in that adorable little *hum* that follows."

"I do not *snore*, but if you think a hum is adorable, I'll own up to that."

He closed his eyes, feeling more vulnerable than he ever had, and that brought on the in- and out-of-control feelings again. He stood up and rolled his shoulders back, trying to regain control of his emotions, and said, "Listen, Abs. I won't get to my hotel in Chicago until after two a.m. I'm not going to call and wake you, okay?"

"Okay, but just so you know, I wore your hat today, and I'm sleeping in one of your shirts."

His chest squeezed. "I love that. Take a picture and send it to me."

"I'll do you one better and take a picture of what's *under* the shirt," she said seductively.

"Baby, you do that and I'm on the next plane home." *Home? Where did that come from?*

"I'm stripping naked right now!" she said with a giggle.

They talked until his plane was boarding. He felt rejuvenated by their call, but as he took his seat on the plane, a knot of longing lodged in his gut. His phone dinged with a text. He was careful to open it with the screen facing away from the guy next to him just in case Abby had gotten bold. But she'd sent something even better than a picture of her gorgeous body—a picture of her beautiful smiling face. A second picture popped up. Abby must have had Cait take it, because her back was facing the camera, his T-shirt hanging nearly to the backs of her knees. She had wrapped her arms around herself, and it looked like someone was embracing her. A third picture popped up of Abby facing the camera with her hand palm up in front of her puckered lips, blowing him a kiss. She looked so fucking sexy and sweet he wanted to crawl through the phone and devour her.

A text message appeared. *Now you can look into my eyes and pretend those are your arms around me. The rest will have to wait.* She added a winking emoji.

His heart squeezed as he thumbed out a response. *I can't wait to hold you. I've never felt this way before. I miss you more than words can express, Abs.* He added a kissing emoji, laughing to himself. *A fucking kissing emoji.* Remi would have a field day with that one.

CHAPTER EIGHTEEN

BY WEDNESDAY AFTERNOON, Abby felt like her father's old boom box. She couldn't tune in to any station except one—*Aiden*. And not for lack of trying. She'd been busy every minute.

Rob Wicked and his sons Zeke and Zander had inspected the building and found a couple of minor issues with the roof and rotted wood in a few parts of the building. They'd also found a leak in the bathroom. It had taken them all day to complete most of the work and had set her back a pretty penny, but the peace of mind had been worth it. While they'd taken care of those issues, Abby had worked with Cait. They'd finalized a simple, classy logo, which they were both thrilled with. *The Bistro* was written in elegant ocean-blue font, with the tails of the *T* and *B* a textured sand color fading into gold at the tips. When they'd shown it to Deirdra, she'd been elated. While Cait set up the accounting, inventory, and scheduling software, Abby had gone through her father's recipes, selecting her favorites for the menu. But her mind kept tracking back to Aiden, wondering if he'd think the lunches she was considering and the dinners she was testing were the best choices.

The kitchen had been her safe haven, the place where the rest of the world faded away. But when she'd been testing recipes, her mind had been all over the place, and she'd burned one of the entrees like a novice. Even though she knew Aiden couldn't text during his meetings, she'd checked her phone like an addict seeking her next fix. It was *ridiculous*.

She never knew it was possible to miss someone so much, carrying out rote exercises became nearly impossible.

Although that wasn't exactly true.

When her father died, she'd missed him like she'd lost a limb. She still kind of did. But missing Aiden was completely different, and ever since Sunday night, she and Aiden had been different, too. Their confessions had brought their relationship to a new level, a safer, more grounded place, where they didn't hold back and single sentences spoke volumes. No one had warned her that falling for someone could create bone-deep longing when they were apart. His morning texts—*Good morning, beautiful. Wish I was waking up beside you. I miss having coffee with my Runner Girl*—and their brief phone calls made her miss him even more. He'd worried over her extra expenditures and offered again to help her out financially, which she'd thanked him for but turned down. When he'd called her from the airport last night before leaving Chicago for LA, he'd sounded tired and she could tell he was frustrated, but he'd still managed to be attentive and interested in hearing everything she had to say. She didn't know if his frustration was caused by work or by them being apart, but she had a feeling it was both, because she was experiencing the same thing.

Cait poked her head into the office, startling Abby. "Hey, sorry to interrupt, but the guys have finished the repairs."

"You're not interrupting." Abby pushed to her feet and waved toward the recipes she'd jotted down, which consisted of about a third of the number they needed. "I swear my brain is a sieve this week. Did they find any other issues?"

"No, but they want to talk with us about the window installation."

"That's good news," she said as they left the office.

"I have more good news. I think I have the staffing schedule worked out using your specifications, but shouldn't you start thinking about putting ads online to find people before the season starts?"

"I already put an ad on the Silver Island community Facebook page. There are always college kids looking for summer jobs. We should be fine. The cook is going to be the hardest person to find."

As they walked through the restaurant, Abby was struck by how much it had changed since they'd started working on it. She could open it as it was if need be. It wouldn't be perfect, but it was clean, with gleaming floors and pretty wooden tables, and once the interior was painted it would look even better. It was missing the elegance of the fancy *lights of love*, but one day—maybe next summer if the restaurant did well—she'd hunt down lights just like the ones her father had used and splurge on them.

Rob Wicked and his sons were a sight to be reckoned with, with their colorful tattoos, shockingly bright blue eyes, and dark hair—Rob's speckled with silver, like his beard.

"There's Caity Cat and her sexy sister," Zander said with a wink. He was as much of a flirt as Wells.

Rob shut him down with a *cool it* look.

"Why did I suggest we hire you again?" Cait asked, but she was smiling, not annoyed.

Abby had immediately noticed the difference in Cait's interactions with the Wickeds compared with the way she was around most everyone else when Cait had allowed Rob to drape his arm over her shoulder as he asked after her. She'd spent a long time talking with Zeke about his volunteering and tutoring at a community center, and she'd asked him to check on Aria, the girl she'd mentioned working with at Wicked Ink, and she gave Zander as much guff as he gave her. At first all of Zander's flirting had made Abby think there might be an attraction between him and Cait, but Cait had made it clear that it was sibling-like affection and nothing more.

Zander flashed an arrogant grin and said, "Because you missed me? You needed some eye candy? You wanted your sister to meet me?"

"More like, your father and Zeke come as a package deal with Cocky McFlirt, and dealing with your mouth is worth the hassle to get a quality job done," Cait retorted.

"I knew you liked my mouth, Caity Cat." Zander blew her a kiss.

"*Zan*," Zeke warned, and Zander chuckled.

Abby got a kick out of the way Zeke, with his crow-black hair and low-key personality, was continually reining in Zander.

Rob motioned toward the side patio and said, "Abby, I asked Cait to bring you out so we could discuss the ordering window. I have a few suggestions. We have restaurants with walk-up windows on the Cape, and I think you stand to lose money with just a walk-up window during the high season. There are too many rainy, cold, windy days, when people aren't on the beach. They might love your food, but standing in the driving rain to order and pick up lunch and sprinting to the car won't be as appealing as ordering from an indoor counter, where they can then sit at a table and enjoy their meal."

"Are you thinking we should build a shelter around the window or screen in the patio? Because I don't really want to screen anything in," Abby said.

"No. An awning over the window as we discussed will be fine. But inside the restaurant you have that counter area outside the kitchen, which is a perfect place for indoor ordering. I think we should replace the countertop, clean up the cabinets, and break through the wall to the kitchen to create a pass-through. That would allow for easier ordering and serving of food and provide shelter during inclement weather. And if you go that route, then I have another suggestion. I know you had your heart set on the window being installed here." He pointed to the area closest to the water on the side of the building. "But logistically, if you shift it toward the parking lot so it's in line with the inside counter area, your staff won't have to run back to the kitchen to pick up the food."

"That makes sense. I can't believe we didn't think about that."

"With all due respect, you're a chef, not a builder. From a consumer point of view, the closer to the beach, the better. But from an efficiency standpoint, the continuity of flow makes more sense."

"I wasn't planning on redoing the counter, but roughly how much would it cost to open up that wall and replace the counter?" Abby asked.

He glanced at Cait with a brief but clearly paternal expression and said, "You're Cait's family, which makes you our family. We can get it done for the cost of materials. The bottom line will depend on the materials you choose. Laminate is a lot cheaper than granite or marble, but it's all about the image you want for the restaurant. It could run a few thousand up to eight or ten grand. My brother is in the restaurant business, and based on his experience, with your setup here on the beach, I think you'd get a high rate of return on your investment. You mentioned you have friends helping you paint and power wash tomorrow. I've made a few calls, in case you decide to go this route. If you go with marble or granite, Justin and Blaine have a selection on hand that they can bring over today. But that decision should be made soon."

"How long will it take to do the work?"

"If you don't mind us working late tonight, and if need be, early tomorrow morning, we can get it done before you paint. Why don't we give you and Cait a few minutes to talk it over?" Rob nodded in the direction of the parking lot and said, "Let's go, boys."

When they were out of earshot, Abby said, "What do you think?"

"I think it makes sense to do it, but as far as going with a cheaper or more expensive product, I don't know. I've never owned a restaurant, and I don't know much about the island economy or what you can expect to earn. All of that is in your hands."

Abby walked into the restaurant and said, "How do you think it would look with the pass-through? Would that make it look cheap? People would see the kitchen staff."

"I think they can make it pretty enough that it won't detract from the restaurant during dinner hours. And there's something nice about seeing your food cooking. Tank took all of his employees to a fancy Italian restaurant last year, and we could see the kitchen staff through the bar area. It didn't take away from the elegance at all."

"That's good to know. I guess we wouldn't have to keep both the counter and the window open at all times, because that would mean more staff and more overhead. But it would give us options, like Rob said. I think it does make sense, and if we're going to do it, we might as well do it right, with a nice marble or granite countertop. I like stainless steel in the kitchen, but it's too cold for customers to see. I wish Aiden were here to give us his opinion." As the words left her lips, she realized *what* she'd said and cringed. "When did I start needing a man's opinion to make my own decisions?"

"I hardly call wanting to get the opinion of someone you trust *needing* it to move forward."

"But the fact that I want it is almost the same thing."

Cait was shaking her head. "You want his opinion because you trust him, and honestly, I think you *should* trust him. He hasn't steered us wrong yet, and there's no doubt he has a wealth of knowledge about business and finance." Her expression softened, and she said, "But I understand where you're coming from. I didn't trust anyone for so long, I wasn't sure I'd ever be able to. But I've learned that there's nothing wrong with valuing the opinion of someone you trust. Especially your boyfriend's, since you trust him with your body and your heart, which are *way* more important than a restaurant."

"You're right, and intellectually I know that. It just feels weird after all these years to have my thoughts turn to someone else for critical decisions. It was the same way yesterday when I was working on the menu. I kept wondering what he'd think about my choices. I know how close Aiden and I have gotten, but I guess I hadn't realized how much a part of this restaurant he'd become, too."

"Does that bother you?"

"No, but it's a little shocking. I've been independent forever, and we just sort of happened. Do you have anyone like that in your life?"

"I never did until I met Tank. But he didn't give me a choice. He has a way of weaseling into people's lives and getting them to open up. To be honest, I called Tank before I called Rob and Justin about doing the work here, and I trust Rob and Justin with my life. But my thoughts went to Tank first because he's *that* person for me."

"He must be very special. Is there something going on between you two?"

"Not romantically. But Tank is the closest thing I've ever had to a best friend." Cait kicked at a mark on the floor with the toe of her peach Converse and said, "But now I feel like I can trust you and Deirdra, too."

"You can, and I feel the same way about you." Abby took a deep breath and said, "Relationship revelations are scary. Thanks for reminding me that that's normal. Let's go tell the guys we want to do both the counter and the window."

"What about Aiden's opinion? Do you want to text him first?"

"My wise big sister pointed out that there's a difference between want and need. I *want* to get his opinion, but I don't *need* it to move forward, whereas I *need* him naked in my bed again before I lose my mind, which I realize also qualifies as a *want*. See? I know the difference."

As Aiden boarded the eleven-thirty flight from LA to Boston, he wondered how he'd ever thought a life consumed with work had been a life at all. The work hadn't changed. Though road shows weren't his favorite thing, strategizing and the competitive environment had always lit his brain on fire, adding to his drive to take over more companies, to help others succeed, and to carry on his father's legacy with the highest level of integrity. But every minute of the last three days he'd spent helping George and Damon raise capital, he'd wanted to be back on Silver Island, helping the woman he was falling hard for make her dreams come true. He'd never put anyone above work besides Remi. He'd never slighted a client, and though he'd never been very involved with a woman, he'd thought himself to be a gentleman, couth enough never to slight a woman.

But here he was, taking a seat beside George Pennington, feeling like hell because Remi hadn't spoken to him since he'd called her Monday morning to let her know where he was, and any way he looked at it, he'd slighted Abby. He'd chosen work over her. She'd texted him pictures of the renovations being done at the restaurant today, and it only made him wish he'd been there even more. She was perfectly capable of overseeing the work, but he'd have loved to be there to see and feel her excitement as the changes came to fruition.

George put on his seat belt and rested his head back with a sigh. "I'm getting too old for this." He was in his early seventies, with snow-white hair, kind dark eyes, and the best business sense of just about any man Aiden knew.

I'm getting too smart for it.

George's eyes opened and he said, "I want to thank you for joining us at the last minute."

"No need to thank me. I'm always here for you—you know that."

"I do, and you've proved it many times over. I knew your father for a long time, and I know how much you and your sister meant to him. He would be proud of both of you, Aiden, but what you did for your sister . . ." George nodded and said, "There are not many men like you, and I'm proud to be among your clients."

"Thank you, George. That means a lot to me," he said, although he didn't feel worthy of that praise after sweating out every minute, wishing he could leave. It was times like these that Aiden wished he could speak to his father again, to gain some of the fatherly advice he'd missed out on when he was younger.

Aiden's phone vibrated with a text. He pulled it out, hoping it was Abby. He'd texted her before boarding, but she and Cait had stayed late at the restaurant, until after the Wickeds had left, and painted the wall Cait was going to use for the mural. He was sure she'd already turned in for the night.

Remi's name appeared in the message. He opened it, and a picture of Remi scowling, eyes narrowed, arms crossed, stared back at him with the message *I'm still not speaking to you.*

George glanced at the phone. "Oh boy, kiddo. It looks like you've upset the applecart with your sister."

With myself, too. "She's not pleased about a business decision I made."

"She's questioning *your* choices." George laughed incredulously. "You're the smartest businessman I know. A real chip off the old block."

Maybe that was the issue. He'd paid all of his attention to the way his father had handled business, but he'd failed to pay as close attention to the way his father had navigated the crossing of paths between work and his personal life. Aiden the businessman was exactly where he needed to be, but Aiden the *man*, Aiden the *boyfriend*, wanted to get the hell out of there and see his girl. "This is one of those times it would be nice to have my old man to lean on."

"I've got a pretty good shoulder. You're welcome to take it for a spin."

He trusted George, and so had his father, so he gave it a shot, keeping it in the realm of business. "Have you ever wanted a deal so badly, you were willing to risk everything for it, even if it's completely different from anything you've ever done? New, uncharted territory, with an overwhelming amount of room for errors? So much room that you weren't sure you wouldn't fuck it up?"

"Me? *No.* I'm far too conservative. But I know what your old man would say."

That piqued Aiden's interest.

George met his gaze and said, "He'd tell you that the most important deals are made with your heart."

Aiden scoffed. "Come on, George. You can do better than that. You know my father didn't allow his emotions to affect his business dealings."

George arched a brow and said, "You're right, because he believed there was only one deal worth risking everything for, and it was one he'd made years before you were born, the one he saw every night when he walked through his front door."

A rush of emotions hit Aiden, and his father's voice blew through his mind. *The best part of my day is coming home.*

"I hope that helps." George eyed him curiously. "This deal you're thinking about must be a doozy, because I've never seen you unsure about anything since the day I met you the summer after you graduated high school. Do you remember that?"

"Yes, that was a great summer." Aiden had spent the summer before college shadowing his father at work, and he'd gone with him to meet George and his team for a quarterly meeting. He could still remember how proud he'd felt in his suit and tie, standing beside his father, his mentor, his *idol*, shaking George's hand—firmly, as his father had taught him, without breaking eye contact. He'd felt like he was on his way, on the one and only path he'd ever wanted. Now he needed to find a way to remain on that path while making room for another one without running them both off course.

"To this day, I've never met a sharper kid," George said, drawing him from his thoughts. "You have always known exactly what you were doing, Aiden."

"While I appreciate that, George, you were around when I was raising Remi. You know I made more mistakes than I can count."

"Sure, but you always did what was best for your sister because you made those decisions out of love. Those are the hardest decisions to make." His expression turned serious, and he said, "You know, we don't get a lot of chances to grab hold of the brass ring and run with it. I'm too old to change my ways, but you're still young enough to jump into something new with both feet."

"Funny, I don't feel young." Although that wasn't quite true. With Abby, he felt spry and excited about everything he did. Whether that was feeling young, or falling in love, he wasn't sure, but it felt fucking fantastic.

"Trust me, you're young," George said. "I remember something else your father said to me once. I was deciding if I should branch out in a new direction, and he said, 'I'm quite certain if you really *think* about what you want, you'll see there's only one right answer, and it's been there all along, waiting for you to accept it.' Your father was right. I had known what I wanted to do all along. I had only been seeking validation because like you, I wasn't sure I wouldn't fuck it up."

"What did you do?"

"I believed in myself and took a leap of faith. That was the year we tripled our earnings." He rested his head back and closed his eyes again. "I haven't thought of that moment in years. I sure treasured your old man's friendship."

"So did I," Aiden said.

When it came to business, Aiden had never had concerns about making the right choices. But now he wondered if what was the right decision one day could be the wrong one the next.

He'd never been good at leaps of faith, but he believed in himself and in his feelings for Abby. He liked the man he was when he was with her. Hell, he liked the whole world a lot more when he was with her. She made him want to live a brighter life, to explore and see her light up with every new discovery. He had less than two weeks left with Abby before he headed overseas and back into the daily grind, spending twelve or more hours each day focused on work. He'd never been able to strike a balance between his personal life and his business life because he'd never *wanted* a personal life.

Until now.

That didn't mean he *couldn't* find a balance. He just needed to figure out how.

He looked at Remi's picture on his phone, and her words came back to him. *Isn't that the whole reason you and Ben groomed Garth and Miller to take over?*

Well, fuck him sideways. His little sister was right.

He thumbed out a text and sent it to Remi. *You were right, smarty-pants.*

Then he composed another text message, one he should have taken care of days ago.

CHAPTER NINETEEN

THURSDAY MORNING STEVIE Nicks blared from the boom box as they painted the interior of the Bistro. Abby swung her hips to "Edge of Seventeen," painting the corner of a wall while Brant used the roller. He and Grant had arrived bright and early, sporting baseball caps, T-shirts, and cargo shorts and armed with a pressure washer and extra paintbrushes. They'd been hard at work painting ever since.

Abby glanced at Brant's slanted brows and intense look of concentration and said, "How can you stand still with this song playing?"

He pushed the roller up the wall and said, "I assumed you wanted us to do a *good* job to go along with the rest of the work you've had done."

The Wickeds had done an excellent job. The granite countertop they'd chosen was worth every penny, and the pass-through to the kitchen and the ordering window on the side of the building made the Bistro feel even more open. Those additions, along with the bright white they were using for the walls, the ocean-blue trim to match the logo, and the colorful mural Cait had started painting gave the restaurant a fresh, welcoming vibe. She couldn't wait for Aiden to see all the changes when he returned tomorrow night.

"Unless you'd rather I paint all willy-nilly like someone else is doing." Brant eyed the area she was painting.

"I'm not painting *willy-nilly*," she said sharply. She couldn't help it if she'd been jumpy since yesterday afternoon. Every time she stood in one place for too long, she'd start thinking about Aiden. Not only did that make her miss him more, but it inevitably brought her thoughts to the following Sunday, when he was leaving again—only this time for good, returning to his real life. She'd tried to counter the ache of missing him by keeping herself busy. But then last night she'd lain in bed over-thinking everything from how little time they had left together to what it would be like when he went back to work for good. Would she be like this the whole time they were apart? How would she survive that? And those thoughts made her uncomfortable because she wasn't a needy person. She'd been up half the night, which had left her jittery, like she'd guzzled too much coffee, and she'd been going back and forth painting three different areas of the restaurant to use up her nervous energy. Two more days, she told herself. Just two more days and he'd be back.

And now she was thinking about Aiden again.

Needing a distraction, Abby continued shaking her booty, and called over her shoulder to Cait, who was hard at work on the mural, "I can paint and dance. Right, Cait?"

"Depends how you define painting." Cait looked cute in what she called her painting jeans. They had tears in the thighs, a hole in one knee, and paint speckles and smears from previous creations. Her black sneakers also showed proof of her experience.

Cait hadn't made it sound like she painted very often, but she was clearly at home behind a paintbrush. She hadn't even drawn the mural on the wall before jumping in and starting with Abby's father's face. It took Abby's breath away to see him brought to life within these walls.

Brant set the roller down and straightened his ball cap as he saun-tered over to Cait and asked, "Where are you going to fit me in?"

Cait kept her eyes trained on the area she was painting. "It's going to be a picture of the Bistro, not the marina. Olivier is here." She pointed to different areas of the wall as she spoke. "Ava will be there, with me,

Abby, and Deirdra. I was going to put a few tables back here and a little of the beach over here, but the other people will be out of focus."

Brant put his back to the wall beside where she was painting, so she had no choice but to look at him, and said, "Show me where you're going to be, again."

She pointed to an area to her left.

"Then I want to be here." He put his finger on a spot beside the one she'd shown him. "You can paint me in my bathing suit. I can take my shirt off and model for you."

"*No*," Cait said flatly, without looking in his direction.

"Would you prefer I'm in my birthday suit?" Brant asked. "Because I've got a really hot one."

Cait's head snapped in his direction. "You're messing up my mojo," she said breathily. "Go *paint* or jump in the ocean. Just get away from me."

Brant grinned and went back to painting.

"Dancing Queen" came on, and Abby twirled across the room to paint with Grant. She sang and danced, bumping against his hip in time to the beat. "I'm so thankful that you guys came to help." *Bump, bump.* "I never had friends like this in New York." *Bump, bump.* "I'm so glad to be back." *Bump, bump, twirl.*

Grant grabbed her hand and stole the paintbrush, giving her a stern look from beneath the bill of his Rock Bottom Bar and Grill baseball cap, his brown hair sticking out the back, brushing his collar.

"*Hey!*" Abby complained.

"When did you start snorting coke?"

Abby gasped. "I would *never!*"

"You're definitely high on something, the way you're flitting around here, yammering on more than Pix does." Grant took a step back, looking her up and down like she was an alien being. "What's going on with you?"

"There's nothing going on with me. I'm just excited about working on the restaurant with you guys. I've even got most of the menu figured out." She reached for the paintbrush, but he lifted it over his head.

"She misses Aiden. Cut her some slack," Cait said.

Grant's eyes narrowed. "Aw, shit. Sorry, Abby. No wonder you're being weird. When does he come back?"

"Tomorrow night, and I'm *not* being weird." *Liar, liar, pants on fire.* She reached for the paintbrush again, but he lifted it higher.

"You want this place to look good?" Grant asked. "Or do you want it to look like we let elementary schoolers loose in here with horse brushes?"

Abby huffed out a breath.

"He's not wrong, Abby," Brant said. "Take a good look at the places where you've painted."

She did, and holy cow, she was doing a shit job. So much for *this* distraction. "Fine. You're right. I'm doing more harm than good with the paintbrush. I'll go power wash the outside."

"I can take care of that," Brant offered.

Abby waved him off. "I'd like to do it. I need something rigorous to do."

"To keep your mind off Aiden?" Brant asked.

"*No.* To get my workout in." She turned on her heel and strode outside.

Brant followed her out. "At least let me show you how to use it so you don't break my machine." As he hooked it up for her, he said, "I enjoyed hanging out with Aiden the other morning when I showed him my boats and he borrowed the pressure washer."

"I'm glad. I enjoy hanging out with him, too," she said cheekily.

"He's pretty hung up on you."

She loved hearing that. "I'm pretty hung up on him, too. But I can't talk about him, because it makes me miss him, and I'm not used to that. So let's change the subject."

"Okay." A coy grin brought out his dimples. "Is Cait seeing anyone?"

"*No*," she said curiously.

"Then I take it Wells hasn't been sniffing around here?"

"Brant Remington, are you jealous of Wells Silver?"

He scoffed. "Are you out of your mind? I know Wells, and so do you, if I recall correctly. I wasn't sure if Cait needed someone looking out for her."

"Uh-huh." She wasn't buying it. "That's really sweet of you, but that's my sister in there, so should I be keeping my eyes on *you*?"

"You know I'm a better man than that." He flashed those dangerous dimples and said, "I leave the playing to the boys."

He showed Abby how to use the pressure washer, started it up, and then left her to work out her emotions by blasting the dirt from the building. This was exactly what she needed to keep her mind off Aiden. She could barely hear the music playing inside the restaurant as she cleaned the front siding. Cool mist dotted her arms, the bright sun warmed her skin, and her mind tiptoed back to the first day she'd seen Aiden sitting on that very patio. She couldn't believe she'd mistaken him for a Nautica underwear model. She smiled thinking of his reaction, so calm and collected, suave in his remarks. She thought about the next morning when they'd shared breakfast. She'd known then how different he was, how attentive and interested but somehow also careful and witty. Memories of their walk through town trickled in, and their first kiss. *Oh*, that kiss. It was pure and magical. She lingered on the memory, remembering the feel of his lips, confident and insistent, the strength of his arms, and her most favorite moment of that whole day, when their lips parted and his breath whispered over her cheek as he'd said—

"Abigail de Messiéres, you just might be my undoing."

Abby whipped around, goose bumps rushing over every inch of her, sending chills through her body, her mouth agape as she tried to make sense of Aiden being there.

"Hey, Abs, think you can drop the pressure washer?" His suit was drenched.

"It's *really* you!" She dropped the tool and launched herself into his arms, unable to believe he was really there, holding her in his arms, kissing her as desperately as she was kissing him.

"God, I missed you," he said between kisses.

"I thought you were a figment of my imagination." *Kiss, kiss.* "What are you doing here?"

"Turns out I forgot something important."

"What?"

"That it was okay to put my work aside and just be a man who's falling madly, passionately, and at breakneck speed for an *incredible*"—he kissed her softly—"*sexy*"—he kissed her again—"*patient* woman during the best vacation of his life."

CHAPTER TWENTY

THEY SPENT SEVEN wonderful days painting, pruning bushes, fixing the fence in front of the Bistro, hanging out with friends, riding bikes, lying in the hammock, trying recipes for the restaurant, and checking off items on their Let Loose list and six beautiful nights taking walks on the beach, romantic drives along the coast, and falling into each other's arms to enjoy dirty, sweet deliciousness into the wee hours of the morning. Coming clean to George and handing the remainder of the road show over to Garth so he could enjoy the rest of his vacation with Abby had been two of the best moves Aiden had ever made. Second only to inviting her to join him for breakfast three weeks ago, which felt more like three months. He felt like he'd finally discovered the man he was always meant to be—businessman, brother, friend, *and* significant other.

His phone buzzed with a text as he and Abby sailed out of the harbor on the boat he'd rented from Brant. They were looking forward to spending the day on the water and the evening in the artsy town of Chaffee. Chaffee was on the island and only a short drive from the house, but Aiden was glad they'd chosen to spend a few hours sailing first. He glanced at his phone, pleasantly surprised to see Brant's name instead of Remi's. Remi had been thrilled that he'd come to his senses and cut his work trip short, and she texted at least once a day to tell him so. He read the text from Brant. *Hope you and Abby have a great day!* Aiden hadn't realized how much he'd missed having a sense of community until Abby had introduced him to her friends and they'd embraced him in their world.

He'd finally found everything he'd never known he was missing, especially the brunette standing beside him at the helm, gorgeous in a coral hoodie with her hair blowing over her shoulders. He pocketed his phone and said, "That was Brant wishing us a great day."

"It's already a perfect day. The sun is shining, we're on this beautiful sailboat, and we have all day together. How does it feel to be back out on the water?"

"It's everything I remember, only better because I'm here with you. I'm definitely going to start making time for this." *And for you.* He didn't want to think about leaving on Sunday, or the weeks they'd be apart until the grand opening. Carrie had sent him all of the documents and reports he needed for his Q2 meetings. Normally, he'd have reviewed them right away, but when he'd gone to the hotel to swap clothing earlier in the week, he'd attempted to start studying the reports, but they were a reminder of how few days he and Abby had left together, and it had bummed him out. He knew how hellish it would be to leave Abby, and this time he had no choice. Real life awaited.

"I haven't been out on the water or to Chaffee in years," Abby said. "I wonder if anything has changed. I know you're still not allowed to drive in the shopping district. That'll *never* change because it's written into Chaffee's bylaws." She pressed her shoulder against his arm and said, "I'm glad we're doing this, Aiden."

"Me too." He put a hand on her back and kissed her, inhaling the scent of the summery lotion Remi had sent her, which she'd bought from Ben's mother, Roxie. Roxie Dalton was known in Upstate New York for her homemade lotions, shampoos, soaps, and fragrances, which she claimed to have infused with love potions. He was sure Remi thought he wouldn't remember that little myth, which Remi and all of the Dalton siblings swore by. But the truth was, not only did he remember it; he *welcomed* it.

They sailed for most of the day, basking in the sun, eating the lunch they'd brought, and enjoying every minute they had with each other. When they docked at Chaffee and walked along the cobblestone streets, Aiden was immediately taken with the charming area. In the middle of town was an enormous square cobblestone courtyard surrounded by vibrant three-story shops with wrought-iron balconies. A small stage anchored one side of the courtyard, and in the center of the courtyard was a fountain surrounding a statue of a man and a dog. A few children were kneeling on the edge, peering into the water, while others were playing tag, running around tables and darting between large planters overflowing with leafy green plants and colorful blooms.

Aiden pointed to the kids playing and said, "Did you do that when you were young?"

"Of course. Every kid who grew up on the island probably did. What else are you going to do when your parents are canoodling at a table?"

He pressed his lips to hers and said, "I'd like to canoodle with you."

They meandered in and out of shops, picking up a few gifts for Patrice and Olive. Abby flitted from one display to the next, commenting on how much she liked this or that. It didn't seem to matter if they were in a candle shop, a boutique, or an art gallery. She found something to love in every one of the shops. She continued to amaze him. She'd spent days stressing over recipes, testing and tweaking, and planned to serve far too many dishes for the tasting with their friends this weekend. The judging of the competition, the biggest day of her life, was less than a week away, and here she was, fully present, carefree, and enjoying every moment. He could watch her all day, survive on her enthusiasm rather than oxygen. But what he really needed to do was *learn* from her. Learn her secrets to striking a balance before he went back to work full-time.

"*Look*, a musician." Abby tugged Aiden out of an art gallery toward the courtyard, where a crowd had gathered around a young guy playing guitar by the fountain. He had shaggy dark hair and wore wire-framed glasses, hemp pants, and leather sandals. A dalmatian lay by his open guitar case. Inside the case was a sign that read DONATIONS FOR AUTISM ARTS APPRECIATED.

As a practice, Aiden donated twenty-five percent of his income to charity. He tossed a few twenties into the guitar case, making a mental note to look up the cause to see if he should add it to his annual donations list.

"That was nice of you," Abby said as he drew her into his arms, swaying to the beat. "Nobody else is dancing."

"That's their loss." He kissed her and said, "This place, this courtyard, reminds me of Salvador de Bahia in Brazil."

Surprise sparked in her eyes. "You've been to Brazil?"

"Mm-hm." He kissed her again. "I do a fair amount of international travel for work, so I bought a little villa there. Maybe sometime in the off-season, when the Bistro is closed, we can sneak away, and I'll show you around. It's gorgeous in February." She was looking at him like she saw puppies again. "What is that adorable look for?"

"You just put us together months from now like we're a given."

"Is that too presumptuous?" They were great together, and while he would come back for the grand opening as he'd promised, he wanted *more*.

"*No*," she said happily. "I want that, too. But you talk about *Brazil* like it's Boston, right around the corner. I've never been anywhere besides New York."

"Then maybe I can show you the world one week at a time, during your off-season, of course."

"Aiden . . . ?" She laughed. "You're *crazy*."

"You should have a chat with my friend Runner Girl. She told me I was too romantic for my own good."

"You *are* romantic. But you're also crazy."

"Crazy about you, that's for sure." He gave her a chaste kiss and motioned in the direction of a row of shops they hadn't yet explored. "Let's go check out the rest of the stores, see what we can find."

"This store has Abby written all over it," Aiden said as they approached a funky little shop with WHIMSICAL THINGS painted on the glass above the purple door and a mannequin out front wearing aviator sunglasses, a floppy woven hat with a pink flower on the front, a white shirt with WHIMSICAL THINGS printed across the chest, and bright yellow pants. Several elegant necklaces and a rainbow boa hung around the mannequin's neck, and its arm was bent at the elbow, hand palm up, as if it were presenting the shopper with a gift. Three expensive-looking bracelets decorated its wrist, and a gold hanging light with pink fringe hung from its fingers.

"Aiden, look!" Abby went to the mannequin and touched the hanging light. "This is *just* like the kind of light my dad would have put up in the Bistro!" She looked at the price tag and exclaimed, "No way! It's only *fifteen* dollars." She snagged the light, clutching it against her chest, and said, "I'm getting this. I wasn't sure where to buy lights, but this is perfect! Let's see what else they have."

She threw open the door, thrilled at the mix of chic and eclectic items before her. Colorful rugs were spread over hardwood floors, creating alcoves of funky chairs and interesting wall hangings. There were candles and pottery bowls, pillows and planters. Several funky lights of varying sizes, shapes, and colors hung from the ceiling, as if her father had sprinkled his magic all over the store.

She moved from one display to the next, checking out fancy wine-glasses and rustic decorations. "Look at the prices. I can actually afford these things." She found another great light and snatched it off the table. "Aiden, I think I'm in *love*."

"You and me both."

The depth of emotion in his voice drew her attention. He was standing a few feet away, holding the bag of gifts he'd bought for the girls in one hand and reaching for her with the other as he closed the distance between them. The emotions in his voice were nothing compared to the ones looking back at her. She clutched the lights against her chest to keep from dropping them as he slid his hand beneath her hair, drawing her closer, and said, "Only I don't *think*, Abs. I *know*. And I'm not falling, baby. I fell. I'm *there*."

She was breathing too hard, tears burning her eyes. "*Aiden?*" came out shaky and unsure, though there was nothing unsure about the way she felt, and that rattled her, but she could no sooner change her feelings than eke out another word.

"I fell in love with you like night takes over day—soaking up every little thing you did and said, until you were all I saw, all I *wanted*. Until you were so much a part of me, I no longer knew how to be me without you."

A tear slipped down her cheek, and a nervous laugh tumbled out.

He brushed the tear away with the pad of his thumb and said, "I love you, Abigail de Messiéres. I love your determination and your vulnerabilities. I love the way you let your heart lead your decisions and how you put your whole beautiful self into everything you do."

She gasped for air, her chest too full to speak. He lowered his lips to hers, kissing her slow and sweet, drawing the words out as their lips parted, and she said, "I fell, too."

Someone sniffled, and they both looked in the direction of the sound. A kind-faced older woman with gray hair was wiping her eyes. "I'm sorry. That was so . . ." She sighed.

Abby laughed nervously and touched her forehead to Aiden's chest.

"Thank you." Aiden kissed the top of Abby's head.

"I'm Beverly. Let me take those lights for you so you can seal those lovely words with a proper kiss."

Aiden held Abby tighter and said, "Thank you, but would you mind taking a picture of us first?"

"Not at all. You want the lights *in* the picture?" Beverly asked.

"Yes, please." He gazed into Abby's eyes as he pulled his phone from his pocket and said, "I want to remember this moment just as it is."

He navigated to the camera and handed Beverly his phone. Aiden gazed into Abby's eyes as Beverly took the picture. He put his arm around Abby, and Beverly took another picture, both of them beaming at the camera.

"Thank you," Aiden said, taking his phone. "I'll text you copies, Abs."

He sent the pictures as Abby handed the lights to Beverly and said, "Thank you. I definitely want to buy those."

"Wonderful. Take your time looking around. I'll be by the register if you need me."

Abby was floating on cloud nine as they looked around the store, kissing, whispering *I love you*s, and holding hands. She wanted to dance, to *sing*, to shout her love from the rooftops. She wanted to call Deirdra, Cait, and Leni and share her happiness with the world! But all of that would have to wait, because as much as she wanted to gloat and celebrate with her friends, what she wanted even more was to be with Aiden, reveling in their newly claimed love and the confessions she hadn't seen coming and couldn't have held back if she'd wanted to.

They found three more fun lights for the Bistro and two great pictures for the walls. When they finally made their way to the register, Beverly said, "You sure do like lights. I wonder if I can interest you in taking a few larger lights off my hands?"

"Larger lights?" Abby asked.

"These are beauties, but they're big and much too heavy for me to get into the showroom. They've been collecting dust and taking up space in my stockroom for years." Beverly glanced at Aiden and said, "Are you in a hurry, or can you take a moment to peek at them?"

"We'd love to take a look," Aiden said.

Beverly came around the counter, and they followed her through a door in the back of the store, into a stockroom where a teenage girl was sitting on the floor texting and blowing a bubble with her gum.

"Honey, I thought you were doing inventory," Beverly said, bringing the dark-haired girl's eyes to them. "This is my granddaughter, Medina."

Medina pushed to her feet and said, "Hi. I *was* doing inventory, but Chip and I broke up again. I was texting him to say we're over for good this time, and don't worry. I'm *fine*. This was my decision."

"I'm glad you're okay. If you want to talk—"

"I don't. I'm *fine*."

"Okay, great. I want to show this lovely couple a few things," Beverly said. "Would you mind watching the store?"

"Sure."

After Medina walked out, Beverly said, "I would not want to be sixteen again. Young love is like a Ping-Pong match."

She led them toward the back of the stockroom, around a row of metal shelves, and stopped by something covered by a tarp. "Here they are."

Beverly grabbed one side of the tarp and said, "Would you mind?"

Aiden took hold of the other side of the tarp, and together they pulled it off, revealing three enormous chandeliers.

Abby's breath left her lungs in a whoosh. She grabbed Aiden's hand, excitement bursting inside her. They were almost identical to the chandeliers her father had used at the Bistro, but each one had colored crystals hanging from the bottom rim instead of clear. One had green, another blue, and the third had pink. "They're *gorgeous*. Where did you get them?"

"I don't recall. I'm sorry. My brain is like the Bermuda Triangle these days," Beverly said.

"Aiden, they're so similar to the ones my dad used at the Bistro." Abby walked around them, goose bumps rising on her flesh as she admired the gleaming crystals. Her father really *had* sprinkled his magic around that store. The café chairs had been delivered, and they definitely enhanced the ambience. The lights would pull it all together. They were the pièces de résistance.

She *wanted* to buy them, but it sure felt more like a *need*. The trouble was, she also needed two months of capital, and she'd spent thousands of dollars on unexpected renovations. She and Aiden had gone over the budget again this week. They'd rerun the staffing numbers and came up with a new estimate of monthly food costs since inclement weather wouldn't necessarily mean fewer customers. She was already skating a very thin line of being able to keep her head above water. There was no way she could spend what she was sure would be thousands of dollars for each chandelier.

"Abs, you need these," Aiden said.

Abby turned away from Beverly and whispered, "I can't afford them."

"I can help." Before she could respond, he said, "Beverly, how much would you like for these?"

Abby glowered at him. She was *not* going to let him pay for the lights.

"Oh, I don't know. I haven't thought much about it." Beverly cocked her head, looking at the chandeliers, and said, "I'd just like them out of here so I can have the storage space back. Do you think three hundred each is fair?"

Abby whirled around. "Yes! I'll take them! All three!" She squealed and hugged Aiden. "I had a feeling when I walked in here that my dad was here with me, and I think he really must be!"

"Good things come to good people, Abs." Aiden kissed her and said, "Thank you, Beverly. You've made my girlfriend very happy."

"I think you made her even happier with three very special words a little while ago." She winked and said, "Let's go work out the details."

They made arrangements for the chandeliers to be delivered and enjoyed a romantic dinner in Chaffee. As they sailed back toward the harbor, neither one wanted their perfect day to end. They anchored outside the harbor and made themselves a nest of blankets beneath the stars. They took off their shoes and got cozy with Abby's back against Aiden's chest, his hands over hers, their fingers interlaced. The gentle waves and the sounds of the sea lulled them into a peaceful silence.

"We should make a wish," Aiden suggested. "It's on our list."

Abby's heart was so full, she couldn't imagine what she would wish for other than Aiden never leaving the island, but she played along. "Okay. You first."

"Let's make them together."

"Mine can't come true. The only thing I want isn't realistic."

"A very special woman once told me that dreams are made of *what ifs*." He kissed her cheek and said, "So tell me, my love. What are wishes made of?"

"Miracles," she said wistfully.

"Then I say we go big." He took her hand in his and kissed the back of it. "Let's shoot for miracles, Runner Girl."

She tilted her face, smiling up at him. "This is a super-big one."

"Then we'll wish extra hard." He kissed her and said, "Close your eyes." When she did, he whispered in her ear, "Wish hard, baby, because I want all your dreams to come true."

She wished as hard as she could, and then she relaxed again, trying not to think about his leaving. But that was like trying not to breathe. Their confessions of love had brought elation and a sense of peace that was stronger than the undercurrent of Abby's worries about expectations and disappointments. But old habits die hard, and those

worries refused to go away, lingering like a slow-moving creek, its bab-
bling nearly imperceptible. A subtle reminder that if a storm hit, the
creek would flood and upend everything in its path—a reminder of
why she needed to be in complete control of her life at all times. She
laughed softly. How could anyone be in control when *love* showed its
all-powerful, beautiful face?

Aiden pressed a kiss to her head and said, "What's funny, babe?"

"Life." She tipped her chin up, shifting so her side was against
his chest and she could see his handsome face. "I was a workaholic,
dedicated to my job above all else. I dated a guy for almost a year and
never gave much thought to when I'd see him again during the times we
were apart. Then you come along and effortlessly change the way I live.
I have spent more time enjoying life since meeting you than I have in
almost twenty years. And somehow we also managed to give the Bistro
a fabulous face-lift and get the entire business almost up and running.
And still we had time to connect with my friends, clean out my mom's
house, get to know Cait, and for this. For *us*. How did we do it?"

He pulled one of the blankets around her shoulders and said, "I'm
at as much of a loss as you are. Before you came into my life, time off
was spent planning or analyzing work. But the truth is, I've barely even
thought about work since our first breakfast together, and while that
should scare the life out of me, it's had the opposite effect. It's made me
appreciate all that I've been missing. And the best answer I can come up
with as to how this happened is that we, two self-professed workaholics,
have finally found someone, *something*—the love between us—that is
more interesting, more meaningful, and more powerful than the work
we'd been hiding behind."

"I don't think I've been *hiding*."

He brushed his lips over her cheek and whispered, "Hiders never
think they're hiding. Myself included." He smiled and said, "I knew
you'd become more important than work when I was at the road show.
Nobody but Remi has ever come before work. But today, as I watched

you getting excited about lights and knickknacks, I thought about all that I'll be missing when I go back to work, and I felt it here." He put his hand over his heart. "Like rocks stacking up, jagged and wrong. I've never been in love before, so I have no basis to compare my feelings to, but love like ours is scary, Abs. We found something in each other we've never found before, and it soothed the workaholic in us. We trusted each other early on, shared the details of the things we've kept locked inside or had told very few people. I think our connection brought us both out of hiding. You were afraid to believe in someone, and I was afraid to let anyone come ahead of Remi. And for the last two years, it was more comfortable to hide behind work than to go out and find the life I never felt I was lacking. But from the moment I met you, hiding and working were the last things I wanted to do."

His words burrowed inside her, touching all the places she had no idea longed to be touched. Then again, Aiden had a way of reading her mind and fixing things before she even had a chance to voice her concerns. Last weekend she'd been silently lamenting their time together coming to an end. On their way to the hardware store to pick out paint colors for the living room, junk room, and her mother's bedroom, he told her he'd made arrangements to come back to stay for the entire week of the grand opening. And just like that, she'd felt better.

"Maybe you're right, and I was hiding so I wouldn't be faced with disappointment," she said. "But as for you, I feel like you worked so much during your vacation, you didn't get any time off."

"It didn't feel like work. It felt like we were building something together, something meaningful that allowed us to get to know each other on more than a superficial level. And that is what allowed us to come out from behind the walls we erected. That made it possible for us to embrace every minute we had together."

"So, what happens when you leave Sunday? Will you go back to being Workaholic Aiden Monday morning?"

"I have *no* idea who I'll be on Monday." He took her hand and said, "I have a few insanely busy weeks coming up with back-to-back meetings. I'd like to think I'll be able to focus when I need to, but if the road show was any indication of what happens to me when I'm away from you, it'll be an uphill battle. But we'll talk every day, and knowing I'll be back next month for the grand opening will make it a little easier."

"For me, too."

"You'll be busy winning the competition and then interviewing and training staff."

There it was again, his endless belief in her. "You're so confident about my winning."

"I'm even more sure of it after tasting all the recipes you made this week. You've got this, Abs. But on the off chance Wells pays off the judges, you have to know how proud of you I am and how proud your parents would be."

She nudged him. "Wells won't pay off the judges."

"That's the only way he'll win. You'll *wow* them with your cooking and mesmerize them with your gorgeous smile."

"And if that doesn't work?"

"Then the judges have no taste, and the competition isn't worthy of your time."

Swoon! "You're really good for my ego."

His eyes turned seductive. "Your ego, huh? I'd like to think I'm good for a hell of a lot more than that." He kissed her neck and swept her beneath him, sending the blankets to the deck.

"Coldcoldcold!" She shivered, laughing as he pulled the blankets over them, blocking the wind.

He lowered his lips to hers, turning her laughter to desirous moans as he took the kiss deeper and their bodies ignited. She loved kissing him, feeling the strength of their passion colliding like two rushing rivers feverishly blending into one. She pushed her hands under the back of his shirt, needing *more*. His muscles were *hot* and hard against her palms. He made a low, guttural sound that sent lust spiking through her, burning hotter with every slick of his tongue. Need pulsed between her legs as his hands moved hungrily over her breasts, and in a complete contradiction to their wild passion, he slowed their kisses to a sensual dance of sliding tongues and grinding hips. Her senses reeled as he eased from one whisper of a kiss to another, so light and tantalizing, she whimpered for more. But he continued tasting and taunting until she couldn't take it anymore.

"Need you," she demanded, and craned up, *taking* more.

He crushed his mouth to hers, and their control snapped. They tugged at each other's clothes. "Love you so much," he said as he tore off her shirt, then ripped off his own. Her bra went next as he moved swiftly down her body, loving her breasts, kissing her belly as he unbuttoned her pants and stripped them off along with her panties. He made quick work of taking off the rest of his clothes and reared up on his knees to find his wallet. Cold air brushed over Abby's heated flesh.

She shivered, crossing her arms over her chest, and said, "*Hurry!*"

His eyes flared predatorily as he sheathed his length, and she looked her fill. He was so damn sexy, all rugged and hard. He tugged the blankets over them as he came down over her, but this man, and his *love*, were all the warmth she needed. He cradled her in his strong arms as their bodies came together. The sheer pleasure searing through her drew a wanton sound from her lungs. His mouth covered hers as they found their rhythm. They both went wild, clawing, nipping, moaning. The blankets slid to a puddle beside them. The cool air whipped over the sheen of sweat they'd earned, heightening every sensation as he stroked over the spot that made her toes curl under. He pushed one hand beneath her, palming her ass and lifting her hips, driving deeper, but slower, lingering over that sensational spot, until her entire body felt electrified.

"*Aiden,*" she panted out.

"I've got you, baby."

He reclaimed her mouth, kissing her so fiercely, loving her so thoroughly, pleasure *engulfed* her. "*Aiden!*" flew from her lips as she spiraled into ecstasy. Her hips bucked, her body writhed, her insides pulsing around him as he followed her over the edge, chanting her name like a mantra. "Abby, Abby, *Abby*—"

He cradled her in his arms as their bodies thrust and jerked, their hearts thundering as one. His mouth covered hers as they came down from their highs, kissing her so slowly and beautifully, she'd never felt so treasured in all her life. Every time they made love, she was sure nothing could surpass the depth of their connection, the strength of their passion. But they always proved her wrong. When their lips parted, Aiden's head dipped beside hers as if the feelings were *that* intense for him, too, and he whispered, "*Jesus*, Abs. Nothing has *ever* felt as perfect as loving you."

CHAPTER TWENTY–ONE

THE SAVORY SCENTS wafting out of the kitchen were almost as heavenly as the woman creating them. It was late Saturday afternoon, and soon their friends would arrive for the tasting. Aiden glanced at Abby through the newly renovated pass-through to the kitchen as he and Cait set the tables for what Abby was calling the *Big Test*. She was totally in her *zone*, chopping vegetables in her white double-breasted chef's coat and hat. He loved seeing her dreams coming to fruition, and he wanted everything to be perfect for all of her *big tests*—the tasting, the judging, and the grand opening. Yesterday they'd ordered the menus, and thanks to Brant's connections, they were able to bring in an electrician to install the chandeliers and colorful lights. They'd also hung the pictures they'd found in Chaffee, along with some of Abby's father's paintings. Cait had finished the mural, and not only was it absolutely stunning, but it really brought the energy of Abby's once-happy family into the restaurant in a big way. Abby had gotten teary-eyed over it, and she must have hugged and thanked Cait at least a dozen times. All of the changes had transformed the run-down restaurant into a romantic, bohemian gathering place, as Abby had hoped they would.

"I need a taste tester!" Abby hollered out to them. She had been a nervous wreck this morning, but a little lovin' had taken the starch right out of her—at least for a while. She'd been buzzing around the Bistro all afternoon, prepping, chopping, getting ready for the taste test with their friends.

"Race ya," Cait said, hurrying past him.

Aiden chuckled as he followed her into the kitchen, where Abby was wiggling to the music streaming from the boom box as she stirred something in a big pot on the stove. Every burner on the two stoves was occupied, as well as the ovens, and four mouthwatering desserts were lined up on a counter, calling Aiden's name.

Abby filled a large spoon with soup and said, "Who's first?"

"Sisters before misters," Cait said, sidling in for a taste. She ate the soup, and her face contorted in disgust.

"*What's wrong?*" Abby asked anxiously. "Is it too salty? Too bland?"

Cait's brow furrowed. "I think I need another taste to figure it out."

Abby grabbed two more clean spoons and dipped one in the soup, watching Cait intently as she tasted it.

Cait closed her eyes, making an appreciative sound. "I *love* French onion soup."

"Cait!" Abby snagged the spoon from her. "You almost gave me a heart attack! Get out of my kitchen."

Cait walked past Aiden with a big-ass grin. He put his arm around Abby as she stirred and tinkered. "Take it as a compliment, babe."

"I am. I'm just stressed and excited, and I'm trying to get everything done before everyone gets here. Deirdra texted that she caught an earlier ferry and didn't bring her car. She's waiting for an Uber. She should be here soon." She waved a spoon and said, "Do you want a taste?"

"Only of you, baby." He pressed his lips to hers, wondering how the hell he would leave her tomorrow, much less make it a month before seeing her again. He was determined not to let his leaving put a damper on her big day and said, "What can I do to help?"

"I love you, but . . ." She pointed at the door.

"Okay, but if the kitchen is your domain, I get the bedroom." He swatted her ass and said, "With you *in* it." He headed into the restaurant to help Cait finish setting the tables.

Deirdra walked through the door a little while later pulling a small suitcase. She looked sharp in tan skinny jeans, a white blouse, and sky-high heels. Her hair framed her face, which was made up like she'd been on a fashion shoot. Wells sauntered in behind her.

"*Whoa*. Am I in the right place?" Deirdra pointed at Cait and Aiden. "*Sister. Other sister's hot boyfriend.* Yup. I'm in the right place."

"It's good to see you, Deirdra." Aiden embraced her, and as she hugged Cait, he offered his hand to Wells. "Good to see you again, Wells. How are you?"

Wells shook his hand and said, "If the gossip around town is accurate, apparently not quite as well as you and Abby are doing."

"I'm a lucky man. What brings you into the restaurant?"

"I was dropping a friend at the ferry when I saw Deirdra waiting for a ride. She told me that you were leaving tomorrow. I thought I'd say goodbye, and while I'm here I'd like to wish Abby good luck in the competition."

"Thanks, man. That's awful nice of you."

"Deirdra said you won't be back when they announce the winner."

Aiden's gut clenched. "Unfortunately, she's right. I'm due overseas for the next couple of weeks. But I'll be back for the grand opening."

"I'll make sure I have plenty of wine on hand for Abby to drown her sorrows when you leave," Deirdra said.

"It's a bummer that you'll miss the announcement ceremony," Wells said. "If Abby wins, I'll be sure to take pictures for you."

"Thanks. I'd appreciate that."

"You mean *when* she wins." Deirdra looked around and said, "This place looks amazing. Cait, the mural is gorgeous. It's so lifelike. You must have used a picture of our mom from ages ago—she looks like I'd like to remember her—and I love that you're in the picture, too."

Cait's expression turned bashful. "Abby insisted."

"Of course she did," Deirdra said. "That's exactly how it should be."

"You painted that?" Wells asked.

Cait nodded.

"That's one hell of a talent you've got there, Cait," Wells said.

"Thanks."

"Where on earth did you find the lights of love?" Deirdra asked as she wove around the tables. "It's like I've been thrown back in time but not quite *all* the way back. The restaurant has never looked this good. I swear, Abby remembered every little thing."

"Aren't the lights great?" Abby yelled from the kitchen. "We found all those lights in Chaffee. I got a steal from this woman who had no idea what they were worth. I felt guilty, actually. Hey, Wells! What are you doing here?"

"Just came to wish you luck," Wells said loudly.

Deirdra ran her hand over the granite countertop. "Abby, the counter, the pass-through, the ordering window on the side of the building. It's all *perfect*. I never should have doubted you."

"Thank you, but Cait and Aiden were a huge help. Let me turn this down and I'll be right out."

"The girls deserve all the credit," Aiden said. "We hung up some of your dad's paintings, too." He pointed to the other side of the restaurant, where they were hanging.

"Where did you find them? I forgot how artistic he was."

"In the junk room closet," Aiden said as Abby came through the kitchen doors.

Abby hugged Deirdra. "I'm so glad you came for the tasting."

"Me too. Malcolm was getting on my last nerve. I needed the break."

Abby smiled at Wells and said, "I'm so glad you stopped by, too. Good luck next week."

"Good luck to you, too, Abby. You've done a hell of a job here. It looks, and *smells*, fantastic."

"Thank you. We're having a tasting. You're welcome to stay."

Wells cocked a grin. "Inviting a wolf into the henhouse? That's awfully brave of you, but I have to get over to the restaurant."

"Thanks for the ride, Wells," Deirdra said.

"Anytime, doll."

"I'll walk you out." Aiden touched Abby's back and said, "Why don't I put Deirdra's suitcase in the office before everyone else arrives?"

"Thanks, Aid," Abby said.

As he and Wells made their way to the front, Wells said, "Listen, I know Abby has friends all over the island, but I'll keep an eye out for her, too."

"Thanks. I appreciate that." When they reached the door, Aiden shook his hand and said, "Good luck in the competition."

Wells nodded; then he eyed Cait and blew her a kiss. "Hit me up sometime, Cait. I'll buy you a drink."

Cait rolled her eyes. Wells chuckled on his way out the door.

Aiden brought Deirdra's suitcase into the office. When he came out, Abby was arguing with a portly man who looked annoyed. Deirdra stood beside her studying a piece of paper, and Cait's eyes were volleying between Abby and the guy as they argued.

Aiden strode over to them. "What's going on?"

"This guy says he has an oven delivery, but I didn't *order* an oven," she snapped.

"Oh shit," Aiden said at the same time Deirdra said, "But Aiden did."

"*What?*" Abby fumed. "You ordered an *oven*? Take it back," she said to the delivery guy.

"Come on, lady. It's paid for. My truck broke down on the way to the ferry, and I've got a kid's birthday party to get to . . ."

Aiden was too focused on the smoke coming out of Abby's ears to hear the rest of what the guy was saying. "Babe, I'm sorry, but you can't open a restaurant with only two oven units. Not for the number of customers you're likely to have. You're using every burner for a *tasting*."

"Aiden! It's *my* kitchen," she fumed. "I know what I can and can't do."

"What is going on? Why are you fighting?" Deirdra asked.

Abby glowered at her. "One of the oven-range combos is broken."

"The biggest one," Cait explained.

"And I am not letting him buy it," Abby snapped.

"Holy crap. Abby, *take* the gift. You'll need it," Deirdra said. "Don't you remember how busy the kitchen used to be?"

"I'm *not* accepting it. You can't walk in here and take over, Aiden. The competition was one thing, but an *oven*? No." She spun around to the delivery guy and said, "Take it back. I refuse the delivery."

"Babe, don't do this," Aiden pleaded.

"*Don't do this?* I didn't *do* anything. You did. A commercial oven-range unit is thousands of dollars that I can't afford right now."

"But I *can*." *And a better one than you'd probably buy.* He knew her well enough to realize she'd purchase a more reasonably priced unit that she'd have to replace sooner and in the long run would cost her more. He wanted her to have the best, which was exactly why he'd purchased the Viking sixty-inch Professional 5 series with grill, griddle, and two full-size ovens.

She crossed her arms, glowering at him.

"Please just hear me out." He took her by the elbow, guiding her away from the others. "Abby, I watched you trying to make do, and you didn't let it stop you when you ran out of space this week as you tried recipes. But you can't work at maximum efficiency without that unit. I know it's not easy for you to accept this kind of help from others, but I'm not just anyone. I'm *yours*, and I love you. I want to see you succeed. Please let me do this for you."

"Oh my God," Deirdra said. "How can you say no to *that*?"

"Aiden." Abby sighed, her brows knitting. "You don't listen," she said softly.

"I *do* listen. I listen to you saying and doing all the right things to prove you can do this on your own. But, baby, you mean the world to me, and I had to listen to my heart, too."

"By buying me an oven unit?"

"Yes." He put his arms around her and said, "I told you my biggest flaw was doing too much for the people I care about. I ordered it and honestly didn't think about it again until now. I'm sorry for not telling you. But when you love someone, don't you love their flaws, too? I love your stubborn streak as much as I love your determination." That earned a small smile.

"But I don't want you to spend all of your money on me. I love you for *you*, not for what you can do for me."

"Abby, I know that, but I could buy you things every day of our lives and still have more money than I could ever spend."

"Some regular guy you are," she said sarcastically.

"Abby," Deirdra called over to them. "This delivery guy has other things to do, and it's a *really* nice oven-range combo unit. Just like the ones you salivated over when you were in cooking school."

Aiden arched a brow, hoping she'd accept it. "Come on, baby."

"*Fine,*" she relented. "He can put it in the back of the kitchen until I can get it installed. The kitchen opens to the parking lot. Dee, Cait, can you let him in the kitchen door?"

The delivery man walked out, and Deirdra and Cait headed into the kitchen.

"The installers are coming Monday," Aiden said. "It'll be ready for you to cook for the judges Tuesday."

"Thank you for everything, but—"

He pressed his lips to hers, silencing her, and said, "I know the *buts*, Abs."

She banged her forehead on his chest. "What am I going to do with you?"

"I can think of about a dozen intriguing things."

With her father's favorite music playing, the lights of love shining down on her, and the chatter of family, friends, and Aiden, Abby was thrilled with the aura of the Bistro. But she had so many butterflies in her stomach, she'd barely eaten a thing all night as her friends devoured their dinners and eagerly feasted on the fancy desserts she'd made. Aiden, Cait, and their friends doled out high praises, while Deirdra had been uncharacteristically quiet since the tasting began. She'd eaten a bowl of French onion soup, a heaping portion of shrimp etouffee, and seconds of the duck and coq au vin. She also had hearty helpings of grilled ratatouille salad and potato gratin. She'd even had some beef bourguignon, and she wasn't a huge fan of beef, but she had yet to say a word. Abby didn't get it. Deirdra was not one to keep her opinions to herself.

"Hey, Abby, can you pass me another one of those cream things?" Daphne asked.

"It's called Paris-Brest, and it's a choux pastry with a praline-flavored cream," Abby said as she passed the dessert plate.

"You can have that. I need this napoleon pastry," Cait said, reaching for another slice of mille-feuille. "How should I eat this? Cut it, or . . . ?"

Brant licked his spoon and said, "Eat it with your fingers."

"Like an animal?" Cait looked at him like he'd lost his mind.

"That way I can watch you lick them clean," Brant said in a hushed voice. Unfortunately, he was not quite quiet enough to keep everyone else from hearing him.

Deirdra pointed her fork at him and said, "Listen here, Bee Gee. That's my *sister*. Watch yourself." She stabbed a piece of the croquembouche and popped it into her mouth.

When Abby had brought out the croquembouche—choux pastry puffs stacked into a cone shape and bound with threads of caramel—everyone had *ooh*ed and *aah*ed, debating whether it was too pretty to eat. But Deirdra had said that nothing was too pretty to eat and had taken the first piece. Abby studied her sister's reaction as she ate the dessert, but her face gave away nothing.

"Or at least make it worth her while, Brant. If you're going to go there, you might as well offer to lick it off *for* her." Grant smirked.

Jules dipped her finger into the cream from a Paris-Brest and held it up for Grant. "You can lick my fingers anytime."

"Seriously, Jules?" Jock shook his head.

Jules narrowed her eyes, though she'd never been able to pull off a fierce look. Her face was too sweet, and her eyes were always happy, even as she said, "He's going to be my *husband*. Deal with it, big brother. He can lick anything of mine he wants."

"*Jules!*" Leni snapped, and everyone else laughed. "This wasn't about you and Grant getting down and dirty. It was about Brant hitting on Cait."

"Oh my God." Cait blushed. "Can we please stop talking about Brant licking anything *or* hitting on me?"

Brant draped an arm over the back of her chair and said, "I didn't mean to embarrass you."

"You didn't." Cait sat up straighter and said, "I'm kind of losing my appetite."

Everyone laughed.

Abby loved how Cait was finding her place among their friends. When everyone began talking at once about the food, the renovations, and how big a splash the Bistro was going to make, Cait was right in the middle of it. Abby hung on every word Deirdra said as she complimented the restaurant and talked with Leni about the marketing plans they'd come up with. But *still*, she said nothing about the food.

Aiden's hand slid over Abby's thigh as he leaned closer and whispered, "You seem on edge. Want to meet me in the office and I'll take care of that for you?"

Heat darted through her with the memories of the delicious things he'd done to her that morning to take the edge off her nerves. "*Yes*," she said, and holy hotness, her stomach flipped at the wickedness in his eyes. She was tempted not to say what she knew she had to, but once Aiden got his hands on her, there would be no hiding the dirty things they'd done. So she put her hand over his, lacing their fingers together, and said, "But as much as I want to, we can't."

"Later," he promised, and kissed her.

"I'm definitely having Abby cater events at the winery," Daphne exclaimed, drawing her attention. "I think this is the perfect place for my book club meetings, too."

Cait asked about the book club, and Grant struck up a conversation with the guys about the bonfire they were having after the tasting. The more everyone chatted, the more anxious Abby became about Deirdra's silence. She wasn't even sure why it was so important to her to know what Deirdra thought of her cooking, but the importance became magnified with her sister's silence.

Deirdra stabbed another piece of the croquembouche and held it up, twirling her fork as she inspected the pastry puff.

Abby couldn't take it anymore and kicked Deirdra's foot under the table.

"Ouch!" Deirdra glared at her. "What was that for?"

Abby leaned forward and lowered her voice to say, "You haven't said a word about the food. Do you hate it that much?"

"*No*, I don't *hate* it. How could you think that?"

"Then why aren't you saying anything?"

Deirdra's expression turned serious. "Because I'm freaking blown away by you, Abby, and I haven't figured out the right words to say. I'm sitting in a restaurant that I thought would never find its legs, eating food that is better than I could get anywhere in Boston, and *you* made it. My little sister, the girl who would rush through homework so she could cook with our dad and never hesitated to take over after I went to college, staying on the island long after she should have. You have done something I never thought possible."

Emotions brimmed in Deirdra's voice, bringing tears to Abby's eyes. She realized everyone else had gone silent and was watching them.

"You astound me, Abby, with your confidence, your courage, and your determination." She glanced at Aiden, and then back at Abby, and said, "With your ability to leave all the bad shit behind and to *love* with your whole self. I'm sorry I didn't say anything earlier, but . . ." She shrugged, tears shining in her eyes. "I'm so damn proud of you."

Abby laughed and cried and practically climbed over the table as they reached for each other. "Thank you," she said through her tears.

"Now, that's one hell of an endorsement," Aiden said, sparking cheers and applause from their friends.

"Thank you, guys." Abby wiped her eyes as they sat down, sharing a warm, silent moment with Deirdra across the table. "Thank you, Dee."

Deirdra sat back with one hand over her stomach and said, "I might have to think about that nasty E word after this meal."

"*Enough?*" Jock asked.

"Exercise." Deirdra feigned a full-body shudder.

"I don't exercise, either, but Jock does. You could jog with him," Daphne suggested.

Deirdra grabbed another puff pastry and said, "Thanks, but I prefer to get my workout in with *single* guys and earn my sweat in more pleasurable ways."

"Damn, Deirdra. Who knew you were so into sex?" Brant chuckled.

Abby rolled her eyes. "Don't let her fool you, Brant. Sex takes time, and Deirdra's got none of that."

"But I have plenty of time for fantasies, and in them I'm super fit and the single guys are as smart as they are hot." Deirdra looked at Cait with a secret smile, as if they'd talked about this very subject, and said, "And they have *off* and *mute* buttons."

Abby laughed along with everyone else. For a minute there she was jealous of Deirdra and Cait, but she and Deirdra had shared the same sentiments about guys over the years. She pushed to her feet to quiet everyone down and said, "Now that you've tasted everything, I could use some help figuring out what to serve to the judges."

"Everything," Brant said.

"Definitely that shrimp thing," Jules added.

"And the duck," Jock chimed in. "That was magnificent."

Daphne grabbed another dessert and said, "And the Paris-Brest!"

"I like breasts, and they don't have to be from Paris," Brant said, causing everyone to *Boo* him, which led to a multitude of jokes.

"What'd I tell you, Abs?" Aiden said as everyone talked over one another. "You might have gotten the magic touch from your father, but"—he motioned to the food, their friends, and the restaurant itself—"this is your *own* brand of magic."

CHAPTER TWENTY-TWO

LATER THAT EVENING, Abby cuddled closer to Aiden on their blanket as laughter and shouts rang out around the bonfire on the beach in front of the Bistro, where they were playing charades. They'd pushed open the glass panels of the restaurant, and the lights of love illuminated the interior. Abby still had so much to do—interviewing, hiring, moving her things from New York—but she couldn't think past tonight. Her last night with Aiden. The pit of her stomach burned at the thought.

"A dead fish?" Leni shouted, drawing Abby's attention.

Brant was standing up with his arms over his head, his hands steepled, wiggling his entire body, and every few seconds he pointed to the water.

"A belly dancer?" Deirdra asked.

"More like belly dancer having convulsions," Grant said.

Brant glowered at him. "Dude. You're not even trying."

Deirdra laughed and said, "Come on, Remington. Use that hot bod of yours in a different way, and maybe we'll figure it out."

Brant did pelvic thrusts, and everyone laughed.

"Love you." Aiden kissed Abby's temple, pulling her tighter against his side.

She rested her head on his shoulder and said, "I love you, too."

Those sentiments had come often, along with yearning and sorrowful looks. How could two fiercely independent people feel so lost at the idea of being apart from someone they'd known only a few weeks? She was done questioning, done worrying. She didn't want to play games or think. She wanted to be alone with Aiden, cocooned within his loving arms for the rest of their time together.

"A mermaid?" Leni guessed.

"Oh! I know!" Jules shouted. "What's that movie where Daryl Hannah is a mermaid?"

"*Splash*!" Leni chimed in.

"I love that movie," Daphne said.

"I know you do, babe. Anything happy." Jock cuddled with Daphne across the fire from Abby and Aiden and said, "Hey, Brant, is it *Mystic River*?"

"No, and I'm not a damn mermaid." Brant raked a hand through his hair. "Come on, Cait, work with me."

"*Me?*" Cait knee-walked forward and warmed her hands by the fire. "I hardly ever watch movies."

Grant nodded toward the Bistro and said, "Hey, Abby, someone's checking out the restaurant."

"Be right back." Abby and Aiden pushed to their feet and headed up to the patio, their friends' voices fading behind them. A young dark-haired guy wearing a striped Baja hoodie with a guitar strapped to his back was peering into the restaurant. When he turned around, Abby recognized his shaggy dark hair, thick brows, and pitch-black scruff. It was the guitarist they'd seen in Chaffee.

"Hi. The restaurant isn't open yet," Abby said. "But were you playing your guitar in Chaffee last week?"

"Yeah, I was." He whistled, and the dalmatian they'd seen in Chaffee bounded around the corner of the building to him. He loved the pooch up, looking more carefully at Abby and Aiden. "I remember you. You danced as I played. Thanks for the donation, man. That was cool of you. I'm looking for Ava. Is she around?"

Abby's chest constricted. Aiden put his arm around her, and she said, "Um, no. How do you know her?"

"She's a friend. I cook for her when I'm in town. I'm here for a few weeks and thought I'd see if she needed my help."

"I'm sorry, but Ava passed away a few months ago. I'm her daughter, Abby, and this is my boyfriend, Aiden."

"Hi." Aiden offered his hand.

"Oh, man . . . That's . . . *Sorry*," he said forlornly, shaking Aiden's hand. "Jagger Jones." He was quiet for a moment, his features sagging as he stroked his dog's head. He lowered his eyes, blinking repeatedly, sniffled, and cleared his throat before meeting their gazes. "I'm . . . I'm sorry for your loss." He swallowed hard. "Ava was a good friend. May I ask how she died?"

Abby wondered about this good friend of her mother's whom she never knew existed. He couldn't be older than about twenty-four or -five. "Cancer. It hit fast. She was gone within a few weeks after she was diagnosed. When was the last time you spoke to her?"

"Over the holidays. She called to check in, which she didn't do very often," he said. "She asked me to play her a song, and I did. She didn't mention being sick. She told me to tell my brother she sends her love, and we talked for a bit."

"She knew your brother?" Abby asked. "I don't recognize you as being from around here."

"I'm not. I'm from Boston. I'm a musician, and I travel a lot. My brother, Gabriel, lives in Boston with our parents. He has nonverbal autism. We do video calls when I'm traveling, and I play my guitar for him. He loved to hear your mom sing."

"She *sang* to him?" A lump formed in Abby's throat. "I'm sorry, I'm . . . She never mentioned you, and it makes me happy that she was singing to *someone*."

Aiden held her tighter and said, "How long did you know Ava?"

321

"On and off for a few years." He looked at Abby and said, "For what it's worth, she talked about you and your sister, Didi, a lot."

"She did?" Abby smiled at the nickname her mother used to call Deirdra.

"Yeah, she was proud of her girls. I guess you took over the Bistro? It looks awesome."

"Yes."

"Well, if you need a cook, I'm not looking to get tied down to a forty-hour-a-week job, but I've got a bit of experience and a few weeks to kill. I haven't worked at any one place for very long because I go where my music takes me, but I filled in at the Empire in Boston for a few months for a chef who was out on maternity leave."

"Wow. Jared Stone's restaurant?" Abby asked. She'd followed Jared Stone's career with awe. He was a well-known chef-turned-restaurateur. His restaurants were top-of-the-line, and he only hired the best staff.

"Yeah, you know him?"

"No, only his reputation."

"He's a cool dude," Jagger said. "I've helped him out a few times there and at his other restaurants when I was between gigs. Some of his digs are a bit pretentious, but they pay the bills."

"Where did you train?" Aiden asked.

"Aw, man." He shook his head, smiling affably. "I figured one of you might ask that. I didn't go to culinary school, but my father's buddy was a chef at a restaurant where I bussed tables in high school, and he took me under his wing for a few years and taught me everything I know. That's how Jared found me. He ate at the restaurant when I was cooking and asked to meet the chef."

"That's a hell of a jump," Aiden said.

He scratched his dog's head and said, "Yeah. The chef who taught me, Ross Denario, is kind of a big deal."

Ross Denario wasn't just a big deal; he was known in the industry for his arrogant attitude as much as he was for his cooking. "You studied under Ross and lived to talk about it?" Abby asked. "That's impressive."

He shrugged again. "You can call him for a reference, if you'd like."

"I'll tell you what. I could use a chef, but this week I'm tied up with the Best of the Island Restaurant Competition. Why don't we do a trial run next week sometime? Do you have time to come in and cook a few things for me?"

"Cool, yeah. I'd love to."

"What type of pay are you looking for?" Aiden asked.

Jagger shrugged. "Whatever. I don't need much. Ava used to pay me two hundred a week under the table and let me live in the apartment above her garage. But I've got my own RV now, so I don't need a place to stay. And like I said, I like to keep things loose. That's kind of how I roll, so I'm not looking to work all that much. But I can fill in, do a few hours here and there, that kind of thing, and play some music on the patio if you're into that."

"We were just talking about that possibility. But I do things differently than my mother did. I'll pay a fair salary," Abby said. "Why don't you come meet my sisters; they own the restaurant, too." She pointed to the bonfire and said, "You can also meet some of our friends."

"Good idea," Aiden said. "What's your pooch's name?"

"Dolly." Dolly looked up at Jagger, and he leaned down and kissed her snout. "Abby, did you say sisters? I didn't realize Ava had more daughters than you and Didi."

"We didn't either until recently. Apparently my mother was good at keeping secrets. Would you like to meet them?"

"Yeah, sure," he said. "We'd love to hang out, if you're sure we won't be imposing."

"It'll give us a chance to get to know you, too," Abby said, and they headed down to the bonfire.

She introduced Jagger and Dolly to everyone and explained that he'd known Ava and had worked at the restaurant. It turned out that Jules, Grant, and Brant all knew who he was and had seen him around a few times over recent summers. That helped to put Abby's mind at ease. Jagger settled right in, and Dolly took a liking to Deirdra, who got up and moved seats four times in the space of an hour or so to avoid having to pet her. Dolly settled in between Cait and Jagger as he began playing his guitar.

Abby headed in to use the bathroom, and when she returned, Deirdra intercepted her before she reached the group.

"How do you know he's not lying?" Deirdra whispered.

"He knew Mom called you Didi."

"Oh my God. Are you freaking kidding me?"

Abby chuckled. "He's nice, Dee, and he's an experienced cook. I like him."

"You like *everyone*." Deirdra crossed her arms, scrutinizing him. "He's a total hippie, and he lives in a *van*."

"An RV, and don't be so judgmental."

"Fine, but he better not call me *Didi*."

Aiden stood as Abby and Deirdra neared the group. Deirdra sat between Jock and Grant, and Aiden drew Abby into his arms, standing a few feet away from the others. "Everything okay with her?"

"She's being her overly cautious self about Jagger."

"I guess that makes two of us. I sent a text to my partner, Ben. He's friends with Jared Stone. Jagger checks out on all fronts. Jared knows his family, says they're good people. He's a hard worker, though as Jagger mentioned, he's never taken Jared up on a long-term offer. The longest stint he's held was three months at a shot."

"Aiden, that was really nice of you, but I could have checked his references."

"I know, but I'm leaving tomorrow, and I wanted to be sure you were safe. I didn't mean to overstep."

"I know you didn't." She went up on her toes and kissed him. "Sending a text to keep me safe is a lot different from buying me a ten-thousand-dollar Viking range and double oven combo."

It had cost fourteen grand, but she didn't need to know that.

"Come on, you two," Leni said. "We're going to play Never Have I Ever."

"Back to my college days," Aiden said, and they went to join the others.

Although Aiden was having a great time with everyone, as the night wore on, he wanted to be alone with Abby. He pressed a kiss to her cheek and said, "Dance with me?"

She glanced at the others, looking a little embarrassed, but she said, "I'd love to."

He helped her up and gathered her into his arms, swaying to the song Jagger was playing.

"Look at Mr. Romance over there," Leni said with an approving smile.

"I want to dance. Come on, hubby-to-be." Jules popped to her feet, dragging Grant up with her. "Jock, get up and dance with your wife."

"I'll never turn down that suggestion." Jock stood and helped Daphne up.

Brant held out his hand to Cait. "What do you say?"

She bit her lower lip and looked at Leni.

Brant offered a hand to Leni, too. "Come on. Let's be the talk of the island. Just me and two beautiful ladies."

Leni stood up, and Cait said, "You two dance. I'm good."

"Come on, Cait," Brant urged.

She stroked Dolly's head and said, "No, thank you. Have fun."

Brant looked at Deirdra. "Dee?"

"I'm good, thanks," Deirdra answered, her skeptical gaze still locked on Jagger.

Brant and Leni danced a few feet away, and Aiden noticed Abby watching Deirdra and Cait as Cait and Jagger struck up a conversation. He loved the way her brow furrowed when she worried about her sisters and her friends. Hell, he loved everything about her. Her all-consuming kisses and loving touch, her laughter and smile, and the way she held his feet to the fire when he gave too much.

"Are you worried about one of them?" he asked. "Or all of them?"

"Neither. Cait looks content. We know she doesn't dance, and Deirdra is more comfortable in her office than on a beach. She's probably thinking of all the work she's going to do when we get home tonight and how much she hates having sand in her shoes."

"You're probably right about that." He gazed into Abby's eyes and said, "Are you having a good time, Abs?"

"Yes. This has been fun, and today couldn't have gone better. I was so nervous, and Deirdra floored me with her compliments. In case I haven't said it enough, thank you for pushing me into the competition. I feel good about it now, and I never would have done it without you." She gasped, and her unstoppable smile cut right to his heart as she said, "I still haven't paid you back for the entry fee. I'm so sorry. I keep forgetting. I promise to write you a check tonight."

He laughed. "Do you have any idea how much I adore you? You have paid me back a hundred times over by making me the happiest I've ever been. I don't want your money, baby. You gave me your heart, and that's the only thing I want."

Her cheeks pinked up, and she said, "So you *don't* want the sexual favors I have lined up for tonight?"

"You are the sexiest woman on the planet." He lowered his lips to hers, kissing her breathless.

Her eyes went hazy with the unmistakable look of love and lust, and she said, "I don't want to sound ungrateful for everything my friends have done, but I'd really like to lock up the Bistro and head home so I can wrap myself up in *you* for the rest of the night."

She didn't have to ask twice.

The girls hugged Abby, and the guys shook hands, tugging Aiden into manly embraces.

"We'll get together when you come back for the grand opening," Grant said.

"Have a guys' night," Jock suggested.

"Or go for a sail," Brant offered.

"That all sounds good to me," Aiden said, realizing he was going to miss them, too.

When the girls hugged him goodbye, Cait hung on longer than the others and said, "I'm going to miss you."

"I'm going to miss you, too. I'm glad you and Abby and Deirdra have each other. Will you be here for the grand opening?"

"I wouldn't miss it for anything."

"Good. I'll see you then." Aiden kissed her cheek and said, "Take care, Cait." He hugged Deirdra and whispered, "Have you figured out that I'm not after Abby for her inheritance yet?"

Deirdra laughed softly. "Yes, and you're actually good for her. I haven't seen my sister this happy since she was a kid. I wish we had more time to get to know each other."

He glanced at Abby and said, "Hopefully we'll have plenty of time for that in the future. Take care of yourself, Deirdra."

"You, too. Cait and I will lock up the restaurant. Get out of here before my sister bursts."

Aiden and Abby headed back to the house, making out all the way up to the bedroom and forcing themselves to remain clothed until they were safely behind Abby's bedroom door. Then their mouths crashed together, shoes and clothes went flying, and the second they were naked, Abby dropped to her knees, taking him in her mouth, stroking and sucking, and *holy hell*, he couldn't take it. Aiden hauled her to her feet, and they tumbled to the bed in a tangle of gropes and hungry kisses. "I'm never going to make it a month without you," he growled, feeling *feral*. He reclaimed her mouth, rough and greedy, and she was right there with him, taking as much as she gave. She arched and writhed, getting the head of his cock wet with her arousal, rubbing her softness against his hard frame. *Fuck*, he was going to miss her. He tore his mouth away, needing to *see* her face. "The *minute* I'm back in the States, I'm coming for you, Abby de Messiéres."

"*Yes*," she panted out, her eyes glistening with sadness and love and so much more.

He grabbed her wrists, holding them by her sides as he moved swiftly down her body, kissing and loving, and finally, *blissfully*, feasting on her sweet, hot center. He wanted to stay right there, pleasuring her for hours, long into tomorrow, and the next day, and the next, but his leaving hung in the balance like a ticking time bomb.

"*Oh Looord.*"

She rocked against his mouth, her wrists pinned by her hips as he took his fill. But just as there was no end to his love, his *need* for her was endless. He moved his mouth higher, using teeth and tongue to make her gasp and mewl. Her thighs flexed, her hips shot up, and with one twist of his tongue, she cried out, loud and unabashedly. Her hips bucked as he released them and moved lower, feasting on her. She grabbed his hair, her hips rocking, a stream of indiscernible sounds flying from her lips.

"*Aiden!* Need you," she pleaded.

He grabbed a condom from the box in the nightstand, sheathing himself faster than ever, and buried himself in one hard thrust. He covered her mouth with his, loving her with *everything* he had. She tasted of sunshine and happiness, sins and seduction, and all the other glorious things she brought to his life, including hopes of a future he so desperately wanted. She squeezed his arms, scratched his torso, and clutched his ass, her nails digging into his flesh. Everything she did— every touch, kiss, and sensual noise—was *exquisite*. Just as he felt her body constrict like a vise, heat shot down his spine, and they spiraled into oblivion together, crying out each other's names, clawing, pawing, *pleading* for more, until they collapsed to the mattress, sated and spent in each other's arms.

"I wish I could stop time," Aiden said against her cheek, kissing her again and again, wishing he had better words, *bigger* words. Words that were as vehement as their love, but his head was spinning, his leaving hovering like a dark cloud.

She didn't respond, just burrowed deeper into his arms.

"I love you, Abby. I love you so damn much."

She held him tighter, burying her face in his chest.

"Look at me, baby." When she lifted teary eyes to his, he felt his heart crack open. He kissed her softly and said, "Two weeks, Abs. In two weeks I'll be back from overseas, and I'll come for a weekend. That's a promise."

"And then . . . ?"

He brushed a kiss over her freckles, knowing he'd miss the sight of them, too, and said, "Then I'll be back again for the grand opening, and we'll figure it out from there. Once I handle my quarterly commitments, I can work from anywhere."

"Here?" Hope glimmered in her eyes.

"Absolutely."

The hopeful smile that had first reeled him in curved her lips, soothing the fissure inside him. They held each other until he had no choice but to take care of the condom, and when he came back to bed, she settled into his arms and drifted off to sleep. He lay awake, reveling in her soft snores and the sweet hum he loved so much, in the feel of how right they were together.

He brushed his lips over her forehead, drinking in her familiar scent, which had become as much a part of him as the air he breathed. He didn't question how far they'd come, or why he hadn't fought his feelings for her even for a moment. He thanked whatever higher powers had brought them together and whispered, "You changed my world, Abigail de Messiéres, and when I come back, I'm going to change yours."

CHAPTER TWENTY–THREE

ABBY AWOKE TO the feel of Aiden's tender kisses, and for a split second she felt like everything in the world was right and wonderful. And then she remembered he was leaving on a nine o'clock flight.

"Abs," he whispered. "Wake up, babe. We have one last thing to check off our list."

She tried to remember what was left on their list. *Skinny-dipping.* She shook her head, snuggling deeper into his warmth, eyes still closed. "I'm not going skinny-dipping, and I'm not ready to go pack up your room at the resort."

"We're not doing either. I promise."

She opened her eyes, his handsome face coming into focus in the dimly lit bedroom.

"Hi, beautiful. Want to throw on a sweatshirt and pants, bundle up in blankets, and watch the sunrise with me from the hammock?"

Just when she thought her heart couldn't get any fuller, he made her shift things around and make room for more. "I'd love to."

They bundled up and headed into the chilly predawn air. The shells they'd collected by the lighthouse were still filled with birdseed. It was a nice thought, but the birds weren't interested. They made their way across the lawn, passing the gardens they'd planted together, and climbed into the hammock. Abby nearly tipped them out as they got situated, bringing laughter, embraces, and more wonderful kisses. When they settled in to watch the birth of a new day, she couldn't help wondering what Aiden would be like when he left the island. She hadn't gotten to see him as the workaholic businessman he and Remi claimed him to be, though given how much they'd done while he was there, it wasn't hard to imagine him in a suit and tie, working endlessly.

"Do you think I would like Workaholic Aiden?" she asked.

"I hope so, but I'm not sure that version could exist around you. Or at all anymore, quite honestly. I like this version of myself better. The guy I am with you."

She melted at that. "I like this version of myself better, too."

"With you I have discovered so many parts of myself that I never knew existed, and the thing is, Abs, I think they only exist with you. And now I'm heading back to work with an even greater task than finding a life."

"What's that?"

"Figuring out how to function after leaving such a big part of myself behind."

Tears welled in her eyes. He kissed her lips, then her freckles, as he'd done so often, and still it felt as intimate as the first time.

"Don't cry," he whispered. "We're a good thing, baby. The *best* thing."

She rested her head on his chest, and they lay in comfortable silence, sharing tender kisses, tight embraces, and heartfelt whispers. Eventually the sun peeked over the horizon, making its slow ascent into the sky.

After a long while, Aiden said, "Come on, sweetheart. Let's get showered. I have a surprise for you."

"It better not be another oven," she said lightly.

They lingered under the warm spray of the shower, making love one last time. Then they gathered Aiden's things and drove over to the Bistro.

"What are we doing here?" she asked as he put his arm around her.

As they walked along the side patio, he said, "I thought it would be fitting to share the last breakfast of my vacation where it all began."

A gust of salty sea air stung her cheeks as they came around the front of the Bistro. Abby's heart swelled at the sight of the table Aiden had been sitting at when she'd first met him. It was draped with a white tablecloth, with all the fancy trimmings of their first breakfast together, including a single rose in a crystal vase. In the center of the table was a covered silver platter.

"Oh, Aiden. How did you do this without leaving the house?"

"I've made a few friends while I've been here." He lifted the top off the platter, revealing several delicious pastries. "Keira's specialties."

She got choked up and hugged him. "You spoil me."

"No, babe. I treat you the way you deserve to be treated."

She remembered how she'd called him a *god* for sharing his breakfast with her the first time they'd eaten together, and he'd told her she should set that bar a bit higher. There was no bar higher than Aiden Aldridge.

They moved their chairs close together, talking and sharing their breakfast treats, soaking in every second together. With the sounds of the sea kissing the shore and the sun warming her cheeks, Abby thought today would be perfect, if only Aiden didn't have to leave.

When they finished eating, they lingered as long as they could, before Aiden said, "I think it's time."

He rose to his feet, drawing her up and into his arms and gazing so deeply into her eyes, she had no doubt that he could *see* everything she felt. He ran his fingers through her hair and said, "I've been trying to figure out how to tell you what I feel for you in a different way, but nothing seems big enough. Some people find their first loves in middle school or high school, and for the rest of their lives, nobody measures up. Others go their whole lives without finding the one person who makes them feel complete. I am so lucky to have found my first, last, and *only* love at thirty-eight."

Tears slipped from her eyes.

"I love you, Abby, and I'm going to keep finding new and different ways to show you and tell you until you hear it even when we're miles apart."

Aiden had made it to almost forty years old without having to deal with the pain of leaving a woman he was in love with behind. Standing on the patio of the Bistro with Abby in his arms, he wished to hell he could go forty more and stay right there with her. But there were meetings to be had, business to be conducted, and arrangements to be coordinated if he hoped to change his life in a way that made sense for both of them.

He gazed into the big, beautiful green eyes that owned his heart and soul and did what had to be done. "We'd better get up to my room to pack up the rest of my things, so I have time to drop you at home before going to the airport."

They drove to the Silver House, and he held her in the elevator, his heart aching anew with every passing minute. He never could have imagined putting anyone or anything other than Remi and her family above work, but every iota of his being screamed for him to say *fuck it all* and stay on the island. He gritted his teeth against the urge, knowing it wasn't a possibility. There were too many people counting on him.

When they walked into his room, it felt like he was treading in someone else's life. He'd slept there only a handful of nights, though his work files were strewn across the desk and dresser. There was a finality to packing his belongings, the last step before heading back to the world that no longer seemed quite as important.

"Where are your suitcases?" Abby asked, putting on a brave face, but there was no hiding the sadness in her eyes.

"Come here, babe." He gathered her in his arms, holding her tight.

"Goodbyes suck," she said shakily.

"They sure do."

"I'm not a weepy girl. I'm sorry I keep losing it."

He leaned back far enough to see her face and said, "Don't you dare be sorry for loving me enough to miss me. I'm sure as hell not sorry for loving you so much I physically ache at the thought of leaving you."

"We're a mess," she said.

"The best kind of mess, but I'm pretty sure love is supposed to be messy."

She pushed out of his arms and huffed. "No more tears. Suitcases?"

He retrieved his suitcase and briefcase from the closet and set the briefcase on the table. "Would you mind throwing my files in the briefcase, and I'll pack my stuff from the bedroom and bathroom?"

"Sure."

He kissed her forehead and went into the bedroom before he lost his mind and hauled her into his arms again. He shoved his clothes into the suitcase, then packed his toiletries. He took one last look in the mirror, barely recognizing the suntanned man staring back at him. He hadn't shaved in days, and his hair was in need of a trim, curling at the edges. But it was the unfamiliar look in his eyes that stopped him cold. He'd always seen a shrewd businessman staring back at him, and while he knew he could recapture that man when he walked into a boardroom, he liked this new look even better. It was a look of relaxation and happiness.

It was the look of love.

He took a quick selfie and thumbed out a text message. *Thank you for forcing this vacation on me. I think you'll agree I've learned how to chill. Love you, sis. I'll be in touch when I settle in overseas.* He sent it off and composed another text. *This is the face of the man who loves you. Xox,* and sent it to Abby.

He zipped his suitcase and headed into the other room. "Ready, Abs?"

She was sitting on the edge of the bed with an open folder in her lap. When she lifted her face, there were tears in her eyes. "What is this, Aiden?" Her voice was filled with hurt and confusion. "Why do you have an entire folder on the Bistro? A copy of the original offer from DRA Capital?"

Fuuck. "I can explai—"

"I saw your signatures on some of the documents. It was *you* who tried to buy the Bistro, and then you tried to get me to put some other deal together to line your own pockets as an angel investor." She pushed to her feet and threw the folder on the bed.

"Abby, *listen* to me—"

"You never said a word." Her entire body was shaking, her eyes casting daggers. "You pushed for me to invest with *you*, the *angel investor.*" She said *angel investor* like a curse. "How could you do that to me?"

"I didn't want you to lose the restaurant or your house, and with a home equity line of credit, both are at risk." He reached for her, but she twisted away. "Abby, come on. You know me better than that."

She crossed her arms, tears streaming down her cheeks. "Do I? Because I'm not sure I have any idea who you really are. You *lied* to me."

"I *never* lied to you."

"You said you were in finance."

"I *am* in finance," he said through gritted teeth, trying to hold his shit together. "Jesus, Abby. *Yes*, before I met you, I saw the restaurant, checked it out, and put in an offer. But then I met you, Abs, and you turned it down. There was no need for me to say anything—"

"Right, because who needs honesty? Obviously not the girl who said it was her number one priority."

"Damn it, Abby," he snapped. "I liked you from the moment we met, and I didn't want you to see me like every other woman sees me— as the guy who could buy them diamonds and yachts and whisk them away to exotic places."

She crossed her arms, the anger in her eyes slaying him. "So you were afraid I was a gold digger?"

"*No!* Just the opposite. You were so different. You were—*are*—real and down to earth. You're kind and funny, and I wanted to enjoy being with you without the pressure of everything else that goes along with being fucking *Aiden Aldridge.* I didn't think I'd fall head-over-heels in love with you. And then I *did*, and you needed money, and I had it. It's as simple as that. I *tried* to give you the money out of my own pocket, but you refused my offer, so I tried to do the *only other thing* I could to ensure that you wouldn't risk losing the restaurant and the house."

"More like you wanted to be there to collect if I screwed up," she said angrily.

She tried to stalk past him, but he grabbed her hand, unwilling to let the only woman he'd ever loved walk out of his life. "That's not it, Abby. If you'd taken me up on the investment, I would have had a separate legal document written up directing every goddamn penny you paid back go into an account for *you* in *your* name, not mine."

"It's easy to say that now, isn't it?" she seethed. "I asked you for *one* thing, Aiden. You knew what I went through with my mother and how many times she lied to me and hurt me. All I asked for was transparency, and you gave me lies."

"I *never* lied to you. Christ, Abby. Do you *really* think if I had something to hide, I would have been stupid enough to ask you to put away my files? Do you even hear what you're accusing me of? I told you how I was raised to believe if I *have*, I should *give*; I should help others. Why, for fuck's sake, would I not give to the woman who I was falling in love with?"

"It's not about *giving*. It's about how you went about it," she hollered. "It makes me feel like I don't really know who you are. The guy who will do whatever he wants and say the hell with my feelings, or the guy who . . . who . . ."

"Who loves you enough to do whatever it takes to make your dreams come true. This is *me*, Abby. The same guy you said you loved five minutes ago. I haven't changed. I haven't lied. If anything, I've told you more about myself, more *truths*, than I've ever told anyone else. I told you about my family and my famous sister. The person whose identity I have guarded with my *life* for years. I *wanted* you to know those things, Abby, because I knew, even then, that there was something special between us."

Her expression softened the slightest bit, giving him a shred of hope.

"Did I screw up, Abs? *Yes*. Do I regret not telling you I was the original investor? You bet. But after you said you didn't want to pitch an investment deal, I didn't even think about it again except to say to myself that I would do everything within my power to make sure you didn't lose your house or your business."

Her eyes narrowed, and her chin lifted in defiance. "I'm perfectly capable of doing that myself."

"I know you are, but it's *business*. Anything can happen, and for as long as you use that line of credit, your house and your restaurant are at risk. And they are as big a part of you as *you* have become of *me*."

Her lower lip trembled, and her shoulders sagged.

"Abby, sweetheart," he said in a gentler tone. "I'm sorry that I hurt you, but if you know me at all, then you know I wasn't trying to."

"Well, you *did*. How can I ever trust you again?" Tears slid down her cheeks.

"Baby, please think about what you're saying. What would I have to gain by tricking you?"

"I don't know," she snapped. "But obviously something. The *house*. The *restaurant*. You said yourself it was worth millions."

He felt like he was climbing a sand dune in a windstorm, her fury whipping the sand out from under him, sending him tumbling backward with his every effort. She might be too angry and hurt to hear him, but he wasn't about to let her obliterate everything they had over a fucking mistake. He clenched his teeth so hard he was afraid they'd crack and gritted out, "You know what? I'm done pussyfooting around who I am. *Yes*, your property is worth millions, but I could buy the whole damn island—*twice*—and still have enough money left to buy three more. You want to persecute me because I'm rich? You go right ahead, but you're making a *huge* mistake, Abby. Think about it." He stepped closer to her, but she stepped back, breaking his fucking heart. "Why can't you believe that I was falling in love with you and I wanted to help?"

She was shaking her head. "I can't . . . I need to think, and you need to catch a plane." She inhaled, loud and ragged, and pulled the door open.

He stepped behind her, his heart shredding. "Please don't do this. I love you, Abby. I'm *not* letting you go."

With her back to him, she said, "I don't know if I'm asking you to. I just . . . I need space to think. Can you listen to me this once and give me that? *Please.*"

Fighting against every action his mind and his heart told him to take, to go after her, to make her understand, he stood rooted in place, determined to listen even if it killed him—and as he watched his whole world walk out the door, he was pretty fucking sure it might.

CHAPTER TWENTY-FOUR

ABBY WALKED HOME in a fog, hoping to avoid running into anyone she knew by taking the long way, cutting through backyards and backstreets the way she'd done as a kid. Anger and hurt battled inside her, making her nauseous and teary and so damn confused she didn't know which way was up. When she finally got home, the sight of the garden nearly brought her to her knees, and when a plane flew overhead from the island airport, her heart plummeted.

She dragged herself into the house, her chest constricting at the sight of the spotless living room, ready for painting and for her furniture from New York to be moved in. She and Aiden had joked about keeping her mother's couch since it was where they'd first made love. Memories of the start to that amazing day when Aiden bit her butt, then wooed her like she'd never been wooed before swamped her. His laughter rang in her ears as fresh as morning dew, turning all those confusing emotions to a throbbing ache of sadness and disappointment. That disappointment fueled a tornado of anger—at herself for letting her guard down and at him for not being one hundred percent transparent with her.

She stormed into the kitchen and right past Cait and Deirdra, who were sitting at the table. She yanked the refrigerator door open, then immediately slammed it closed.

"Hey," Cait said. "You okay?"

Abby paced, feeling like she was breathing fire. "Fine!" She grabbed a pot from the cabinet and banged it on the stove with a *clank*.

"Looks like someone is ready for a mimosa." Deirdra lifted the pitcher sitting in front of her and filled the three empty glasses before her. "I'm not leaving until later, so we've got plenty of time to drown your sorrows."

"And I'm here until Friday, so if you need to curl up in a ball and cry, I'll take care of everything, including being there to meet the installer for the oven tomorrow. While I can't cook for the judges, I did make you these." Cait handed her a sketchbook. "I know they can't replace Aiden, but hopefully they'll help cheer you up a little."

Abby opened the sketchbook and trapped a sob in her chest at the drawing of her and Aiden at the Bistro the first day he'd shown up to help in his short-sleeve button-down, khaki pants, and those stupid loafers she loved. Her hands were on his chest, his arms wrapped possessively around her. Cait had captured the wolfish grin on his face just as Abby had remembered it seconds before they'd realized Cait had walked in. She flipped the page, finding a sketch of the first night she'd cooked him and Cait dinner. He was gazing adoringly at her, and she was smiling so big, it hurt to see it.

She closed the pad and groaned as she slapped it on the table. "Thank you, but . . . *Ugh!*" She fisted her hands. "I'm so mad right now I can't see straight."

"That's what the mimosa is for." Deirdra thrust a glass in her direction.

"I don't *want* a mimosa!" She stalked a path beside the stove. "Wait until you hear what he did!"

"Bought you a Lamborghini?" Deirdra smirked.

"This isn't funny, Dee! *He's* the investor who tried to buy the restaurant, *and* he's the investor he was pushing me to use for that frigging angel deal. I found copies of the original offer when we were packing up his hotel room. Thank *God* I said no. He's been lying to me this *whole* time." She stopped pacing, staring angrily at Cait's and Deirdra's gaping jaws. "He told me he was in *finance*, and I bought it hook, line, and sinker. Frigging idiot. I let him get to me." Tears spilled from her eyes, and she began pacing again.

"That *asshole*," Deirdra snapped. "He's lucky he's gone because I'd like to give him a piece of my mind. I thought he was after your inheritance at first, but now it all makes sense. He was after *everything*. Fucking greedy prick."

Despite her hurt and anger, Deirdra's accusations stung. "He's not a *prick*."

"I said *greedy* prick," Deirdra seethed.

"Wait," Cait interrupted. "Can we slow down a minute? I know lots of manipulative, greedy pricks, and I'm sorry, but Aiden doesn't strike me as one."

"He tried to force her to take an investment deal and never said *he* was the investor. If that's not the very definition of a greedy prick, then I don't know what is," Deirdra snapped.

"He didn't try to *force* me," Abby exclaimed. "He had offered to invest personally, and when I turned that down, he *suggested* that I put together a deal and present it to the investor. But he didn't push hard when I said I wasn't doing it. He just explained why it wasn't the best idea, because I could lose the house and the restaurant."

"Did he tell you why he never said that *he* was the investor?" Cait asked.

"Does that even matter?" Deirdra spat.

"*God*, Deirdra. *Yes*, it matters. I saw them together way more than you did, and there is no way he could have faked the way he looked at Abby. I felt his love for her from across the room *every* time they were together, and if you don't believe me, it's all right here." She shoved the sketchbook across the table. "Proof of two people falling in love, not a conniving asshole and a duped woman."

Cait flipped open the sketchbook, paging through one picture after another. Several depicted Aiden looking at Abby when she was unaware, with so much love in his eyes, it jumped off the page. Each image hit Abby like a knife to her chest.

"If he's a dick, then he totally had me fooled, because all I saw was a guy who believed in you, fell in love with you, and would move mountains to make good things happen for you," Cait said. "And if that's the case, you should run in the opposite direction, because I'm pretty damn good at judging people, and that would mean he's a master manipulator."

"I *know* he loves me," Abby said vehemently through tears. "I *know* he believes in me and wants good things for me. That's why it hurts so bad."

Cait reached for her hand, her eyes pleading as she said, "You're my sister, and I want to be wholly on your side with this, but I'd love to hear what he has to say, because it makes no sense to me."

"I don't even know what *my* side is. I *love* him, and I *know* he loves me." Sobs stole Abby's voice.

Cait embraced her.

"Abby, you can love him and still believe he'd hurt you. Look at Mom," Deirdra said.

Abby gasped to fill her lungs, stepping out of Cait's embrace. "He *isn't* Mom! He said he never told me that he was the investor behind the original offer because he wanted me to see him as a regular person, not some rich guy who apparently could buy the whole island if he wanted to."

"If that's true, then it makes even less sense as to why he would bother trying to take the house and the restaurant," Cait pointed out. "They have sentimental value to you, but if he's a cold-blooded investor with no attachment to you or the island, much less this house or the restaurant, then why waste three weeks acting like he's falling in love with you?"

"I don't think he *acted*," Abby fumed. "I said I know he loves me, and I believe he wanted me to think he was just a regular guy at first, because when he told me who his sister was, he said he usually made a point of *not* telling women about Remi. He said once women found out he had a famous sister, it changed everything, negating him as anything more than a means to an end. He didn't say it in those words, but that's how I took it. And I believe that, too." She flopped into a chair, crossed her arms on the table, and *plunked* her forehead on them. "I *hate* this."

"I guess it makes sense why he didn't tell you about the original offer," Deirdra conceded. "But what about the other deal, the one you said he *suggested*?"

Abby met Deirdra's scrutinizing gaze. "He said if I had gone forward with an angel investor deal, he would have had a legal agreement written up indicating that the money I paid back would be set aside for me."

"Now, *that* sounds like Aiden," Cait exclaimed.

Deirdra gave her a deadpan look. "Or a really good manipulator."

"*Don't* villainize him," Abby warned.

"*Me*? You're in tears over him not telling you the truth."

"Yeah, but that's *my* boyfriend, *my* choice. I'm hurt, and I'm mad, and I'm trying to figure out if I'm walking down a path with a guy who's going to lead me to a lifetime of lies, or if his fucking heart is too big and he's so used to making things happen, he doesn't realize gray areas don't work for me. I need crystal-clear lines."

Deirdra held her gaze and said, "The fact that you even have to say that worries me."

"Deirdra, this is the same guy who believed in Abby enough to enter her into the competition and help her every step of the way to get there," Cait said angrily. "He even went to the bank with her to make sure she didn't get screwed. And did you notice the gardens? Or that he power washed the house? Do you know that he's the one who had your dad's paintings framed for the Bistro? Or that he was filling those little shells on the porch with birdseed every day just so Abby could see the birds?"

A sob burst from Abby's throat. "I thought the birds weren't eating it."

"He was like the flipping birdseed fairy," Cait said. "I saw him doing it when you were cooking dinner one night, and he asked me not to say anything."

"You didn't find that curious?" Deirdra accused.

Cait crossed her arms, eyes narrowing. "*No.* I found it sweet and romantic that he wanted Abby to see the birds but not worry about maintaining the feeders."

"So you're on *his* side?" Deirdra shook her head.

"I'm not on either *side.* Abby has a right to be pissed that he didn't tell her. But come on, you guys. This is *Aiden.* The guy who basically lived with Abby for three weeks, stuck by her side working his perfectly manicured fingernails to the bone for her. Abby said she turned his money down, so it's not like he was hiding the fact that he wanted to help her. It sounds like he tried to help her in another way."

Deirdra snapped, "That's called a lie of omission—"

"No shit, Deirdra, but it's not like he was lying about another woman or having a wife, for Pete's sake!" Cait snapped. "He lied to try to help her, and in doing so, to help *us,* too. We're all in this restaurant together, whether you're a silent partner or not."

"Okay, I can see that," Deirdra relented. "But I'm on Abby's side, first and always, and right now I'm pretty pissed at him for hurting her."

Abby pushed to her feet, feeling sick and exhausted. "This is all too much. I'm going upstairs to lie down." She picked up the sketchbook and said, "Thank you for these. I really love them."

"Want to take the pitcher?" Deirdra asked.

Abby shook her head and went up to her bedroom. She kicked off her sandals and lay on her bed. Aiden's cologne lingered on the pillow. She rolled onto her side, catching sight of a framed picture of her and Aiden that hadn't been there before. It was the selfie they'd taken the first day he'd helped her at the Bistro, right after she'd agreed to help him work through his list.

She sat up to pick up the picture and found a handwritten note from Aiden along with the letter from her mother tucked beneath it. Setting the letter from her mother aside—she didn't need to go down that rabbit hole—she read Aiden's note.

Dear Abs,

This is one of my favorite pictures. I would have kissed you then if Cait hadn't walked in. I never knew three weeks could feel like three wonderful years. I probably didn't say this enough while I was there (I was too busy falling in love with you), but thank you for helping me with my Let Loose list and for bringing a new level of happiness and true love into my life. These next two weeks can't pass soon enough.

Yours always, Aiden

Abby's tears fell onto the note. She pressed it to her chest as she lay down and closed her eyes, wishing she could rewind time. Wishing he had told her he was the investor. Wishing she could *believe* he was the liar she accused him of being, because that would give her the clarity to walk away. But in her heart she *didn't* believe it, and walking away would mean losing the truest love she'd ever known and the only love she wanted.

CHAPTER TWENTY-FIVE

ABBY WALKED UP to the Bistro Tuesday morning feeling like she'd lived a hundred years in the last forty-eight hours. Thank God for Cait. She'd not only met the installer yesterday, but she also had the patience of a saint. One minute Abby was vehemently upset about Aiden risking their relationship by not telling her that he was the investor, and in the next, she was poring over the sketches Cait had drawn, missing him so much she could barely move. It hadn't helped that when she'd finally checked her phone Sunday night, she'd seen a text Aiden had sent hours earlier with a picture of his handsome face and the message *This is the face of the man who loves you.* That had only made her cry harder.

She stared at the door to the restaurant, and for the first time since returning to the island, she didn't want to walk in.

But she had to.

The judges were coming in a few hours, and she had a competition to win.

She filled her lungs with as much courage as she could swallow and headed inside. When she flicked the light switch, bringing to life the colorful lights and elegant chandeliers, a pang of sadness moved through her. She swallowed hard against it, refusing to fall apart. She was *not* her mother. She didn't need a man to make her whole.

Looking straight ahead instead of up, she strode into the kitchen, her pulse quickening at the sight of the gleaming oven unit Aiden had bought. She ran her fingers along the cool stainless-steel edge, and memories of the day the stove had arrived trickled in.

I do listen. I listen to you saying and doing all the right things to prove you can do this on your own. But, baby, you mean the world to me, and I had to listen to my heart, too . . . I told you my biggest flaw was doing too much for the people I care about . . . When you love someone, don't you love their flaws, too? I love your stubborn streak as much as I love your determination.

Tears welled in her eyes. "*No,*" she said through clenched teeth. "I am *not* crying again."

She threw her shoulders back, grabbed the packet of information the installers had left, and stalked into the office. She riffled through the packet, setting aside the warranty card information, and scanned the receipt. *Fourteen thousand dollars?* She blinked several times, sure she'd misread the numbers, but as she looked more carefully, she realized that with delivery and installation, the unit had cost Aiden almost *fifteen* thousand dollars.

Holy. Fudge.

She sank down to the chair, her heart racing. She *never* would have bought such an expensive unit. What was Aiden thinking? Her gaze moved to the receipt for the chandeliers on the edge of the desk. She picked it up, remembering how happy she'd been when she'd found them. She went to the file cabinet and dug out the old article they'd found with the pictures of the lights her father had used, and she carried it into the dining room. Her pulse quickened again as she compared the pictures to the chandeliers she'd bought. They were almost identical, with the exception of the colored crystals. Aiden's voice whispered through her head. *This store has Abby written all over it.* Her stomach knotted with an uncomfortable thought. She headed back into the office and didn't give herself time to back out as she called the number on the receipt.

"Whimsical Things. This is Medina."

"Hi, Medina. This is Abby de Messiéres. I was in the other day and bought three chandeliers that your grandmother had in the stockroom and a few other lights and pictures."

"I remember. Hi."

"Hi. I love the chandeliers, and I'm curious about where they came from. Is your grandmother around?"

"She's not here, but I can check the files. Hold on."

Abby became more anxious with every passing minute as she waited for Medina to return. On the heels of the anxiety was guilt, thick as sludge, for even making the call.

A few painful minutes later, Medina came back on the line. "Hi. Sorry that took so long, but I found the paperwork. It says they were a custom order. Let's see . . . They were seventy-two hundred dollars each, paid in full. Hold on. This is weird. It looks like there were a bunch of smaller lights custom ordered at the same time, but they're all different prices—fifty, forty-six, twenty-nine, seventeen, thirty-two, and twenty-four dollars, all paid in full. And there was a refund given for . . . *Oh.* Huh. The refund was given the day you bought the lights, for the total amount you paid." Medina quoted the amount and said, "I'm sorry, what did you want to know again?"

"Um." Abby swallowed hard, trying to make her brain think past *Holy shit, Aiden!* "Nothing. Thank you." She ended the call and sank back in the chair, flabbergasted.

"Abby? Abby honey?" Shelley's voice rang out. "Are you here?"

Shit. She loved Shelley, but she was too rattled to fake being normal, much less happy. *Lord give me strength.* "I'm here!" Abby feigned her best smile and headed into the dining room.

"Hey, darlin'. Guess someone's beau is missing her." Shelley motioned to a man standing behind her carrying two of the most enormous bouquets of roses Abby had ever seen. "I know my bouquets, and that's a lot more than two dozen roses."

"Six, to be exact, for Abigail de Messiéres." The man pronounced her name as *de Meh-sears*.

"That's me. Thank you." Abby took one of the vases and set it on a table. "You can put that one here, too."

He set the vase on the table and said, "You must have done something right. Have a nice day."

After he left, Abby snagged the card from the plastic holder.

"You've got yourself one heck of a classy beau." Shelley leaned in to smell the flowers.

Abby tried to smile, but her thoughts were whirling as she read the card. *Good luck, Abs. You've got this! Love, Aiden.* Even after the way she'd gone off on him, he still believed in her?

Shelley plucked a card from the other bouquet and handed it to her. "I guess he has too much love for just one card."

Abby took the card out of the tiny envelope and read it. *Hey, beautiful, please don't let my mistakes sidetrack you today. Let your magic shine, babe. I'm sorry, and I love you. A*

Do not cry. Do not cry. Tears brimmed in her eyes. *Shit.* She turned her back to Shelley as tears slipped down her cheeks.

"Aren't they lovely?" Shelley said cheerily.

Abby's breathing hitched. "Mm-hm."

"Oh, honey." Shelley embraced her. "It's okay to miss him. Let it out, baby girl."

"It's not *that*." Abby stepped from her arms, swiping at her tears. "I mean it *is* that. I do miss him, but I'm so *mad*, Shelley. I'm so *hurt*! First he entered me into the competition; then he bought me an *oven*. And that's not all."

"No?" Shelley asked, her face riddled with confusion.

"Oh *no*. I found out that he spent *thousands* of dollars on those chandeliers because he knew how much my father's meant to me." She thrust her index finger up toward the lights. "*And* he tried to lend me money for the restaurant."

"Oh, sweetheart." Shelley's brows furrowed. "*Now* I understand why you're so upset."

"Right?" She wiped her eyes. "*Thank* you!"

"Oh, yes. What a bastard, doing all those things to help you." Shelley leaned closer and said, "If you don't want him, can I get his number for Sutton or Leni? Because thoughtful men are hard to come by."

"*Ugh!*" Abby threw her fists in the air. Shelley was looking at her like she'd really lost her mind, and that was *exactly* how she felt.

"Come here, sugar." Shelley took her by the shoulders and guided her into a chair. She sat beside Abby and said, "Now, how about you take a deep breath and tell me why those things are so horrible."

Abby told her the whole story, every little detail, and then she slumped against the back of the chair, depleted. Shelley didn't respond. "Aren't you going to say anything?"

"Yes. But before I do, honey, you've always trusted your heart. What does your heart want right now?"

"That's not a fair question."

"Love isn't fair, honey."

"So I'm learning. I love him, Shelley. I love him so much I can barely breathe when I think about not being with him. But I don't want to spend my life wondering if I'm being told the truth or not."

"I understand that. But to be sure we're on the same page, you're not talking about if he's with other women or has a criminal background, right?"

"He'd never cheat, and he's not a criminal."

"Okay, then we're talking about wanting him to tell the truth about if he does something special for you, right? Like having the chandeliers made and paying for most of them?"

"*Yes*, exactly."

"Then, honey, don't let yourself fall in love with *anyone*, because the very nature of being in love is wanting to do what no one else can for the person who means the most to you. And if you don't want that, then maybe you don't want to be in love."

"But—"

"Hear me out, Abby. For some couples the stakes are different, because they might not have much in the way of money. The guy might buy his girlfriend a dress she'd had her heart set on, or a pair of earrings. Let's say you're dating one of those guys, and they want to buy you earrings, but they're pricey, so you say no thank you, and you go on your merry way. Then one night you're getting ready for bed, and lo and behold, you find this pretty little gift box on your pillow with no note. You know who put it there, but when you ask him, he says he didn't do it. Do you end the relationship over that?"

"No, but we're not talking about hundred-dollar earrings."

"You're right. We're talking about a man who has much more to give than most men. I understand why you're upset. He made a big mistake, and he made it to *you*. Trusting doesn't come easily for you because of what you went through with your mother, which is completely understandable. I love you like my own child. You know that. If I thought Aiden did something malicious, I would tell you. Actually, I'd hunt him down and make him wish he'd never set foot on this island. But nothing you've told me changes my opinion of him. He didn't try to steal your money or lead you astray. He found a way to give you the *earrings* that had mesmerized you from the time you were a very little girl."

"But what if it's not just lights and money? What if there's something more he's after?"

"Oh, believe you me, honey. There *is*. What that man is after is worth a *lot* more than lights or money. Aiden Aldridge is after your beautiful, stubborn, *scared*—and rightly so—heart. That man wants forever with you." She touched Abby's leg and said, "I think the real questions are, do you want forever with him, and can you forgive him for his mistakes?"

Abby lowered her eyes and said, "Other than these flowers, he hasn't even reached out to me to try to fix things since our fight. Maybe I ruined us by being such a hothead, and he's done with me."

"Or maybe he's giving you time to figure out what you really want." Shelley pulled Abby up to her feet and said, "I can still see you at five years old following your daddy around the restaurant and gardening with your mama. Your gorgeous hair all wild and tangled, wrist deep in dirt, and always a smile to make everyone's day. You were a special girl, Abby, and you're an extraordinary woman. Listen to your heart, darlin', and you can't go wrong."

"I'm trying," Abby said, drying her eyes.

"I didn't get to tell you how great this place looks. You've really outdone yourself. Your parents would be proud of you and thrilled *for* you."

A sliver of guilt hit her. "I still haven't read my mom's letter."

"That's okay, sweetheart. You will when you're ready."

Abby looked at the roses and the lights, and her eyes filled with tears again.

"What's wrong, honey?"

"You said the very nature of being in love is wanting to do what no one else can for the person who means the most to you." She swiped at a tear. "Aiden did so much for me, but I didn't do anything for him. We checked off things on a list he had, but they were silly things like bike riding and going to the beach. I didn't do anything *big*."

"Honey, Aiden has had a lifetime of *big*. You gave him the one thing money can't buy. You gave him love with no strings attached." Shelley drew her into a warm embrace and said, "Now, you have to promise me something."

"Anything."

"This is your special day, and I know it will be hard, but you have to put these worries about Aiden aside and allow yourself to focus on making the best damn meal of your life. We're all counting on you to win this one." Shelley lowered her voice and said, "I love Wells Silver and I always will, but it's time a queen wore the best restaurant crown." She hugged her again and said, "We're all pulling for you, sweetheart, and those roses tell me Aiden is, too."

Cait showed up shortly after Shelley left, which was luckily enough time for Abby to do as Shelley said and tuck away all of her heartache and pull herself together. Abby and Cait pulled out all the stops, draping the tables with linen, using their best place settings, and thanks to Aiden, they used roses for centerpieces. Abby cooked like her life depended on it, using her father's recipes with her own touches, and Cait was right there by her side, keeping her company and helping her with anything she needed—including talking out her feelings. Cait was much better at it than their overprotective attorney sister, whose parting words yesterday had been *Call me if he needs his ass kicked, and if you two make up, he'd better do some big-time groveling.*

Sometimes Abby wondered if Deirdra ever let her guard down.

Abby and Cait changed into nicer clothes before the judges arrived. The four highly acclaimed food critics from Boston and New York hardly said a word before sitting down to eat. Abby served the meals wearing her chef's coat and hat, and then she and Cait stood off to the side watching anxiously as the judges ate. The two impeccably suited older gentlemen with salt-and-pepper hair stared straight ahead as they ate, their stoic expressions giving nothing away. The two women, one older, tall, and thin with short gray hair, the other a middle-aged, short, stout blonde, wore conservative dresses and slightly less unyielding expressions. Abby felt like she was eight years old again, waiting for her turn to see the principal after she and Leni got caught passing notes in class. She was glad Cait was there, but Aiden had become such a big part of her life—of *their* lives—and of the restaurant, she felt his absence like a missing limb.

Cait grabbed her hand and whispered, "Do you think they like it? I think they do. They have to. What do you think?"

"I'm trying not to think," she said quietly. "We did the best we could."

Finally, what felt like two hours later but in reality was probably one, the judges set their napkins beside their plates. They shared a practiced glance and a confirmatory nod, rising to their feet in unison.

The taller of the two gentlemen said, "Thank you, ladies. We appreciate the fine meal."

"We hope you enjoyed it. Thank you for taking the time to judge the contest and for eating here." *For eating here?* Abby shook his hand, wishing she'd been more eloquent.

"It was our pleasure," the short blonde said. "Have a nice afternoon."

As soon as the door closed behind them, Abby and Cait both exhaled loudly.

"Did you hear that?" Abby asked excitedly.

"The pleasure thing? Yeah! That's got to be good!"

Abby let out a squeal and hugged Cait. They jumped around and wiggled their hips.

"Look at you! You're dancing!" Abby exclaimed.

"I'm celebrating!"

Abby reached for her phone to share the news with Aiden—and froze, remembering their fight.

"Are you texting Deirdra?" Cait asked.

Abby tried to hide her discomfort. "Uh-huh." She thumbed out a text to Deirdra. *Went well!*

"Aren't you going to text the chandelier fairy?"

Butterflies swarmed in her belly. "I was thinking about it. He worked *so* hard for this."

"You don't have to explain yourself to me. I *want* you to text him."

"Oh, good. I thought you were climbing into Deirdra's boat."

"Nope. I'll start clearing the table. You get texting."

Abby did just that and typed, *Thank you for the picture of us. It's one of my favorites, too. I was so happy to find your letter, and I love the roses. They're beautiful. The judges just left. I have no idea how it went, but I hope it went well. Fingers crossed. I'm so nervous about the competition, and about us. I miss you. I wish you could have been here today. I wish I hadn't gotten so mad at you. I wish we had talked more before you left. I'm so confused and scared. You really hurt me. I don't believe you did it on purpose, but I don't know what to do with all the hurt or how to make sure it doesn't happen again.* She stared at what she'd written, wanting to push *send* and barrel through that door, to believe Aiden was everything he claimed to be, but there was a tiny voice in her head warning her not to be her mother, not to rely on a man for her happiness. She needed to work this out in her own head and heart before she could even begin to work it out with him. With a ball of lead in her gut, she deleted most of the text and sent it off before she could overthink it.

Cait picked up a stack of dishes and said, "The hardest part is done. In less than forty-eight hours we'll know if you're the reigning queen or not." They were announcing the winner at eight o'clock Thursday morning.

"You mean if *we're* the reigning *queens*."

As they cleaned up, Abby was acutely aware of her phone *not* vibrating with a response from Aiden. She told herself not to overthink that, either, and decided to drown her confusion and heartache with her drug of choice. "When we're done, what do you say we treat ourselves to queen-size sundaes?"

"I thought you'd never ask."

Aiden hung up the phone with Ben and walked into his hotel room from the balcony. He was sick of hotels, sick of meetings, and sick of phone calls. He was sick of everything that had once ruled his life.

He sat on the couch and checked his messages, uttering a curse. He'd missed three texts from Remi and one from Abby. He opened and read the text.

Thank you for the roses. They're beautiful. The judges just left. Fingers crossed.

He sat back, staring at the message, missing Abby's excited ramblings. He was debating how to respond, when Remi called.

Shit. He'd been avoiding her since he'd called her Sunday night, when he told her about his fight with Abby. He didn't want to discuss it again, but he couldn't continue avoiding her, or she'd make his life hell.

"Hi, Rem."

"Hey. How are you?"

"Fine."

"*Aiden.* You don't have to pretend with me."

He didn't respond.

"Listen, I'm going to call Carrie and book a flight. I don't want you to be alone."

"*Don't*, Remi," he warned. "You know I have one meeting after another."

"Then talk to me. I'm worried about you. You're the guy who fixes things, not the guy who gets broken. *Please* talk to me? It's hard for me to be a good mom to Olive and Patty when I'm worried about you."

He scrubbed a hand down his face and said, "That was low."

"It was honest."

"*Fine.* You want to know how I am?" Too agitated to sit still, he pushed to his feet and paced. "I feel like I have a black hole in my chest. I can't eat. I can't sleep. All I can think about is how much I hurt Abby. Okay? Feel better now?"

"No." Her voice cracked, and he knew she was crying.

More guilt landed on his shoulders. "I'm sorry, Remi. That wasn't fair."

"Yes it *was*. It's *my* fault. I sent you to Silver Island. I pushed you to get a life."

"Jesus, Remi. Don't do that. Those were the best three weeks of my life. I should be singing your praises, not dumping my shit on you. I'm the one who fucked up. Not you."

"Then fix it. Go see her!"

He gritted his teeth. "That's not the answer. I can't change who I am. You of all people know that. I've done enough damage. Bullying my way in to try to convince her I'm someone I'm not isn't going to do anything but make her angrier. This time I'm doing things the right way."

"Then you have a plan?" Remi asked hopefully.

"Yeah. Nose to the grindstone and get my shit under control. Listen, I have to go. I love you. Kiss the girls for me." He ended the call and called Ben again.

"I'm in the middle of changing a diaper. What's up?" Ben asked.

"Pull the trigger on the schedule we outlined."

"I thought you wanted to think about the international travel and—"

"I'm done thinking. *Do it.*"

CHAPTER TWENTY–SIX

"WHAT DO YOU think?" Cait asked as she walked into Abby's bedroom Thursday morning wearing the green floral sundress Abby had lent her for the announcement ceremony. Her feet were bare, and she curled her toes under. She crossed one arm over her stomach, the elbow of her other arm resting on that arm's wrist, her fingers moving nervously over her mouth.

Abby pushed to her feet in her pajama shorts and Aiden's T-shirt, which she'd found when she'd done laundry, and said, "*Wow.* You look fantastic. Move your arms. Let me see."

Cait lowered her arms and said, "Are you sure?" She looked down and immediately crossed her arms over her belly. "*Ugh.* I'll just wear my jeans."

"No, you will *not*. You have a great figure, and you look beautiful. Please wear the dress. In fact, you should keep it because you look better in it than I ever did."

Cait tucked her hair behind her ear and said, "I feel naked."

"That's because you're used to the feel of denim hugging your skin. You don't look naked." Abby bumped her shoulder and said, "But I have a feeling Brant wishes you were."

"He does *not*. He's a big flirt."

"Actually, he's never been a big flirt. Wells is way flirtier than him. But for what it's worth, I like them both a lot, so if there's any interest on your part . . ."

Cait scoffed. "I'm not looking for a guy."

"Okay, I get that. But I wasn't looking when I met Aiden, either." Anxiety prickled her limbs. She'd fielded good-luck texts from friends all morning, but she hadn't heard from Aiden since Tuesday evening, when he'd texted, *You've got this, Abs. No finger crossing necessary.* She'd had no idea how to interpret such a generic response. But given her ricocheting emotions, she guessed that he was either on the same roller-coaster ride or he'd given up on her, which was why she hadn't responded. She wasn't ready to hear the latter.

Hope rose in Cait's eyes. "Did you talk to him?"

She shook her head, and disappointment washed Cait's hope away.

"Are you thinking about reading the letter from our mother?" Cait glanced at the letter Abby had forgotten she was holding.

"Maybe. I've been thinking about Mom and my dad a lot. I wish they were here." She wished Aiden were there, too.

"They're here in spirit." She pointed at the letter. "Do you want me to be with you when you read the letter?"

Aiden's voice traipsed through Abby's mind. *Do it when I get back, so you have me to lean on.* She'd spent her life making sure she was never in a position to be so reliant on a man that she couldn't stand on her own two feet if he left. And now here she was, standing on her own, doing all the things she needed to do, and doing them well.

Well enough, anyway.

But still she was swamped with longing, drowning in an emotional abyss caused by his absence.

"Abby?" Cait touched her arm, jerking her from her thoughts. "Do you want me to stay while you read it?"

"No, thanks. I think I need to read it alone." *To prove to myself I can get through anything.*

"Okay, then I'm going to finish getting ready."

Cait walked out, and Abby looked at the letter. She ran her finger beneath the sealed edge, opening the envelope, and heard the sound of tires on gravel. *Aiden!* She ran to the window and saw Brant's truck backing down the driveway with a boat on a trailer. He was probably there to wish her luck. Or maybe he was there to see Cait.

She went downstairs and headed outside, waving as she descended the porch steps.

"Hey, Abby," he said as he climbed from his truck. "Good luck today."

"Thanks." The grass tickled her bare feet. "That boat looks like my dad's dinghy, except I think his is in dire need of repair."

"I'm guessing Aiden didn't tell you he asked me to clean her up for you?"

"He . . . ? No," she said, choked up for the hundredth time in the last few days.

"Yeah, the morning after we all had dinner a couple of weeks ago. When he borrowed the pressure washer. The house looks great, by the way."

"Thanks," she said absently, trying to remember when she'd told Aiden about her dad's dinghy.

"The trailer's yours, too."

"He bought me a boat trailer?" That was so *Aiden*. She blinked repeatedly to keep the tears burning her eyes at bay.

"Can't get her down to the water without one. Fixed up the sail, too." The sail was rolled up and secured to the boat with bungee cords, as were two new oars. "This little gal sure is a beauty. It was a pleasure cleaning her up. Where do you want her?"

"Um . . ." She was still hung up on the fact that Aiden had arranged for all of this and had never said a word about it. "You can leave it there. My garage is a mess."

Brant unhooked the trailer from his truck and said, "Did Dee come in for the announcement?"

"No. She couldn't get the time off work."

"And Cait?" Interest sparked in his eyes.

"She's inside getting ready."

He straightened the bill on his blue baseball cap, grinning as he said, "I'll be there pulling for you two. I promised Aiden I'd video the whole thing. He's pretty bummed that he can't be here."

"You talked to him?" she asked, hope rushing through her veins. If he wanted Brant to video the event, then maybe he hadn't given up on her.

"Not since he left. He just texted to confirm that I was still planning on videoing it for him."

"Cait offered to video it for him," Abby said as the thought popped into her mind.

"She can't do that if she's onstage with you accepting the award, can she?" He winked and said, "Good luck. I'll see you there."

"Thanks."

As he drove away, Abby ran her hand along the wooden edge of the boat. It looked brand-new, with the upper third newly stained and gleaming and the lower section painted forest green. She realized she was still holding the letter from her mother. She'd been thinking about her parents so much, the boat felt like a sign.

She climbed carefully into the dinghy, settled into a small space between the sail and the side, and opened the letter. As she read, she heard every word in her mother's voice.

My dear, sweet Abby,

If I know you as well as I hope I do, you're reading this letter long after I'm gone. You've taken your time getting to a place in your life where you feel you can handle it. You've always been so sure of yourself and known exactly

*what you wanted and what you needed to do to get there.
I was a little jealous of that. I'm sure you're shaking your
head right now.*

Abby realized she was, and tears slipped down her cheeks.

*Your downfall is putting others—and the need for stabil-
ity (which is my fault)—ahead of your own dreams. But
you're stronger than you know, sweetheart. Even stronger
than Didi, which I'm sure you won't believe. The difference is that you face your insecurities head-on, and Didi
has never been able to. Maybe one day you can help her
with that. Like you, she's terrified that some of my bad
traits have rubbed off on her. (Yes, I am aware of your
insecurities. I'm your mother, after all.)*

*Don't worry, honey, they haven't. They couldn't.
Neither of you is broken in the way I am. I'm not talking
about alcoholism—that's just a by-product of never really
healing from my past. By now you've met Cait, and I'm
sure you have a lot of questions. I'm sorry I'm not there
to answer them. I had never loved anything or anyone as
much as I loved Cait until I met your father. He saved me
from myself. I started drinking right after I was forced to
give up Cait. Your father gave me what I had always been
missing. Unconditional love. He gave me a purpose and
helped me live my life instead of hiding from it.*

Abby thought of Aiden and the way he'd said they'd both been
hiding behind work.

*When we had you and Didi, I learned that I could love
each of you as deeply as I loved Cait. But I'm not strong*

362

like you girls are. I was a troubled kid, and while I found my way with your father, when we lost him, I lost myself. I drank to numb the pain of missing him, and you girls paid the price for my weakness.

To say I'm sorry for what I put you through would be a gross understatement, but I'm going to say it, because I am sorry for letting you down, for making you grow up far sooner than you should have, and for all the emotional scars I left you with.

Abby swiped at her tears.

You girls are the light of my life, and I'm so very proud of you. Despite my mistakes, you've grown into bright, independent adults, which is why I chose not to tell you I had so little time left when I found out how sick I was. I'd given you enough heartaches. I know you, Abby, and you would have wanted to come home and take care of me, to make sure I knew you loved me. I couldn't do that to you, but rest assured, I know you love me despite my flaws. That's your greatest gift, seeing the heart and soul of a person rather than only seeing what others see. I hope you never lose that ability. You remind me so much of your father. I hope one day you'll work a little less and allow yourself time to find someone as wonderful as he was. Someone who appreciates and supports your strength to stand up for yourself and who's not afraid to challenge you, because you need that, too. You don't do well with pushovers.

Abby moved the letter out of the path of her tears.

You know who you are, Abby. Don't ever doubt that. I hope you will continue to dream, to be stubborn, and to follow your heart wherever it may lead because a strong, determined woman like you can't get lost the way I did. Your light is simply too bright. It will always guide you down the right path.

Live on, sweet girl, and don't waste your energy looking back. Chase your dreams and make them all come true. Daddy and I will be cheering you on from above.

All my love,
Mom

Abby looked up at the sky through a blur of tears and said, "Thank you. I needed this."

The front door flew open, and Cait walked out looking beautiful in the sundress. "Abby? Whose boat is that? We have to leave in twenty minutes."

Shoot! Abby scrambled out of the boat and ran toward the house in her bare feet and sleeping shorts. "It was my dad's boat. Brant brought it over."

"You're not even showered yet?" When Abby got to the porch, Cait said, "Oh no, you're crying. Are you okay? Is it Aiden? What can I do?"

"It's . . . *everything*, but I'll be fine," Abby said quickly.

Cait looked at the letter. "You read your letter?"

"*Yes.* You should read yours."

"It made you cry. I think I'll wait on that. You sure you're okay?"

"I will be. No more looking back. It's time to chase our dreams."

Cait nudged her through the front door and said, "Okay, but first I'm chasing your ass upstairs. You need to get ready, because one of my dreams is seeing Wells Silver's face when they announce the Bistro as the winner!"

♥ ♥ ♥

There was standing room only at Majestic Park, where Patrick Osten, the mayor of Silver Island, was preparing to step up to the podium. A banner reading BEST OF THE ISLAND RESTAURANT COMPETITION hung across the back of the amphitheater, and red and white balloons bobbed from strings tied to the railing of the steps leading up to the stage. Abby stood with Cait, fidgeting with the plunging neckline on her peach maxi dress as they waited for the contestants to be called up for the announcement. Cait was equally nervous. She'd been tugging at the hem of her dress since they left the house.

They were both overwhelmed by the number of people who had already wished them luck today. Abby hadn't even known half of them. As much as she wanted to win the competition, even if they lost, it was enough knowing so many people were cheering on the Bistro and welcoming her and Cait into the community with open arms.

"Why are we so nervous?" Abby asked. "We already did the hard work."

"I have some more to do," Cait said.

"What do you mean?"

Worry riddled Cait's brow. "I've been thinking about this a lot. I love working with Tank and everyone at Wicked Ink, but I also really love being here with you and working at the Bistro together. Would you mind if I tried to do both, but got involved here in a bigger way? I can handle the accounting and inventory, maybe hostessing?"

"Are you kidding? I would *love* it if you could be here more often."

Cait exhaled loudly, putting her hand over her heart. "That's great."

"How could you even think I wouldn't want that?"

"I didn't really, but I was nervous about it. I don't want to step on your toes or for you to feel like you have to let me do more."

"Trample on my toes, *sister*. The Bistro is yours as much as it's mine and Deirdra's. Now I'm excited! Tell me what you're thinking."

"I don't have it all figured out, but I could work here more over the summer and with Tank over the winter. Or possibly start doing tattoos and piercings here and also work more at the Bistro, and then work with Tank a couple of days a month. I don't know the best way to schedule my time, but we can talk about it, and I'll definitely figure something out."

"This is going to be *fabulous*." Abby hugged her.

"There they are!" Shelley waved, pushing through the crowd with Lenore and Faye Steele, Shelley's ex-sister-in-law.

"Can you believe how many people turned out for the announcement?" Shelley exclaimed. "Abby, you remember Faye."

"Of course!" Abby threw her arms around Faye, whom she would recognize anywhere. Faye was a voluptuous woman, like Shelley, with thick, layered blond hair, apple cheeks, and big brown eyes. When Abby was younger, she'd had a crush on Faye's oldest son, Reggie. "I haven't seen you in so long."

"I know, darlin', and that's my fault," Faye said. "I haven't been out to visit in a while, but Shelley has filled me in on *everything* that's been going on with you, including a new beau and a new sister. Those green eyes tell me you're Cait, right?"

"Yes. Cait, this is Faye, Shelley's ex-sister-in-law, and this is Lenore, Shelley's mother."

"Faye was married to my husband Steve's brother Jeffrey." Shelley shielded her mouth and said, "But we don't talk about him."

"He's an ass," Lenore said.

Cait smiled at that. "It's nice to meet you both."

"Faye, how long are you in town?" Abby asked.

"Forever," Faye said. "Shelley and Lenore have convinced me to move here."

"That's wonderful," Abby exclaimed.

"It only took us a decade," Shelley said. "Faye has spent the last several years working as a cook at a fancy restaurant in Trusty, Colorado. She needs a job, and you gals need a cook. I thought you might want to talk."

"We have someone who might be able to fill in here and there, but we definitely need a full-time cook," Abby said. "They're going to start the announcement soon, but I'd love to get your number."

"I'll text it to you," Shelley promised.

"The Brigaders and I are excited to get back to having our luncheons at the Bistro," Lenore said. "And remember, if you ever need help, we're excellent waitresses."

"Thanks, Lenore," Abby said. "We'll keep that in mind, but *no* free labor."

"We can talk about that another time." Lenore raised an eyebrow in Cait's direction and said, "Right now I'd like to get to know our lovely Cait. Rumor has it a few of our island boys have already cast their hooks in your direction. Have any reeled you in yet?"

Cait's smile faltered, her eyes darting nervously to Abby.

"That's island gossip, Lenore," Abby said, giving Cait a reassuring nod. "But can you blame them? I mean, look at my sister. She's not only beautiful, but she's also a talented artist. She painted a gorgeous mural in the Bistro. You'll have to come see it."

"Shelley told me it was stunning. I look forward to seeing it." Lenore eyed Cait's tattoos and said, "And my granddaughter Leni told me that you're a tattooist. Maybe I should make an appointment. I'm thinking of—"

"I think my mother is having a late-life crisis," Shelley said, pushing in front of Lenore. "Yesterday she tried to talk Brant into selling her a motorboat." She took Lenore by the arm and said, "Abby, I'll text you Faye's number. Good luck, ladies."

"Fingers and toes crossed!" Faye waved her crossed fingers.

"Thank you," Abby and Cait said in unison as Faye disappeared into the crowd behind Shelley and Lenore.

"Are people really talking about me?" Cait asked nervously.

"I know I am," Wells said as he walked between them and draped an arm around each of them. "Good luck today, ladies."

"Thanks." Cait slipped out of his reach.

"Thanks, Wells," Abby said. "Good luck to you, too."

He looked sharp in a dress shirt and slacks. "Word among our friends is that I've got pretty tough competition."

"We're hearing the same thing. Who knows, maybe we'll both lose," Abby said, but she was pretty sure that wouldn't happen. While the other restaurants were good, and some were even considered great, she'd been told that there was nothing *remarkable* about the food or the dining experiences at any of them. And although she loved the romantic, bohemian experience of the Bistro, that didn't mean the stoic judges did. Wells was a tough contender, and she wasn't about to count her chickens before they hatched.

"That's not going to happen," Wells said, and then his face went serious, and he pulled Abby aside. "I hear you and Aiden got into a tiff before he left. You guys okay?"

Her stomach plummeted. "How did you hear that?"

"Not much gets by me."

Fitz. She felt her cheeks burn. Had they been that loud when they were arguing? She lifted her chin and said, "I'm fine."

"I really like the guy, but more importantly, you two seemed great together. Is *he* okay?" Wells asked.

Startled by the question, she thought about it and answered honestly. "I don't know. I hope so."

"Let me know if I can do anything to help," Wells offered.

The mayor's voice boomed through the speakers. "We'd like to invite the contestants up to the stage, please."

Applause and cheers rang out as people began heading toward the stage, where Tara Osten, the mayor's daughter and a local photographer, was taking pictures.

Wells said, "After you, ladies."

When they were out of his earshot, Cait whispered, "What did he say to you?"

"He asked about Aiden." She forced a smile as they ascended the steps, and Tara took their pictures.

"He's just trying to make you nervous or something," Cait said.

"I don't think so. He's not mean like that."

They stood on the stage with the other six contestants as the mayor gave a speech about Silver Island and the competition. Abby looked out at the sea of new and familiar faces, feeling honored to be back among the community that had not only helped raise her but had also helped her family more than she'd ever known. She was thrilled that Cait was sharing in her journey to building a new life there and also starting her own. But even the support of the community and the excitement of the day couldn't quell the ache of missing Aiden. If not for him, she and Cait wouldn't be standing on that stage.

Had he stepped on her toes and spent too much money on her? *Yes.* Had he made a freaking *huge* mistake by not telling her he was the investor? *Absolutely.* But no matter how much she tried to believe he'd done those things for his own gain, she couldn't. It didn't add up. His face—the face she'd grown to love, the one she'd already imagined mapped with wrinkles and framed by gray hair—flashed in her mind, bringing with it a pang of longing. They'd been apart only a few days, and it was far too long. She thought of her mother missing her father so much she'd given up trying to push past the pain and had chosen to give up on life instead. As much as it broke her heart to know how badly her mother had hurt, her mother's weakness and her mother's letter gave her the courage to do what her heart wanted to do. To obliterate the fears of turning into her mother, the fear she'd carried for as long as she could remember, and to chase *all* of her dreams. Because Abby *wasn't* broken, and she wasn't about to give up on *anything.*

Not on this competition, not on herself, and *especially* not on Aiden.

Her mother had needed her father to survive. Abby didn't *need* Aiden in that way. She knew who she was—Abigail de Messiéres, sister, friend, chef. But she *wanted* Aiden in her life, because being with him made everything that much better.

Cait nudged her, startling her out of her thoughts. Everyone was applauding and cheering, so Abby applauded too, wondering what she'd missed.

"We won!" Cait exclaimed.

"Wha . . . ? We *won*? We won!" She hugged Cait.

Wells leaned in and said, "I think you need to make a speech."

"Oh, *right!*" Abby exclaimed, and grabbed Cait's hand. "Come on, Cait!"

There was a rumble of laughter and shouts of *congratulations* as they shook the mayor's hand and stepped up to the podium. Abby's heart raced. She'd been so consumed by her and Aiden's troubles, she hadn't prepared a speech.

She looked at Cait, wide-eyed and smiling from ear to ear, and said, "Would you like to make the acceptance speech?"

Cait closed her mouth and shook her head, elation glittering in her eyes.

Abby leaned closer to the microphone and said, "Thank you so much." The applause quieted. "This is a great honor for me and my sisters, Cait"—she motioned to Cait, who waved—"and Deirdra. Unfortunately, Deirdra couldn't be here today. Deirdra and I grew up at the Bistro, watching our father cook, paint, and sit down with customers while they ate and watching our mother hostess, waitress, and mingle. Back then all I wanted was to be part of that world." She found Shelley's friendly face in the crowd and said, "It took a push from a special friend for me to finally leave this beloved island and find my way through culinary school and into the restaurants of New York City. What I didn't know while I was gone was that the people here, the community in which I'd grown up and loved, helped to keep the Bistro afloat. My sisters and I couldn't possibly thank everyone who had a hand in that, but you know who you are, and we will be forever grateful for all that you have done." She looked at Cait and said, "Now it's our turn to give back to the community."

She scanned the crowd, wishing Aiden were there, because not only did he deserve the most thanks, but this was *their* moment. He'd wanted this for Abby even more than she'd wanted it for herself. Struggling to push past those thoughts, she said, "When we first came back to the island, the Bistro was a mess. It was run-down and a reminder of the hardships our family had dealt with. Some people thought the Bistro should be put out to pasture, but I still felt the magic it once held, and I saw the beauty in it, flaws and all. And with the help of my sisters and our friends, we brought it back to life. Unfortunately, someone else who is very special to me and who deserves the most gratitude for this *win* isn't here today. Funny enough, he came into my life the same day the Bistro and Cait did. When I told him about the magic the Bistro held for me, he looked past the run-down structure and past *my* flaws—my stubbornness and my fear of entering this competition—and he saw things in me that I didn't. He believed in me and my dreams, and he moved mountains to help me make those dreams come to fruition." Tears sprang to her eyes as she said, "Without him, we would not be standing on this stage."

Murmurs rose from the crowd, which parted before her like the Red Sea as Aiden stepped to the front, a sight for Abby's aching heart, in a navy button-down, khaki slacks, and *loafers*, holding a bouquet of flowers.

Tears spilled from Abby's eyes. "You're *here*?"

"I never left," he said.

Sobs burst from her lungs as a collective "Aw" rang out. Abby ran around the podium and leapt from the stage right into his arms, causing gasps, cheers, and applause.

"I'm sorry," he said between kisses.

"No, *I'm* sorry. I was hurt and scared. But I'm not scared anymore. I *know* everything you did came straight from your heart, and I *love* your heart, Aiden. I love *all* of you!"

He kissed her again, eliciting more cheers. As he set her feet on the ground, his loving eyes found hers, and the crowd quieted as he said, "I love you, Abs, and I promise to be as transparent as glass from now on. These last few days were the worst, but they made one thing very clear to me. I don't want to figure out how to function when half my heart—and everything I need and want—is right here on this island."

Tears slipped down her cheeks. "You're going to stay for a while?"

"I had something a little more permanent in mind. Do you think you can stand being with a workaholic who's sure to make mistakes but will do his very best not to?"

"Yes! Can you stand being with a stubborn chef who has a chip on her shoulder about doing things herself?"

The devastating grin she loved lit up his eyes, and he said, "Not only can I stand her, but I want to make her mine forever." He got down on one knee, sending Abby's heart into a wild flurry, and pulled a gorgeous diamond ring from his pocket, causing another round of gasps and commotion. Abby couldn't believe her eyes. The ring had two diamond-encrusted gold bands with an enormous teardrop-shaped diamond between them. A row of smaller teardrop diamonds arched around the peak and the rounded bottom of the center diamond. Tiny strands of diamonds ran between the gold bands on either side of the center diamond, like the lights-of-love chandeliers. "You are my light and my love, Abigail de Messiéres, and I want to build a life with you. I want to have stubborn little girls with flyaway hair and adorable freckles and nerdy boys who wear the wrong shoes and prefer numbers to race cars."

Tears streamed down Abby's cheeks. She had no idea how her wobbly legs were holding her up as she imagined adorable little boys with Aiden's serious eyes and cute little loafers, and nervous laughter slipped out.

Aiden took her hand, his teary eyes smiling back at her, and said, "I want to show you the world one week at a time during your off-season, and ride our bikes to Keira's for breakfast when we're running late because we've stayed in bed too long. I want to take long walks on the beach and get sand in our sheets, tangle up kite strings, and add a million more memories for us to make to our list. I want to hang out with our families and friends and hear your carefree laughter for the rest of my life. And I promise I will never, *ever* hold anything back. Will you marry me, Runner Girl? Be my wife, the mother of our babies, and let me cherish and love you forevermore?"

Abby could barely think past the love thundering between them. But she didn't need to think, because everything she wanted—the beautiful man who had not only changed her world but had become her world—was right there waiting for her to say "*Yes!* Yes, Chair Guy, I *will* marry you!"

Aiden shot to his feet and lifted her off the ground, kissing her *hard.* "Yes?"

"Yes!" She pressed her lips to his again, and an explosion of cheers rang out.

"I'd say we have more than *one* winner today," the mayor said into the microphone, and they both laughed.

As the crowd converged on them, Aiden put the gorgeous ring on Abby's finger and said, "I love you, Abs, and I'll spend the rest of my life showing you how much and probably getting into trouble by showing you *too* much, then making it up to you again and again."

With laughter and tears and more love than she ever thought possible, Abby said, "And I'll overreact and love you through every mistake and for every single second of the rest of our lives."

CHAPTER TWENTY–SEVEN

GUITAR MUSIC FLOATED in from the patio through the open glass doors of the Bistro, mixing with the heavenly scents coming from the kitchen and the chatter of customers celebrating the grand opening. The restaurant had been packed since they'd opened at eleven, and while Abby had been cooking all day, she'd made a point of popping out of the kitchen several times to greet customers, like her father used to do. But Aiden was so damn proud of her, he needed another Abby fix.

He pushed through the kitchen doors, the hair on his arms rising with the electrical charge in the air, buzzing louder than the classics coming from the boom box. Abby was in her happy place, moving feverishly from one pan to the next amid sounds of meats searing, fish and vegetables grilling, and soups simmering, barking orders in coded chef language, which her staff expertly carried out. She was working her magic, like a maestro choreographing a symphony as controlled chaos ensued around her—servers delivered and picked up orders, bussers cycled in and out, and meal preppers washed, peeled, cut, and seasoned. Faye Steele, a jubilant, motherly type who had taken Abby and Cait under her loving wings, winked from the stove, where she was cooking.

Aiden waited until Abby took a breath and said, "Abs? Everything okay here? Do you need anything?"

Abby turned, her face glistening from the heat of the stove, her radiant smile lighting up the room. "Just a kiss."

He quickly pressed his lips to hers and said, "Love you, babes."

"Me too, you. How are things out there?" she asked, turning her attention back to the stove.

"Every table is full inside and out. The patio is packed, shoulder to shoulder, and everyone is raving about the food."

It had been three wonderful, busy weeks since the competition, and even before the opening, the Bistro had become the most talked-about restaurant on the island. But that hadn't stopped Abby from worrying over every detail of her big day. Earlier that morning, she'd been so hyped up, Aiden had kept her in bed for an extra hour, knowing just how to take the edge off. He'd lavished her with love until she lay happily sated in his arms, too spent to stress over anything. He'd known she needn't have worried. Abby never did anything halfway. She and Cait had hired and trained competent and friendly staff and had planned the event perfectly.

"And Jagger?" Abby asked.

"He and Dolly are a big hit." The laid-back guy was as good a cook as he was a musician, and Abby had hired him to do both—on a *loose* schedule, of course, because that was how Jagger rolled.

"I'll zip out when I get a chance." Abby looked over her shoulder and said, "Dessert at our table later?"

"You know it."

They'd set the table Aiden had bought when he'd first come to the island on the patio with a sign that read RESERVED FOR ABBY AND AIDEN, which would change to read RESERVED FOR MR. AND MRS. ALDRIDGE after they were married that fall. News of their impending wedding had spread like wildfire. It seemed all the women on the island were aflutter with wedding talk.

Aiden took one last long look at Abby, his heart overflowing with love for her and for the life they were building together. Over the last few weeks they'd transformed her mother's house into a bright new beginning for the two of them, with newly painted walls, refinished floors, several of her father's paintings, and pictures of Aiden, Abby, and their families. They'd turned the junk room into a glorious master bedroom and her mother's bedroom into an office, complete with the couch where they'd first made love. They'd moved Abby's things from New York and some of Aiden's things from his house in LA, filling in the rest with furniture and art they'd chosen together from local shops. Like with any couple, it wasn't always smooth sailing, but they were learning to navigate troubled waters together. Aiden still had a lot to learn about not trying to do everything for Abby all at once, but she was gracious with her teachings. When he had surprised her with the conversation pit she'd admired at the furniture store for the Bistro, she'd started to give him a lecture. But she'd stopped herself and surprised him by thanking him for being so thoughtful instead. When she'd come home that evening and found another conversation pit on the deck out back, she'd simply laughed and said, *What am I going to do with you?* She'd approved of the sensual ideas he'd come up with, and he'd happily endured his punishment.

He was looking forward to surprising her with a new kitchen for their house as a wedding gift—and *suffering* through the penalty for doing so.

Smiling with the thought, Aiden made his way back out to the patio.

He spotted Shelley and Steve chatting with Leni, Jules, and Jock and felt a wave of gratitude. He'd confided in Shelley when he'd decided to stay on the island and work from Silver House after his and Abby's argument last month. Staying away from Abby had been the hardest thing he'd ever done, but she'd asked for space, and he'd wanted her to know he'd heard her. But he'd been losing his mind with worry, and he'd needed someone he could trust to check on her and make sure she was okay. Shelley had graciously done the deed without exposing his whereabouts.

On the other side of the patio, a swarm of young women was gathered around Jagger, who was sitting on a stool playing his guitar with Dolly at his feet.

Deirdra sidled up to Aiden in her high heels and silk blouse, giving Jagger what Abby called the *stink eye*. "Can you believe the hippie has a harem?"

Aiden chuckled. While he, Abby, and Cait had become good friends with Jagger, Deirdra still refused to call him by his name. "He's definitely a welcome addition to the Bistro."

She scoffed. "I can't even imagine what he and my mom had in common."

"From the things he's said, it sounded like he and your mom were just unlikely friends. I think he's a good guy."

"Yes, well, we both know your judgment needs *tweaking*." Deirdra arched a brow. "I still can't believe you didn't have me sign a nondisclosure agreement when you sent me your life history."

Aiden had called Deirdra the morning of the competition announcement to apologize for upsetting Abby and to let her know he'd planned on proposing. While Deirdra was chewing him out, the package he'd sent her detailing the names and addresses of every business and property he owned, as well as a formal background check, for which he'd paid, had arrived.

"I trust you, Deirdra, and I wanted you to know that you could trust me."

She sipped her wine. "I do trust you, and after Abby told me what you'd done and why she was so upset, Cait took me aside and filled me in on everything you'd done for Abby. I knew in my heart you were a good man. But it was Cait's sketches that sealed the deal, not those documents."

"She could have made up the way I was looking at Abby." He and Abby had framed and hung up Cait's drawings. He'd had no idea Cait had captured so many moments between them. They were better than photos, because their love had touched another person so deeply, she'd said she *had* to put it on paper.

"No frigging way. Nobody has that good of an imagination."

As if she'd been summoned, Cait hurried over and squeezed between them, looking cute in a Bistro tank top and jeans, with all her tattoos on display. She was still figuring out a more permanent schedule between working at Wicked Ink and the Bistro, but she and Abby had hired enough staff to cover the times she went back to the Cape. Tonight she was hostessing, and Aiden had been keeping his eye on several guys he'd seen checking her out.

"You'd think it was a full moon or something," Cait said. "All the wolves are out tonight."

He followed her gaze to Wells and Brant, talking with Mason and Ben across the patio. Ben was holding his son, Christopher, and Mason's watchful eyes were on Olive, who was sitting on the beach in front of the Bistro talking with a teenage boy whose father was eating dinner on the patio. Brant's gaze was locked on Cait. Wells winked in her direction, and Cait's arm slid across her belly. Brant glared at Wells, then flashed his dimples at Cait. Aiden imagined cartoon sparks appearing beside those dimples. He had seen Wells ogling Leni all night and wondered if his flirting with Cait was more about getting under Brant's skin than getting into Cait's pants. But what did he know? He was no expert on love. Although he sure hoped to become an expert on loving Abby.

Cait scoffed. "Do I have a sign on my forehead that says flirt with me, or have Wells and Brant lost their minds?"

"I'm going with the latter," Deirdra said. "*Oh!* There's Sutton. I want to talk to her. I'll catch up with you guys later."

"Uncle Aiden!" Patrice, adorable in a pink fluffy dress, ran ahead of Remi.

The adoption for the girls had been approved two weeks ago, the same day Remi found out she was pregnant. Life was getting more beautiful by the day.

"Hi, Cait! You're going to be my aunt one day!" Patrice exclaimed as Aiden lifted Patrice into his arms.

"I'm looking forward to it." Cait tickled Patrice's belly, earning the cutest giggles. "But if you'll excuse me, I have to go put blinders on."

As Cait walked away, Patrice said, "What are blinders?"

"That's code for Cait doesn't want to see guys looking at her," Aiden said as Remi glided gracefully to his side, gorgeous in a long orange tank dress, with a warm smile in her eyes that never failed to remind him of their mother.

Patrice wrinkled her nose. "I wish Olive wanted blinders. She hasn't spent any time with me tonight."

"She's at a funny age where boys start to look like sugar rather than salt," Remi said. "But don't worry, peanut. She'll spend time with you when we leave. She's already asked if you could stay up late with her tonight."

They were staying in a suite at the Silver House. Aiden and Abby were thinking about putting an addition on the house so they would have more room for family and friends.

"Yay!" Patrice cheered. "Uncle Aiden, Mommy says you're going to have babies with Aunt Abby, too. Then me and Olive and our new baby will have cousins. But Daddy said not to hold my breath because you want Abby all to yourself for a while."

"I think your dad is right, Patty Cake." Aiden spotted Abby walking through the restaurant, stopping at tables to chat, and his heart thumped harder.

"That's selfish," Patrice said.

"*Patrice*," Remi chided. "Sorry, Aiden. I'm learning that five-year-olds are a little unfiltered."

"Actually, sis, Patrice is right. As you love to remind me, it took me almost forty years to find Abby. I want to enjoy giving her my undivided attention before adding little ones into the mix." Since they'd decided to wait to have a family, Abby had gone on birth control. Their lovemaking had always been incredible, but *nothing* compared to loving Abby without anything separating them.

"Olive says you want time to kiss Abby." Patrice made kissing noises, and they all laughed.

"I'm not going to lie, Patty Cake. I do love kissing Abby. But it's also important to me that she has a chance to do *all* the things she wants to before we have babies, because babies need a lot of love, and they take a lot of time and energy. But don't worry. One day you'll have cousins to play with."

"*Fine*," Patrice said dejectedly. "I guess I'll wait. At least Mommy's having a baby."

He tapped her nose with his index finger and said, "Thanks."

"Maybe Cait or Deirdra will get married and have babies before you and Abby do."

"I kind of doubt that," Remi said. "Cait pays no attention to the guys checking her out, and Deirdra is a tough cookie. She's *all* about work, like someone else I *used* to know. I think I need to send *her* on a vacation."

Abby's eyes found Aiden's as she stepped onto the patio, and love filled the space between them like a ribbon drawing her forward.

Patrice wriggled out of Aiden's arms. "I want to go see Aunt Abby before she goes back to the kitchen!"

He watched Abby scoop up Patrice, giving him visions of her holding their children one day. He definitely wanted babies, but he was in no rush to complicate their lives when they'd only just begun to make room for each other. Aiden had met with Ben and Garth and had redelegated much of the work he'd previously taken back, with a promise not to renege again. He'd also worked out a schedule where most of his travel would take place during Abby's off-season, when they could travel together. He had no interest in giving up too much of his work. His love of investing would always be his mistress, and Abby seemed okay with that, just as he was with her affair with the Bistro.

"I've never seen you so happy," Remi said with damp eyes.

He put his arm around her and said, "Then why are you crying, Rem?"

"Because you're in love, and I wasn't sure you'd ever have your happily ever after, and I'm pregnant, and pregnancy hormones have turned me into a teary mess. And that's so frigging awesome!" She threw her arms around him and said, "I love you, and I know Mom and Dad are so proud of you, and they're with us tonight. I can feel them."

Aiden's eyes dampened. "Me too, Rem. Thank you for forcing me to get a life when I thought I already had one." He wiped his eyes as Abby came to his side, holding Patrice's hand.

"Are you sad, Uncle Aiden?" Patrice asked.

"No, Patty Cake. I'm the happiest man alive because I have all of you." He drew Abby into his arms and said, "And I get to spend the rest of my life coming home to the woman I love."

Long after they'd shared their dessert at their special table and everyone had gone their separate ways, Abby changed into shorts and her CHILL sweatshirt, and she and Aiden took the dinghy out to Lover's Cove. Abby was still riding high from the grand opening, which had been even more spectacular than she could have imagined. Her life was shaping up just as wonderfully. When she'd quit her job, she hadn't known what the future would hold, which should have terrified her, given that her mother had just passed away. But she'd somehow known she'd done the right thing. She might never understand why she'd had that level of certainty, but as the brisk air whisked over her skin and the love of her life rowed them to the middle of the cove, she knew one thing for sure. The mother who had taken so much of her childhood had given her another sister *and* the future she'd always wanted. Coming back to the island to claim that future had blessed her with a career that filled her with happiness, more friends than she could ever hope for, and an unexpectedly glorious love that was more magical than anything she'd ever known.

Aiden set the oars inside the boat and dragged his fingers in the water. "It's chilly. You sure you're up for this?"

"Yes. At least I *think* I am." They were going to scratch skinny-dipping off their list. Abby looked nervously back at the island, where tiny yellow lights shimmered in the windows of cottages and houses.

Aiden leaned forward and took her hands in his. "Before we do, I brought something for you."

"A bathing suit?" she said hopefully.

"Not a chance, beautiful." He reached into his bag and pulled out a flat package. "When we had our goodbye ceremony for our parents, we lit paper lanterns and let them float up to the heavens. This was such a big, magical night for you, I thought it might be a nice time to say a private goodbye to your parents."

He handed her the package, and she realized it was a paper wishing lantern. A lump clogged her throat. She'd learned that Aiden's gestures always had deeper meanings than she would have guessed. Like when he'd told her what the colored crystals on their new lights of love symbolized. *Green for your eyes, which captured my heart the first time I saw them. Pink for the blush on your cheeks when you called me an underwear model, and blue for the first blueberry Danish we ever shared.* She thought of those memories every time she walked into the Bistro.

"You are the most thoughtful, loving person I know," she said. "Thank you for thinking of this. Knowing you used paper lanterns for your parents' goodbye ceremony makes using them for mine even more special."

"Why do I hear a *but* coming?"

"You know me so well. I've been thinking about it, too, and after I read my mom's letter, I felt so much better and saw myself and my life so much clearer, I'm kind of hoping that when my sisters read theirs, they'll find the same closure. If they do, then I think it would be nice if we all said our goodbyes together. I know that might take years, because Deirdra is *Deirdra*, and that's okay. I'm beyond happy, and I've had my closure."

"That makes perfect sense."

"You're not upset?"

"Of course not. I love you, Abs, and I want you to do all the things that make you happy and that feel right to *you*. I was trying to be supportive, not push it on you."

He reached for the package, but she held it tight. "I have another idea I'd like to use this for tonight, if that's okay."

"Anything's okay. What do you have in mind?"

"How about instead of using the lantern to say *goodbye* to our pasts, we use it to *welcome* our lives coming together and our bright new future?"

"Aw, Abs. I love that idea."

"Yay!"

He pressed his smiling lips to hers, and they got the lantern ready. Aiden held the lantern up as Abby lit it, and she said, "You've become my best friend, the sun that lights up my days, and the fire that heats up my nights. You're my sounding board, my shoulder to lean on, my dance partner, and my favorite finger foodie. I love you with all of my heart, and I can't wait to spend forever chasing our dreams together." *And a lifetime of hearing your whispers of love to me when you think I'm sleeping. I treasure each and every one of those heartfelt confessions.*

He was gazing so deeply into her eyes, she was sure he could see every beat of her heart. He swallowed hard, as if he were trying to rein in his emotions.

"Don't you want to say something?" she asked, butterflies fluttering inside her.

"I can't believe you're mine. Ditto, Runner Girl, to loving you, chasing dreams, and everything in between." He released the lantern, took her in his arms, and kissed her breathless.

He held her as they watched the lantern float into the clear night sky. When it was nothing more than a twinkle in the distance, Aiden turned desirous eyes on her and said, "Ready to get naked, beautiful?"

She shivered with trepidation and excitement.

"We don't have to do this."

"Actually, we do," she said cheekily. "Remi promised to make us another list once we finished this one."

He ran his hands over her butt, giving it a squeeze, and said, "I think we can come up with a much better list of our own, starting with making love in Lover's Cove on a very special night."

Her body flamed. "You win!"

She whipped off her sweatshirt, and they kissed as they stripped naked, shivering against the brisk night air.

"Ready, sweetheart?" Aiden asked as he took her hand.

"With you by my side, I'm ready for anything!"

Just as they'd jumped into their relationship and the Bistro with both feet and eyes wide open, they leapt out of the boat and plunged into the cold, dark water. Aiden found her underwater, his strong arms circling her as they broke the surface, legs kicking, mouths kissing, and hearts beating as one.

A NOTE FROM MELISSA

I met Aiden and Remi while writing *The Real Thing*, the first book in the Sugar Lake series, and I have waited years for him to be ready for his happily ever after. Once Remi found hers (in *This Is Love*), I knew it was Aiden's turn. I also knew he'd need a very special woman to accept his quirks and overindulgences. I met Abby and Deirdra through a mention of their mother when I was writing Jock and Daphne's story, *Tempted by Love*, the first book in The Steeles at Silver Island series, and I knew after all Abby had endured, she needed Aiden as much as he needed her. I hope you enjoyed their story as much as I enjoyed writing it. If you'd like to get to know the Steeles, the Silvers, and the Remingtons, pick up *Tempted by Love*. If you enjoyed the Silver Island setting, pick up *Searching for Love*, a Braden & Montgomery novel featuring treasure hunter Zev Braden and chocolatier Carly Dylan. In *Searching for Love* you can get to know the Bradens and the Silver Island Remingtons.

Ben Dalton's book, along with the books of each of Ben's siblings, is available for your binge-reading pleasure in the Sugar Lake and Harmony Pointe series. I hope you'll also check out the rest of my Love in Bloom big-family romance collection, starting with *Sisters in Love*, the first book in my beloved Snow Sisters series. Each of my books may be enjoyed as a stand-alone novel. Characters from each series make appearances in future books, so you never miss an engagement, wedding, or birth. A complete list of all series titles is included at the start of this book, and downloadable checklists, free series starters, and family trees are available on the Reader Goodies page of my website (www. MelissaFoster.com/RG).

Be sure to sign up for my newsletter to keep up to date with my new releases and to receive an exclusive short story (www.MelissaFoster. com/News).

Happy reading!

Melissa Foster

ACKNOWLEDGMENTS

Writing a book is never a solo adventure. I am grateful for the inspiration I receive from fans and friends and to all the kind people who patiently answer my never-ending research questions. Heaps of gratitude go out to Kristen Roberts of Truro Vineyards for her help with vineyard-related questions. As always, I take fictional liberties with my stories and any errors are not a reflection of misinformation provided by others.

It's not often that my stories serve as inspiration for other artists, but I am honored that Aiden and Abby's story was the inspiration behind the song "Billionaire" by Blue Foster. Blue is my youngest son Jake's professional name. Jake writes his own music and lyrics, and it was thrilling to watch "Billionaire" come to life.

If you'd like sneak peeks into my writing process and to chat with me daily, please join my fan club on Facebook. We talk about our lovable heroes and sassy heroines, and I always try to keep fans abreast of what's going on in our fictional boyfriends' worlds. You never know when you'll end up in one of my books, as several members of my fan club have already discovered (www.Facebook.com/groups/MelissaFosterFans).

Follow my Facebook fan page to keep up with sales and events (www.Facebook.com/MelissaFosterAuthor).

I'm forever grateful for my assistants and friends Sharon Martin, Lisa Filipe, Lisa Bardonski, Missy Dehaven, and Shelby Dehaven. Thank you for always having my back.

A special thank-you to my incredible editor Maria Gomez and the fantastic Montlake team. As always, my books would not shine without the editorial expertise of Kristen Weber and Penina Lopez and my capable team of proofreaders. Last, but never least, I am grateful to my family for their ongoing support and encouragement.

ABOUT THE AUTHOR

Photo © 2013 Melanie Anderson

Melissa Foster is a *New York Times* and *USA Today* bestselling and award-winning author of nearly one hundred books, including the Sugar Lake series, The Steeles at Silver Island series, and the Harmony Pointe series. Her novels have been recommended by *USA Today*'s book blog, *Hagerstown* magazine, the *Patriot*, and others. She has also painted and donated several murals to the Hospital for Sick Children in Washington, DC.

She enjoys discussing her books with book clubs and reader groups, and she welcomes an invitation to your event. Visit Melissa on her website, www.MelissaFoster.com, or chat with her on Instagram @MelissaFoster_Author, Twitter @Melissa_Foster, and on Facebook at www.facebook.com/MelissaFosterAuthor.